Prophecy of the Eagle I

THE STORY OF A NATIVE AMERICAN BOY AND LACROSSE

Mike Celeste

ISBN: 1494291428
ISBN 13: 9781494291426
Library of Congress Control Number: 2013921968 Registration # Txu 1-885-183
Certification 10/8/13
CreateSpace Independent Publishing Platform
North Charleston, South Carolina

To the Iroquois National Lacrosse team, who, some with their wooden sticks of old, continue to play this Game given to them by the Creator with gratitude, and who continue to assert their human rights of independence as representatives of a free and sovereign people.

To Oren Lyons, lacrosse player, Faithkeeper, and one of the most influential spiritual leaders of America's indigenous people, who courageously and relentlessly continues the fight to preserve the sovereign rights of native peoples, and who continues to remind us all that we are but tenants on Mother Earth, our rights to which were given us by the Creator on the condition that we treat her and all living things with respect and dignity.

CAST OF MAIN NAMED CHARACTERS

In Order of Appearance

Pontiac – Chief of the Ottawa
Red Fawn – Interpreter for Pontiac and the English colonel at Fort Michilimackinac
Sweet Willow – Pontiac's wife
Strong Hand – Sweet Willow's Iroquoian husband
Strong Oak – Son of Sweet Willow and Pontiac
Benjamin Fallen Tree Harwood – Jake's Grandfather, Sachem, Faithkeeper of the Onondaga
White Pine – Jake's deceased mother
Mary (6), Molly (13), Maggie (15) – Jake's sisters
Jake Harwood (17) – The protagonist of the story
Miss Doolittle – Beloved schoolteacher on the reservation
Old Thunder – The family horse
Firefly – BIA agent on the reservation
Hiawatha – First Sachem of the Haudenosaunee
Bear – The family dog
Johnny Big Nose – Jake's friend on the reservation
Little Crow – Jake's friend on the reservation
Sarah Sweetwaters – Jake's girlfriend
Youngblood – Jake's rival on the reservation
Sonny Two Weasels – Youngblood's henchman

Mrs. Charlotte Graham – Haughty older woman in Syracuse, mistress of Madeline, and Grandfather's reading teacher when he was a boy

Madeline – Half-breed young woman whom Jake saves from assault in Syracuse

Brown Otter – Jake's teammate on the Onondaga team

Leo Man Killer – Jake's teammate on the Onondaga team

John Fast Elk – Jake's teammate on the Onondaga team

Little Johnny – Cross-eyed ball boy on the reservation

Running Bear – Old spiritual leader of the Onondaga lacrosse team

Gray Wolf – Sachem and coach of the Mohawk lacrosse team

Weeping Willow – Grandfather's deceased wife

William Brave Bull – Mohawk lacrosse player

PROPHECY OF THE EAGLE

BOOK 1

CONTENTS

PROLOGUE

North America's native population has been at war with the white man since the moment Columbus set foot in the New World. The extermination of the Carib and Taino Indians of the Caribbean Islands by the Spanish became a prelude to the misery to be visited on the red man by the white man's march across North America as the fulfillment of Manifest Destiny. In contrast, the natives' destiny became either extermination or reservation. As a result of war and disease, the Indian population in the Americas fell from an estimated fifty million in 1500 to less than one million by 1900.

History is written by the victors in war, as evidenced by the many stories recounting the quest to tame the savage North American frontier. Even by the turn of the twentieth century, other than the battle of the Little Big Horn, acts of Indian courage and determination to defend their culture, tribal lands, and identity remained untold.

But now you will read an amazing story of one small victory by a young boy that will live on as a source of pride and inspiration, not only for the Iroquois Nation but also for all people who hope to walk the path of a human being. This story begins with the Prophecy of the Eagle, a powerful prophecy that could not be denied even though its fulfillment would take generations.

1

THE GREAT CHIEF, PONTIAC

I stand, a solitary figure upon a hill rising up from the great lake. Beads of sweat form on my body and glisten in the moonlight. A summer lightning bolt streaks across the evening sky, momentarily illuminating me against the backdrop of the dark hills and the black water beyond. My arms extend to the heavens, both hands grasping the sacred stick meticulously carved by my father. I sing of honor and thanks.

"Oh, Gitche Manitou, Great Spirit and Creator of all things, look kindly upon your faithful son, Pontiac. Give me strength and wisdom, for tomorrow I must lead the people anew. When the sun next rises, we shall honor you with the great Game."

I am Pontiac, and these are my words as written by an English missionary new to our country. I see him place a feather upon paper, using the kind of ink my people use to paint their bodies. I speak English only a little, so I must trust that most of what I say, most of what I mean, is put upon the paper accurately.

My prayers finished, I slip through the dark pine forest to my people's campsite. Like a deer seeking the cover of night to feed, I unflinchingly glide through thorny underbrush that marks my bare legs with many cuts. But pain is no stranger to me. Stopping momentarily to examine a particularly deep cut, I swipe my finger over the wound and touch it to my lips, silently acknowledging that tomorrow much more blood will be shed.

My path now illuminated by the many campfires that dot the hillside, I calmly survey our camp. Excitement shimmers in the air, unusual for this time of night, typically a time of solace and calm.

As chief of the Ottawa, I proudly stride into the campsite. My tribe has gathered at the foothills located by the great lake to play our Game in honor of the white father, the king of England, whose birthday will be celebrated the following day, which the missionary tells me is June 4, 1763. The Great Spirit gave the game *Bagadowe*—the name the people of the great lake use for lacrosse—to his people at the time of creation.

Fort Michilimackinac is one of a string of thirteen forts built by the French around the great lake during the French and Indian War. After their defeat, the French abandoned the forts to the victors. According to my scouts, the English fort is a small garrison of some fifty soldiers. Although the tribes who live around the great lake had been allied with the French, they are now neighbors of the English, sharing an uneasy truce.

The people slowly begin to stir as I walk among them. I pause a moment to watch some of my warriors, their faces already painted, slowly dance around a campfire to the beat of a soft, rhythmic drum. Trancelike, these shadowy figures dance to songs of honor and bravery that they hope to earn the next day. Most of the warriors have already unwrapped their deerskin war bundles, carefully laying the contents upon blankets. So closely is *Bagadowe* associated with warfare that the braves wrap their game sticks along with their war clubs, tomahawks, and knives.

I gingerly step over the outstretched legs of warriors, some of whom sit quietly, backs against trees or rocks, carefully adjusting the deer hide laces of their game sticks to form the most perfect pocket within which to carry and pass the ball. I remember the queasy feeling in my own stomach in anticipation of battle or of the Game when I was a young brave. I smile as I move quietly among some of the men who lie on bear and buffalo hides, controlling the rhythm of their breathing, completely relaxing their bodies, and most likely visualizing their movements on the field the next day.

The older men tell somewhat embellished stories of past great games, not only to entertain but also to inspire the young warriors to greatness. They playfully challenge the veracity of each other's stories and are certain that their past deeds of glory can never be replicated.

The women eagerly participate in pregame rituals too. They sing songs that taunt imaginary opponents with insults to their skill and manhood. Some women softly whisper words of encouragement into their husbands' ears. Others meticulously fix their warriors' tufts of hair by applying generous amounts of bear grease to coax every strand perfectly upright. The women enjoy primping their men for battle, weaving eagle or hawk feathers into their men's hair and inserting metal rings into pierced noses, ears, cheeks, and eyelids—hoping to earn bragging rights for the handsomest man. How proud the women are of their men! To be the wife of a great warrior is honor enough, but to be the wife of a skilled *Bagadowe* player exalts a woman and her family above all others. Each of the women crows about how handsome and brave her man is, some in song and some in banter.

I stop behind a group of children who sit wide-eyed around a fire, listening to their elders tell tales of animals playing the Game against men and of the first men who played against giants. In every story, bravery, heroism, self-sacrifice, and honor are common themes.

Humility is also a virtue that every warrior is careful to respect. A warrior must never extol his own virtues as a player. Rather, he who confers honor upon a teammate, or even on a brave opponent, is respected. Nearly every boy dreams of the honor of being invited to play *Bagadowe.* Aside from the profound spirituality of the Game, the older warriors and chiefs determine a young man's readiness to participate in a raid or in battle by his performance in the Game.

After patiently waiting for a tribal elder to finish one of his tales, I then step forward out of the shadows. The children squeal in delight and are hushed to silence by their parents as I position myself to where all can hear my words. I too have a story to tell. When all is quiet except for the crackling of the campfires, I slowly raise my head. The glow from the fire illuminates my face, making me look like one of the supernatural first beings on Earth from the tales of the elders. I suddenly crouch, turn my head slowly, and scowl menacingly, startling the children. But just as quickly, a wide, warm smile spreads across my face. The children sigh in relief and smile back.

"At the beginning of time, when man had not yet come upon the earth, there lived monsters of tremendous size, covered with dirty hair and smelling worse than a dead elk's carcass," I begin.

Disgusted by these imaginary beasts, the children chorus loudly, "Eww," some burying their faces into their mothers' arms.

As I lithely move among them, I continue. "Gitche Manitou, our Creator, could not put man upon the earth until these monstrous demons were banished to caves deep beneath the ground. So the Father devised a plan to rid the earth of these creatures: he challenged them to *Bagadowe.* The loser was to crawl underground, never again to return to the surface. When the monsters learned that Gitche Manitou alone would play against them, they eagerly accepted the challenge."

"But these monsters were unaware that Gitche Manitou possessed the attributes of each animal he had created: the speed of the deer, the strength of the elk, the power of the bear, the ingenuity of the beaver, and the piercing eyes of the eagle, among other skills. Yet the monsters, owing to their great size, walked all over Gitche Manitou and scored many goals. It looked as if our Creator would lose."

So moved by my story of the imminent demise of their beloved Creator, one of the little boys begins to sob. His mother pulls him into the warmth and comfort of her embrace and looks up at me with a smile to apologize for her little boy's interruption. I reassuringly return her smile and beckon the children closer.

"Feeling sorry for Gitche Manitou, soon all the animals of the forest came to urge him on. They each reminded our Creator to use his special gifts to overcome the advantage of the monsters' size. And so with the swiftness of the deer, he darted amid the lumbering giants and scored a goal. With the ferocity of a stampeding buffalo, he courageously ran headlong right at the monsters, but at the last minute, like a coyote, he ducked and ran between their legs."

The children erupt in a rousing cheer.

"But that is not all. Gitche Manitou ran so fast that he ran out of his moccasins. His legs moved so swiftly that he was lifted into the air as if he had wings and flew over the monsters' heads. So high did he fly that he captured the sun in his own *Bagadowe* stick. Coming back to earth, and with one last burst of the bear's power, he hurled the sun at the monsters and burned them to ashes."

"Aiee!" the children mimic the adults in high-pitched voices.

"After defeating the monsters, Gitche Manitou returned the sun to its place in the sky and, as a reward for its help, he permitted the sun to sleep every night, just like many of the creatures of the earth. Then, when he created man, Gitche Manitou gave this new creature the game *Bagadowe* to honor him and to develop the skills, strength, and speed of his brothers the animals to defeat any monsters that might come upon the earth again."

"And so, my children, whenever you feel the shaking of the ground and the rumbling of the earth, it is the monsters trying to escape their cavernous tombs. But fear not, for you have been given the Game to vanquish the monsters and any of your enemies. For it is he, Gitche Manitou, who has promised that playing our Game will, in time, cure all ills."

The children cheer, clap, and jump to their feet. The closest few fling themselves onto me, hugging my now dried blood-streaked legs. Bending over, I lovingly pluck them from my legs, return them to their mothers, courteously bow to my audience, and move along.

I think of the night before I played in my first *Bagadowe* game with the men of my tribe. I had dreamed of the first *Bagadowe* game, envisioning myself in the role of Gitche Manitou. Induced by the heat of the sweat lodge, which burned all day, visions often come in the form of dreams to a warrior who is preparing himself for the Game.

Our sweat lodge is framed with flexible saplings covered by animal skins in the round shape of a teepee, commonly seen in the villages of our brothers to the west. The round shape symbolizes the circle of life. We are uncomfortable, even sickened, in the white man's buildings with their square shapes and sharp angles.

The hole in the ceiling of the sweat lodge not only permits the smoke from the smoldering rocks to escape but also invites the Creator to look upon his people who purify themselves in his honor. We believe that cleansing the body in such a way frees the mind from worldly matters. Some of us smoke pipes of herb or hemp to induce a vision before battle. To produce heat in the sweat lodge, we layer stones over burning coals. The occasional sprinkling of water and herbs upon the red-hot stones produces a cloud of steam, releasing a pleasant aroma and eliciting more sweat from our warrior bodies.

Hardly a word is spoken in the sweat lodge other than the drone or chant of an elder or medicine man or the occasional musings of a warrior who may be experiencing a vision. So sacred is the sweat lodge that only men participate in its rituals. Women, the usual keepers of the fire, are not permitted to enter the sweat lodge. Boys are forbidden entrance until they pass into manhood. Warriors bond in the sweat lodge, creating the sense of brotherhood that is necessary for victory.

The dream that would haunt me for the rest of my life first came to me during my purification in the sweat lodge a night ago. I dreamt of an eagle that held a bloody stick in its talons as it flew over the earth, its massive wings casting a great shadow over the land. Although its meaning is not yet clear, I believe that the dream is important to my cause or to the Game I will play the next day. I have shared this dream with the elders of my tribe, all of whom but one do not understand its meaning but agree that it is a powerful message sent to me from the Creator.

However, the oldest of the elders remembers hearing stories of his grandfather encountering white-bearded men wearing metal breastplates and metal hats and riding the first horses into our country. He recalls a prophecy that speaks of a time when the people witnessed a great eagle, largest of all the birds, flying over the land, casting a shadow, carrying in its talons a stick dripping with blood that drove these white bearded men from our land. The eldest is perhaps too old for he or anyone to remember how many winters have passed since he came upon the earth; he is a man with long, white, braided hair. He believes that a warrior who plays the Game with the greatest passion can summon the great eagle—to what purpose only the warrior knows.

Is there a connection between my vision, the prophecy, and the next day's Game? I wonder. These thoughts are much too vexing to ponder the night before the Game. Shaking my head, I hope to rid myself of thoughts of the great eagle so that I can mentally prepare in my traditional way for the next day's events.

After leaving the adoring audience of children, I continue to walk proudly among my people, enjoying their preparation. I momentarily stop by the campfire of my immediate kinsmen. I sense that they are ready. But am I? Although outwardly confident, I am burdened by the many responsibilities of a chief. Will my strategy work? I sigh and am comforted that joining with my brothers in the sweat lodge and offering prayers to the Creator will eventually lead me to wisdom.

On the way back to my lodge, I stop to help a young brave struggling to tighten the webbing of his stick. With my hand on the obviously frustrated brave's shoulder, I smile as if to say *I know you are nervous. Be calm. Let the strength of my hand guide you.*

I look into the eyes of my braves, each of whom look up in respect as I pass. In some, I see courage; in others, I see fear. To those who radiate courage, I crouch down and whisper a request that they use their strength to fortify the resolve of the inexperienced players. For one young brave trying to mask the fear that I see in his eyes, I grasp his trembling hands with my own, instantly conveying a calm strength that stills his trepidation.

"Steady, my son," I begin. "Be brave in the face of adversity. Be calm when confronted with chaos. Be wise in the midst of confusion. In the end, know that you are one of my warriors. Draw on my strength, for I have much to give. Now close your eyes and breathe deeply. Imagine us running together, our hearts beating as one, running so swiftly that we barely touch our feet to our Mother Earth's breast. We fear nothing, for we are one. One in the Game. One in spirit. Brothers in the stick!"

The young man breathes deeply, his spirit nourished by my words. His trembling subsides and a confident smile forms over his lips.

I come upon a granite outcropping three times a man's height. I climb it so that all may see, my face and body reflecting the glow of the camp's fires. I gaze stoically as, without signal, the people begin to drift to this spot and settle into their places. When all have gathered, I speak.

"My people, tomorrow will be a time that will be remembered in songs for generations to come. It will be the dawning of a new time, when the traditions of our fathers will meet a new age and when the people will recover all that has been taken from them since the arrival of the white man into our country. The Creator has spoken to me tonight on the hill overlooking our ancestral lands and the great lake. He has reminded me of our sacred cause. He has promised me that our warriors will be given the swiftness of the deer and the strength of the bear. He is well pleased with us and will bring victory to our people!"

Yelps and cries ring out as my voice reaches a crescendo of confidence and pride. The men jump to their feet, holding their prized sticks in their raised hands and, as one, shout, "Aiee!"

Hushing the crowd, I continue in barely a whisper, "Now sleep, my people. Dream of your Game and of the battle. Calm yourselves and save the powers divinely given to you by the Creator this night. Women, keep your children quiet lest they disturb their sleeping fathers. All of you, never forget who you are. You are the children of the lake, the bounty of which is the Creator's gift to us.

Then, speaking more loudly, my blood's passion rising in my throat, I shout, "The white man can never take from us—from our hearts, from our minds—who we are as a people. We are his people who will rise again. Believe in me who carries the sacred stick through which his will be done."

With the roar of a waterfall, I beseech my people, "At the sun's rising, gather with me at the fort's gate, and let us fulfill our destiny."

The tribe's cheer is so great that it must startle the soldiers at the fort. The warriors are stirred to a frenzy. To the people's delight, I fling a handful of black beans into the fire, a custom widely believed to cause confusion in one's enemy. I also toss gunpowder into the fire, which explodes in a puff of smoke. As the smoke clears, the startled people return their eyes to my former perch upon the granite rock, but I have disappeared—for now.

—

Morning dawns with its usual sounds of the world coming to life: the squirrels chattering, the crows cawing, the horses neighing, and the babies crying. Some of the warriors slept calmly. Others twitched nervously through the night. Many did not sleep at all. As the sun rises, the clamor of children playing, the crackle of fires burning, and the smell of herbal tea brewing awaken me.

Undisturbed by dreams of eagles carrying bloody sticks, I slept well. I feel lighter yet stronger, even though I am fasting as part of our pregame ritual.

I am chief, but on this day I will not be a spectator. I will play in the Game with my warriors as fiercely as if we were together in battle.

Although I have been on this earth for more than forty winters and clearly am one of the oldest players, I am determined to amaze even the youngest warriors with my strength and stamina. The passing of the years has probably cost me the loss of a step or two, but I make up for any age-related shortcomings with skill, anticipation, and tactics.

The people are excited too, not so much because this day marks the English king's birthday, but because they are playing their Game in the Creator's honor. They are anxious as well, because the outcome of this Game, more than any Game ever witnessed, will mark their destiny as a people.

Silently staring at the morning fire, I occasionally sip hot tea, in which steeps a piece of buffalo jerky, hoping that the spirit of this great animal will strengthen my physical resolve. My concentration breaks as I glance up at my mother, who busies herself around the camp. The upcoming day's events race through my head.

I watch her, smile, and say, "Thank you, my mother, for all that you have given me."

She returns the smile and says nothing as she packs up the family's bowls, pots, and utensils.

I am comforted by my mother's presence. She is a slender woman, the hair on the top of her head turning white like the snowcapped mountains in the West.

"You still move as quietly and as gracefully as the lake stork," I note lovingly.

She laughs and kindly replies, "Someday you will marry again, my son. Then you can watch your wife perform these chores and lie to her as well."

I chuckle at her wisdom and, after a moment's silence, offer, "I am sorry, my mother, if I have caused you any unhappiness or pain."

Momentarily stopping her chores, the older woman slowly arises from a stooped position, reaching back with both hands to locate the pain of many years of hard work, and responds, "It is not pain I feel for you, my son, but sadness."

Sensing my troubled thoughts as only a mother can, she offers unsolicited wisdom. "Listen to and follow your heart. Guidance comes to us in many forms, my son. Wisdom comes in prayers, in dreams, in times of quiet solitude, and in the words and deeds of wise elders and friends. Use all these to your advantage."

I smile. I want to help my aging mother, whose back has stiffened over the years from performing typical camp labors, but that would bring shame to her, for only a woman does such chores. A man has his own duties. Such is the efficiency of the people. Each has a role in the tribe. Older members of the tribe teach the children—a communal asset—their respective duties. And so it has been for generations.

My mother disappears into our lodge, which, along with the dwellings of the rest of the tribe, had been erected only yesterday with a swiftness that any white general forced to make camp along his march would envy.

She emerges with a bright smile, reverently holding a deerskin sack. I slowly stand and proudly receive the package from her rough outstretched hands—nails worn down to the nubs and skin patterned with many prominent veins like the tributaries of a great river. She stands unusually erect, shoulders back, her wrinkled but loving face beaming with pride. The rest of the camp stops to behold this solemn moment as I remove the sacred stick from its deerskin covering.

Inspecting the stick for any cracks or loose lacings, I turn it gently in my hands as if admiring a newborn son. But what I hold is nothing other than wood, leather, and string. The nicks and gashes on the wooden shaft tell stories of great Games past. The smoothness of its shape reminds me of my lost love, my wife. Its firmness, in spite of its years, reminds me of my mother. Its strength is like the heart of my father, killed in war long ago.

I slowly and firmly caress the stick in my hands, feeling the wood's grain. I close my eyes and imagine the stick becoming an extension of my arm. I gaze upon it with such intensity, as if wishing for it to tell me what to do and to explain the meaning of the eagle. Then, if only in my mind, the stick does speak: *I shall be the instrument of death in the hands of the warrior who holds me.*

Reassured that I am on the right path, I then turn to my awaiting tribesmen. I hold my stick with one hand outstretched to the sky and cry, "Gitche Manitou! Bring us victory!"

The communal response alerts the soldiers in the fort that we are coming. The women quickly decamp, gathering up the morning's wares and packing them away in assorted satchels and skins. Also gathering their children, some carried in backboards, they stuff deer hide sacks with chunks of venison and strips of buffalo jerky, strapping these provisions across one shoulder and water-filled deer and buffalo bladders across the other shoulder. The women also carry knives sheathed in decorative deer hide in the smalls of their backs and secret steel hatchets under their dresses. Then the people await my signal to approach the fort.

Smiling with supreme confidence, I raise my stick and shout, "Follow me, my children, for the hour of our destiny is upon us. Remember to look to me for the signal."

"Aiee!" the people respond in unison as they follow me, their leader.

2

PONTIAC'S RUSE

The sounds of the tribe's trampling feet upon the dried ground and the jingling of bells that many warriors have affixed around their ankles announce the people's march. They move as a wave on a distant shore. A cloud of white dust arises to what was otherwise a clear, blue sky. Two hundred paces from the fort, as if previously choreographed, the women and children begin to peel off to the sides, forming two long parallel lines that extend to the fort's gate. Through the middle of both lines, the warriors proudly stride, their bodies shimmering with sweat and bear grease. Their faces and bodies are painted red to distinguish themselves from our brothers—but on this day, our competitors—the Ojibway, who are painted yellow. Their metallic face rings reflect the sunlight, transforming their heads into twinkling stars. Exaggerating their fierce countenances and nervously switching their prized *Bagadowe* sticks from hand to hand, the braves confidently march behind me, their chief and teammate.

Again without signal, the warriors stop their procession twenty paces from the fort. Proudly and slowly, I alone walk toward the English, who have opened the large wooden gate as a sign of friendship and respect.

The English commander, a middle-aged man with a round, red face and a big belly, stands inside the fort clothed in red and wearing a white wig. Beads of sweat begin to form into little streams on his brow in the sweltering sun. His honor guard stops at the gate, but the commander continues to march to the sound of fife and drum until he stands across from me.

The commander, I am told, is a lieutenant colonel who served in His Majesty's army during the time when French, English, and Indians fought each other and is well versed in the customs of the native people. He raises his left arm, the arm closest to the heart, toward me as a universal sign of friendship. I return the gesture, holding my Bagadowe stick in the crook of my right arm much like a hunter carries his musket.

Moments later, a slender Indian woman emerges from a group of Indians of different tribes who have taken up residence around the fort. Through these contacts she learned the languages of the French, English, and the people of the great lake.

"I am Red Fawn," she softly introduces herself to me. As she speaks, she casts her eyes to the ground, not having the temerity to look a great chief in the eyes. She explains she had been married to a French trapper and later was traded to the English storeowner at the fort for a musket and ammunition.

Understanding her purpose, I speak. "I have come with my people, at your invitation, to celebrate the white father's birthday. In his honor, we offer you and your men the entertainment of our Game. We shall play *Bagadowe* until the Creator is satisfied. Afterward, we shall feast, sing, and dance...together," I explain, holding out my arms as if to gather both people together.

Patiently awaiting the translation, the British commander graciously accepts with a smile and replies, "In His Majesty's name, I hope that this gathering will be the first of many in which our people shall openly and honestly meet and trade in peace." With that, he removes his triangular hat and broadly sweeps it across his body as he deeply bows. But before the commander returns to an erect position, I turn and begin to walk away, not out of rudeness but rather because I am preoccupied, as any warrior is before playing the Game—and impatient with the white man's formalities.

The English colonel looks at Red Fawn and commands that she beg me to listen. He foolishly shouts to me even though Red Fawn stands next to him. She translates: "Tell the great chief that we welcome him and his people, and we look forward to this magnificent game about which we have heard much from the French trappers and traders. Please ask the great chief if he wishes to view the game from the parapets of the fort or perhaps the corner sentry posts, which are higher and more comfortable."

Taking a moment to understand Red Fawn's translation, I stop, laugh to myself, turn to face the dumbfounded commander, and reply, "A great chief never watches his warriors in battle. He leads them."

We both smile, albeit uncomfortably, and with a slight bow, leave to prepare for the day's events. The English garrison, now having finished their morning mess, are ordered to keep the fort's gates wide open as a token of their trust and friendship toward their Indian guests. The soldiers seem to worry little about attack after witnessing the peaceful parley between the two leaders and observing that the warriors do not display any weapons, only the curiously constructed *Bagadowe* sticks that obviously do not have sharp edges or metal points as opposed to the typical Indian war club. Little, if any, notice is given to the Indian women who are well armed.

After completing their morning duties, the English soldiers gather high up on the fort's parapets for a better view of the Game. The field of play extends from the fort's gates, where two vertical stakes have been driven into the ground about ten paces apart, and about four hundred paces to the foothills from where we emerged earlier. The parallel lines of the Indian women and children, about one hundred paces apart, delineate the width of the field of play. Thus, the field, which measures approximately four hundred paces by one hundred paces, can be plainly seen and enjoyed by the English spectators.

Below the fort's walls are gathered Indians of various tribes, French traders, hunters, and scouts. Their Indian women, each chattel to be traded at her man's whim, typically do odd jobs around the fort. The French traders, who do business with the fort's merchants, have witnessed the playing of this fabulous Game previously.

New to the Game, the English soldiers shout many questions to the Frenchmen below, who, in turn, shout answers back up to them.

"Monsieur, what are the rules?" an English soldier asks.

"How does one win?" another chimes in.

"Are there penalties for misbehavior?" an officer inquires with a sly smile.

The Frenchmen laugh while passing a jug of whiskey among themselves. After taking a voracious swig from the jug and wiping his mouth on his buckskin sleeve, one of the Frenchmen yells back up at the English soldiers.

"Rules? Zere are few, *mes amis*. It seems chaotic at first, but after a while, you will appreciate ze skill and ze stamina of ze players."

Another soldier asks, "What is the purpose of the pieces of wood with stitching that the Indians hold?"

A French trapper explains, "Ze sticks are made of hickory. I have seen zem made. Ze wood is boiled for hours to soften it. It is zen bent in ze crook of a tree so zat, after zis process, ze stick looks like ze *crosier*, or *crosse*, of a French bishop. Zat is why we French call ze game 'lacrosse.'"

Grabbing the whiskey jug with one hand and balancing it on the crook of his elbow and arm, another trapper takes a long draught and continues, "A player can only carry or pass ze ball wiz his stick. He cannot touch ze ball wiz his hands. Ze players zen orchestrate as best as can be determined, out of ze midst of zis chaos, an attack or charge toward zere goal, against which zere opponents do evreezing in zere power to stop."

"Can a player strike another player with his stick?" a soldier asks.

"Do players get hurt badly?" another inquires.

The Frenchmen heartily laugh and slap each other on their backs, as if to warn the Englishmen of the impending mayhem. "Watch, *mes amis.* Just watch."

All is ready. I look toward my warriors, the women, the children, the English, and all the spectators. I pray that I have embarked on the right course. After positioning myself at the center of the field, I raise my stick, look to the sky, and shout, "Gitche Manitou!"

In unison, the warriors on both sides raise their sticks and similarly shout, "Gitche Manitou!" signaling commencement of the Game.

I hold a ball made from the knot of a pine tree where the sap gathers that my people call *pikwakwad.* Half the ball is painted red, representing warmth, light, and spring; the other half is painted blue, symbolizing cold, death, and winter. The thin yellow stripe around the diameter symbolizes the path of the rising and the setting of the sun. The ball is punctured with many small holes that cause a whistling sound when it is tossed through the air. With a great heave, I throw the ball toward the clouds. As the ball seems momentarily suspended in the air, the shouting warriors rush madly, gauging its imminent return to earth.

Amid a deafening clash of bodies and sticks, the ball falls to the ground. Emerging from the cloud of dust, a red-painted warrior carries the ball as the yellow-painted warriors excitedly pursue him. Whooping, hollering, and wildly swinging their sticks, the yellow warriors savagely strike the red player's arm and his stick countless times. The vicious sound causes some English soldiers to cringe in disgust. One English soldier shouts, "I say, is that yellow-painted chap attempting to dislodge the ball or break the ball carrier's arm?"

A Frenchman laughs, "A little of boz, I t'ink."

As the red warrior miraculously eludes his yellow tormentors and tosses the wooden ball between the wooden wickets, the English soldiers burst into a mighty cheer and wave their three-cornered hats in the air. The soldiers prudently do not fire their flintlocks in their exuberance lest they scare us away or, even worse, rouse us to violence. But it will take more than a few shots to do that on this day.

It quickly becomes apparent that the teams are distinguishable by their red and yellow paint. The Ottawa braves, led by me, are painted red. The Ojibway, who are Ottawa allies, are painted yellow. Although brothers-in-arms, the tribes play this Game as fiercely as if in battle against one another.

After the first goal, the Game ebbs and flows, each team alternately possessing the ball but unable to reach the goal. Both sides are evenly matched. This will be a contest of attrition. Who will tire first? Scores of fights and wrestling matches spontaneously break out among the warriors, each accusing the other of a violation of some unwritten rule, of which there are few. The combatants curse and hurl insults at each other as deftly as they hurl the ball to their teammates. Wounded braves with cut heads, broken arms, and hideous gashes of all kinds limp or are carried off the field to a nearby brook where medicine men apply mud and herb packs to the players' wounds.

The air is filled with the ringing of the warriors' ankle bells, the whistling sound of the ball, and the swooping of the sticks, melodic amid the cacophony of moans and screams of agony. It is not difficult to understand the uneasiness that some of the English soldiers, particularly those newly arrived in America, must feel in watching a game that so simulates battle. They must surely hope that they will never have to face these warriors in battle one day.

During the few lulls in the Game when I was not directly involved in the action, messengers informed me of the general condition of the fort's soldiers. I was advised that the Frenchmen are generous in sharing their whiskey with the English soldiers, who sneak draughts while their officers are distracted by the Game. After all, this is a celebration. I am told that the English soldiers, are drunk and openly waging anything of value, from British coin to furs and whiskey.

The braves take no respite from the Game for food or water, even after three hours of playing. Nor does a warrior dare slow down, for if he begins to lag behind, any of the Indian women, not necessarily of his family, are permitted to urge him on by beating him with saplings and switches. This is the only circumstance wherein an Indian woman is permitted to strike a man, although a man striking a woman is not prohibited. Few braves, unless gravely injured, chance lagging behind for fear of being publicly chastised and bringing dishonor to themselves and their families.

Just as the Indians do not stop for water or food, I am told that the British do not take their customary afternoon tea, so enthralled with the magnificence of the Game are they.

Where am I amid this frenzied melee? Discerning one brave from the other in the chaos and dust is nearly impossible. After several hours, however, clearly a handful of braves stand out from the others as the strongest, the swiftest, and the most skillful. I am proud that I am among this group. Blood trickles from my nose, the side of my mouth, and the shaved side of my temple. My slashed, bloody hands and arms resemble jerked venison rather than flesh and bone. Several broken or dislocated fingers appear more like an eagle's crooked talons than a man's hand.

Yet despite pain and injury, I am determined to hold my stick no differently than if uninjured for fear that my opponents may sense weakness.

As are all the warriors, I am sweating profusely. A combination of red face paint and blood drips onto my neck and shoulders. A thin layer of dust coats my body. The bottoms of my feet are raw since I, like many other teammates, play the Game barefoot. No protection covers any parts of our bodies. The sound of a stick striking a human body with full force must send shivers up the English soldiers' spines. So violent are some of the blows that the English are often compelled to avert their eyes from the carnage.

On this day, Gitche Manitou looks upon his people with pride. His game, *Bagadowe*, is being played with the ferocity and vigor expected of all men who call themselves warriors.

As the hours pass and the sun begins to descend in the afternoon sky, signaling that we are coming to the end of the game, the Frenchman who has been keeping score announces that the Game is tied ten to ten. The score is important only to the whites who gamble on the outcome. Although some of the people have, on occasion, wagered goods on the outcome of a game, to the warrior participants, playing with all of one's strength to honor the Creator was of greater importance. My team has just recovered the ball at the far end of the field and is on the move toward our opponent's goal at the fort's gate. With bloodcurdling war cries, my braves and I, a sea of red, muster every fiber of our beings and mount one last surge.

Although gasping for air, I am resolved to inspire my exhausted teammates to victory. "My brothers," I begin and pause to gather my breath, "beseech the Creator for strength. Reach into your hearts and find the stamina for one more run at the goal. We must and will score now and end this. Now, to your feet...breathe as one...feel the power...raise your sticks...Gitche Manitou!"

"Gitche Manitou!" they shout in unison.

My teammates flawlessly pass the ball back and forth and, with renewed vigor, charge the goal at the fort's gate. Our yellow-painted opponents poke and prod the red ball carriers to no avail. Just before a yellow warrior physically assaults our ball carrier, the red player passes the ball to his teammate, who quickly separates from a yellow defender and advances the ball up the field. The ball never falls to the ground. The red warriors time their passes perfectly, cutting in and between their yellow defenders, who are clearly on their heels and retreating.

"Guard against Pontiac, my brothers," shouts an Ojibway warrior whose yellow-painted face sports red dots on one cheek as drops of blood ooze from a gash above his left eyebrow. "He is favored by Gitche Manitou."

"You had better have the wind at your backs, my Ojibway brothers, if you hope to stop us now," I warn as I lead one last fearsome attack toward the goal.

Only a handful of red-painted braves remain at my side. The others fall behind, utterly exhausted and unable to keep the pace. The women, respectful of the warriors' courage and endurance, do not beat or urge them on; instead, the women hand the warriors gourds of water and, surreptitiously, the hatchets they had secreted under their dresses.

Most of the remaining warriors have now been on the field for much of the day. A handful of yellow warriors, barely able to stand, are left to stop my advance. Their teammates, like their red opponents, drift toward the sideline with the women and other spectators. The English and French spectators cheer wildly and vigorously, urging me to score the winning goal.

"Stay with me, my brothers," I encourage my warriors. "Pray that the Creator brings us strength. One last charge. Aiee!"

With all spectators' eyes focused on my final surge, I dodge my pursuers or run through them as if I were running a gauntlet. The English soldiers do not notice the many players, either genuinely exhausted or feigning exhaustion, straggling along the sidelines yet slowly edging toward the fort.

About fifty paces from the goal, bleeding and with battered limbs, I close my eyes, take a deep breath, and, with an undeniable determination, make the last play.

I pass the ball to a teammate, who quickly passes it back to me. I must stretch to reach the dangerously high pass, perilously exposing my ribs to a vicious body blow. I catch the ball at the apex with one extended arm, momentarily suspended in the air like a hawk floating on the wind.

Pain sears through my legs. Three Ojibways viciously smash my legs with their sticks, one player breaking his stick across my shins. A lesser man may have been crippled, but not I. Descending to the ground, I begin to whirl my broken body rapidly, spinning through my opponents like a tornado with blood and sweat flying from my body. One yellow warrior hurls his body at my knees, but at the last moment before impact, I jump up and execute a forward flip over the yellow brave, who falls face-first into the dirt.

Thinking that no man could possibly endure such punishment and keep possession of the ball, the English mercifully beseech me to toss the ball to a less-besieged teammate. But I neither ask for nor give mercy. Raising my stick, I feign a pass to a teammate on my right. I quickly turn my wrists at the last moment so that the ball magically remains within the deer string-webbed pocket of the stick, even though I have fully extended my arms forward as if to pass. Deceived, all the players and spectators turn their eyes to the right. Seeing no ball in flight, they realize that they have all been duped by my trick. Still carrying the ball, I continue my advance alone.

Now only three yellow-painted warriors remain on the field standing between the goal and me. The three yellow warriors drop their sticks and interlock their arms in front of their goal, determined that I will not get by them to score. I must breach that yellow wall.

My muscles ache with pain, my fingers are numb, and blood drips from my flayed arms onto my stick, trickling down the shaft and leaving a blood-spotted trail in my wake. My chest heaves, I can hardly breathe, and my mouth is so dry that the blood dripping from my nose and upper lip is welcomed moisture.

Only twenty paces away, I summon my last ounce of strength. Just then, an ominous shadow falls over the fort. Looking up, I think I see a magnificent eagle, larger than any eagle I have ever seen before. *Does no one else see it?* I wonder. *Is it real? Is this the bird of my dreams? Is this the eagle of the prophecy?* Whatever the truth, this is the sign I have been waiting for.

With one final burst, I run headlong toward the fort and the goal alone. Blood and sweat spray from my body, and dust floats up from my feet as I pound the ground with every step. Anxiously awaiting their foe, the three bloody, exhausted, terrified Ojibway are determined to block my way. There are no chiefs in *Bagadowe*; all warriors are equal. Victory or defeat depends on skill and teamwork, not on status.

Just as I approach the seemingly impenetrable yellow wall of defenders, who scream for my blood and dare me to try to score, the teammate to whom I had faked a pass sprints back onto the field and executes a quick flanking cut toward the goal as if leading interference for me. But at the very moment when the cutting teammate confronts the three defenders, he unexpectedly falls flat on his belly. In an instant, he scrambles to his hands and knees, whereupon I leap upon his tired back, push off with both feet, and sail through the air over the heads of the astonished yellow defenders, who impotently wave their sticks at me.

I fly as the great eagle of my vision, carrying a bloody stick in my talons and casting a shadow over my enemies below. I still see everything clearly. The spectators' mouths drop open in amazement. No one speaks a word nor even draws a breath as all eyes are transfixed upon me in flight. While suspended in the air, I whisk my stick behind my head and in one fluid motion move my arms and hands forward, hurling the ball with all of my might. The ball flies through the two goal sticks and rolls into the fort's open gates before I hit the ground. I can hear all voices—white and Indian—mightily cheer for the winning goal.

My exhausted, bloody, seemingly lifeless body crashes to the dirt in a heap. I do not stir. The crowd grows silent, wondering if the great chief—the great eagle—is dead. But after a few moments, I slowly raise first my head to see whether I have scored the winning goal and then drag myself up to my knees. Realizing that I have scored, I thrust my stick to the sky and burst into a war cry that echoes across the lake. A thunderous cheer arises from every player and spectator: Indian, French, and English alike.

What a magnificent game-ending goal! Now all the Indians rush toward me. However, they do not stop to touch me or to sing my praises, as is customary after such an amazing feat. Rather, they rush past me and pour into the fort, whooping and shouting. The soldiers assume this wave of Indian bodies is a mad rush to retrieve the game-winning ball, a trophy befitting any man's lodge. The unsuspecting spectators chatter and roar with laughter.

Soon, however, the white man's sounds of glee turn into cries of anguish. The players who had lagged behind feigning exhaustion during my last surge had actually gathered steel tomahawks and knives from the Indian women on the sidelines. The English soldiers unknowingly are rushing headlong down the stairs from the parapets to greet these fabulous athletes who were, a short while ago, their entertainers but now have become their executioners.

As death screams fill the air, I realize that my ruse has worked. I had earlier devised this plan to capture the fort by offering to play *Bagadowe* in honor of the king's birthday. This victory today is the beginning of a grander campaign to eradicate the English from our country.

The unsuspecting soldiers fall victim to my masterful plan. The Ottawa and Ojibway, opponents in the Game, now become allies in a common cause: destruction of the fort and its garrison. My brother warriors now wield their tomahawks as skillfully as their *Bagadowe* sticks.

Stunned by this sudden turn of events and realizing my deception, the stout commander desperately orders his men to arms. But the usually organized and disciplined English soldiers manage only a feeble response in their disheveled, confused, and drunken condition. Desperate pleas for mercy replace the English shouts of encouragement during the Game. The Indians take their war trophies in the form of English scalps. They scrape English skulls with their knives and tear off a scalp of hair as the victim lays dying. The trickles of blood that spot almost every Indian player from the brutal contest of flesh versus stick starkly contrast with the torrents of blood from the dead and dying within the fort.

Fort Michilimackinac will be the first of twelve forts in the great lake to fall in the summer of 1763. "Pontiac's Uprising," as it becomes known, begins not with a gunshot, but with the simple-yet-savage Game that the Great Spirit gave to his people to heal the sick, to grow the crops, to train for war, and, ostensibly, to honor the English king on his birthday. Following the fall of Fort Michilimackinac, I become leader of a confederation of many tribes, including the Ojibway, the Saux and Fox, the Assiniboine, the Potawatomi, the Huron, and others who will sweep across the great lake region like an icy storm, dispatching one fort after another, although never again under the ruse of the Game.

I believe that the story of the fall of Fort Michilimackinac will become legend, remembered in song around the campfire. But is this victory the fulfillment of the prophecy of the great eagle told to me by the elder or just the enactment of a dream? I leave the truth to the Creator, who reveals all things in due time.

3

PONTIAC'S BETRAYAL

During the war between the French and English that came to be known as the French and Indian War, the Indians around the great lake were mostly allied with the French. The French had traded with our people many years before the English came into our lands. The French introduced to our people steel knives, pots, pans, bits of metal used to make arrowheads, and, most prized of all, steel tomahawk heads in return for blankets, beaver pelts, and provisions.

The early French traders did not trade the flint musket, which they held in their exclusive possession as a kind of guarantee of safety against the overwhelming number of native people. But in time, and as a result of the white man's war, the French, who were outnumbered by the English, enlisted Indian allies and taught us the art of musketry. The French lost that war, and many of them left our lands.

Following the English victory, Lord Jeffery Amherst, commander of all the post-war English forces in America, made no secret of his distrust of the Indian people, whom he regarded as treacherous heathens forever allied with the French. Lord Amherst ordered an embargo on trade of almost all European goods with the Indians until they could prove to his satisfaction their loyalty to the Crown.

This edict angered many of the Indian peoples, who had grown accustomed to the trappings of European civilization. Those who had long since abandoned their stone tomahawks and wooden and gourd implements for gleaming steel were reluctant to return to the old ways. The cessation of trade in muskets, powder, flint, and ammunition caused a rift between the Indians, who lacked the capacity to produce these goods, and the English. Hunting, whether a deer or one's enemy, was a far more daunting task with stone implements or bow and arrow than with musket and ball.

Many native people began to grumble over the loss of their European luxuries. Others, like me, lamented the loss of our traditional ways. Whatever the motivation, the English were hated and had to go, either voluntarily or by force.

Before the French and Indian War, my people and I enjoyed a relatively peaceful relationship with the French, who were interested in trade and who treated the Indians with respect. Many Frenchmen took Indian women as brides. The English, on the other hand, openly declared that as a result of their victory over the French and their Indian allies, and pursuant to the Treaty of Paris in 1763, they now "owned" the land over which the spirits of the people's ancestors dwelt. Wisely, the French had never openly declared that they owned a piece of land; rather, they were more interested in "controlling" a swath of land for trade purposes.

Soon after cessation of hostilities between the French and English, and before the fall of Fort Michilimackinac, the tribal chiefs from the great lakes gathered in an area near Fort Detroit to discuss the English problem. Here is my recollection of that day.

"People of the great lakes," I say, "our French brothers in this region are few now. They have either been killed or driven off by the English. The English are not friends of the Indian people. They take without asking. They abuse our women. By merely stepping on the land of our fathers, they claim to own it."

This last statement particularly stirs the chiefs. I continue.

"You ask why it is that they withhold trading goods from us. It is to show that they are superior to us."

The chiefs nod in agreement.

"When the white man—French, Dutch, or English—came to this land, darkness fell upon us. The white man has given us diseases against which we have no defense. He has scattered the buffalo and has driven off the elk. Only our brother, the elusive deer, remains. And like the deer, we must be swift in our actions. To delay will give the English time to reinforce the forts and permanently settle in our land. I say to you, we must not hesitate. We must drive the English from our lands before they become too strong and too many, and we become too weak and too few."

Most of the tribal chiefs yelp in agreement. Some are less than enthusiastic, perhaps hoping that Lord Amherst can be convinced that trade can benefit both cultures. But those entreaties have been rebuffed time and again, and the dissenters are shouted down.

—

I have emerged as the leader of both camps: the "traditionalists," who long for the return of the ways of their fathers, and the "traders," who want steel, musket, and powder, which they think will be easily procurable if the French return. Each group's objective can be achieved if the English are eliminated from Indian lands. I do not hate all white men—most, but not all. But my reason for hating the English goes deeper than anyone knows—not political as much as personal. My heart burns with revenge.

During the French and Indian War, Indians fought not only the white man but also each other. Often a tribe used war as a pretext to raid another tribe for goods and captives. Most often the French and English sanctioned these raids as long as they were made upon the opponent's ally.

Allied with the French were most of the great lake tribes, including the Huron, whose many clans extended between the great lake into what I learned was called the Ohio Valley and up into New York. The Iroquois Nation, composed of the Mohawk, Oneida, Onondaga, Seneca, Cayuga, and their Algonquin brothers of the Eastern forests, were allies of the English.

Regardless on whose side they had fought, the Indian peoples now fear that no matter what we try to do to stave off the onslaught, the whites will continue to pour into our lands. I believe that left unchecked, the whites will become as many as the stars in the sky.

The European view of war is too complicated to understand. We Indians view war simply as an opportunity to advance our fortunes in muskets, captives, scalps, and honor. Neither any Indian chief I know nor I have ever started a war for possession of land or power. In fact, words for the possession of land are absent from our native tongues. We do not crave trade routes, gold, and power as the white man does. We have no maps to measure our ancestral lands. We roam the lands of our fathers whose bones are the surveyors' marks.

This is not to say that, like all men on Earth, we Indians do not engage in treachery. In the autumn of 1761, a confederation of Ottawa, Ojibway, Fox, and Sauk had joined with most of the Huron of the great lakes region in an expedition east against the Iroquois. The Huron leaders had convinced the people of the great lake that if they did not attack the Iroquois first, the Iroquois would become too strong and, with the help of their masters from England, would sweep west across the great lakes lands like the pox that had decimated their brothers to the east.

During this trek eastward, just before the expedition crossed the small mountains the whites call the Alleghenies, some of the Huron warriors who had remained behind raided the villages of the warriors who'd traveled eastward, including the Ottawa, where my wife, Sweet Willow, remained.

These cowardly Hurons, who exploited the absence of warriors, stole Sweet Willow and other captives, carrying them north and east not to join in the fight, but to trade with some of the English who did not abide by Lord Amherst's prohibition of trading with the Indian people.

I am told that Sweet Willow was traded to an English trapper for two steel hatchets and a steel knife. I am also told that this Englishman was exceptionally cruel to my beloved wife. Being cheaper than a mule, she was forced to carry over one hundred pounds of material on the trail. Tired of her resisting him at night, the Englishman traded my Sweet Willow to the Iroquois.

I have learned about the Iroquois mostly from the Huron who have fought them many times. I was told that the Iroquois village where Sweet Willow was taken was located in a place the whites call New York near some lakes east of the river that connect to the great ocean south of the lands the French call Canada. The Iroquois villages are formidable fortresses, usually one hundred wooden lodges surrounded by a triple-walled wooden stockade twenty feet high, in the middle of which stands their great longhouse where the council of Sachems and venerable women gather. The Iroquois are hunters, gatherers, and agriculturists. Rich natural resources, including fertile lands, plentiful game, and streams filled with fish, contribute to the prosperity of the Iroquois nation.

Although Sweet Willow was an Iroquois captive, she, like other captives in Iroquois tradition, was not a slave in the typical sense of the word, for she could become a member of the tribe. She could not escape, and I could only imagine her desperation.

My warriors and I returned home from our eastern expedition with little to show for our efforts. Snow flurries forced us to return home to prepare for the winter. Little did I know that Sweet Willow and I had crossed paths by not more than a few miles apart as I traveled west to home while she was taken east as a captive.

Upon arriving at my village, I was stunned to learn of the Hurons' treachery and heartbroken at the loss of my wife. Taking my knife from its sheath, I repeatedly cut my chest as a sign of mourning over my loss. My heart hardened, I was obsessed with revenge.

I hated all things Huron and English. I set out with a small band of warriors, hunting down the Hurons who had raided my village and had stolen my wife. Although some of the braves recovered their wives, I did not. My brothers and I took pleasure in roasting some of the Hurons alive over an open fire. The rest we tied to stakes and meticulously skinned alive. A warrior's courage is measured by his not crying out as his skin is flayed from his quivering body. But some are weak. In return for a quick death, one cowardly Huron revealed what had happened to Sweet Willow.

But fortune sometimes finds a friend in tragedy. I learned from white and Indian traders that many Iroquois women died during the winter of 1761 from an outbreak of smallpox. Most of them had been infected and died before Sweet Willow's arrival. Desperate for wives, Iroquois warriors raided other villages for women but came up short as the pox decimated the land, infecting friend and foe alike. Once a captive accepts the customs of her captors, she is adopted into the tribe, treated with affection, accorded rights, and expected to fulfill the same duties as any woman born of the tribe.

Many seasons passed before I learned what happened to my beloved Sweet Willow from this missionary who now writes my story. He lived among the Iroquois and came to know my wife.

I know in my heart that Sweet Willow never stopped loving me, and I do not begrudge her trying to make the best of her captivity. Sweet Willow had learned she was pregnant with my child after I had departed east to fight the Iroquois. Knowing that her worth as a wife would be diminished if it were discovered that she carried another man's child, Sweet Willow consented to be married before her belly betrayed her. Strong Hand, war captain and son of a Sachem, took Sweet Willow as his bride. She later gave birth to a boy, the labor so painful and complicated that she could bear no more children. I never knew that my kidnapped wife was pregnant when I departed east. Strong Hand believed the boy was his. Thus, my son was saved.

Like the Indians in the lands around the great lake, the Iroquois also love *Bagadowe.* Each tribe of the Iroquois has its own name for the Game. For example, *Tewaarathon,* meaning "little brother of war," is the Mohawk name. The Iroquois warrior's playing stick is as much a prized possession as a musket or a fine steel tomahawk. Many a man sleeps with his stick, which he holds as tightly and as lovingly as his own wife. A newborn boy's first gift is a small stick in his cradle. As soon as an Iroquois boy can walk, he is given a larger playing stick, not by his father but by his mother, whose father, uncle, or cousin constructs the stick. In this way, the bonds with the wife's family are fortified. As the child grows, a larger stick is made for him. An Iroquois boy's first taste of battle is usually in his first lacrosse game, a sacred rite of passage for the young man. When he dies, an Iroquois man and his stick are buried together. As I learned more about the Iroquois, I was strangely comforted that if my wife were to be taken anywhere, it would be among these impressive people.

So revered is a man's lacrosse stick, even to an enemy, that although a woman is forbidden to touch a man's lacrosse stick, the Huron brave who stole Sweet Willow did not object when she carried her husband's stick from their burning lodge. Sweet Willow carried that stick through all of her travails until she married again. Her Iroquois husband, already possessing a fine stick given to him by his mother's family and made by his maternal uncle, had no need of the stick she carried. Might he have changed his mind had he known that the stick she carried belonged to me, Chief Pontiac, whose name is spoken with reverence even among the people of the Eastern Woodlands? What a splendid trophy that would have made!

I am pleased to learn from this missionary that Sweet Willow passed my Bagadowe stick to our son, whom she named Strong Oak, hoping that he would become as strong and skilled a player as I, his true father. It is my hope that upon her Iroquois husband's death or well into the autumn of her own life, Sweet Willow will reveal to Strong Oak, who by then will be a grown warrior, the identity of his real father. I hope she regales him with stories of my exploits. I hope Strong Oak is proud, not only of the father who raised him but also of his heritage as my son!

And what of me, the great Chief Pontiac? My rebellion was quelled in 1763 by the English, who sowed the seeds of betrayal among some of my allies by providing them with English goods. I was forced to sign a treaty with the English in Canandaigua, New York, only a few miles from where I later learned my lost love had been taken. I agreed to bury the war hatchet or risk losing all of my ancestral lands to English trading companies.

In 1769, a renegade Indian, who blamed me for the death of his parents when the English burned his village as punishment for my uprising, ambushed me at a trading post and has caused me grave injury. I have lived for forty-nine winters. It is a good time to die. With my last breath, I tell this story. The English have come into our lands, so I suppose that my dream and the prophecy of the eagle told to me by the elder at Fort Michilimackinac are unfulfilled. As I lay dying, I pray my son or his sons or those future sons in our bloodline remember me, fulfill the prophecy, and restore the land to our people.

4

THE RESERVATION, 1909

Despite years of war, famine, disease, removal, and murder, Pontiac's *Bagadowe* stick has been passed down from our mothers since the days of Sweet Willow. I may not look like it now, but in my youth, I was the tallest, strongest, fastest, most skillful player on the reservation. I am an Onondaga, meaning "people of the hills." We are one of the six tribes of the Haudenosaunee, named for the longhouses in which we had once dwelt as keepers of the council fire of the once mighty Iroquois Confederacy. I am a Sachem, one of the twenty-five chiefs appointed by our venerable clan mothers. I am a Faithkeeper, responsible for ensuring that our cultural ceremonies are kept and performed correctly. I am a member of the deer clan, one of many such clans that are also named after the turtle, bear, wolf, beaver, hawk, and heron. I am a proud descendant of Pontiac, Sweet Willow, and Strong Oak. Like Strong Oak, I am named for a tree.

I am Fallen Tree, so named by my mother, who had watched loggers steal trees from the fringes of our sacred forest in the 1830s to construct rail ties and wooden pipes to move salt from the marshes in the northern part of the reservation. My Christian name is Benjamin; our Christian surname is Harwood. My father was called "Hardwood," but with the passage of time, the missionaries shortened our name to "Harwood," claiming easier pronunciation.

It is 1909. I have lived on the reservation south of Syracuse, New York, through many winters, most probably seventy-five or more. My only daughter, White Pine, died of whooping cough five winters past. My daughter's husband died in a logging accident a year after her death. I am grandfather to Jake, the oldest, and his three sisters: Mary, the youngest; Molly, the middle child; and Maggie, the eldest of the three girls.

You may wonder why descendants of Pontiac, Sweet Willow, and Fallen Tree have Christian names. The girls' names are easy to explain: my daughter loved the shape of the letter "M," which reminded her of the rolling hills of our country.

Jake's name is a longer story, but I will tell it anyway. When Jake's mother, my daughter, was ready to give birth—which typically occurred within our cabins with the aid of our midwife clan mothers—Jake, it seems, was impatient to enter the world. White Pine was working in the fields when Jake announced his arrival. She did not have time to summon the clan mothers or to seek the comfort of her bedroom, so she held onto a skinny but sturdy tree in private, where she struggled, pushing and moaning, to give birth to her baby. As the baby's head breached, a snake slithered along the grass between White Pine's legs. She was too far along to stop her labor, despite her fear that the snake might bite her or her newborn infant. With knees bent and legs as wide apart as possible, White Pine pushed her baby into the world and onto the grass. She held her breath as the snake's tongue flickered upon the glistening child. After a moment or two, the snake slithered around the crying baby without baring its fangs. Our people believe that the Creator placed his protective hand over this baby who had come so close to instant death with his first breath of life. As was our people's custom, my daughter named her son after a curious or significant event at or near the time of his birth. What could be more curious a sign than that of birthing a baby nearly on top of a snake?

As the boy grew older, the missionary teachers were loath to tolerate such a name as Snake Runs Over Him Harwood, fearing that the boy would be cursed by his namesake, which in the Bible tempted Eve in the Garden of Eden. He was renamed John, which soon gave way to Jake, a logical mix of "John" and "snake." Thus, the boy's name pleased both his people and the missionaries.

What a fine grandson! He is tall like his mother and his great-great-great-grandmother Sweet Willow, as well as straight and strong like his great-great-great-grandfather Pontiac. He is tallest of all the boys on the reservation. Yet even with his great size, no swifter a runner have our people ever seen.

"Look, Grandfather! Look at me!"

Out of the corner of my eye, I notice a deer gracefully leap a crumbling wooden fence. In hot pursuit, the boy jumps the fence without missing a stride, almost catching the deer in midair but instead ending up with a mouthful of grass as he plunges headlong into the hayfield.

Slapping the ground in disappointment, Jake marvels over the magnificent grace of the deer as it leaps away through the field. "Grandfather, will I ever be swift enough to touch our brother the deer?"

With a comforting laugh I answer, "The time will soon arrive when your brain catches up to your natural speed. It is not a man's speed alone that allows him to catch our brother the deer but his wits as a man who can outthink his prey. It is the ability to think that marks us as men."

Out of breath and missing one moccasin—dangled in the fence—Jake wraps his sinewy arms around me and whispers with a sly grin, "Grandfather, what makes you so wise? Are you blessed by the Creator above all men?"

I embrace my grandson. The smell and softness of his long black hair reminds me of my daughter. Suspicious of this unsolicited compliment, I suddenly jerk back, leaving Jake alone with his arms still outstretched, and jokingly ask, "What are you up to? What other than wisdom do you wish from me?"

"You know, Grandfather," Jake urges impatiently. "Please. You promised me many summers ago that you would take me to the city, to Syracuse, when I turned seventeen."

"Many summers ago?" I ask.

"Well, two summers ago," Jake concedes.

Syracuse is the closest city, about ten miles north of our home, which is located at the southwest part of the Onondaga reservation. I have been to other cities before: Albany, Oswego, even Montreal, Canada. The city holds nothing good for an Indian, especially a young, curious Indian boy.

"Please, Grandfather. You promised that if I did all my chores, studied hard in school, and helped my sisters in the fields, you would take me to Syracuse," Jake begs again.

"What is it about the white man's city that fascinates you so? Do you not know that there are dangers in the city?" I rejoin, hoping to dissuade him.

"Yes, but I have heard of many new and wondrous things in the city not seen on the reservation. I have read about the great cities of the world—Paris, London, and even Washington, our nation's capital—places I know I shall never see. But Syracuse is so close." Without missing a breath, and now trying to impress me, Jake continues, "Did you know that Syracuse was the name of an ancient Greek city?"

"What a smart boy. Have the missionaries taught you children something other than the burning fires of hell?"

"Stop, Grandfather. When do we leave? Besides, you know the missionaries do not teach us anymore. How many times do

I have to remind you that our teacher is Miss Doolittle from Boston?"

"Oh, yes, Miss Doolittle, the new teacher from the East." How could I have forgotten? Perhaps I am getting old. I shake my head and dispel any such notions. "Jake, you have kept your end of the bargain. Your sisters tell me that you have worked hard in the fields, even though you constantly complain that you are doing women's work. And I'm also told that you have studied very hard and are at the top of your class. In the next two days, when the moon is full, we shall hitch old Thunder to the wagon and journey to the big city."

"Oh, thank you, thank you, thank you, Grandfather!" Jake cries, hugging me so hard that I lose my breath. Jake departs, leaving me to regain my breath as I bend over with both hands on my knees. Arising, I can hear Jake's war cry as he runs down the dusty road, over a hill, and out of sight, his presence betrayed only by his Indian calls, which grow fainter in the distance, and his one remaining moccasin still dangling in the wind, which I lovingly retrieve with a chuckle.

The one main road, the central artery of the reservation, mirrors the meandering Onondaga Creek that flows north toward Syracuse and into Onondaga Lake. Many a spring floodwater has washed out the road and left it pock-marked like the dark spots of the moon. On a hill almost in the center of the reservation, off the road and near the creek, stands our sacred longhouse, and around it the church, the blacksmith and shoemaker shops, and the schoolhouse.

The Bureau of Indian Affair's agent, whom we call Firefly, promises to organize a road crew to repair the road. Each worker is to receive two dollars a day. But as with most of Firefly's promises, these are empty words. We complain to him that the coming of the winter snows and the spring melt will wash away what remains of the winding, bumpy road unless road crews are assembled and put to work immediately, but to no avail. BIA money earmarked for reservation improvements always seems to end up someplace else.

The Bureau of Indian Affairs is the federal agency that exercises exclusive jurisdiction over Indians relocated onto the reservation. The New York agency conducts BIA business from offices in Buffalo and Syracuse. The BIA is empowered by the federal government to manage Indian affairs, enforce policies, and maintain peace, although, for the most part, we manage our own affairs without government interference.

The BIA's inefficiency and corruption is notorious in reservation life, not only here, but, from what I have read, across the country. There is little, if any, oversight, and sharp dealing is rampant. The disrepair of the main road is not for lack of available men. More than half the men of working age on the reservation are unemployed and would gladly take up shovels. We continually reject overtures from the New York State Assembly to build more roads into our country for fear that the whites will exploit our resources, but the lasting repair of our one main road is essential to intra-reservation transportation. We hear the usual excuse from Firefly that the BIA budget does not include funds for construction projects. It is expensive to truck in loads of dirt from the sandpits around Lake Erie that are necessary to repair what Firefly calls the "pathway to civilization."

This is truly a road that would cause the fleetest of deer to stumble. And as for the road being the "pathway to civilization," well, for the Indian, that usually means the pathway to misery and despair. Perhaps a road in disrepair that may impede an exodus from our country is in our best interests after all.

You may wonder why we call the BIA man Firefly. A firefly flickers its light on and off as nature dictates. The elders tell a story of a firefly that was caught by Hiawatha, the first Sachem, or chief, of the Haudenosaunee people many centuries ago. As a condition of its release, the firefly was to lead Hiawatha through the dark forest. But when they came to a sunny clearing, the firefly's natural light flickered out, and it flew away. Hiawatha, still lost, cursed his little insect brother: "I followed you through the dark woods, but when we got to the light, you stopped showing me the way." The tiny firefly replied as it flew away, "Great chief, it is not out of disrespect that I do what I do as much as it is in my nature to do so." Our BIA man is like the firefly. He promises our people much but never leads us to anything good, for it is his nature to speak to us with two faces.

"Grandfather!" I hear my grandson shout from the distance. "Can you not walk more quickly? My sisters do not believe that you and I are going to Syracuse!" Jake shouts excitedly as he stands by the screen door that has as many holes as the road.

I try hastening my step, but my knees crack and crunch as I walk. The white doctor who visits the reservation once a month calls my condition "arthritis." I call it old age.

"Feels like rain," I mutter as I rub my knees before grabbing onto the porch railing. With one hand, I painfully haul myself up the wooden steps, which creak as loudly as my knees. *Some of these boards are as old as I am,* I think.

"Grandfather, can we go too?" A cacophony of shrill voices fills the air as three imps, my usually sweet and respectful granddaughters, assail me. Nearly in tears, wringing their hands and stomping their feet, they look like they are wailing over a dead relative.

"Has someone died and passed to the Sky World?" I inquire.

Shocked into silence, they stop, looking at each other with puzzled faces and obviously not understanding the joke. "No. Why do you say that?" the eldest, Maggie, asks with deep concern.

"Because you sound like the old women who might someday be grieving over my grave," I reply lightly.

"No, Grandfather. We love you. Please do not talk like that," whimpers Mary, the youngest.

I pick Mary up under her arms and hoist her over my head, her legs and arms flailing as she giggles uncontrollably.

"Grandfather, look at me. I'm a sparrow."

"You are as cute as a sparrow," I agree.

Mary is her Christian name, but I sometimes call her "little rabbit" or "little squirrel" or "little toad." This last name she so protests that she will not respond when I call her with it. Mary is six years old and as carefree as a bird. She laughs readily with a happy heart.

"What about me?" implores Molly.

"You!" I begin as I gently return to the porch my little squirrel, who scampers into the house so quickly that the holey screen never even comes close to spanking her on the backside as she disappears inside.

I bend slightly forward to brush the tip of Molly's nose with my finger. "You are the peacemaker. You are my levelheaded little girl, the wisest of all the girls your age. You are destined to be a clan mother like your aunts—my sisters. But here you are screeching like an owl."

Looking down in shame, she whispers, "I am sorry, Grandfather. It is unbecoming of me to beg and whine. I know a clan mother must be wise and in control of her emotions, for it is she and her clan sisters who select the Sachems, like you, and her judgment must be clear."

Slowly bending on one creaking knee to the creaky porch, I gently hold her shoulders and assure her. "Molly, my sweet daughter, you will be a wise clan mother someday. But for now, you are a girl of thirteen years who is allowed to whine and cry like her sisters once in a while. Now get along and help your sisters with dinner," I say kindly, giving a pat on her backside as she too scampers through the squeaky screen door.

"Grandfather!" speaks Maggie—short for Margaret—who stands firmly, arms folded across her chest as she impatiently taps one foot. "Have you forgotten something?" At fifteen, Maggie is tall like her brother, with piercing, dark eyes. She is the most accomplished seamstress on the reservation for a girl of her age thanks to the Quaker women, who teach sewing before church on Sundays.

"Forget something?" I echo with feigned ignorance. "Oh!" Fumbling around in my pockets, then reaching under my tattered jacket, I produce a small bolt of white cloth with a blue-and-yellow flowered design and proudly hand it to her. "Did you think I would forget my most industrious granddaughter?"

With a sigh and a smile, Maggie impulsively embraces my tender shoulders and repeatedly kisses my cheek. If not fortified by the strength of her love, I would surely have tumbled over. "Thank you, oh, thank you, Grandfather," she says lovingly. "You did not forget. You are the best grandfather. I love you."

"I could never forget you, Maggie. After all, a seamstress without cloth is like a lacrosse player without his stick."

"Oh, Grandfather," Maggie responds with exasperation. "Must you always make comparisons of life to the Game?"

"Our game, *Dehuntshigwa'es,* is the gift of the Creator, and playing it is our way of honoring him and our ancestors," I explain. "It is our life."

Not really wanting to hear the explanation she has heard me recite many times before, Maggie interrupts, "I know, I know," she says teasingly as she holds her bolt of cloth closely to her chest with one hand and, with her other arm, kindly escorts me into the house.

Since their mother died, Mary, Molly, and Maggie have done their best to keep house, cook, tend the fields and animals, and go to school and church. They have chores and obligations from sunup to sundown, a life little different than most other children on the reservation.

We live in a freestanding wood-framed house that I built with the help of my brothers, who passed to the Sky World long ago. But when I was first married, I went to live in the longhouse of my wife's mother, as has been our custom since the beginning of time. Today there is but one longhouse (used for ceremonial purposes) located near the center of our reservation just off our bumpy main road.

In the old days, when a man and woman married, the man and his wife lived in the longhouse of the bride's mother along with their children until the children were old enough to marry themselves. A grown son who married would leave his mother's longhouse and live with his wife's mother and her clan in the matriarchal longhouse. As the female children grew and married, sections were added onto their mother's longhouse. Proud were the people who dwelt within the longest longhouse, for that family was blessed with many children.

My mother-in-law's longhouse was constructed of bowed pine saplings covered with elm bark. Hemlock, basswood, ash, or cedar bark—which was fastened to the frame with strips of inner bark—could also be used. I remember cutting the bark from the trees in the spring with my brothers when the leaves were the size of squirrel's ears and the flowing sap made the bark sheets easier to peel. Most longhouses were fifty or sixty paces long and about twenty paces wide, shared by as many families as there were daughters on either side. Campfires were kept down the middle of the longhouse. Several holes cut in the roof allowed the smoke to escape.

I built our bed by weaving evergreen boughs for the mattress, on which my wife placed mats of reeds and cornhusks topped by furs. Strings of braided corn hung from the rafters along with strips of dried pumpkin, squash, apple, herbs, and sweet grass, producing a pleasant scent.

The missionaries, who had been successful in Christianizing some of our people over the years, eventually dissuaded us from living communally in the longhouses. They believed that people living in such close proximity were subject to unchristian temptations. At first, many of our people refused to live in single wood-framed houses because they felt alone and isolated. Some claimed that the square shape of the dwelling blinded them. To the Indian, all that is true and right is contained within the "circle of life." The squared houses stood in stark contrast to the longhouse, which more resembled a circle. Some of our people erected teepees like our wild brothers in the West. But the harsh winters of the north country soon drove our people within the confines of the squared houses like the ant is driven underground when the first snows blanket Mother Earth.

Our house was built with pine and oak taken from the surrounding forest and milled into clapboards at our rudimentary sawmill. The Haudenosaunee were one of the first tribes to agree to live on a reservation. We agreed to bury the war hatchet and live on a reservation so long as it encompassed at least part of our ancestral lands. Much of the land on which our fathers hunted was gradually taken by the whites through deception and outright thievery, however, unlike most of the other tribes in America, who were removed to foreign and hostile land, we are proud to say that we still hunt, fish, and live on lands in which our fathers are buried.

Paint is one of the commodities that flow in abundance in the white man's world, yet the BIA can never procure even a bucket or two for our houses. The Methodist Church gleams a fresh white; in contrast, the people's houses are stark gray or white as faded as the white birch tree. Thankfully, the walls of the schoolhouse, which we agreed to allow the state of New York to build in our nation rather than risk our children being forced into off-reservation schools, are always freshly painted.

Every roof of every house on the reservation leaks. People generally cover their roofs with pine shakes cut into small squares from scrap pine procured at the sawmill. Each succeeding top shake overlaps the bottom shake before being nailed down. But pine shakes, like all things made of wood, grow old and splinter. They often blow off in storms, precipitating a song of raindrops in the odd collection of tubs, pans, and buckets spread about on the oak and pine floors of these ramshackle dwellings.

Had the girls not dressed our windows with beautifully handmade curtains and adorned the walls and shelves with beautifully carved wooden ornaments, bowls, and gourds, our home would look stark indeed. My eyes particularly prize the glow of the sunlight shining through the light blue curtains in the girls' bedroom windows.

Although we are by no means an opulent family, we want for nothing. Our income derives from Jake's part-time work at the mill and Maggie's sewing. I have also prudently saved some money from my many years working as a lumberjack to use in unexpected or extreme emergencies. We are self-sufficient otherwise with our crops and our animals. Our few extra dollars are spent on minor extravagances such as some of the girls' jewelry, tables and chairs built by artisans on the reservation, a sturdy wagon, tack for our horse, and, of course, the white man's clothes that the ministers insist the children wear when they attend church on Sundays.

Our gathering area and kitchen are one great room anchored by a deep stone fireplace with cooking irons and a stout chimney without any cracks. Last winter, a family tragically died from a chimney fire that started when the pine tar caked on the walls of their chimney ignited, spreading through the cracks in the chimney mortar and into the house, engulfing them all in flames while they slept.

We are one of the few families that owns a potbellied stove, which I purchased in Syracuse after my last job as a lumberjack in Canada. I was a "topper," the highest-paying job in the woods. I climbed the tree, shearing branches as I ascended, attaching pulleys and riggings to the top of the tree as a spar so that logs could be skidded onto the landing. This was an exceptionally dangerous job: some of the trees were 150 feet tall, strong winds could blast unexpectedly, and safety equipment was nonexistent. The white man is afraid to climb high into a tree, but the Indian does not fear heights, particularly in a tree. Its branches are like Mother Earth's hair, floating in the wind which keeps our people secure—unless she is angry and shakes us out.

We also count ourselves fortunate to have secured glass from Firefly to fill the openings in our windows. This was not provided as a result of the BIA agent's generosity but rather in trade for a beautiful communion dress Maggie sewed for his daughter. Jake and I have built sturdy shutters to protect our glass windows from winter gales. At night, we use kerosene lanterns for light—that is, when kerosene is available as part of our BIA rations. Otherwise, we light candles made from beeswax or animal fat.

Our wide pine floors are covered with braided rugs produced in the woolen mills that dot the rivers of upper New York State and New England. Some women weave mats of sweet grass to cover their floors.

My most prized furnishing is a brown bear rug that lies in front of the fireplace. I killed that bear with a bow and a two-and-a-half-foot arrow during the spring after I married. The girls love doing their schoolwork on that bear fur. They often fall asleep there, huddled together like three beans in a pod. So as not to disturb their slumber, I simply wrap the edges of the bear rug over them and let them sleep there during many a cold fall or winter night.

About twenty paces from the house we have an outdoor deep well with a rusted pump that requires priming before use. In the winter, priming requires that we keep a jug of water near the fireplace, unlike in the summer, when it is kept outside by the pump. I have promised the girls that I will investigate extending the pump into the kitchen so they can pump water into a basin by the kitchen window without having to trudge through heat, rain, and snow for water. That is another house project that I hope to live long enough to accomplish.

We have an outhouse that is sturdy enough to withstand winter's winds and airy enough during the hot summer. One of Jake's least favorite chores is to pour lye into the toilet, a hole in a pine plank worn smooth over the years. Receiving a Sears catalogue is always a time of great excitement. Not only are the many pictures of the white man's goods offered for sale within its covers fascinating, but the pages are also used in the outhouse for personal cleaning. The night pots are kept under our beds and emptied each morning.

Through my last labors in the mill and Jake's part-time work, we've secured enough milled planks of pine and oak to construct a barn. Not every family is fortunate enough to have a barn. Our barn is actually bigger than our house, containing a hayloft, a stall for our horse, Thunder, a special room to secure our tack and tools, and our wagon, which I purchased in Syracuse. Under the rafters, several guinea hens roost at night. Attached to the side of the barn stand a goat pen and wired chicken coop. The girls tend a rabbit hutch that they continually secure so our mangy cat, who lives in the barn to rid it of mice and rats, is not tempted to supplement his diet with these furry friends. We have also dug a root cellar to store preserved fruits and vegetables that will sustain us through the winter.

When Jake was a baby, I received a mixed-breed pup, whom I named Bear. He was a fat, brown, furry pup, resembling a bear cub more than a dog. Bear is old now, blind in one eye and missing part of his right ear and tail, bitten off during a scuffle with several coyotes. His hips are as arthritic as my knees. In spite of his handicaps, this dog has been loyal to the children and has followed them wherever they go on our land. The myriad holes around our house are not gopher holes; Bear digs these holes strategically so that he can cool off during the hot summer months while keeping his good eye on the children whenever they are outside doing their chores.

Our home is cozy, clean, and pleasantly scented by the herbs that the girls have planted in a grow box outside the kitchen window. The girls have learned to sing in three-part harmony in church, which, accompanied by their incessant laughter, brightens our home more than the sun. We are never hungry and have but few holes in our clothes. Although our surroundings are modest, we are rich with love. Of course, the children miss their mother and father. I have tried to be both, appropriately stern like a father and comforting like a mother. I can only pray to the Creator that I have been successful.

Ownership of land had been a foreign concept to the Indian people throughout North America until the reservation system began. As a result of the Dawes Act of 1887 (from which the Haudenosaunee were exempt), Indians on reservations throughout the United States were doled out parcels of land and given farming tools. The wild warrior hunters of the Great Plains had the most difficulty in adjusting to a sedentary, agrarian way of life.

But we, the Haudenosaunee, traditionally both hunters and agriculturalists from the earliest days of our history, have not found adjustment to reservation life difficult. We do not believe we own the land on which our home sits; rather, we are the caretakers of parcels of land over which we have influence. We grow our own crops and are self-sufficient. We share what we have with families whose crops are not harvested in abundance. We trade for items that we do not possess sufficient skills or resources to produce ourselves. Unlike our brothers in the southwest United States, who were placed onto arid, unproductive parcels of land, for over one hundred years we Haudenosaunee have remained on our ancestral lands, which are fertile and rich with game and fish. Although reduced by the white man's treaties and treachery, we thank the Creator that we live on the land on which our fathers have lived and in which they are buried.

5

JAKE'S DREAM

As the summer days are hot even in upper New York State, so are the nights pleasantly cool. Sleeping with the windows open during the summer is usually comfortable. So you can imagine my shock to see and feel Jake's sweat-soaked long johns as I comfort him in my arms one troubling night.

"Easy, easy, my son. Easy. Breathe deeply of the night's air. Smell the scent of the tall pines outside your window. Listen to the owl and the crickets sing to us," I whisper soothingly.

Jake's breathing begins to slow from its rapid pace. His body's twitching quiets as I stroke his long black hair. I feel his heart begin to beat in rhythm with mine as I hold him close to me. I gently lay his head back upon his goose-down pillow. The straw-stuffed mattress held up from the floor by woven rope crinkles under his body's weight. The cotton sheet and a knitted yarn blanket envelope him, as safely and as securely as if he were in his mother's womb.

Satisfied that Jake has calmed from whatever fitful nightmare tormented him, I attempt to quietly remove myself from his bedside. But the creaky floor gives up even this stealthy hunter, who had been taught from boyhood to walk lightly on his toes.

"Grandfather?" a faint voice comes from the darkness. "Please, do not go."

I sense an urgency in Jake's voice that I take seriously, for he is no longer a little boy afraid of monsters and demons in the dark. I return, sit on his bed, and let him speak first.

"Grandfather, I had a dream."

I smile as I brush his moist hair away from his warm forehead. "Many are the times when a boy who is becoming a man has dreams come to him as a guide into manhood."

"But Grandfather, it was so frightening."

"Becoming a man who must now assume greater responsibility to his family and his people can be frightening," I assure him. "Do you wish to tell me of your dream?"

Jake draws a deep breath and stares at the beamed ceiling with distant eyes as if he is somewhere else or sees something imaginary there. I look up to the ceiling but see nothing.

With hesitation Jake begins. "I saw a large bird. I believe it may have been an eagle, soaring high over the land. Something dripped from his talons and his wings. I could not see clearly, but I believe it may have been blood. The bird was not wounded, for he could still fly. In his talons he carried a wooden branch or stick that was spotted red from the dripping blood. He flew over a great longhouse many times larger than our own and then over a white man's village, casting a large shadow over it and the people below. The white people fled in terror and then disappeared. After he flew by, he looked back and saw that the white people had vanished from the land."

I sit pensively, begin to chuckle, and then roar with laughter.

"Grandfather," Jake says angrily, "you make fun of me. Have you not said that a man's dream must be viewed seriously? That it may point him in his life's direction? So why do you mock me?"

Catching my breath, I readily reply, "I am sorry, my son. I am not laughing at you. I am laughing at the notion of eliminating the white man with a single swipe of an eagle's wing."

Although momentarily confused, Jake also breaks into laughter. He understands my meaning. We laugh together so loudly that we awaken the girls.

"What is wrong?" Mary tiredly asks, rubbing her big eyes with both fists.

"What are you two doing?" queries Molly, as she stretches and yawns.

"Do you wish to wake the dead?" Maggie scolds as she struggles to keep her eyes open.

"Quiet yourselves, my little flowers. Nothing is wrong," I assure them. "We apologize for waking you." Then, turning to Jake and winking an eye, I continue, "Jake and I just figured out how to remove the white man from the land once and for all."

The girls, standing there barefoot in their long cotton nightgowns, look at each other with puzzled faces. I slap Jake on the backside, tuck him in, and turn to herd my little urchins back to bed.

"Come, my darlings. Kiss your grandfather so that if the Great Spirit should take me in my sleep tonight I will travel to my ancestors' council fires in the Sky World content with such sweetness."

The three immediately run to me. The littlest, Mary, tackles me around my thighs, causing all four of us to fall back on top of Jake in his bed.

"Hey," Jake complains good-naturedly, "you are crushing me! Get up! Get off!"

The three scurry away like field mice. Their long nightgowns float behind them, ghost-like in an otherwise dark but moonlit room.

I turn to Jake, who has settled back onto his pillow. "My son, do not fear your dreams. Come to accept and understand them. Dreams are not meant to frighten you as when you were a little boy. For a man, a dream must be viewed as a guide, even if it is frightening."

"But what does my dream mean, Grandfather? What is it trying to tell me?"

"You must find that out for yourself, my son," I reply. "I am here as your teacher and as your guide. I am sure there will be a time when the meaning of this dream will reveal itself to you."

Seemingly not quite reassured, Jake takes a deep breath, closes his eyes, and slowly returns to the world of dreams. Hearing him breathe deeply and seeing peace wash over his face, I slowly remove myself from Jake's bed, this time avoiding the squeaky board that betrayed my departure before. Passing through the bedroom doorway without a sound, I marvel at my stealth over such a creaky floor and think, *Hmm, still got it. The hunter is always quiet. Not bad for an old Indian.* As I head for my bedroom, I stop and ponder why the dream has come to him now.

I smile. Although my bed beckons me, I am not sleepy. I slowly open the squeaky screen door lest I awaken my precious gems within. Easing into my old, oak rocking chair, I reach underneath and feel around for my pipe, which I fashioned from boring out a corncob. From the pocket of my comfortably tattered jacket I retrieve a deerskin pouch of homegrown tobacco. Lightly packing the tobacco into my pipe and striking a match with my thumbnail, I slowly inhale the smoke that scrolls around my face. I sit, rock, smoke, and wonder if Jake's dream is the prophecy of old. Too tired to think clearly, I let my mind wander, noting how useful the corncob is in absorbing the tobacco juice so that it will not enter my throat. One of life's simple pleasures is a good smoke on a cool summer's night.

6

THE HAUDENOSAUNEE

As the rooster announces the day's beginning and the sunlight peeks through the curtained windows, the girls are the first to emerge from their bedroom. They can hardly contain their excitement, for this week is the most special of the year.

August is the month in which the people celebrate the coming harvest. This time is marked with ceremony, song, dance, the hunt, and, of course, the Game. This is the time of the Green Corn Festival, one of the four principal festivals that coincide with the seasons: the Mid-Winter Festival in January, the Maple Festival in spring for when the sap rises, the Strawberry Festival in June for when the strawberries ripen, and the Green Corn Festival in late summer.

The sound of bacon sizzling in the frying pan and the smell of cornbread baking over a fire awakens me. The creaky sound of the water pump crank just a few feet from Jake's window and the laughter of the two youngest girls splashing themselves with cool spring water awakens Jake.

"Can you not be more quiet in the morning? Can you not see that I am still sleeping?" Jake bellows.

"Time to get up, you lazy brother. Are you still dreaming?" they giggle in chorus.

Molly sassily adds, "Dreaming of Sarah?" They all giggle again.

"No, he is dreaming of the hunt. Me mighty hunter," Mary chimes in with a feigned deep voice as she pounds her little chest with her little fists.

Now standing outside on the porch, I clap my hands as if to scare off a stray dog. Getting the girls' attention, I urge them to stop dallying and to get on with their chores. As I carefully descend the steps, which creak in tandem with my knees, I slowly head to the outhouse.

Still giggling, the girls fill their buckets and continue to playfully splash each other as they run toward the house.

"Girls, please! Can you not let your brother sleep? Do you not realize that he is nervous about whether he will be called upon to play in the Game?"

Instantly ashamed, the girls quiet themselves. They are proud of their brother and immediately understand the meaning of my words. For a young man, the hunt and the Game are the most important events in his life. Failure or success in either can mark him for life in terms of securing a bride and in assuming a respectful position in the tribe. Success in either or both events brings honor not only to the young man but to his family as well.

"Where is the Sears catalogue?" I desperately shout. The scampering of six little feet and a squeaky screen door betray the girls, who are fleeing my wrath. I am without the pages that serve as both my reading and my cleaning.

Of all the months of the year, August is the barometer of the people's well-being. By August, the people know whether the crops will come in strongly for that year. This has been a good year—no pests and plenty of rain. The corn is already as tall as a man.

The Green Corn Festival is also a time for courtship. Many romances have been sparked during the celebratory singing and dancing. Fall is the perfect time for young people of age and in love to marry, for they will provide warmth to each other over the coming winter months. Late spring and early summer usually bring the cry of many newborn children. During this festival, when all the clans of the Onondaga people gather, marriages are encouraged between men and women of different clans to keep the bloodlines strong.

During the Green Corn Festival, the tribe's elders and Faithkeepers usually attend to traditional ceremonies, the children play games, and the men tell stories of the hunt and the Game. The women gossip about relationships, food, and who wore the finest traditional dress. The young men bet among themselves on who will be called upon to play in the Game with the men. That all-important decision will be made in the next day or two. Only one of the young men will be chosen this year.

But before the Green Corn Festival comes the tedium and the drudgery of daily living. The girls patiently braid each other's hair, put on dresses with aprons, and carry personal items in side bags that Maggie has sewn and embroidered for all of them. The girls usually wear moccasins made of deerskin, which they decorate with colorful beads embroidered with a distinct pattern. They sometimes wear bonnets, mostly on Sundays, looking more like little white girls than Indian girls as a result of the missionaries' influence on the reservation. At first, the girls shunned such nontraditional headgear over their traditional kerchiefs, believing that the bonnet was just one more example of the white woman's tendency to wear much more than is needed. However, as lighter skin is considered more attractive, the bonnet, which shields the girls' faces from the sun, has been readily adopted for its practical use.

The girls run through the squeaky screen door and bound down the steps toward the barn, where they feed the goat, the chickens, and the rabbits. They put out hay for old Thunder. Molly milks the goat, occasionally squirting a stream of milk into the patient barn cat's mouth. When barn chores are completed, they make their way to the field with shovel, hoe, and rake in tow.

The girls are proud to see that their crops are far ahead of last year's growth. Our family tills about two acres. We plant corn, tallest of the vegetables, on the south side of the field so that its growth will not block the sunlight from the other vegetables. We plant each corn seed in the eye of a fish head and bury them both about a finger's length deep under our rich brown soil. We plant bean seeds in mounds of dirt, placing poles in the center of each mound for the vines to climb. Some of the people plant their beans in such a way that the vines climb the cornstalks. Various yellow, green, or purple squash grows around the edges on the east side of our plot. We grow alfalfa, oats, potatoes, and tobacco too. We keep fallow another two acres, on which we spread horse manure and rotate with this year's fields for growing next year. Our stock of hay grows on an additional two acres. Our house stands on another two acres with our orchard of apple, pear, and cherry trees. Our strawberry patch provides the sweet berries for homemade jam.

In 1909 the BIA counted about five thousand Haudenosaunee on a patchwork of reservations comprising twenty thousand acres in New York State. About twelve hundred of these people were Onondaga. During the height of the Iroquois Confederacy before the Revolutionary War, the Haudenosaunee—composed of the Mohawk, Oneida, Seneca, Cayuga, Onondaga, and later the Tuscarora, who joined us from North Carolina—numbered over one hundred thousand on lands that stretched west into Ohio, south into Pennsylvania, and up into New York State as far north as Canada. Now the Onondaga live on about seven thousand acres, half of which is suitable for cultivation.

Before the war between the Americans and the English, during the time when the French and English brought war to our country, we aligned ourselves with the English, with whose help we defeated our mortal enemy to the west, the Huron. We fought back incursions by our Algonquin neighbors in the east. The Iroquois Confederacy was an economic and military juggernaut among the native peoples in the Northeast.

After the Revolutionary War, the Mohawks, under the leadership of Chief Joseph Bryant, who had sided with the English, fled New York and settled on a large grant of land in Canada offered by the grateful king of England.

The remainder of the tribes who either sided with the Americans or tried to remain neutral were decimated by General Sullivan and two thousand regular troops, who destroyed the Iroquois capital, Onondaga. That was the darkest period of our history: the council fire was extinguished and the six tribes of the Iroquois Confederation disbanded. The Americans took most of our land in New York and Pennsylvania. We were permitted to remain on land in perpetuity around the Finger Lakes region pursuant to the Treaty of Canandaigua in 1794.

We are guardians, not owners, of the land. Any land that can be tilled but has been left fallow for more than two years becomes open land on which any capable person is permitted to grow crops. Disputes about who possesses the privilege of tilling the soil and harvesting the crops from a particular parcel are brought before the council chiefs for resolution.

Ultimately, the people share in each other's bounty. We hold a farmers' market at our longhouse during the weekend before the white man's holiday, Thanksgiving, at which excess vegetables are traded, sold, or just given away to less fortunate families under the auspices of the clan mothers. In that way, no one goes hungry during the coming winter.

Although farming is traditionally women's work, in which the women work together in each other's fields under the direction of the clan mothers, Jake and I are not averse to blistered, dirty hands. The girls are genuinely proud of the straightness of their rows of vegetables, the symmetry of their crops, and, by the Creator's grace, the bountiful harvests over the last several years. Neither my three girls nor the women toil in drudgery; their work is a labor of love. I believe that the beautiful female voices heard in song in the fields so delight our plants that they are pleased to grow taller and stronger. Just as Jake's three little sisters are the joy and sustenance of our house, corn, beans, and squash are the three sisters of the life of the people. Jake too is proud of our bounty, however, at this time in his life, he has but three things on his mind: the hunt, the Game, and Sarah.

7

THE HUNT

Other than the Game, the hunt is often the first test of a boy's readiness to enter manhood. If not called upon to play in the Game, Jake is determined to prove himself in the hunt.

A successful deer hunt is as important to the people as a good crop in weathering the winter. The does are in estrous and the usually cautious bucks are running wild to mate making them and their herd easy targets.

I position myself with the boys in the forage line but have bow and arrow at the ready. Sensing Jake's eagerness, I keep an especially keen eye on him this day.

Holding a finger over his lips, Jake whispers, "Shh. Wait here, my brother."

Jake's friend, Johnny Big Nose, anxiously answers in a strained but hushed voice, "Where are you going? The men, the hunters, told us boys to form a forage line along this ridge. We are to stay together and push the deer toward their day bedding at the swamp, where our hunters wait in ambush. Why do you move ahead?"

Pretending not to hear his friend's entreaties, Jake crouches and inches his way into the underbrush ahead of the other boys.

I, who am part of the forage line to keep the boys in order, suddenly notice Jake's moving ahead of his comrades but do not beckon to him as we await the imminent signal to move.

"Jake! Please! Come back!" beseeches his friend, who waves his arm, beckoning Jake to return, and looking at me for support. I just shake my head.

Not often does an Indian's name have much to do with his eventual appearance. After all, a baby goes through many physical changes as he or she journeys through life. In this case, Big Nose is an appropriate name for Jake's friend, who has as prominent a nose as one may find in any caricature of a "Wild West Indian" on the cover of a dime-store novel. Jake always defends his friend, who is often the object of some teasing, telling all who will listen that the bigness of Johnny's nose is matched by the bigness of the courage of his heart.

The sun begins to peek through the trees. Clouds of breath come from the boys' anxious mouths and noses as they lie in wait on the cold ground for the signal to move. In the distance a whistle blows, the signal that the boys are to begin banging their metal pots and pans with wooden spoons, whooping and hollering as they walk together in a long line of about three hundred paces, hoping to drive the night-feeding deer back to their daytime shelter in the thick brush of the low-lying marsh about a half mile from where the hunters lie in wait.

At the entrance of the marsh, the Indian hunters have erected a long line of nets designed to entrap the frightened deer, thus making their prey easier targets for the men with traditional bows and arrows perched high up in trees.

But it seems Jake has another idea. We have discussed that at age seventeen he may be considered too young to play in the Green Corn Festival Game with the tribe's finest lacrosse players, most of whom are in their twenties and thirties. I know he is confident that he possesses the skill, but recognizes his age is a hindrance. Most young men are not given an opportunity to play in the Game until they are at least nineteen or twenty. But it seems Jake is determined to show the men, the hunters, and his young brothers that he is the swiftest of all runners of the tribe and deserves to play in the Game.

The boys' voices and banging grow louder as they approach the hunters up in their trees. The clouds of breath exhaled by the hunters' mouths and noses make the trees appear to be smoking. The hunters, otherwise invisible in their traditional buckskins and leggings—that blend in with the surroundings—stand motionless, bows and arrows poised, awaiting a shot at a deer that will either become entangled in the net or turn to escape the unnatural barrier across its safe haven.

I notice Jake crawls on his hands and knees ahead of the banging boys. He is too far ahead for me to chase after him so I determine to track him for a while then to take a short cut towards the hunters and await the driven prey. Peeking his head above a bush and seeing no deer as yet, Jake pops to his feet and swiftly runs from tree to bush. He occasionally stops, crouches, and surveys the misty horizon. Jake too has blended into his surroundings with his buckskin shirt, buckskin breechcloth, leggings, and moccasins, all unadorned with beads or silver so as to remain undetected as he travels through the underbrush.

Jake quickly moves a few steps and stops. He repeats this sequence of swift-but-deliberate movements that resembles a dance more than a stalk: a few steps, stop, a few more steps, stop. Having observed deer in the woods on many occasions, Jake has become attuned to the sounds they make, especially bucks before the mating season—which has ushered in early this year thanks to a few unseasonable night frosts.

Suddenly, Jake and I notice a twig from a low-lying bush move horizontally. The twig's movement is contrary to the wind that blows in his face. Jake freezes in his tracks and holds his breath. Surely this movement is that of a deer peeking his nose into the wind to smell danger. Since Jake and I are upwind and undetected, the deer smells nothing. Confident of no danger, the deer exits the thicket into the forest clearing. However, this deer is a doe—fat, happy, bleating away without a care in the world, and prancing through the thicket. Jake is apparently not interested in a doe but awaits the buck who is most likely moving her along.

Jake stands up and exhales and is about to return to his friends when suddenly a magnificent buck with a huge chest and a broad rack leaps into the clearing. The buck snorts loudly, as if to command, "This is my doe. All others stay away." I count twelve points with two broken off, undoubtedly the result of combat with a rival. A buck of this stature cannot have amassed such size and developed such a magnificent rack unless he has lived at least eight seasons. Jake also most likely realizes that the buck has not lived twice as long as normal by being stupid. This magnificent buck is smart, cunning, and swift, able to smell and see a human easily at a hundred paces I am sure. Hopefully this buck may have forfeited some of his senses due to his rather amorous pursuits. But such is not the case.

My heart begins to pound, the skin of my chest vibrating with every heartbeat. Concerned that his thumping chest may betray his presence, I notice that Jake takes some deep breaths, trying to regulate his breathing to calm his heart.

Jake slowly drops to his hands and knees, moving only when the buck drops his head to forage for acorns. The doe meanders slowly through an oak hummock, and the buck follows. Jake now moves only when the deer moves. The buck, hearing the crunching of leaves under Jake's hands and knees, stops, alerted. Jake holds his breath and stops as well. Even when inadvertently coming to rest on a viciously thorny vine, Jake does not move because the buck is looking directly his way. Just before his presence is betrayed, the renewed banging of pots and pans draws the buck's attention. First the doe then the buck begin to evade the methodical approach of the banging boys.

Jake is about twenty paces from the buck. The wind is still in his favor. Suddenly the buck freezes. Jake can see his nose sucking in big gulps of air. His ears begin to twitch. Sensing danger the buck stops short and is about to bolt. Jake springs from his hiding place like a mountain lion. The buck snaps his head toward Jake and freezes for an instant. Realizing Jake is not a doe or another buck invading his territory, the animal springs away.

Armed with bow and arrow, I break from the forage line and do my best to follow Jake through the woods. Jake chases the deer over grassy knolls, between maple saplings, and through a thicket of blackberries. He runs as fast and as frantically as he can, despite the vines and bushes that tear at his buckskins. The buck gracefully darts right, then left, easily leaping a group of fallen trees that Jake is forced to run around. But Jake is relentless. I hope he remembers my hunting advice: *Always think like your prey.*

Jake most likely knows that the buck will seek refuge in the thickness of the marsh, his bedding area by day. He notices a funnel between the hills to the marsh. Jake has to arrive at the exit of the funnel before the buck. Circling away from the buck, Jake takes a shortcut to the funnel by nimbly crossing a wide stream on a fallen log over which the deer cannot tread.

I can see from a distance, Jake lies down behind a log and begins to cover himself with leaves. Just then, this majestic buck leaps into the clearing about ten paces ahead. Sensing something amiss, the buck grunts, snorts, and pounds the turf madly with his two front hooves. This is the moment of truth. Jake springs from his lair. The buck crouches in fear and is poised to flee. As the buck whirls from his human predator, legs cocked to spring to freedom, Jake, in one last desperate lunge, reaches out to touch him.

Just as the buck's white tail is within his grasp, Jake hears a snap and a swoosh. Something flies closely over his left ear.

Hearing a thud, Jake quickly turns his head and sees an arrow, my arrow, sticking into the buck's side behind his shoulder and high near the spine. The buck jumps upon impact just as his erect white tail is within Jake's grasp. The buck bolts toward what he thinks is the safety of its bedding area only to become entangled in the waiting net. Jake runs to the bleeding, exhausted buck and reaches for his knife to cut the terrified animal free.

"Jake!" I shout. "You foolish boy! Do you not know where you are? Do you want to be killed? Do you not realize you are interrupting the hunt?"

Jake is stunned.

"Why did you leave the other boys? Why are you running with the deer? Did you want to die today? I did not hear you sing your death song this morning."

Jake is speechless, embarrassed by my public scolding.

Nearby hunters, looking grim, jump from their trees and surround Jake. Other hunters down the line begin to harvest the other deer that had run from this commotion into their trap. Now all of the men chide Jake for his foolishness. But Jake hears only noise. He is more concerned about the buck.

"Grandfather! Please! Can you not end the misery of my brother the buck? He spits blood, and his breathing is labored. Please, he suffers."

Handing Jake the hunting knife given to me by my father, its handle carved from a deer antler and its blade larger and sharper than Jake's cutting knife, I say solemnly, "If you had not disturbed our hunt, this would have been a clean, fast kill. But because of your interference, my arrow went astray, missing the heart. You must end the buck's suffering."

Jake looks at all the men, who, with stern faces, nod in agreement. I halt the arrival of the banging boys by extending my arm so that Jake may address the agonized buck.

"I am sorry, my brother, for your death," Jake begins as tears stream down his cheeks. "Thank you for giving up your life for the people's sustenance. We will honor you at the feast, I promise." Jake holds the buck's antlers with one hand to keep him still and with the other plunges my knife deep into the buck's heart. The buck rears its head, almost plucking out one of Jake's eyes with the tip of an antler, and splits the air with a ghastly cry. Blood and spit fly from his mouth onto Jake's face, causing Jake to rear back and tumble onto the leafy forest floor.

Jake's friends arrive on the scene, proud that their friend has dispatched this magnificent buck with such courage. As Jake regains himself, his friends jump around him, mimicking the warriors' war dance. Little Crow, Big Nose, and the others proudly pat Jake, the great hunter, on his back for his obvious heroics. However, Jake is without joy. He has caused the suffering of his brother the deer. He is sad and embarrassed. Falling to his knees and sobbing, Jake puts his arms around the deer's neck and lays his face on his chest. Blood flows from the buck's open wound onto Jake's clothing, arms, and face.

I approach Jake and gently help him to his feet. Looking down, still sobbing, Jake whispers, "You were the one who said I was not ready to play in the Game. You were the one who said that my brain had not caught up to my legs. You were the one who said I was not yet fast enough. You were the one who said I would not be ready until I touched the tail of the deer."

Astonished by his explanation, and now ashamed over my words, I shake my head, and reply, "My son, I never meant that you should one day actually touch a deer's tail. I simply meant that when you achieve the speed, the grace, and the agility of the deer, you will be ready for the Game."

Jake raises his head and sheepishly asks, "Are you not mad at me for being foolish, Grandfather?"

Gently taking the bloody knife from his shaking hand, wiping it on my leggings, blood-stained from many hunts, and returning it to its sheath on my belt, I embrace the boy who has so desperately wished to prove he is a man and say as comfortingly as I can, "No, no, my son. I can see that you did not understand my words. Perhaps your misunderstanding means that you are still thinking like a boy and not ready to play the Game with men. Or perhaps, as I age, my words are less clear."

Now realizing why Jake is sad, Little Crow attempts to uplift his friend's spirit. "But Grandfather"—all children call their elders "grandfather" or "grandmother" as an expression of respect—"did Jake not prove he is fast enough to play in the Game? We saw him touch the tail of the deer just as the arrow struck its mark."

I ponder Little Crow's defense of his friend and admire his loyalty. Seizing the opportunity to share some wisdom with all of the boys, I reply, "Jake was not running at the moment he touched the deer's tail. He cleverly ran the deer into a funnel between the hills, forcing the deer to run to him as he lay in wait. That shows something more than speed. That shows cunning and daring, which every warrior needs in battle and which every brave must demonstrate in the Game."

"Aiee, aiee!" the boys all shout in unison to honor their friend.

"I am sorry I almost ruined the hunt, Grandfather," Jake apologizes. "By my actions, I could have scared other deer away from the hunters."

"Do not worry, my son, for it was my arrow that felled the beast. Thank you for running him towards me and the other hunters. Without your cleverness, I may never have had a shot."

The boys laugh; then so do I. Finally Jake joins in, although his laughter is more in relief than in joy. The boys slap Jake on the back with approval. However, still being boys, they turn away as the hunters begin to gut the buck. The smell and sight of entrails still make young stomachs queasy.

"Jake," one of the men calls out. As Jake and the boys turn toward the voice, they see in the hunter's outstretched hand a bloody orb of meat that the hunter passes to me.

"Take it." I pass the heart of the fallen buck to Jake. "To the hunter goes the heart," I say proudly.

"But, Grandfather, I did not shoot the buck."

"I know, but your speed and cunning gave me an opportunity for the kill. I simply drew back the string and let the arrow fly at point-blank range. You did all the work."

Careful not to drop it, Jake reverently takes the heart from me with both of his hands. As he draws the steaming heart to his mouth, I clear my throat as a reminder.

"Oh, thank you for reminding me, Grandfather. Thank you, my brother deer, for wandering our woods and creating many like you. You will feed many. I hope that eating your heart will give me your strength and speed."

Jake looks at me before he takes a bite, waiting for my approval of his words. With pride, I nod my head.

Jake hesitates, closes his eyes, and just before he bites, I add, "And you can play in the Game."

Jake's companions whoop, yell, and jump up and down. With a huge smile on his face, Jake eagerly tears into the buck's heart. He rips off a huge piece of meat with his teeth. Blood dripping from his mouth, he raises the bloody organ to the sky and shrieks, "Aiee!"

The other hunters momentarily stop their slaughter to witness a boy's first taste of a deer's heart. The boys turn toward the hunters, who look approvingly upon Jake. The boys look back at Jake, aware that somehow he has changed: bigger, stronger, more confident than before. The boys have witnessed their friend take a giant step toward manhood. They are happy for him. I look upon a young man, now a hunter and a future provider. The hunters had looked upon a boy earlier this morning, now a young man and their teammate in the great Game.

Only one person apparently disapproves. Youngblood, already an accomplished hunter and a veteran player in the Game, stands silently, staring at Jake with menacing, jealous eyes. But why? Small matter. This is Jake's moment in the sun. I shall not let my suspicions dampen his joy.

8

SARAH

Sarah is an only child. Some say she is a lonely child. She lives on the parcel north of our farm with her father. Her mother died bringing her life on a frightful, rainy and cold night. The clan mothers and midwives chanted, sang, and shook their turtle rattles to speed Sarah's birth. They burned sage and urged Sarah's mother to push strongly. But something was wrong. A midwife reached up into Sarah's mother. Extracting her hands, she woefully examined her bloody fingers as if they could speak to her. Using a knife with healing powers, one of the women cut Sarah's mother to widen the opening for the baby to emerge. But the baby was turned around. Reaching in with both hands, another midwife turned the baby, who then came to us, but at the expense of her mother's life.

So broken was Sarah's father at the loss of his wife that he disappeared into the woods for weeks. His agonizing shrieks could be heard for miles in the stillness of the night's air. When he finally emerged from the woods, his hair had turned as white as snow, not a fleck of black remaining. His normally piercing eyes were blank. He never spoke a word again.

The clan mothers believed that the Great Spirit had taken his soul to be with his wife, leaving only a shell of a man. Sarah's father spent many a day wandering the woods, searching for his wife's spirit, returning home only when he was too hungry or too tired to continue.

Sarah's birth is an example of the privations of the people. There are no medical facilities on the reservation. In the past, missionaries attempted to dispense medications and elixirs for certain ailments, but only in return for the people's willingness to accept the Christian God. Desperate for care, some of the people accepted the missionaries' teachings, at least until the medicine bottle ran dry.

The Hospital of the Good Shepherd in south Syracuse near the Kirkwood Park Harness Track is the only hospital in Syracuse that will treat Indians. Dr. S. Ellis Crane of East Onondaga is the official Indian doctor, but his visits to the reservation are limited. Because the ten-mile trek is too long for emergency treatment, the people rely on home remedies extracted from roots, berries, and herbs, the extraordinary medicinal effect of which baffles most chemists. I remember my mother giving me a pinch of doorweed, which she urged me to put into my future wife's tea as a love potion. It worked: I was married shortly thereafter. I also remember my mother boiling wild indigo, which she rubbed on my sore, bruised arms and legs after a Game in order to take away the sting of pain. In a day I was as good as new.

For more serious illnesses, medicine men wearing sacred masks conduct "sick feasts" to cure the gravely ill. A sick feast is a two-edged sword for our people: if the gravely sick person recovers, the medicine man's prestige and power is enhanced; if the ill person does not recover or, even worse, dies, the medicine man usually ascribes some other nefarious reason, such as witchcraft, for the poor outcome. I do not believe in witches, but some of the more gullible of our people do, a practice that often ruins the reputations of innocent people. The high mortality rates of mothers giving birth and of newborn babies are accepted as part of the circle of life.

The medicine men and the clan mothers set broken bones, stop bleeding, and sew torn flesh. However, they possess no magic to fight the white man's diseases, such as whooping cough, smallpox, yellow fever, and tuberculosis. These diseases—and whiskey—are a plague on our people.

The clan mothers who alternately lived in her house raised Sarah and took care of her demented father until she became a teenager. Now Sarah is permitted to live alone with her father—under their ever-watchful eyes, of course. Sarah spends much of her little free time playing with the girls at our house, which is a short walk through the fields and up a path that I cleared for her.

Sarah is strong yet graceful. She is tall—not as tall as Jake but taller than most girls her age. Her hair is as black as midnight, straight, shiny, and hangs to the small of her back. The color of her skin and the color of her eyes reveal a mixed-blood heritage. Sarah is light-skinned, darker than a white girl but lighter than most of her peers. Her eyes are deep blue, almost purple, and so dark that the eye's black dot is barely distinguishable.

Sarah is a special girl. The loss of her mother has served to broaden and strengthen Sarah's character and talents because she has learned much from each of the clan mothers who took turns caring for her. Sarah has learned the medicinal arts from the women who delivered her. She has learned how to cook all the traditional meals as well as how to wisely stretch government rations until the next delivery. She has become an accomplished seamstress, teaching Maggie many of the fine decorative stitches known to only a few. Sarah knows how to raise crops and animals. She can preserve and can food for the winter. She can chop wood and make a fire without matches if needed. Sarah is a beautiful singer and dancer. Truly, Sarah is a gifted young woman. And, although unknown to me at this time, Sarah's heart beats for Jake.

—

I was summoned to meet with Firefly to discuss future work projects that never seem to materialize, so I walk with Jake toward the longhouse and schoolhouse until we cross the Onondaga Creek. The morning air is fresh and still cool. The fragrance of honeysuckle sweeps over us. Three crows fly overhead, squawking incessantly as if to announce our arrival. Jake suddenly stops as he rounds the bend. There on a weathered rail of the old wooden bridge that crosses the Onondaga Creek sits a most beautiful figure, her eyes closed and her face smiling as it tilts up into the warm sunlight.

"'Bye, Grandfather," Jake utters quietly as he bounds down the hillside. "Sarah!" he then shouts. Jake's call so startles her that Sarah almost tumbles into the creek.

"Jake, you scared me."

Sarah eases off the rail slightly, catching her buckskin dress on a nail and revealing more of her legs than Jake has ever seen.

"Wait, let me free you before you tear your dress," Jake calls as he runs to the bridge. With long strides, Jake leaps onto the rail and then executes a front flip over her head. As Sarah quickly turns around, certain that Jake has fallen into the creek, there he stands before her, arms proudly folded across his chest.

"Jake, must you always run and jump when you approach me? You should be careful lest the white man's circus steal you and make you one of their acrobats."

"I must stay in training for the Game," Jake quickly replies.

"Do you mean…? Are you saying…? You made it…?" Sarah excitedly asks.

With a big smile, Jake proudly nods, waiving to me as if to say, *Time to move along, Grandfather.*

"Oh, Jake. I am so proud of you!" Sarah lovingly exclaims, warmly embracing him.

I smile as I shuffle along.

Later that evening Jake embarrassingly but earnestly recounts his feelings to me of his first embrace of Sarah. He closes his eyes and tells me that she smells like the lilacs that she has preserved in a jar of water and uses to brush onto her long black hair. Jake explains that he really wanted tell Sarah how he felt about her. He frustratingly explains that he had chosen and practiced the correct words many times, but they wouldn't find their way to his mouth. He thought about telling her how beautiful she is, that her smile lifts his spirit, that her eyes shine into his heart. He wanted to tell her that her movements are like a grazing deer, graceful and quiet. Her voice is like soft music. Instead he stood silently, listening to the creek.

"Then what happened?" I softly ask.

Jake dreamily explains what happened next.

"Jake? Jake? Where are you?" Sarah asks.

Jake snaps to the present, quickly shaking his head. Has he told her all of these things or has he been dreaming?

"Jake, are you in another world? Come back to me," Sarah begs, as she spins him around.

"Yes, yes!" he shouts.

"Yes? Yes? Yes, what? Why are you shouting?" Sarah asks with a smile. She holds her breath, hoping that he will say the sweet things that she has longed to hear.

"Yes, I am always thinking of the Game," Jake stupidly replies.

"Oh!" Sarah moans angrily. She stomps her right foot and quickly pivots to the left. Forgetting that her dress is still caught up on the nail, she tears her dress again, frustrating her even more than Jake's inability to express his love. Snatching her books off the rail, Sarah runs over the bridge and up the road toward the schoolhouse. Jake stands dumbfounded.

Realizing that he has missed his opportunity to profess his love, Jake smacks himself on the side of his head with his open hand as if to beat some sense into his slow-moving brain. Then he gives chase. *I shall make light of the situation,* Jake thinks, counting on his manner of apologizing.

"You cannot outrun me," he shouts, as he catches up to Sarah and begins running backward as fast as she is running forward. Sarah refuses to acknowledge his immature antics, but she cannot stay mad at Jake for very long. Sarah loves him so much that it is not hard for her to overlook most of Jake's boyish shortcomings.

With a slight smile, indicating her amusement, she sasses, "Do you think that you are a deer?"

"I have already touched the tail of our brother the deer in the hunt," Jake boasts proudly.

"Well, do not think you can touch my tail anytime soon," Sarah warns teasingly. "I am not your brother the deer."

I chuckle and wonder whether the day will come when Jake sweeps her up into his arms and carries her away?

"And so I hope you both made it to school on time?" I earnestly inquire. Jake joyfully continues his story swept up in the moment. Jake and Sarah both begin to laugh as they come up the hill upon which the two-storied red schoolhouse is perched. They arrive just as the teacher begins to ring the bell announcing commencement of class.

"Quickly, children, quickly, or you will be late," the teacher beckons.

The smaller children scamper into the schoolhouse first. Sarah and Jake, the two oldest students, customarily enter last and then are followed by the teacher. Closing the door behind her with a firm slam since the wood swells in the summer, the young teacher tucks a few strands of loose hair into her bun, straightens her long dress, and brushes some dust off of her white blouse sleeve. Now gathered, hands folded in front of her, she looks upon the class, counting them.

I am told by one of the clan mothers who is especially close to her that Miss Doolittle is the new teacher from Boston. She is the daughter of Irish parents who immigrated to America some thirty years earlier. Despite a drunken father, brawling brothers, and a sickly mother who spent nearly every waking moment with her hands in soapy water as a washerwoman, Miss Doolittle excelled in the public schools and received a scholarship to Wellesley College, one of the finest women's colleges in the United States. She had been determined to be her own woman and not to be subservient to anyone unless it was by her own choice.

Miss Doolittle was a gifted student, independent-minded, and attractive in a girlish way with bright blue eyes, a few freckles over her nose and checks, and red-orange hair. Her announcement that she would leave Boston upon graduation and travel west to the Indian reservations to become a teacher caused much consternation to her family and friends. Most Americans, her family included, knew little about Indians save what they learned in dime-store novels and Buffalo Bill Cody's Wild West show. Surely, they thought, she would be scalped, burned alive, or, worse yet, taken by a savage as his wife. Such were the prejudices of an ignorant nation that viewed the Indian people as a nuisance at best and a pestilence not fit to inhabit the earth at worst. Some people would not care at all if the Indians were exterminated altogether.

This clan mother who interviewed Miss Doolittle advises that she had not accepted this teaching position for the money; teachers on the reservation are paid much less than teachers in white schools. Apparently she is a crusader. Had slavery still existed, she surely would have been an abolitionist so I am told. As it is, she is an avid suffragette and speaks often of Indian citizenship. Amazingly, we, the first inhabitants of this land, are not considered citizens under US law.

Attending class as a helper, the clan mother further recounts some interesting observations. Clapping her hands, Miss Doolittle entreats her charges to settle down and take their places. "Children, I know you are excited about this coming weekend's festival. I know it is important to you and your families. But I do not want you to be distracted. Let us study extra hard this week so that the weekend will be seen as a gift and a reward for your diligence. Thus it will be more fulfilling for you."

The children spontaneously applaud. Apparently astonished by their reaction, she quickly realizes how easily excited they can become at the slightest mention of the Green Corn Festival.

"All right, please be quiet," she implores, holding a single finger over her lips. "Sarah, will you assist me by helping the primary graders while I tend to the intermediate graders?"

"Yes, Miss," Sarah replies obediently and with a slight curtsey.

At seventeen, Sarah is the oldest girl in the class and expected to help the teacher, who is charged with instructing students from ages seven to fifteen. Rarely does a student attend school beyond the age of fifteen unless he or she is of such scholarly inclination as to attend a college or university. Sarah is gifted. Miss Doolittle has expressed her hopes that Sarah will pursue higher learning. Not all of the tribe's children attend school. Some of the more traditional people think that school is another of the white man's evils. Some think that learning to read and to perform mathematics is useless, for how can these skills help their children till the field, hunt, fish, and raise a family?

A minority, myself included, believes that the education of our children in the white man's universities is essential to our people's survival. Many of our people who once roamed and hunted this land freely have been reduced to a life of poverty, disease, unemployment, alcoholism, and despair. We are surrounded by the white man, who has cheated us and refuses to trust us in white man's jobs except those that are menial or dangerous.

You may wonder how it came to pass that I speak and write as well as any educated white man. I have never attended a university, but my love of reading all subjects—from literature to philosophy, geography, and science—has opened my eyes to the importance of higher education for our children. After I completed seventh grade, the missionaries chose me to live in Syracuse with a Methodist minister's family for a year. My father feared for my safety in the white man's world and at first refused to let me go. But after he was bribed with tobacco, sugar, salt, and a quart of whiskey—in addition to my mother's ceaseless entreaties—I began my tutelage.

Upon arriving in Syracuse, I was struck by the size of the white man's world. The city was so crowded. It smelled. People moved too quickly, always in a hurry. I jumped eagerly from the carriage with the minister's young son and daughter, overjoyed that I would be living in a magnificent house and would wear beautiful clothes like them. But then an Indian's reality set in.

"Aye, where de ye t'ink yer goin', laddie?" the carriage driver asked as he grabbed me by my shirt collar and dragged me alongside the mistress of the house. The minister's house was indeed grand: we could fit five of our longhouses within its walls. I was marched through the hall of the grand house, where I saw pictures of white people, including children, on the walls and was led straight away to the carriage house and barn at the back of the house, where I was told I would live.

"Welcome te yer new home, laddie," the carriage driver said with a hearty laugh. "Don't be t'inkin' of runnin' away for dere's no place for an Indian boy te run te. You'll be stayin' wit' da horses an' da groomsman. Maybe he'll teach ye te ride."

So I made do, not in the grand house but in the carriage house. It was not so bad. The carriage house was actually bigger than most of the other houses that lined the street. I slept in the tack room on a cot fitted with a mattress and a pillow, both stuffed with straw. The room included a simple chair, a table holding a bowl and pitcher of water, and a tin bucket in the corner for obvious purposes.

I was never allowed to play with the children of the grand house, so I stayed with the horses, which became my only friends. I brushed them until they shone. I spoke and sang to them. The groomsman was an old black man, thin and almost blind. He spoke little but knew everything there was to know about horses. He taught me to ride. I cleaned the stalls and cleaned the barn. It was my home, and I was determined to make it as tidy as possible.

I remember hearing piano music, laughter, and merriment in the grand house at night as I sat shivering in the tack room, which was lit by a small kerosene lantern and slightly warmed by a potbelly stove, against which the groomsman and I jostled for closer position before one of us inevitably had to get up and pee—usually him. When even my blankets were too few to keep me warm, I climbed up on one of the horses and slipped under its blanket, keeping us both warm.

During the winter months, the Negro cook brought me into the house, where she let me sleep on the kitchen floor by the wood-burning stove, which she kept lit all night. She was a very kind woman who gave me biscuits and gravy in the morning, making sure she cleared me out before the master, mistress, and their children awoke.

I was treated as a slave in all ways but for one splendid thing: my reading lessons. The mistress of the house promised my mother and father that she would give me an education. She did that.

Over that year, I learned not to trust the white man, who considered Indians no better than the livestock that I slept and conversed with. Finally able to take no more, I ran away.

But before my inauspicious departure, I learned to read. Oh yes, I learned to read very well. I learned history, philosophy, and literature. The mistress taught me grammar, spelling, punctuation, and syntax. I even learned what a dangling participle was. She taught me to speak like a gentleman and hit me when I regressed to what she called the "pidgin" English from the reservation. The mistress took me into the big house every day for my lessons after I completed my chores. Other than the Negro cook and the groomsman, she was my only human contact. The Irish carriage driver, who checked in on me every day to make sure that my chores were completed, said nothing other than, "Still here, laddie? I'll be!"

The mistress usually took me into the garden in the summer, where we read on a rocker in the gazebo. In the winter, we read either at the kitchen table by the stove or in the parlor on a beautiful, large leather chair facing the fireplace.

I was small for my age. The mistress often insisted that I sit on her lap but only after I was properly bathed, groomed, and sprayed with perfumed water. The Irish carriage man was tasked with that unenviable job, and I struggled under his rough scrubbing with a horse brush in a tin tub of cold water. As the mistress read to me, I sometimes watched and admired her soft, white face and the small ruby-red lips that mouthed her words. Her smooth face was starkly different from that of my own mother, whose youthful beauty had been sapped by the rigors of reservation life. I sat mesmerized by the movement of the mistress's painted lips. When her hair was arranged on top of her head, I could see her neck, as white and as slender as that of a swan. She smelled like lilacs. Her thin waist was hard, as if she wore thin strips of wood under her dress. I later learned that this undergarment, a corset, was customary for white women.

My one anticipated comfort of the day was when she lowered my head upon her chest as she softly read to me. Her breath was sweet and tickled my ear. She held the book in her right hand by the lantern or the fire and with her left hand stroked my hair as she pressed my face to her bosom. Her chest heaved as she breathed. I could hear her heart beat. The combination of my head gently bobbing up and down, plus the warmth and softness of her body, often brought me into that twilight world somewhere between sleep and consciousness in which I heard her words and dreamed that I was one of the characters in the story that she read.

Sometimes after I'd read a particularly difficult passage without error, she rewarded me with a warm hug, sincere praise, and hot apple pie topped with vanilla ice cream. She said such things as, "My smart little Indian boy. My bright little red man." Then, with gentle laughter, she would press my face to her breast, squeeze me, and hug me as if I were a cloth doll.

And so through my experience with the minister's family, I learned to love three things in life: horses, books, and a woman's bosom.

For an Indian in America just after the Civil War, I received an education that few other Indians could dream of. Eventually I ran away, as the master of the house became increasingly agitated over the mistress stroking my hair and pressing my head to her chest. At the conclusion of my reading and speech lessons, I often heard them arguing as I shuffled back to the carriage house. Realizing that I may have worn out my welcome, I ran away, heading north into Canada, where, through contacts with relatives on the Mohawk reservation, I found work in woolen mills as a spindle boy. As I grew older, I worked as a lumberjack in the Canadian woods. I finally returned to the reservation and worked in the salt marshes around Onondaga Lake. One summer I floated rafts of tall white pine used to make sailing ship masts down the west branch of the Susquehanna River to Williamsport, Pennsylvania.

In Canada, I experienced many lonely nights in the dark, cold woods of the North. The lumberjacks stayed in barracks. Some of the men played cards. A few played the banjo or flute. Others dove into a whiskey or rum bottle. I, on the other hand, read every book I could buy or borrow. The older men used to bark at me to turn off the kerosene lantern that I read by into the wee hours of the morning so that they could get some sleep.

My love of reading allowed me to leave the drudgery of daily life, if only for an hour or two. Through reading I learned about the white man and his world. Through my love of books I resolved that education was my grandchildren's only hope of happiness, and perhaps even survival.

—

"Jake, will you please remove the boys to the play yard while Sarah and I review today's lessons with the girls?" Miss Doolittle politely asks.

This is Jake's cue to leave the girls to their privacy. Jake has told me that Miss Doolittle has a special book regarding manners, etiquette, and the workings of the female and male bodies that she reads only to the girls and after the clan mother departs. This book is Miss Doolittle's secret, for if anyone from the BIA, the church, the missionaries, or the parents knew of such teachings, she surely would be instantly dismissed. To discuss or teach anything regarding human sexuality is forbidden. But Miss Doolittle believes that education about the human body is the only way that the girls can protect themselves from unwanted pregnancy and disease. Even more, it is her way of teaching our young women to be proud of their bodies and independent in spirit so that they may not become a man's chattel.

Jake confides that Sarah often whispers some of Miss Doolittle's teachings to him upon sworn secrecy. She implores Jake to speak to no one about this for fear of losing Miss Doolittle's trust. Miss

Doolittle explains that women, most particularly Indian women, have been exploited for their bodies and sexuality over the centuries, and she is determined not to let that happen to her Indian wards. Jake is an unintended beneficiary of Sarah's education. He believes she can teach him things that he will never learn from any of the older boys, let alone from me.

Jake gladly takes the younger boys to the playground, leaving the girls to their studies, and wondering what new things they—and he—will learn today.

The clan mother, who accompanies Jake to the play yard before her departure, especially loves watching Jake and the younger boys interact in the school yard. The younger boys love their playtime with Jake, for among them he really shines. Jake carries his lacrosse stick with him wherever he goes. Most of the people now call the Creator's game lacrosse. Jake is, without question, the most skillful, the most exciting, and the most creative lacrosse player the young boys have ever seen. His unique skills with his lacrosse stick seem magical.

The clan mother also describes a spark kindling between Jake and Sarah.

Sarah momentarily looks up from her studies and peeks out the window, where she sees Jake playing with the younger boys. She seems to muse over how handsome he is: tall, with long black hair, a muscular body, and a beautiful face. She smiles as she sees the boys fawn over Jake, who is naturally comfortable around them.

Sarah and the clan mother watch Jake snatch a lacrosse ball from a little boy's hand with a quick snap of his stick. With a mighty heave, Jake spins his stick in the air and then bends over towards the little boy, holding out his hands as if to ask where has the stick gone. Shrugging his shoulders, the little boy's eyes follow Jake's finger, which points up. Jake then reaches out and snatches his stick without looking up, which magically keeps the ball within its leather webbing. The little boy squeals with delight at Jake's trickery, hugging Jake's legs as Jake bends over to return the ball.

Sarah chuckles as she watches Jake regale the younger boys with more tricks. The clan mother remarks at how wonderful Jake is with the children. She sees in Sarah's eyes the love and confidence that Jake will be a good father one day. Jake, more than any other boy his age, seems to be gifted in his interactions with children. They are drawn to him as if he smells like baked bread or tastes like honey. He is so kind and patient with them. The clan mother intuitively knows that Sarah dreamily looks at Jake as the man she will marry one day and have children of their own.

"Sarah? Sarah?" Miss Doolittle entreats. "Please return to your studies."

"Yes, Miss. Sorry, Miss." Sarah quickly returns her eyes to her book. As Sarah looks down, the clan mother tells me that Miss Doolittle stretches her neck to glance outside. She smiles as she sees the object of Sarah's romantic gaze: Jake.

9

THE RIVAL

It is the Tuesday of the third week in August. The Green Corn Festival is celebrated for four days, but Saturday is the most festive. During the afternoon, the Game is held; at night, singing and dancing are enjoyed. The week leading up to the festival is truly an exciting and busy time for the people, especially the children. School is dismissed early every day at one o'clock instead of the usual three o'clock so that the students have time to complete their chores and prepare for the weekend. My three girls race home every day from school, tend the fields for a few hours, quickly prepare supper, and then secret themselves in their room. Jake and I barely finish our own meals when the girls' busy little hands whisk away our plates, plunge them into a tub of soapy water, dry them with a single swipe, and practically throw them into the wall shelves. The girls then hurry to their room, shut the door, giggle, and gossip, as they busily sew their dresses for the weekend.

Maggie does most of the sewing. Molly measures and cuts the appropriate amount of cloth. Mary assembles the decorative beads for their dresses and moccasins. Girls and women wear the same type of dress. Typically, the Onondaga women wear dark-blue skirts with distinctive embroidery along the bottom and vertical embroidery along the edge where the wraps meet. A white blouse with an embroidered collar covers the upper torso. A leather belt or sash fastens at the waist. Under the skirt, they wear deerskin leggings with side fringe and beads, plus deerskin moccasins, richly decorated with beads of all colors. Many strands of necklaces adorn their necks, and earrings line the outside of their ears. Atop their heads sit white triangular kerchiefs with two corners tied under the chin. Colorful ribbons are woven into their braided hair.

People tell me that they observe Sarah and Jake usually hand in hand running home from school every day. It seems that everyone but me notices a strong fondness between the two. They laugh the whole way, each taking turns pulling the other along. With her long hair streaming in the wind, Sarah runs swiftly. Her hands are strong, with long, delicate fingers. Sarah keeps her hair in either one or two braids. Jake, however, rarely braids his hair, usually keeping his long black hair, which extends beyond his shoulders, out of his eyes with a bandana tied around his head.

Both Jake and Sarah run to Sarah's cabin first. One of the clan mothers who occasionally stop by to lend a hand marvels at Sarah's dedication and she remarks about Sarah and Jake's closeness. She smiles as she watches Sarah and Jake do their chores together. Sarah dutifully kisses her father on the forehead as he blankly stares into space while slowly rocking in his chair. Jake always makes sure to greet the old man respectfully even if he can't hear Jake's greetings. Jake helps Sarah with her chores. He chops and gathers wood. He draws buckets of water and pours adequate lye in the outhouse. After Sarah prepares dinner and is assured that her father is comfortable, she lights the porch lantern and throws a few extra logs on the fire. Then she and Jake race through the fields and up the pathway to our house.

Jake never goes anywhere without his lacrosse stick, which is like another appendage to him. He even sleeps with it. When the end comes, Jake, like me, will be buried with his lacrosse stick. As Sarah and Jake race through the fields, he scoops up small stones, pieces of wood, and even a squash or two with his stick, playfully tossing them at Sarah, who races ahead.

Covering her head under the hail of falling objects, she laughingly begs Jake, "Stop, stop. Do you wish to hurt me?"

Jake instantly, incredulously, stops. The thought of hurting Sarah in any way makes him shudder. "I can never hurt you," he shouts. "I will never hurt you. I…I…I…" He hesitates.

Sarah stops, looking at him with imploring eyes. *Please, please, say the words I long to hear,* she thinks.

Jake stammers on, "I…I…I…"

Sarah's eyes urge the words from Jake's mouth. She silently mouths, "I love you."

"I…I…I…shall…always…protect you," Jake finally blurts out.

"Oh!" Sarah cries in anguish. "What am I going to do with you, Jake Harwood?"

Did I not say I shall always protect you? Jake thinks. *Are you not pleased?*

"What?" Jake asks, puzzled.

Sarah picks up a small, rotting squash and hurls it straight at Jake's face. But at the last moment, he quickly moves his head to the side and simultaneously catches the squash in his lacrosse stick with such aplomb and with such a light touch that it does not puree against the leather webbing. Sarah, even more frustrated now, turns in a huff and races toward our house, where she is greeted with hugs and kisses by Mary, Molly, Maggie, and I.

"Come, Sarah," coaxes Maggie, pulling her along. "Look at the beautiful dress I have made for you. Try it on so I can alter it to fit you perfectly."

"Look what I have made for you, Sarah," Molly interrupts proudly, "a shell-and-bead choker. It will attract the eyes of all of the boys to your most beautiful neck."

Not to be outdone, little Mary brandishes a pair of moccasins. "Look, Sarah!" Little Mary squeals with excitement, holding over her head a pair of beautiful, high-ankle moccasins with front flaps, the tops skillfully decorated with an array of colored beads.

"Molly cut the deerskin. Maggie sewed the skin and beads. But I picked out the beads and designed the pattern," little Mary explains proudly.

Beaming with joy, Sarah hugs all three girls. "Thank you, thank you so much, my sisters, for your generosity and kindness. You are truly my three sisters. Your love will always be in my heart."

All three turn as Jake approaches. Sarah whispers to the girls, "If only your brother will show me as much love."

Mary retorts, "Him? He is just a dumb boy who thinks only of holding his lacrosse stick instead of the tender body of a maiden."

"Mary!" Molly admonishes. "How does such a little girl know of such mature things as love?"

"From Miss Doolittle, who reads us stories of handsome princes who were once frogs until kissed by a princess."

Sarah looks for Jake. Jake, who is chopping wood at the woodpile, has removed his shirt and is beginning to sweat. Sarah loses her breath at the sight of Jake's sinewy body. Again she whispers to the girls, "Perhaps if I kiss that frog, he will turn into a dashing prince?"

All three stare at Jake, who drops his ax to ask, "What? What? What are you looking at?"

Mary shouts back, "A frog!" as all four girls giggle and dash through the squeaky screen door.

—

Jake is now old enough to work at the sawmill, a small and rudimentary enterprise that employs about fifteen men from our part of the reservation. The only other industry involves the blue limestone quarries located in the northeast part of our nation. The mill is a ramshackle building with a water-powered vertical band saw that cuts trees into planks and fence rails. This mill is one of the last sawmills of the once-thriving western Susquehanna lumber business that extracted timber, mostly white pine, to build sailing masts. We have long claimed that white men plied some of our chiefs with whiskey and stole this land from our people. When engines replaced sails on boats, the lumber business declined. The white owners abandoned the mill and never set foot on that part of our land again. Now we selectively cut timber for local use on the reservation. I worked in the mill for many years, as have many men on the reservation, until age, injury, or death removes us from it.

The people do not permit anyone younger than sixteen to work in this very dangerous place. We are more enlightened than the white man, who still works boys as young as ten in their many woolen mills and other factories that dot the mill rivers throughout New England and central New York.

A sawmill worker can earn two dollars a day for a full day's work. Jake works as many hours as the boss will give him. Not possessing the skill of a lumberjack or a saw man in the mill, Jake mostly cleans up, carries small logs to be milled, and helps half-plank the big logs that are cut by the huge vertical saw that is powered by a waterwheel over the Onondaga Creek.

Jake always wears the leather gloves I have given him to protect his hands from cuts or splinters that may affect his soft touch with his lacrosse stick.

Jed (short for Jedidiah) Youngblood has been working in the mill since the day he turned sixteen. Although he completed the eighth grade, he has little use for education. He has followed his father into the woods to learn the life of a lumberman. An Indian boy who lives on this part of the reservation has two choices for employment: work as a lumberman in the mill or work outside the reservation in the white man's world.

The BIA man, Firefly, forever tries to persuade our young men to leave the reservation for the white man's cities, where, he promises, many opportunities for riches await. He tells us stories of our Mohawk brothers who have left the reservation for New York City and earn four dollars and fifty cents per day, working high up in the tall buildings where the white man is afraid to go. But I have yet to meet an Indian who leaves the reservation for the city and does not return a lesser man, if he returns at all.

Our women have even fewer choices. Some leave the reservation to work as maids or cooks. Some marry lumbermen or quarry workers on the reservation. Others put in with Indian men who carve out a subsistence living growing crops and raising livestock. Some marry white men. Most who leave are never heard from again.

As reservation men go, Jed Youngblood, now twenty-four, is a suitable specimen for a husband. Although not handsome, he is not ugly. Short and stocky like a badger, he is neither elegant nor graceful, but he is strong and healthy. Jed is not book-learned but is as cunning as a fox. He is not considered wise, for his heart guides his actions before his brain. When riled, Jed is as mean as a wounded bear. People say that an accident at the mill hardened Jed Youngblood's heart.

A few years back, Youngblood fell victim to a piece of wood that shot out from the saw and into the corner of his left eye. None of the people, not even the medicine men or clan mothers, dared remove the protruding stick for fear of tearing his eye. Desperate, they loaded Youngblood into a wagon. His cries of pain were heard for miles as they hurried him to Syracuse. But he was refused treatment there because he was an Indian. Youngblood was so angered by this rejection that he pulled the stick from his eye in front of the white doctors, threw it at their feet, and spit on it. Shortly thereafter, Youngblood lost sight in that eye, which glazed over with a grayish-white film. Also, his face bears a three-inch scar along his left jaw, earned from a blow to the face by an opponent's lacrosse stick. That scar and the clouded left eye frighten little children. Indeed, Youngblood's stare can freeze any person in his tracks.

Youngblood never has missed a day of work. He is said to be as skillful a lumberman and millworker as any of the old bucks. It is rumored that he will someday run the mill, if he survives.

Of equal importance, at least in the eyes of the young men, Youngblood is the fiercest lacrosse player on the reservation. What he lacks in finesse or speed Youngblood makes up with cunning, daring, and brute strength. He prefers to use his lacrosse stick more like the war club of our ancestors than an instrument of skill.

Excepting his rough appearance, Youngblood is considered a good catch for any Indian maiden. His wife will not have to beg for goods from the BIA or hope for largesse from her neighbors or the missionaries. Youngblood earns fifteen dollars a week, a fortune to most.

The clan mothers and some of the men at the mill tell me that upon reaching that time in life to take a wife and start a family, Youngblood has focused his good eye on only one Onondaga maiden, Sarah.

"I am going marry that tall, pale-skinned girl by the end of the year," Youngblood boasts to his coworkers, who all gawk at Sarah as she passes the mill on her way to school.

"Does she know that yet?" teases one of the older men, bringing a chuckle from the rest.

Quickly turning his head, Youngblood crossly gazes at the man who dares question his plans. The men freeze, hushed.

"You watch. Just you watch," Youngblood scowls menacingly.

"Lighten up, Youngblood," barks the shop foreman. "Get back to work, men."

The shop foreman has worked the mill for thirty years. He is missing bits and pieces of his fingers, walks with a limp from an untreated knee injury, and has a crooked back from one of his other accidents, of which there are too many to remember. Now in his last work season, he fears no one, least of all Youngblood, for what could Youngblood do to him that time and the mill have not already done?

Youngblood and his companion, Sonny Two Weasels, a young man weak in body and spirit, carry a large log to the saw conveyor belt.

"What magic will you use to turn the attention of Sarah Sweetwaters to you, my brother?" Sonny asks with feigned interest after they drop the heavy piece of wood on the belt with a thump.

"What you see, my friend," Youngblood replies proudly, standing tall with his arms folded across his chest.

"Yes, you are strong. You are a great lumberman. And no finer a lacrosse player do the people boast. But she sees you not," Sonny reminds Youngblood.

Angered by this perceived slight, Youngblood menacingly steps up to Sonny's face and sternly reminds him, "She will see plenty of me in the Game, as I shall single-handedly crush our opponents."

"We all await your glory, my friend," replies Sonny, "but it is the schoolboy, Jake, who blocks Sarah's gaze from you."

Youngblood peers with squinted eye at Jake, who is helping the men unload a wagon of freshly cut timber.

"That boy?" Youngblood asks incredulously. "He is nobody. He is…a boy."

"The people say that he is the best young lacrosse player to have emerged since…" Sonny searches for a name that quickly comes to him as Youngblood stares him down, "since you…since you, my brother."

"The best lacrosse player since me?" Youngblood whispers half to himself as he scratches his chin with his rough hands.

"Look, my friend," Sonny blithely continues. "See how tall he is. See how handsome he is. See how his muscles are long and strong. And it is said that he is the best student in Miss Doolittle's class."

"Shut up, you idiot," Youngblood snarls with a scowl.

Youngblood realizes truth in this fool's words. Jake is indeed a formidable rival for Sarah's affections, but not for long if Youngblood has anything to do with it.

"Hey, Harwood. Bring a bundle of kindling to me to tie up for delivery," yells the foreman.

The men load up Jake's outstretched arms so high with scrap wood that he can barely see over it. Shuffling cautiously over the sawdust-laden floor, kicking pieces of wood aside as he carefully maneuvers through the debris, Jake could never have seen what was about to happen. Youngblood takes this opportunity to derail his rival.

"Come on, Jake, move it," shouts the foreman.

When nobody is looking, Youngblood sticks out his leg, causing Jake to trip forward and fall on his face. The kindling scatters across the floor.

The men burst into laughter as Jake embarrassingly picks his head up and meets the foreman's unforgiving gaze. Still on his belly, his arms outstretched on the floor, Jake quickly swings his head to see whose errant foot has caused his fall. Most likely the foot belongs to the person who is laughing the loudest. Youngblood.

"Get back to work," the foreman barks. "Jake, pick yourself up and regather that wood."

Getting to his feet and brushing off his pants, Jake dutifully replies, "Yes, sir. Sorry, sir."

"You had best be more careful around here, son, or you can get killed. Look at that vertical saw. What if you had fallen into it?" The foreman makes a slashing motion with his right index finger across his neck.

Jake looks at the saw and at Youngblood, who simply smiles and then turns away.

—

That night Jake tells me that he felt embarrassed, even angry, by the day's events. On his way home, Jake scoops stones up with his lacrosse stick and angrily targets every fence post he encounters on his way home. He dodges trees in the twilight as if they are opponents in this coming Saturday's Game. Our Grandmother the Moon rises slowly from her slumber and shines her bright light upon the dirt road that guides Jake through the dark forest. Given his haste to return home and his mind awash with the events at the sawmill, Jake pays little attention to where he is going except to follow the dirt road. Then, out of the mist, Jake notices a shadowy figure walking toward him.

"Stop, spirit. Come no closer. Let me pass without incident," Jake implores.

We Indians believe in the Creator or Great Spirit much like the white man believes in one God. Like the white man, we also believe that evil lurks about, intending to do good people harm. Some choose to walk with evil spirits. Others beg to pass them by.

"Jake! Jake! Is that you?"

"Sarah?" Jake asks, relieved it is his love and not an evil spirit. "What are you doing on the road in the darkness alone?" Jake asks breathlessly. "I thought you were an evil spirit."

"I was at your house with your sisters, preparing my dress for Saturday night, and I lost track of the time. I must get home to care for my father. But I want to see you first. Jake, is everything all right? Did something happen at the mill today?"

Momentarily taken aback, Jake asks, "What are you talking about? Nothing happened at the mill. Why do you ask?"

"Johnny Redman came to your house on horseback to give your grandfather money to purchase some goods in Syracuse and told Grandfather of your fall and of how perilously close you were to the saw."

Embarrassed and annoyed that this story had traveled out of the mill and into the community even before he arrived home, Jake replies, "It was nothing. I tripped and I fell. I was not even close to the saw blade."

Sensing his embarrassment, Sarah deeply sighs, reaches up, and gently touches her crestfallen love's face. "Be calm, Jake," she whispers soothingly. "Please be careful. I could not bear to lose you."

Jake looks down, ashamed at his own anger. "I…I must go."

Sarah begins to slowly walk away alone. I am sure she was most likely disappointed that Jake had not taken the opportunity to reciprocate her tender feelings toward him.

"Sarah, wait. I will walk you to your home," Jake calls after her. She whisks by him and calls back, "It is only around the bend. I shall be all right." Jake shakes his head and frustratingly muses, "Girls."

Hearing footsteps in the darkness, I look up. Instantly I see Jake leap over the four steps and bound onto the porch. He flies by me as I sit back in my rocking chair and bursts through the screen door, shouting, "What is for dinner?"

Quickly backtracking and punching open the screen with his backside before his sisters can answer him, Jake turns to me. "Hello, Grandfather. I am sorry I did not greet you as I arrived."

"Is something other than food on your mind, my son?" I ask.

Jake catches his breath as he bends over with his hands on his knees, then sits on the porch steps, wiping his sweaty brow with the sleeve of his shirt.

"Grandfather," he begins hesitantly, "I am facing many new things, feeling new emotions for which I do not have an explanation or answer. I wish for wisdom to come to me in my dreams, but only the eagle, carrying a bloody stick and casting his shadow over the land, fills my head. That dream does not provide answers. It only creates more questions in my mind."

While Jake is in midsentence, Mary backs through the screen door, holding a bowl of soup in both hands with a piece of cornbread stuck in her mouth, as if she were a starling who has just stolen this tasty morsel from a picnic basket. Mary hands Jake the bowl and begins mumbling. When Jake removes the cornbread from her mouth, Mary continues, without missing a beat, "I kept your soup warm for you, Jake. My sisters wanted to put it away to teach you a lesson for coming home late, but I beseeched them to keep it hot, for I know how hard you must have worked today."

Jake is about to thank his little sister profusely and begins to reach up to kiss her on the forehead when he realizes that another purpose may explain this overt kindness.

"You little devil. What game is this? What do you want of me?" Jake insists as he jabs her playfully in the ribs, causing her to giggle.

"I am just trying to be a nice and obedient little sister," she says sheepishly, looking down at her feet with her hands clasped behind her back, slightly twisting her body side to side, as if to say *How can you possibly question your sweet sister's motives?*

"OK, you are a respectful and loving sister. Thank you. Now, good-bye," Jake mutters as he kisses her on the forehead.

Seeing her opening, Mary continues. "Because I am now your favorite sister, will you...? Can you...?"

"Stop!" Jake snorts impatiently. Smiling at her longing eyes, he hesitates. She breathlessly awaits his answer. "Yes, I will get you something in Syracuse."

With a wink and a smile, I affirm Jake's generous offer. Quite beside herself, little Mary jumps into Jake's arms, almost knocking him from the porch steps to the ground.

"I love you, my brother," she squeals, kissing Jake all over his face.

Mary is like an overly affectionate dog licking her master's face. Trying to avoid being smothered by this exuberant little cherub's gratitude, Jake finally stops her by laughingly shouting, "I love you too, my little scheming sister."

At that, little Mary skips back through the screen door into the kitchen, singing, "Jake is buying me a present! Jake is buying me a present! Jake is going to Syracuse in the hills far away! Jake is buying me a present because he loves me today!"

Peace seemingly restored, Jake asks, "Grandfather?"

But before he can seek my counsel, both Molly and Maggie now burst through the squeaky screen, screaming. "Jake! Have you forgotten us? Do you not love us as much as that little devil inside?" they implore, scowling at their impish sister peering through a hole in the screen.

"Girls, do you not see that I am trying to talk with Grandfather? Can you not leave us alone for a few moments?" Jake begs.

"As a Sachem, I am called upon to mediate disputes, some less daunting than the petty jealousies of three little girls," I offer. "My son, the best pleasure in life is giving. Promise your sisters each a gift, which will lighten your heart and uplift their spirits."

"OK, OK, I shall look for something for both of you girls in Syracuse," Jake confirms obediently.

The elder girls immediately fall into their brother's arms and hug him. But Jake is quick to remind them that they should never fail to keep his soup warm in the future, as their little sister Mary has done.

Looking at each other with puzzled faces, Molly replies, "Yes, we did. We made sure that Mary kept your bowl near the fire while we finished our dresses."

"Why, that little rascal Mary!" Jake exclaims as the girls then jump up and disappear inside the house.

Shaking my head with a big smile, I knock my old corncob pipe against the heel of my boot to remove the spent tobacco and then turn my attention to Jake. "You know, my son," I begin, as I lean over and whisper so as not to be overheard, "another reason to promise a woman a gift is to shut her up."

We laugh together as Jake hungrily devours his soup and cornbread.

After some silence, Jake begins again, "Grandfather?"

"Wait. Hush. Why don't you get some sleep. You have one more day at the mill before we go to Syracuse. I have spoken with Miss Doolittle. You can work the whole day for some extra money tomorrow. I have one more thing to do today."

Jake rises unusually slowly, his muscles likely aching from a hard day's work in the sawmill. He simply touches my shoulder as he quietly walks past me and through the screen door and into to his bedroom.

—

With daylight fading but our Grandmother the Moon illuminating my way through the woods, I come upon Sarah's house. I offer a wicker basket full of green apples to my silent friend, Sarah's father, and begin up the path toward home. Suddenly Sarah, who had been sewing and surely gossiping with my girls, whisks by with a polite, "Hello, Grandfather!" apologizing for her haste, explaining that the hour grew late and she needed to tend to her father. I could barely utter a reply as she flies by me. Standing atop the path, I look back and observe two shadowy figures standing on the porch next to Sarah's father, who apparently arrive after my departure. I recognize Jed Youngblood and Sonny Two Weasels. Both pretend to converse with Sarah's father, which is impossible because the poor man has not spoken a word since her mother's death.

As Sarah approaches, both men rise. "Sarah, my friend, your father, and I have been awaiting your arrival," Youngblood says loud enough that I could hear.

"It is late," she politely replies, brusquely brushing by Youngblood's outstretched hands to enter the house.

Youngblood quickly turns and roughly snatches her arm with one hand before she can reach the house door. Seeing her look of terror, he smiles that jagged smile in an attempt to allay her fear and asks most sternly through clenched teeth, "Why do you disrespect me in this manner before your father's eyes?"

"My father understands little and says nothing, which is how I have known him since I was a child," Sarah explains, looking down at the pitiful man. "You cannot offend a man who does not understand your words." She then gazes down at her arm held tightly by Youngblood's strong, rough hand and complains, "You are hurting me."

I begin my approach to intervene but stop as I observe Youngblood remove his hand quickly as if he had touched fire. Peering into her face with his one good eye, Youngblood loudly apologizes. "Forgive me. But I am here to ask you a favor," he states, more as a demand than a request.

"Favor? What favor?" Sarah replies, undoubtedly hoping that he will quickly explain and leave.

"I ask that you cheer for me at the Game on Saturday. It is for you that I shall play my best."

I could tell by the expression on Sarah's face that she feigns interest and asks, "Do you not play to please the Creator?"

"Yes, well, that too," Youngblood responds with annoyance. He is eager to ask the next and most important question. "I also ask that you favor me in the Fish Dance, when the young maidens choose the bravest and strongest men as their partners."

Sarah quickly corrects him. "A young woman looks for many qualities in a man. Bravery and strength are but two of them."

"What other qualities do you seek? I will give them to you!" Youngblood demands to know.

Sarah stands erectly, brushes a few strands of hair from her face, and, in a lecturing tone, explains, "You cannot possess what the Creator has not given you. All men cannot be all things. You are what you are. To be something else is like the beaver trying to run as the deer. Be satisfied in who you are. Perhaps that may be good enough to catch some maiden's eye."

His passions now rising, Youngblood viciously grabs both of Sarah's arms with both of his strong hands, roughly pulling her to him, and commands, "I, and no other, shall be the man you choose."

Sarah begins to struggle and weep. Suddenly, her father angrily mutters something, causing all to look to him. Taking the opportunity to wrest herself free, Sarah runs through the door, crying, "I cannot be with you. I love another. I love another!"

Youngblood angrily swirls away and stomps down the porch stairs.

"Now what are you going to do?" Sonny asks, somewhat enjoying Sarah's rebuke of his rough friend.

"You will see, my friend! You will see!" Youngblood angrily replies. With an evil sneer, he shouts more loudly, "I will have no rivals! Do you hear me? I will have no rivals!"

Sonny stands silently with a perplexed look undoubtedly pondering what Youngblood's outburst means. Noticing that the woods are dark, and the hour grows late, Sonny shouts, "Hey! Please wait, my brother," as he nervously surveys the woods for evil spirits. "Wait for me!" Sonny begs as he chases after Youngblood like a lost pup.

I turn away and slowly trudge up the path toward the comfort of my rocking chair on our cabin's porch. As I am disturbed by Youngblood's disrespectful behavior, I am equally impressed with Sarah's handling that potentially hostile situation. I hope that Youngblood gets the message…but something tells me it will not be so.

10

THE "ACCIDENT"

Only three days remain until the Game and the festival. Tomorrow is Syracuse. Jake and the girls can hardly contain themselves. Their excitement overflows in everything they do. Jake has one more day to work at the sawmill to earn a little more money for his trip to the big city.

Miss Doolittle has closed the school for the rest of the week. She knows how important the Game and the festival are to the people, especially the children, and realizes that much still remains to be prepared. She tells the children that she has a surprise for them on Saturday. But try as they may, even as they beg and tug on her dress, she keeps her secret with a big smile.

Jake can work at least ten hours at the sawmill if he arrives at five o'clock in the morning. Excited by the prospect of earning two dollars and twenty-five cents, he sprints to the mill without stopping. I have given Jake permission to work a few extra hours in the sawmill if the foreman has work available. I now wish I had not been so quick to give Jake my blessing after hearing the account of what transpired that day as later told to me and the elders by Sonny Two Weasels.

Jake enthusiastically approaches the open-air building. But the foreman greets him with disappointing news: no work for him this day. Jake is crestfallen.

Jake walks slowly and dejectedly toward the door, head bowed, tears welling up in his eyes. But his sadness is interrupted by Youngblood and Sonny Two Weasels who were just walking in when the foreman breaks the bad news.

"I need an extra hand in the south woods," Youngblood announces. "Many fallen trees need branch cutting, and I need to finish felling a big one or two. I cannot do it with just this meadowlark here," he declares, shoving Sonny Two Weasels with his elbow.

"Is that what you think of your friend?" Sonny Two Weasels asks. "Your only friend," he reminds Youngblood.

The foreman glances at Jake, who returns his attention with longing eyes. He is apprehensive about sending a greenhorn such as Jake into the woods with just two men instead of a full crew of more watchful eyes.

Sensing the foreman's concern, Youngblood feigns reassurance. "Don't worry. Jake's my teammate. I shall look out for him."

"All right, take Jake, but be careful. He has never been on a cutting crew before. Don't want to lose him before his grand debut in the Game," jokes the foreman.

"I shall watch the little babe as if I were his mother," Youngblood vows disingenuously. "Get your gear, Softwood, and follow me."

"My name is Harwood, not Softwood," Jake quickly corrects.

Youngblood suddenly stops, quickly whirls around, and grabs both of Jake's hands before he can protest. Examining Jake's hands as if he were a doctor, Youngblood looks up without letting go, and sneers, "Humph. Just as I thought. Soft. Is that why you wear those leather gloves?" Youngblood pointedly stares at the gloves folded under Jake's leather belt.

Calmly but with slight embarrassment, Jake replies, "I wear the gloves to protect my hands from splinters or cuts so I can properly feel my stick in the Game."

Seeing this opportunity to add kerosene to the fire, Sonny Two Weasels uninvitingly chimes in, "More like you want to keep your hands soft for Sarah Sweetwaters."

Both Youngblood and Jake angrily scowl at Sonny Two Weasels, who defensively puts up his hands to protect himself from what he thinks may be a quick blow to his head.

"Ok, Ok, knock it off, you three," barks the foreman. "Time's a-wastin'. I've got no horses to get you into the woods, so it looks like you'll be hoofin' it on your own."

"Hey, Softwood," commands Youngblood, "grab that ax, file, and water jug. And don't forget your gloves. Wouldn't want you to develop a man's hands," he mocks, as he proudly waves his calloused hands in front of Jake's face. Sonny Two Weasels laughs.

"What are you laughin' about, you idiot? Grab the saw," Youngblood snaps. Sonny Two Weasels rushes to find the large two-man saw. In his haste to catch up, he drags one end of the saw along the dirt.

"Pick it up, you stupid fool," Youngblood shouts. "Do you want to dull it up before we get to the woods?" Youngblood shakes his head in disgust. "How is it that the village idiot is my only friend?" he asks himself under his breath but loud enough for Sonny to hear him.

Youngblood shouts again, "Pick it up. Move faster," as he strides off into the dark woods.

Jake, Sonny and Two Weasels are amazed at how fast Youngblood walks through the woods. Youngblood is, indeed, strong and fearless. Sonny Two Weasels struggles to balance the large saw, which bends over his shoulder, as he runs after Youngblood, who has disappeared into the woods ahead.

The sun is fully up now. Jake estimates that they have been travelling for about an hour. Jake and Sonny Two Weasels never really see Youngblood as they trek through the woods. It is as if he wants to lose them. The two are guided only by Youngblood's distant voice. Jake is also amazed that Youngblood finds his way to the exact spot where they will labor without use of a compass or navigational stars. Jake sincerely respects Youngblood's woodsmanship. But something menacing about Youngblood's demeanor causes Jake trepidation.

Coming into a clearing, both Jake and Sonny Two Weasels find Youngblood sitting on a stump, wiping his brow with a bandana. "Thought I had lost you two. Pass that jugga' water over." After each man takes a mighty swig from the jug, Youngblood barks out orders. "OK, Sonny Two Weasels, come with me ta fell that oak yonder. Softwood, you go down the hill into the valley below and start branchin' those felled trees. Take the long ax and the file."

As Jake begins to trudge down the mountainside, Sonny Two Weasels shouts back, "Young brother, wield that ax away from your body, for if you miss a branch you can cut your leg. I did that once and I—"

Youngblood slaps Sonny Two Weasels across the back of the head. "Shut up, you fool. Nobody wants to hear your stories. Let him figure it out himself."

"But…but…Jake is new. He may hurt himself," implores Sonny Two Weasels. "Then he will be lost to us for the Game."

Making his way toward the giant oak, Youngblood shouts back, "We do not need him in the Game. We have me," he boasts, pounding his chest with one hand, "and that is all we shall need ta win on Saturday!"

Sonny Two Weasels whispers to himself, "The Great Spirit does not look kindly upon one who boasts so."

Youngblood hears Sonny Two Weasels speak under his breath and angrily responds, "The Great Spirit chooses me ta lead the Onondaga ta victory. Who else possesses my strength and courage?"

Not waiting for an answer, and scanning below, Youngblood locates Jake. With his shirt removed, Jake's sinewy muscles glisten in the early morning sunlight. Both Youngblood and Sonny are surprised at the young man's skillful handling of his ax and, for a moment, wonder whether Jake can handle his lacrosse stick with equal dexterity.

Sonny Two Weasels could tell by Youngblood's expression that he is curious about how formidable Jake will be on the lacrosse field, but he resolves that Jake will not be the shining star on the field on Saturday. As Youngblood stares at Jake, jealousy wells up in his throat. But something else perplexes Youngblood. Is it self-doubt? Sensing this about Youngblood, Sonny Two Weasels cannot resist. "That young Indian swings his ax with strength and finesse. He must surely handle his lacrosse stick with equal ease."

Youngblood spits and barks out, "Get the saw! We need ta get ta work."

Youngblood trudges up the hillside, viciously knocking saplings to the side like an angry bear. Sonny Two Weasels smiles at the thought that he has perhaps placed a bit of self-doubt in his overly confident friend's mind. The look of worry that had briefly flashed across Youngblood's face oddly pleases Sonny Two Weasels. At least for now, Youngblood does not seem quite that invincible.

Sonny Two Weasels walks more erectly and with a slight grin on his face, so proud is he to have taken Youngblood's arrogance down a notch. But his momentary feeling of superiority is quickly dashed as a booming voice echoes down the hillside, "Move it, or I'll cut you in half with that saw!" Sonny scurries up the hillside like a weasel in the underbrush. Looking back, he spots Jake laboring as ordered. But a sense of inexplicable dread sweeps over Sonny.

The three loggers work nonstop for three hours. Not unnoticed, Jake never stops once to rest or to take water. Youngblood and Sonny Two Weasels take a break. Sonny uneasily observes Youngblood's foreboding gaze directed at the boy.

Gathering up the courage, Sonny takes this opportunity to offer another jab. "The boy is strong. Incredible stamina. Quite an addition to the team."

Youngblood spits out some water, wipes his mouth with his dirty shirtsleeve, grumbles, and returns to the tall oak they have been working on all morning.

The three are working an area known as the south slope. Many trees, mostly red and white oak, have already been felled and piled up by men and horse teams that dragged, or "skidded," them through the woods. Once that task is completed, the pile of wood will be set loose down the slope into the river below, which flows north toward the sawmill. Jake's job today is to clear the branches from fallen logs below so as not to impede the stacked logs as they tumble down the mountainside toward the river. The idea is that the fallen logs below will form a wooden "floor" in the forest that will facilitate the movement of rolling logs down into the river.

With the sun at its highest point in the sky, the three estimate that it is close to noon—lunchtime. Each man carries a small satchel of jerked venison, a biscuit, and a green apple.

Sonny Two Weasels stands to invite Jake up the hill to join them for lunch. But Youngblood, with one strong snap, quickly pulls him back down to the ground.

"Let him eat alone," Youngblood snarls.

A half hour later, Youngblood, now finished with his lunch, throws his apple core to a squirrel chirping nearby and barks, "Hey, Softwood. Do you take all day ta eat? Get back ta that ax. You too," he shouts back at Sonny, who is taking the final bite of his apple.

Sonny throws what remains of his apple down the hillside toward Jake to catch his attention. Seeing the apple bounce near him, Jake looks up to see Sonny smile and wave. Jake gratefully waves and smiles back.

—

By three in the afternoon, all three men are dead tired. Sonny is nearly delirious with fatigue. Working the two-man saw with Youngblood is an arduous task. Youngblood and Sonny have felled an oak and two tall pines. They work on another pine that is perilously close to the stacked trees. Sonny is too tired to notice the danger.

Wiping the sweat off his brow, Sonny drops to the ground. "Can we not take a rest?" he begs, lying on his back with one arm over his eyes.

"No, not now! Just one more tree. Just one, and we'll call it a day," assures Youngblood.

Motivated by the prospect of finishing the day, Sonny struggles to his feet, puts his hand over his eyebrows, and looks down into the valley, where Jake is still swinging away. "Amazing!" Sonny Two Weasels whispers under his breath.

"What? What are you saying?" barks Youngblood.

"Nothing. Let us saw," Sonny unenthusiastically responds.

Sonny does not notice that they have cut the great pine at an angle that will cause it to fall in the direction of the stacked logs. After two hours of their sawing and chopping, the great tree is ready to fall.

"When we hear three crackles," Youngblood begins to explain, "we must quickly pull the saw and run opposite the cut." Too tired to realize that the tree will fall dangerously close to the stacked logs, Sonny just nods in agreement.

With every ounce of their remaining strength, both men saw vigorously. Spit flies from their mouths and sweat cascades from their faces. The palms of their hands are bleeding. Their breathing is labored. Suddenly, a crackle. They stop.

"Keep sawing!" shouts Youngblood. They saw, they saw, and then they hear the second crackle. "One more to go," Youngblood shouts.

Crackle…crackle…crackle.

"Pull the saw and run!" Youngblood screams.

The two men yank out the saw before the tree begins to topple. Both men hurriedly run from the falling tree and fall to their knees, scrambling the last few steps until sheer exhaustion causes them to fall on their backs, chests heaving for air. The tree begins to fall away from them so slowly, as if it did not want to fall.

Sonny lies exhausted. Hearing the steady crackle, he props himself up with both arms to watch the giant tree fall. But something is wrong. Terribly wrong.

Adrenalin surging, Sonny springs to his feet. Youngblood remains on his back, exhausted, trying to catch his breath. Sonny senses danger. Ahead of the fallen tree, he notices two great oaks, already branched and smooth, lying on the forest floor. The oaks are adjacent to the great pile. Sonny looks at the slowly falling pine, then at the two fallen oaks, then at the pile, and realizes that the tree they have just cut will fall onto the two smooth oaks that pave the way into the great pile of stacked logs.

Now Sonny screams, "Danger, my brother! Get up! I see danger!"

Youngblood slowly rises to his feet. Thinking this is another of Sonny's pranks or nervous ramblings, Youngblood unenthusiastically follows Sonny's pointing finger to the falling pine and at the stack. Youngblood smiles, stands silently, and does nothing.

Frustrated, Sonny pushes Youngblood to the ground and runs by him to the edge of the glen to warn Jake. He cups his hands over his mouth. "Jaaaake!" he bellows. But he sees no movement, no hand motion of acknowledgment. Jake is nowhere to be seen. Sonny looks back at the pine, which is but a few feet from crashing upon the fallen oak trees that slope down to the pile of logs. "Jaaake!" he shouts again.

Suddenly Jake appears. Happy to hear a human voice, he looks up the hill with one hand cupped over his eyes to block the blinding sunshine and waves with the other hand.

Jake is oblivious to the impending danger; Sonny is panic-stricken. He must warn Jake. Sonny begins jumping up and down, madly pointing at the crashing tree.

Jake looks toward the tree and then back at Sonny. Jake waves more vigorously as if to acknowledge Sonny's achievement. But Sonny continues jumping and pointing madly.

Then, with a thunderous crash, the tall pine falls upon the fallen oaks. It bounces nearly four feet, momentarily suspended in the air before returning to the oak rails leading down to the great pile of stacked logs. Once landed, the mighty pine begins to roll down upon the fallen oaks toward the pile of stacked logs, branches snapping off as if shorn by a buzz saw.

Taking but a moment to process this information, Sonny, with all of his strength, thunders, "Ruuunnnn!"

Quickly realizing the impending danger, Jake does not need further warning. The fallen pine picks up speed as it rolls toward the pile of stacked logs. With a thunderous crack, the pine tree crashes into the pile.

Jake does not wait to see what will happen next. He knows. The pile of stacked logs come undone and begin to roll down the hill over the floor of fallen trees that he has just branched. Jake's work that day facilitates the speed of the wall of wood that ominously rolls toward him.

"Run, my brother!" Sonny Two Weasels shouts.

But Jake cannot hear Sonny's words. The logs crash down the hillside with a roar. Like a wooden avalanche, the loosed logs crush everything in their path.

The rolling logs pick up speed as they carom down the hillside. Jake looks back as he feels the rumbling of the speeding logs. The valley has no upright trees to impede the thunderous herd of wood.

The tumbling logs close in on him. Even Jake, the boy who touched the buck's tail, cannot elude these wooden pursuers. He struggles to keep his balance as he runs with long strides down the hillside. Jake leaps stumps and fallen trees as if he were a deer being stalked, but it is only a matter of moments before he will be overtaken and crushed.

Just as Jake is about to collapse from exhaustion, his legs burning with pain and fatigue, he notices a granite outcropping that forms a ledge to his right. Jake darts for that ledge, jumps from it, and scrambles on all fours back under its lip just as the wooden tidal wave washes over him. Snug under the outcropping, like a hibernating bear in its cave, Jake cups his hands over his ears to protect them from the deafening sound of the logs pounding the top of his granite tomb. Miraculously unscathed, Jake watches in relief as the logs tumble down the hill and crash into the river below with a mighty cascade of water.

Never having witnessed such a spectacle, and still paralyzed with fear, Sonny Two Weasels expects the worst. He stands motionless atop the hill, hoping to see any movement, any sign of life, now that the forest is still. He cups both hands over his eyes, carefully scanning the landscape.

Forlornly about to give up hope, Sonny suddenly spots a solitary, gloved hand grab the top of the granite ledge. Then another gloved hand reaches over. After a few breathless moments, Jake's head pops up. Jake struggles to prop himself up on the ledge.

Succeeding in boosting himself up and over, Jake collapses face-down, exhausted from the day's work, his perilous run, and his near-death experience. Sonny joyfully bounds down the hill to offer Jake aid.

"My brother! My brother! You are alive!" Sonny shouts excitedly as he rolls Jake onto his back. Sonny carefully picks up Jake's head, which he cradles in the crook of his elbow, and pours water over Jake's face and onto his lips.

Jake chokes and gasps for air as he focuses in the sunlight. Shielding his eyes, he asks, "Sonny Two Weasels, is it you, my brother? Or am I with my ancestors at the Creator's council fire?"

"I am not a ghost, my brother. It is I, Sonny Two Weasels. I tried to warn you."

Jake reaches up with both hands and grabs Sonny Two Weasels's shoulders. He pulls himself up and breathlessly murmurs, "You did. You did warn me. You saved my life."

Sonny helps Jake to his feet and brushes off his trousers. "Can you walk? We should climb the hill and grab our gear, for the day is coming to an end," Sonny advises.

Still shaking, Jake takes a step forward on wobbly legs.

"Are you hurt, my brother? Can I help you?" Without waiting for a reply, Sonny swings Jake's arm around his shoulders, places his arm around Jake's waist, and half-carries him up the hillside.

As both trudge over fallen logs, they hear Youngblood shout, "What are you two doin'? Dancin'? Can you not see the night will soon be upon us? Hurry up! Gather our gear and follow me out!"

Sonny and Jake look at each other incredulously and shake their heads. As he helps his young brother up the hillside, Sonny now wonders whether the fallen tree had truly been an accident. How could an experienced woodsman like Youngblood have cut the tree so close to the two fallen oaks that formed a path to the stacked logs? As Sonny struggles to help Jake, he looks up and meets Youngblood's cold eyes. *Am I right? Was this Youngblood's plan to eliminate his rival in the Game and for Sarah's affections?*

Struggling to the top of the hillside, both Jake and Sonny collapse with exhaustion at Youngblood's feet. "You must learn to be careful in the woods, Softwood," Youngblood warns with a scowl. "This is not a game. This is not *the* Game." Looking down the slope where Jake could have met his end, Youngblood adds, "Let us see how you perform in the Game now that you have cheated death."

11

TO SYRACUSE

I tiptoe—you know, walk like an Indian is supposed to—toward Jake's bed. It is about four o'clock on Thursday morning. The rooster has begun to stir but has not yet crowed. Only the crickets and frogs are chirping. I slowly bend over to awaken Jake, but, to my astonishment, his bed is empty. In a moment of panic, I quickly scan the room. With great labor, I stoop to my knees to look under the bed. Still no Jake. My heart begins to race. Did some evil spirit take my precious boy? I scramble through the house, whispering Jake's name so as not to awaken the girls. Still no Jake. I resolve to scour the outside. Surely that darn old squeaky screen door will betray my stealth. As I carefully open the screen door, I spy a light coming from the barn. Thankfully, the girls do not hear me.

Approaching the barn, I am instantly relieved to see Jake grooming Thunder. With brushes in both hands, Jake softly sings an Indian song as soothing to Thunder's ear as the soft brushes are to his coat.

"What do you sing, my son?" I ask.

Startled, Jake quickly turns around. Relieved that it is I, Jake replies, "'Witchee Kno,' the song of the traveler."

"Ah. Did I teach that song to you?"

Jake smiles and continues his grooming, for it is I who taught him most of the songs that he knows.

"I shall come up in a few minutes to help gather supplies for our journey," Jake cheerily assures me.

I return to the cabin. Try as I may, no matter how slowly I open that screen door, it squeaks. Surely the girls will never sleep through two squeaks in the early morning.

"Grandfather? Is that you?" little Mary asks sleepily as she stands in her flannel nightgown, gently rubbing her eyes.

"Yes, it is I," I reply.

"Where are you going?" another voice speaks. No sooner does Molly ask that question than Maggie appears. All three quickly realize that today is Thursday.

"Is this the day, Grandfather?" Mary asks, not yet realizing that a new day is about to dawn.

"Is it Thursday?" Molly asks with a big yawn.

"Do you need any help in preparation, Grandfather?" Maggie inquires semi-audibly.

"No, I do not need help, and, yes, today is Thursday. Your brother and I are going to Syracuse," I patiently answer.

"Syracuse! Syracuse! Syracuse!" all three sing together, suddenly awakening from their daze.

"Shh! You will wake our dead ancestors," I whisper. "Well, if you are not returning to bed," which I know is impossible now that the girls' excitement fills the house, "get dressed and help us load up the wagon," I decide with a smile.

"Aiee!" little Mary yelps like a young warrior.

The three scamper into their room, each complaining that she cannot find a moccasin or a belt or a kerchief.

After brushing cow fat onto the harness and reigns, Jake hitches the wagon. Tack and horse are ready. Jake greases the wheels, bangs a couple of sideboards back into place, and pats old Thunder's neck. Satisfied that all is prepared, he turns toward the house.

"Go and wash up, Jake," I comment. "We do not want the white man thinking that Indians smell like cow fat and horse manure. When you are finished, come here. I have something for you."

Jake ducks behind a tree and quickly bathes by pouring a bucket of cold well water over his head and naked body. With a small bar of lye soap, he quickly skims his body, rinsing off the soapsuds with another bucket. He pulls his long black hair back and squeezes the remaining droplets over his shoulder. Now dried, arching his back and throwing back his head so the remnants of his bath will not fall upon his lower torso, he stands there in the morning sun, looking like I imagine our great first Sachem, Hiawatha might have looked like.

The rooster cries his first crow. It is time to get on the road.

The girls patiently wait on the top step of the porch as I proudly hand Jake a new blue jacket I obtained in trade with Firefly for some canned squash. I hope it will fit.

"Take off that old horse blanket jacket, Jake," I beseech, "and try this on."

Jake rips off his old jacket, which is now too short in the sleeves, tattered at the collar, and sporting holes at the elbows. Turning the jacket inside out as he takes it off, Jake does not throw it to the ground where it probably belongs. Instead, he reverently slings it over the porch rail. It has been a good jacket to him for these past two seasons. Perhaps the girls can use it for scrap material, patches perhaps. Jake holds up the blue jacket and admires its newness. He quickly puts it on, willing it to fit.

"Fits!" he exclaims with satisfaction.

"Your sisters altered it as a surprise," I reply.

Jake lovingly looks at Maggie, the seamstress, for he knows this is her handiwork.

"Thank you, my sister."

"How handsome you are in your new jacket," Maggie answers.

The other two girls coo around Jake as he faces Maggie.

Molly lifts his collar and jokingly asks, "How are we ever going to get our brother back on the reservation after all the pretty girls in Syracuse feast their eyes upon him?"

I interrupt the girls' fawning over their brother. "Many white people have never seen an Indian at all, and they may never if we do not get a move on."

"All right, all right, my sisters," Jake begs as they continue to fuss over him. "I can dress myself," he notes as he finishes buttoning his jacket. "Thank you. Thank you," he whispers as he hugs all three.

"That is not all, Jake," I say, tossing one last surprise to him.

"A Stetson!" Jake excitedly exclaims. Jake has never owned a hat other than a stocking hat, which he wore in the winter, and certainly never a quality name brand like Stetson. He reverently brushes imaginary dust off the brown, wide-brimmed felt hat with his elbow sleeve and carefully shapes it with both hands.

"Got the best of that deal," I boast. "One can of squash for a coat and a bag of salted beans for the hat. The white man may know how to steal our land, but he cannot trade worth a darn."

All the children laugh in unison.

Jake gently places the hat on his head. He rolls his eyes up to locate the front of the brim and runs the fingers of both hands around the brim to make sure it is straight. Finished, he stands proudly, with arms folded across his chest, pretending that he is as important as the president of the United States.

"Jake, Jake!" I shout, startling him from his self-admiration. "Let us get going. It will be light soon."

I reenter the house through that squeaky screen door one final time to gather the money some of the people have given me in order to buy them odds and ends in Syracuse. I have refused no one. My only condition is that I will not buy whiskey, for that, as much as the white man's diseases, has debased many of us.

I walk around the wagon and horse for one last inspection before our long journey. All seems to be in order.

"Good job, Jake," I comment. "The horse and wagon are ready."

The girls run up to Jake one more time, each giving him a package. Mary gives him some venison jerky in a deer hide pouch. Molly offers four apples—a bit green but juicy enough. Maggie hands him two dollars and fifty cents that she has earned sewing curtains for the minister's wife.

On tiptoes, Maggie whispers into Jake's ear, "I know you have money to spend on us. Please do not spend all of it, my brother, for we never know when hard times may fall upon us." Although Molly is the practical one, clearly Maggie is the most frugal. "Do you have money to buy something nice for Sarah?" she thoughtfully asks. "Think of her, my brother, before us. She has little, and she so admires you."

"Thank you for your wisdom and your kindness, my sister. And yes, I will buy something special for Sarah."

"Take this money," she continues, taking his hand and folding it over the money she has placed in his palm, "and buy Grandfather some leather gloves with fur in them to keep his hands warm through the coming winter."

"I will, my sister," Jake replies with a smile.

Maggie then hugs her brother and again whispers in his ear. "Be careful, my brother. I hear there are many evil spirits in the white man's city."

"I shall be fine," Jake reassures Maggie, kissing her on the forehead.

"Jaaake!" both Mary and Molly sing out, patiently awaiting their turn.

Jake drops to one knee and opens his arms. The girls fling themselves at him, giggling as he hugs them both and kisses each on the cheek.

Both girls stand with their hands behind their backs, occasionally looking up, batting their eyelashes, and gently swaying from side to side. Their postures betray their intentions. They both call for their brother as he is about to pull himself up onto the wagon.

"Jaaake!" they impatiently implore.

Jake stops, one foot still on the ground, and faces them. "Have I forgotten something?" Jake asks playfully. They both shake their heads affirmatively. "Is there something you need?" Both girls, now annoyed, but with longing eyes, madly shake their heads again.

Jake is teasing his sisters.

"Is there something you want?" he continues with his game. Now obviously annoyed, both girls stand motionless, arms folded across their chests and noses in the air. "Can it be something pretty for you?" Jake inquires as he quickly takes out a shiny silver dollar and holds it up to his smiling face.

"Yes!" both cry out, clapping their hands and jumping for joy.

Finished with his teasing, Jake promises, "I will not forget you, my sisters!"

Jake carefully returns the silver dollar to his pants pocket, spins around, and continues his climb onto the wagon when he meets my eyes.

"Where are you going?" I playfully ask.

A look of great disappointment falls over Jake's face.

"Oh, no, Grandfather," Jake murmurs dejectedly as he bows and shakes his head. "Not again."

I hesitate a moment and then, with a hearty laugh, reach my hand down to help him up.

"No, ride up here with me," I assure him.

And with one great leap and an "aiee!" Jake leaps up onto the wagon seat.

You see, the last time we went to Syracuse four or five years ago, Jake was about twelve. I made him run behind the buckboard the entire trip, about ten miles, as part of his lacrosse training. He slept on the return trip and could not walk for two days.

"Thank you, Grandfather," Jake says earnestly as I cluck old Thunder on and snap the reigns.

"Thank you for taking you to Syracuse?" I ask.

"No, thank you for not making me run behind the wagon," Jake responds with a sigh of relief.

We both laugh. Jake holds onto his hat with one hand and turns to wave to his sisters with the other. All three girls are huddled together in a blanket wrapped around their shoulders to protect them from the cool morning air, and they wave, somewhat sadly—more likely apprehensively—as we disappear down the dusty road. Perhaps they intuitively understand that a journey to the city is filled with danger.

Jake shifts forward again, facing me with a look of pride and anticipation. I simply pray to the Creator that we will journey well and without incident.

As we turn at the bend in the road, I notice Jake leaning back, stretching his neck to look around me toward a light coming from the cabin in the dark woods where Sarah and her father live.

My eyes on the road ahead, I casually say, "She is up early."

Jake does not hear me. He longingly looks at the light, hoping to catch at least a glimpse of Sarah's silhouette. His gaze is transfixed so intently that when his head can turn no more, Jake twists his body, nearly losing his balance and falling over the side of the wagon.

"Are you trying to see how far you can turn your head before it twists off?" I inquire playfully.

Jake rights himself with a snap, says nothing, and bends forward as if in pain.

"Every young man feels his first pangs of love in his stomach," I affirm.

Jake glances up in embarrassment. "I think the milk I drank this morning was curdled," he foolishly offers. Indians cannot tolerate cow milk, but we have never had a problem with our goat's milk.

I say nothing, for I drank the same milk and am sitting tall.

We journey for an hour and a half over the bumpy, pockmarked road. We are about halfway there. I curse Firefly for every pothole we drive over. My sore back and creaky knees have a name for every pothole we hit. The road follows the Onondaga Creek, which flows north and empties into Onondaga Lake in Syracuse. We speak hardly a word. Jake is slumped back, his eyes closed, arms folded over his chest, new hat moved forward over his eyes, resting the back of his head on a folded blanket on the seatback.

"Let us stop and rest awhile," I suggest. "Jake, wake up."

"Are we there?" he sleepily asks.

"No, we are about halfway. Let us rest."

Stretching his arms high over his head and looking around to gather himself, Jake admits somewhat embarrassingly that he must have dozed off for a few minutes.

"More like a couple of hours," I retort. "But that is all right, because you will need to stay more alert as we continue our journey."

Beginning to alight from the wagon, Jake freezes. "You mean? Are you saying? Do I get to drive?"

"Yep," I reply.

Jake jumps onto my back as I bend over to check old Thunder's hooves.

"Aiee!" Jake yells as he waves his hat in the air, pretending to ride me like a wild horse, much like the white cowboys in Bill Cody's Wild West show, which I once saw in Albany.

I buck Jake off, hurling him to the ground.

Lying on his back, Jake looks up and laughs, "You sure are strong for an old buck."

Jake suddenly stops his joking, realizing he has referred to me as "old." I can see in his eyes that he does not mean to disrespect me. Jake does not yet understand that for the Indian, "old" does not carry the negative connotation as it does in white society; in our culture, age is venerated.

"Grandfather," Jake begins, picking himself up from the ground and dusting off his pants and coat with a few swipes of his hat, "I am sorry I called you…old. I did not mean…"

I put my hand reassuringly upon his shoulder. "I know you mean no disrespect, my son. Do not apologize. I am 'old,'" I state, "and I can still kick your backside if I have to."

I pull him over my outstretched leg. Jake pulls me down with him. As we laughingly wrestle to the ground, our moment of merriment disappears as we both notice a large shadow fall over us.

Still lying on the ground, we apprehensively look up. No eagle. Instead we observe a covered black carriage that contains a white man, a white woman, two little girls peeking out from their bonnets, and a little boy looking out from under a felt hat so large that it seems propped up on his folded ears. Relieved we are not dead, the white man, sporting a large handlebar mustache and wearing a long, black, dusty coat with a stylish, wide-brimmed hat, cracks the whip over the ears of his two horses, jolting his family back into their seats. As they pass, we hear him mutter in disgust, "Damn drunken Indians!"

When they are out of sight, Jake and I burst out laughing. We help each other up, dusting off the backs of each other's trousers. Jake asks, "Are all white men that stupid?"

"Most," I reply. "Most. Let us have a bite to eat. Then we will see how good a driver you really are."

"Aiee!" Jake shouts excitedly.

Jake handles the horse and wagon well. There really is not much to handling one horse. I recall driving a four-horse team, dragging logs out of the woods up in Canada near where my daughter's husband died. I have always felt partly responsible for his death because I introduced him to the logging business.

"Tighten the reigns a bit. Keep your thumbs up. Do not tug on the reigns to turn. Move your fingers," I urge.

Jake replies exasperatingly, "Yes, Grandfather."

I realize I have admonished him about handling the reins before. "I apologize to you, my son, for repeating myself."

Jake speaks kindly. "It is all right, Grandfather. You have always been my teacher, even more so than my father."

"Well, do not blame your father for not teaching you many things. The wilds of the North Country had a compelling draw upon your father. I believe it was the wildness of the place that made him happy," I muse.

"Your father loved you, your sisters, and especially your mother, but he knew he could not make ends meet on the reservation. He was not satisfied with merely tilling the land for survival. He wanted more for all of you. He knew that the only way to improve your lives was to earn money as a lumberman."

"Why do Indian men choose that kind of work, Grandfather?" Jake asks.

I patiently answer, "The white man is afraid of many things in the natural world. They are taught from childhood that the forest, the rivers, and the mountains are places where only wild and savage things live."

"Including us?" Jake asks.

"Yes, many whites consider the Indian people nothing more than wild animals. We, like our sacred forest, stand in the way of the white man's canals, railroads, farms, and settlements. I have read that the white man's Manifest Destiny is to subdue or kill all wild things from coast to coast."

"But the Haudenosaunee believe that it is wrong to kill without reason, and it is wrong to feel superior to another. Does our religion not teach us that all people must respect each other and live in harmony with our wild brothers of the forest? Is that not true, Grandfather?"

"You have learned well, my son," I reply, as I proudly put my hand upon his shoulder.

We quietly drive a little while longer, when Jake mumbles, "My father."

"What?" I ask.

"My father. You were telling me the story about my father."

"Oh, yes. Your father." It is time that Jake learns the truth about his father. I struggle to tell the story. "Your father, like many Indian men, was hired by the white man's logging company as a topper."

"Topper?" Jake asks.

"Yes, a topper is the man who climbs to the top of the tallest tree, cutting off all the branches as he climbs, chopping the top off so that this tree becomes the center of the logging operation—attaching pulleys and riggings to skid logs onto the landing for loading."

"Were you not a topper? How does one climb such a tall tree, Grandfather?"

"Toppers wrap a leather strap around the tree and the lower part of their backs. When a topper leans back against the strap, it becomes taut, which holds him up, along with the aid of long metal cleats strapped to his leather boots. After climbing to the top and affixing cables and ropes, a topper then inches his way back down the tree"

"Sort of like a caterpillar, Grandfather?"

"Yes, like a caterpillar, my son."

"This is very dangerous work. Some of these trees are over one hundred fifty feet tall. The white man is afraid of heights. Most white men refuse to top trees. But it pays well, which is why your father did it."

Jake thinks about how dangerous this job must be. "Grandfather? How did my father die?"

I hesitate, but Jake is seventeen, old enough to know the truth.

"Your father worked for days without much rest. The white man is always in a rush to do things. That is why they never do anything well. The white man had to produce so many feet of lumber for a building project near the St. Lawrence Seaway; if they did not meet their deadline, they would be penalized on their contract."

"Contract? What is that?" Jake asks.

"A contract is a piece of paper on which the white man finds it necessary to write his promises," I explain.

"But, Grandfather," Jake asks with a puzzled look, "is not a man's word spoken to another enough to keep a promise? Why must it be written on paper?"

"I often wonder about that too, my son. When I was a young man like you, I thought that the white man must be very forgetful because he had to write everything on paper. As I have grown older, I have learned that the white man's papers are the way that they cheat each other and the Indian people."

"Then why bother, Grandfather?" Jake asks, shaking his head in disgust.

"If a man is not as good as a handshake and his word, then he is not a man. Do you hear?" I ask, my voice rising in anger as I remember the many times our people have been cheated by the white man's paper.

"Yes, yes, Grandfather. Why are you shouting? Why are you angry?"

"I am sorry. Let me breathe deeply. It is all right," I reply as I compose myself.

After I am calmed and breathing more easily, Jake continues, "So…my father?"

"Yes, your father." I hesitate, for I realize I must be sensitive in how I speak of this so as not to offend the dead and the living alike. "He had worked for five days, twelve hours each day, in cold, windy weather. The boss man would fire anybody, especially an Indian, if that worker complained, was sick, or was tired. Your father's legs were as hard as stone. His arms and hands were as big as a bear's. But even he began to tire."

"Then the rains and wind came, cold and biting. Yet your father still climbed. One day the wind came in from the north, blowing so hard that all the men, even the Indians, refused to work under those conditions. The boss man screamed at them and threatened to fire all of them. Exasperated, he shouted, 'I'll pay double to any man who climbs!' That was eight dollars for the day. The men talked among themselves but still refused. Their lives were more valuable than the money. All turned away except your father, who stepped forward. All he could think about was his leaky cabin roof, his lack of a wood-burning stove, his rickety wagon, his horse on its last legs, and, of course, school for you children."

"School?" Jake questions.

"Yes, school," I respond.

"School for whom?" Jake asks.

"You, my son. You," I reply.

"Why school for me, Grandfather?" Jake queries.

"Your father saw how the white man, and even some Indians who were educated in universities, live. They wear handsome suits and hats. They walk with fine ladies on their arms. They ride in fancy black carriages with painted wheels and horsehair seats, pulled by majestic white horses and driven by a colored coachman who takes them to the theater and on trips. This is what your father wanted for you."

"What about my sisters?" Jake asks. "Did he not wish for them to attend school as well?"

"He never mentioned that. His hope was that each would marry well, perhaps marry an educated Indian."

"Well, what university will accept an Indian, Grandfather?" Jake presses on.

"I have read of a college in New Hampshire established by a Reverend Wheelock over two hundred years ago just for the Indians."

"What is it called?" Jake asks curiously.

"If memory serves me, it is called Dartmouth College. It is supposed to be one of the finest universities in the country," I explain.

"If it is so fine, why does it accept Indians?" Jake asks ironically.

"My son, not all white people are bad. Many, but not all. Some, for whatever reasons, care about the Indian people. The problem is that those who care about us always have a condition attached to their deal."

"Condition?" Jake asks. "What is a condition?"

I ponder that question for a moment. The Indian people have no such word in their language.

"A condition," I start as best as I can, "is an untruthful reason for one's action."

Jake looks puzzled as I struggle to continue. I have to think of an example or forever miss teaching this point. "It is like when the white man promised the black man in Africa a trip to a new and beautiful land on the condition of performing some work.

Upon his agreement, the black man was put in chains and taken as a slave."

"The white man wishes to enslave us?" Jake asks in horror.

"No, no," I reassure him, although the white man of the Carolinas tried to enslave our brothers the Tuscarora two hundred years ago, which is why they joined the Iroquois Confederacy. "No, the white man no longer wishes to enslave us, but he promises things, worldly goods, if we will join his church, worship his god, and promise to be good Indians and stay on the reservation. That is a condition."

I wonder if I am offering the boy too much information. However, often a long trip is the best opportunity to speak of things that otherwise go unspoken.

"Anyway, back to your father. Your father braved the storm. Pain and fatigue racked his body. But he thought only about his family and you in college as he fastened on his spiked cleats and wrapped his leather strap around himself and the tree. The leather slipped many times on the wet bark, but he held on. As the wind gusted, the tree perilously bent over, almost to the point of breaking, and then snapped back, nearly slingshotting him off. But your father held on."

"My father must have been very strong to hang on under such conditions," Jake states proudly.

"Yes, that is true. After several hours had passed, your father was so high up in the tree that he disappeared into the clouds. None of the men below could see him. They worried and began to sing for your father. The white men, who were usually annoyed with Indian singing, understood the gravity of the situation and let them sing without interruption or their usual cursing. And then..." I hesitate as I struggle to push the words from my throat, "a cry in the darkness."

Jake pulls the reigns and stops our wagon.

"My father?" he asks.

I hesitate again, and then simply acknowledge, "Your father. The Indian men returned your father's body to us, which we buried in the customary way."

"I remember," Jake states softly, blankly staring off into the distance and clucking old Thunder to move again. "I remember crying for a man I never really knew," he muses.

"Such is the life of our people," I explain. "We work hard, and we die."

"Grandfather?" Jake asks as he snaps the reigns over Thunder's rump. "Do you wish for me to attend college?"

I hesitate before I speak. "I have always thought of this with a troubled heart. On the one hand, if you go off to the white man's university, we may never see you again."

"But, Grandfather—" Jake interjects.

"Hush, let me finish," I continue. "Why would an educated man return to the reservation where there is no work befitting someone with a diploma? Only despair and frustration are available to an educated man on the reservation. However, on the other hand, you could become somebody with your university diploma."

"I can be a great Sachem like you, Grandfather," Jake eagerly asserts.

"Yes, my son, you can be a Sachem. But I am one of many Sachems of a very small part of the world. I have much responsibility. But other than respect, what do I have to show for it?"

Jake looks forlornly as he drives. I wait for him to speak first.

"Grandfather, you forget to mention the most important reason for me to attend college."

"What is that, my son?" I patiently ask.

"It was my father's wish for me. He died to make that dream come true for me. I cannot let him down."

I smile at my grandson, whose wisdom grows each day. "Yes, it is true that honoring your father's wish is important. But you must live your own life. Attending college should be your own choice."

After some silence, I begin singing "acha wowya" as we roll along. I wonder if I have discussed too many new ideas with Jake and if the importance of each may have been lost in volume. However, Jake is brighter and more intuitive than most boys his age. I convince myself that we have conversed appropriately. But how inadequately I have prepared Jake for the white man's city! His education regarding the white world is about to enter a whole new dimension. Jake will learn many of its lessons the hard way. I hope he will not be too hurt in the process.

On the horizon, the faint silhouette of Syracuse's buildings rises unnaturally into the sky, beckoning us on.

12

BIG-CITY WONDERS

Just before we arrive at Syracuse, Jake and I switch places on the buckboard. The city is too chaotic for a boy to drive through. I drive us into south Syracuse just before eleven o'clock. We pass the Erie and Oswego Canals. We stop awhile to watch Negro and Indian men load up the many floating barges with salt mined nearby. Jake marvels at the grand houses perched on the hill overlooking the waterway across Onondaga Lake in the distance. We watch the New York Central Railroad's train pulling into the station. Jake has seen only pictures of a train before this day.

I have not visited this place for almost three years, and I am amazed at how much it has grown since that time. South Salina Street is bustling with activity. Wagons, horses, and people move about in all directions like bees buzzing around a hive.

We see elegant women wearing long gray, blue, black, and white dresses all puffed up around their backsides—probably to hide their wide bottoms—gracefully strolling along on raised wooden sidewalks. They mostly wear long-sleeved white blouses, the collars of which creep up their necks. They wear large-brimmed hats, some adorned with long feathers. They carry umbrellas, although I do not understand the necessity of doing so when there is no sign of rain.

The men wear pants that are sharply creased in the front and stretch into their shoes. They have wide ties tucked neatly into their vests. Gold chains extend from a vest button to a pocket, at the end of which lies a gold watch. Most of the men sport mustaches of all sizes and shapes. The men talk, walk, and some twirl silver-tipped canes. Upon meeting a woman, they politely tip their derby hats—one of the few instances of politeness I will see this day.

Young boys are dressed like their fathers except that their pants stop at their knees, meeting their long stockings. Young girls wear loose-fitting short dresses that resemble what I once observed American sailors wear.

I remark how the streets are less dusty. I am told that the town fathers have authorized spreading onto the streets a black, sticky substance called "oil" that is apparently produced in abundance in Pennsylvania. Oil is extracted from under the ground and into wells. *Leave it to the white man to take not only what Mother Earth has to give on her but also to dig into her body and extract her blood. Is there no end to the white man's greed?* I wonder.

Jake is as wide-eyed as a schoolboy at his very first circus freak show. He perches on the raised buckboard seat, his mouth agape with wonder, looking right, then left, then right again. Every minute he shouts, "Do you see that, Grandfather?"

"You had better sit still before your head swivels off," I joke.

"Grandfather, I have never seen so many wondrous things. Look how long their lodges are."

"Those are called stores, where men trade different goods. They are close together so that the white man does not have far to walk to purchase his things. White men don't like walking far," I explain.

Jake shakes his head in disbelief at the white man's laziness.

"This is not like the reservation where people produce much of what they need," I add. "For those goods we cannot produce on the reservation—like salt, spices, sugar, coffee, good tobacco, iron, and certain types of cloth—we gather at the longhouse every month or two, where Firefly and his BIA minions dole out government rations or offer for trade goods that were promised to us to begin with." I'm not sure Jake is listening, as his eyes survey and his ears hear so many new things more exciting than the familiar drone of my voice.

Jake points up to long black ropes strung between poles. "Grandfather, is this the white man's way of snagging birds from the sky?" he asks.

I pause a moment, for I have forgotten their purpose. Then it comes to me. "I believe the white man sends messages to each other through the black ropes, but I know not how."

We pass a saloon seconds before a man comes flying through swinging wooden doors, rolling headlong into the street, menacingly followed by a large man with a handlebar mustache, rolled-up white sleeves, and a white apron around his waist. This very tough-looking fellow claps his hands as if he has just thrown out trash. Then, firmly planting two fists onto his hips, he bellows, "We don't serve half-breeds here. Move down the line"—he points—"and drink with the darkies by the canal."

Appalled by such a display of cruelty, and pointing to the crumbled mess of a man lying in the dirt, Jake beseeches me, "Grandfather, let us help this man. He looks to be hurt."

"I am sorry, my son. But there is no helping a man who has taken to the bottle and does not know in which world he belongs: white or Indian."

I snap the reins and move past this pathetic wretch lest Jake and I be brought into this unfortunate affair. Jake looks at me with wanting eyes, silently pleading for me to help. Tormented as I drive by, pretending to ignore this man's suffering and humiliation, I too am humiliated.

"Grandfather, what are you doing? Please stop so we may help this man," Jake pleads again.

"Jake," I bark, "turn around. Do not even gaze upon this man unless you wish for those white men, plied with whiskey, to pull you from this wagon and harm you for interfering with their business or pleasure or whatever it is they are doing."

"But, Grandfather," Jake implores, "have you not taught us to help the defenseless and those in need?"

I am silent. My heart pains me, for the boy's words are true. My pathetic attempts to explain my inaction are thankfully interrupted by the sudden appearance from around the corner of the saloon of a monstrous, black iron carriage without a horse. Sitting in the front are two men in long white coats, wearing floppy, brimmed white hats and large circular glasses around their eyes. In the back seat are two women holding onto their large floppy hats, each loudly laughing as Thunder rears at this frightening-yet-wondrous sight.

"Whoa, whoa, Thunder. Whoa down, boy," I repeat forcefully but calmly.

"Grandfather," Jake stammers breathlessly, holding his hat and pointing to the loud machine with his other hand. "Do you see that? What is it? How can it move without a horse?"

I have read about the horseless carriage in one of the many books I have secured from the missionaries who have sought to civilize me. But I have never seen one other than in a picture.

"That is a horseless carriage," I explain. "I am not sure what makes it move. I believe it drinks that black liquid that they put on the roads." I had read that a local bicycle maker, John Wilkinson, built the first horseless carriage in these parts and that the Franklin Manufacturing Company produces these machines, thus becoming Syracuse's largest employer.

We can barely see the livery stable sign ahead through the canopy of multicolored store awnings. Since we have been on the road for three and a half hours, Thunder needs water and hay.

Jake remains full of questions. "Grandfather, why are so many barrels lining the street? Does the white man possess so many goods that he discards them in these barrels?"

Before I can answer, Jake points, asking, "Grandfather, what are those round glass balls on that iron tree?"

Before he asks another question, I quickly answer, "Those are streetlights. They become bright at night and light the dark streets."

"Like the stars?" Jake asks.

"Yes," I answer with a smile, "like the stars."

Jake suddenly sits erectly and obviously disturbed, as I see his exuberance of only a moment ago wash from his face. He uncomfortably gazes upon an awful sight: a woman walking on the road ahead of a white man, who prods her along as if she were a mule with the tip of his cane, depositing a dot of dirt on the back of her black blouse with every poke. She is laden with many bundles. Her sad eyes are affixed to the ground.

As we draw near, we hear the white man shouting at her. "Move along, you cow. You've become lazier and slower over the years. What happened to the comely, eager Indian maiden I traded for years ago? Now look at you: fat with sagging skin. For two bits, I'd sell you off."

"Hey, Jake! I'll buy her for one bit," slurs a scruffy, drunken white man sitting on a chair outside the saloon.

"Hey, Jake! I'll take her off yer hands, but ya have to throw in a bottle of whiskey," shouts another.

Shaking his head in disgust, perhaps half willing to let her go for a bottle of whiskey, the man concedes, "No, no, I suppose she's better than a mule."

"I'll bet a mule smells better," another man chimes in.

They all laugh as the crude white man strikes her with his cane, this time squarely across her back with a thump—for what infraction we cannot tell. Caring nothing for her feelings, he seems to think it is he who is humiliated by being in the company of this woman.

"Grandfather," Jake observes, "they call that man Jake, like me."

"You are nothing like that man and can never be," I reply. "Although still a boy, you are more of a man than he. You share nothing of him but his name."

"Grandfather, why would any man beat a woman?" Jake continued. "Are we not to watch over our women and children like they were treasures from the Creator? Do not the white man's missionaries preach the same to him?"

"Jake, my son, there are laws that protect white women from such horrible things, but those same laws do not apply to Indian women."

Shocked, Jake looks back. "She is an Indian?"

"Yes, she is Indian. Can you not see her braids tucked into the back collar of her blouse?" I ask.

"Yes. But why does she hide her hair? Should an Indian woman not be proud of her hair?" Jake asks.

"My son, when an Indian woman leaves the reservation and her people, she is sometimes treated well at first. She is given things by her white husband that she can never have on the reservation. But in time, both she and her white husband come to realize that she can never fit into the white world. Rarely is she fully accepted by his family and friends. Her white husband soon loses interest in her as a wife, even as a human being. He then treats her like any other white man's thing: a horse, livestock, or sometimes even worse."

Saddened by the cruel treatment of the Indian woman, Jake looks back once more, catching her eye as tears stream down her dusty cheeks. Casting her eyes downward, the Indian woman plods along—helpless, hopeless, another lost soul who had thought that life off the reservation would be better.

Not surprisingly, this exhibition of cruelty dampens the excitement and enthusiasm Jake had enjoyed moments earlier. Deflated now, Jake slouches back in the buckboard, not in exhaustion but in pain and revulsion. He leans his head back onto the buckboard seatback and tilts his hat forward over his face to hide from the foreign, cruel world into which I have thrust him. He quietly sobs.

Jake explains that he is ashamed not to have helped that poor woman and that he covered his face to hide his guilt from the Creator. I do not believe that I shall ever be able to restrain Jake again should he witness another such act of cruelty.

—

Thankfully, the livery stable is just ahead.

"Howdy, sa. Horse need tendin' ta?" a black man asks as we pull up.

Jake perks up, swiping his hat from his face.

"Good boy. Good boy," the man croons to Thunder. "I'se take good care a' him," he says to us.

Jake has never seen a black man up close before. He has read about slavery in school but thinks the black man, freed by President Abraham Lincoln, lives mostly in the South or has traveled back to Africa.

"Kin I help ya down, young sa'?" the black man asks Jake.

Almost embarrassed that another man might help him off the buckboard as if he were a child, Jake politely replies, "No, thank you," and jumps off.

"Only be'n polite," the black man comments with a smile and a tip of his tattered straw hat.

"Ulysses! Ya shifty nigga. Get a move on dere. Ya don't have time for no conversation. Unhitch dat horse an' get him fed," growls a fat white man with long side-whiskers, a balding head, dirty boots, and a checkered vest.

Who I assume is the owner of the livery struts up to me, his hands not fitting into the shallow pockets of the dirty, checkered vest that nearly bursts over his protruding belly. He stops, looks me up and down, and states the obvious: "Injun. Ain't cha?" Rubbing his chin as if pondering something important, he finally blurts out, "So dey let cha off the rez, chief? Well, don't tarry in dis town. People don't like Injuns much, 'specially after dark. The fine white people of dis village t'ink dat Injuns come in da dark ta steal der chillen and take scalps. Ha ha ha," he laughs heartily, slapping me on the back. "Me, I got no problems wit Injuns. So long as dey got money." He laughs again, jabs me in the ribs with his elbow, winks, and spits a wad of tobacco juice on the ground by my feet.

Jake and I both look at the juice and then each other in disgust. I am sure Jake wonders whether every white man in Syracuse is as cruel and as dirty as those we have seen thus far.

"How long ya stayin' in town, chief?" the livery owner asks.

Exasperated by this obvious disrespect, Jake frustratingly blurts out, "My grandfather is not the chief. He is a Sachem who proudly sits with the council of chiefs!"

I snap my head toward Jake and look him sternly in the eye, imploring silence.

Seeing his opening, the livery owner walks over to Jake, the first two fingers of both hands still tucked into his bulging vest.

Ashamed, Jake looks down and realizes he has spoken out of turn.

Too close for comfort, the liveryman begins, "So, he ken talk. Da Injun boy speaks English."

With a great laugh, he shouts over to Ulysses, who is bent over picking out Thunder's hooves, "Hey, Ulysses, ken ya imagine? First da bleedin' heart Quakers taught ya niggas English an' how ta read. Now dose same bleedin' hearts are teachin' de Injuns. What's next? Horses?"

"Yes, sa, they surely kin," Ulysses quickly agrees.

"Ah right den," the owner says as he walks away. "Dat'll be two bits, chief. Give 'em der money's worth, Ulysses," he adds as he waves his hand and disappears around the corner, returning to the saloon from which he apparently does his morning's business.

After checking that the boss man has really left, Ulysses scurries back. "Don't ya worry none, sa. Ulysses take good care of ya horse. Yes, sa."

I produce a Barber quarter from my pocket. Ulysses freezes, wiping his hands on his leather apron, wondering whether this coin is for him.

"This is for you, Ulysses. I shall pay the livery owner separately. Thank you, sir, for your kindness," I say with a smile.

In disbelief, the black man snatches the coin and bites it to see if it will bend. Realizing this is a genuine quarter, Ulysses grabs my hand with both of his and shakes it madly.

"Oh, t'ank ya, sa. T'ank ya," he says gratefully. Then he stops talking. Looking at me with wonderment, he whispers, "Ya called me 'sa'? Ya called me sa! Nobody ever called Ulysses sa befo.'"

Jake and I both tip our hats to the kind black man and begin to walk north on Salina Street toward Fayette Street. We marvel at the goods displayed in the windows of the various stores.

"Grandfather, I am sorry I spoke out earlier. I do not understand why that fat, dirty white man kept calling you chief. He does not even know you. For if he did, he would know you are a great Sachem and the Faithkeeper of our people."

About to respond, I instead quickly push Jake to the sidewalk, where he falls flat on his face. Shocked, Jake raises his head, wondering if I have gone mad, only to see his first streetcar clanging down the street track. As he slowly rises, Jake embarrassingly asks, "Is that a train, Grandfather?"

"In a way," I answer. "It is called a streetcar. It is moved by lightning, which flows into the ropes you see overhead." I point to the silver wires above us.

Still shaking from such a close call, I put my arm around Jake's trembling shoulders as we meander down the sidewalk, not only to keep him close but also to urge him on as he gawks into every store window. We stroll by a woman playing a piano at the entrance of a shop. She and Jake smile at each other as she plays a lively tune. She moves her arms so quickly and taps her feet so rapidly that she appears to be dancing while sitting.

As we walk by a fruit and vegetable stand, a puny, bespectacled white man with a single tuft of greasy gray hair on the top of his head sneers at us, "Don't get any ideas of filching any of my produce, ya dirty savages." I wheel around and quickly extend my arm toward this pipsqueak of a man. Perhaps fearing that I have drawn a knife, he stands motionless and speechless, exhaling only after I open my hand to produce two Liberty Head nickels.

"Is this enough for two apples?" I inquire. Nodding, he tremulously snatches the coins from my hand, and I choose two apples. As we continue along, enjoying our juicy apples, Jake asks me why that man called us "dirty savages." I explain that the white man calls the Indian many things, sometimes out of ignorance, but mostly out of fear.

"Fear?" Jake asks, puzzled.

"Yes, fear. The white man fears what he does not know. Rather than admit he does not know or understand something, he simply hides that ignorance by pretending to be superior. Most white people have never met an Indian. Many know only the image of the Indian they see on the cover of a dime-store novel, scalping a helpless settler out west. Others know only what they hear from Christian ministers, who call Indians they cannot convert 'children of the devil.'"

Jake interrupts, "But, Grandfather, Miss Doolittle is white, and she does not say such things."

Nodding in agreement, I continue, "You are right, my son. Miss Doolittle is white. But she is different. She has come to live among the people. She has never feared us. She has never treated you and her other young charges with an air of superiority like Firefly and some of the Christian preachers have done. She listens to the people and has come to hear the voices of our ancestors, who whisper to her on the wind."

Jake smiles. "Do you think Miss Doolittle has become an Indian?"

With a chuckle, I explain, "Although she respects the ways of the people, she can travel back into the white world without difficulty. Someday she will leave us. Rejoice that she will never be beaten or prodded along the street like that helpless Indian woman we saw."

We walk together, safe in our closeness, Jake with his arm around my shoulder, and I with my arm around his waist.

Jake marvels at the pictures drawn upon the stores' brick walls. I am not certain of the purpose of such pictures, but I think they are drawn to incite the white man to purchase the depicted items for sale within their walls.

One wall shows a smiling man in overalls walking behind a mule and a "Syracuse Chilled Plow."

"'The hardest blade ever made,'" Jake reads out loud.

On Wyoming Street, another pictures a man with a whip sitting on a wagon made by Bradley & Company. Yet another depicts a woman in a dark skirt and a white blouse sitting at a table with both hands on a machine called a Monarch Typewriter. I cannot explain the purpose of such a contraption.

We continue to walk in the street rather than on the sidewalk to save Jake the humiliation of having to step aside every time a group of white men or women walk toward us. But he does not care.

"Grandfather! Look!" Jake shouts with excitement. "Pictures that move!" Standing by a dark doorway, a finely dressed gentleman beckons us to enter and view the moving pictures that jump about on a white wall. I simply shake my head and wave him by. A dark building is certainly not a suitable place for two Indians to enter. Furthermore, I have no power to fend off whatever evil spirit is able to flatten people and make them jump along a wall.

Pulling Jake away from that evil place by the back of his collar, I see we have finally arrived at our destination.

13

THE GENERAL MERCHANDISE AND DELIVERY STORE

"What is this place?" Jake asks.

"Well, read the wooden sign above the doorway," I reply.

"General Merchandise and Delivery," Jake reads carefully. "What is here, Grandfather?"

"Everything that we have come for," I answer. "Now wipe your feet on the mat outside the door. Remove your hat when you enter. Speak only if spoken to. Do not look any of the white women in the eyes. Remember to say please and thank you. And keep your braid tucked into the back of your shirt."

"I think I can remember my manners, Grandfather. But why not look a woman in the eye? Did you not always teach us to look into a person's eyes when talking with him or her? Did you not always say the eyes were the pathway to the heart?"

I am pleased and yet perturbed that this boy remembers so much of what I have taught him. "The white man believes that if an Indian looks into the eyes of a white woman, he must be putting a spell upon her that will cause her to leave the white man and walk with the Indian."

"But that is nonsense, is it not?" Jake states and asks at the same time.

"Yes, but we are not here to correct the white man of his superstitions. Now come along."

Jake stops in the General Merchandise and Delivery Store doorway. He dutifully removes his hat, wipes his feet, and enters a world filled with an unimaginable abundance of goods. His mouth agape, Jake looks all around him. He has never seen so many things stocked and shelved from the floor to the ceiling. Who I suspect is the proprietor, a bespectacled, balding man wearing a blue apron and white shirt with black garter bands at his elbows, climbs a ladder that wheels horizontally along the walls on tracks to retrieve items stored high by the ceiling.

I take out my list of needed items as Jake strolls around, looking at and touching everything. Pots and pans of all kinds hang on the wall. Beautifully crafted Colt pistols, some with ivory handles, are locked behind a glass case. Shiny repeating rifles and shotguns hang on the wall behind the pistol case. Sturdy barrels of gunpowder, seeds, flour, sugar, salt, pepper, and herbs stand invitingly open. Jake delights in watching the bald man grind coffee beans for a woman. Opening the container box, he assures the impatient shopper, "Just a few more turns."

"Well, be quick about it," she shoots back. "I have many appointments today and can't be waiting on your arthritic hands to turn a few cranks."

"Yes, ma'am," the bald man replies obediently, a few beads of sweat now forming on his brow.

This woman's voice rings familiarly to me. But how can that be? Other than Miss Doolittle, I have known only one white woman in my life, and that was many years ago.

Although tending to my business, I keep a vigilant eye on Jake, who by the look on his face appears mesmerized by the abundance of white man's things. Jake marvels at the stacks of blankets and many bolts of cloth. Perhaps he imagines Maggie flinging herself upon all this material in rapture. He does not recognize one type of cloth that seems to shimmer in the light. No such cloth exists on the reservation. He cannot help reaching out to touch so fine a fabric. I know this cloth, which feels colder than the air. Jake closes his eyes as he gently strokes this fabric, most likely imagining Sarah's skin. But then Jake is suddenly shocked from his musings; his silly smile quickly disappears as the salesclerk, a stocky woman in a long gray dress with a white apron, sternly warns him, "Don't touch unless you are prepared to buy."

"No, ma'am. Yes, ma'am," Jake quickly apologizes.

I chuckle at his politeness.

The salesclerk half smiles at Jake as she walks toward the shopper who is still scolding the proprietor.

Carrying a bolt of that shiny cloth, the salesclerk offers, "This will make a lovely gown, Mrs. Graham." Leaning toward the shopper, she whispers just loudly enough for me to hear, "And if you don't mind my saying, with a figure like yours, at your age, I would fit this as snugly as your corset permits and even cut the fabric low to reveal your shoulders."

The woman snaps back, "Do you think that I'm an old fool who will fall for your flattery?"

The salesclerk awkwardly looks down in silence. Mrs. Graham admires herself in a mirror, holding the cloth to her neck. "I still do have that certain something though, don't I?" she declares with a self-satisfied smile.

"Certainly, Mrs. Graham," the salesclerk quickly agrees.

Tossing the beautiful cloth at the salesclerk as if it were a burlap sack, the haughty woman sashays by me with upturned nose and commands, "All right, wrap it up with my other goods, and be quick about it. I have tarried here much too long."

Mrs. Graham glances at me and smiles. I dare not return the smile as I hand my list to the storeowner.

Jake wanders up and down the store aisles, as orderly as his sisters' straight cornrows. Finally, he finds what he is looking for: ribbons of all colors, spooled and hanging from the wall on wooden pegs. Jake has thirteen dollars and fifty cents in his pocket, including Maggie's two dollars and fifty cents: a veritable fortune for an Indian boy. He has no idea how much ribbon—or anything else, for that matter—costs since he has never purchased anything before.

"May I help you?" the stout salesclerk inquires. Jake replies as courteously as possible, "Yes, ma'am. May I please purchase this ribbon?"

"All of it?" she jokes. Sensing Jake's unease at such a prospect, she quickly allays his fears. "How much do you want?" she inquires with an easy smile.

"I wish to buy ribbon for each of my three sisters, my friend Sarah, and my teacher, Miss Doolittle," Jake replies.

"All right, then," she muses as she counts to herself, "that will be five pieces of ribbon. Correct?"

Confirming five in his mind, Jake simply answers, "Yes, ma'am. Five, please."

Patting her apron as if she has lost something, the salesclerk says under her breath, "Where is that pair of scissors? Oh, there it is by that spool of thread. Excuse me." She walks across the aisle to retrieve the scissors.

Jake is now confronted with choosing the right colors and length. He has never purchased ribbon before.

Returning with her scissors at the ready, the salesclerks asks, "What colors and how long?"

Jake points. She follows his finger. "This color?" she asks, holding a purple ribbon. Jake shakes his head affirmatively.

"This color?" she asks again, holding a bright red ribbon. Jake again nods.

Holding out a golden ribbon, the woman comments, "Now this would be pretty around any young Indian girl's rich, dark hair."

"Excuse me, ma'am," Jake asks in a hushed, surprised voice, "how do you know that I am an Indian?"

She cautiously bends closer to him and whispers, "The braid is a dead giveaway."

Embarrassed, Jake reaches up and feels his braid, which has come out from under his jacket, unnoticed in the excitement of the day.

"Don't be embarrassed," the salesclerk says. "If only the white boys in this town were as polite as you."

Jake smiles with relief and graciously murmurs, "Thank you."

"Have you decided on your final two colors?" she inquires.

Jake looks bewildered.

Sensing his dilemma, the salesclerk asks, "Want some advice?"

Jake eagerly replies, "Yes, ma'am."

"You say there are five girls in your life," she restates. Jake has never thought of it that way, but it is true: his three sisters, Sarah, and Miss Doolittle are indeed the five girls in his life.

"Yes, ma'am," Jake answers.

"Well then," the salesclerk explains, "it's easy. We'll cut five lengths of ribbons of these five different colors, each long enough to weave within their braided hair—let's say an arm's length." Not waiting for an answer, she continues, "Here are a white and a navy blue."

Jake interrupts, "Excuse me, ma'am, but how will I know which color ribbon to give to whom?"

"Simple: let the girls figure that out for themselves," the salesclerk replies as she begins to cut the ribbons. "Gather them together, hand them the bundle, and let them choose. Believe me, each will always make the right choice."

Jake is not sure that is a good idea, but trusting her wisdom, he smiles as the salesclerk snips away, humming a merry tune.

"Now then, what else can I get for you?" she asks, rolling each ribbon and fastening them together with a string.

"Please, ma'am, I must purchase something extra special for someone."

My ears perk up. *Someone special?* I muse.

"Who and what?"

"Ah…ah…well…you see…" Jake falters.

"A girlfriend," the salesclerk quickly deduces.

"Yes…well, not yet. But soon. At the Green Corn Festival," Jake affirms confidently.

"I trust she is about your age," the woman surmises.

"Yes, ma'am. I think." Jake is suddenly embarrassed that he does not exactly remember Sarah's age.

"Follow me. I'll find that special someone something special."

Eagerly following the salesclerk up and down many aisles, Jake finally arrives at a large glass case.

Putting on her glasses as she excitedly scurries behind the glass case, the salesclerk inquires without looking up, "See anything you like?"

Jake's eyes rove throughout the case of jewelry. Everything is so exquisite and most probably more expensive that he can afford. Then his gaze freezes. Noticing his fixated eyes, the salesclerk looks over her spectacles. "You found it, didn't you?"

Jake eagerly points to something I cannot yet make out.

"Oh, these are beautiful," the salesclerk coos as she removes a set of silver earrings shaped like stars from their box and places them on the glass counter for Jake's closer inspection.

Satisfied that she has a sale, the saleswoman offers, "These earrings are meant to be the North Star, which is the one true star in the heavens. When she wears them, like the North Star, your love will always be guided only to her."

The kindly salesclerk reaches out and gently grasps Jake's hands with her own hands. Save the memory of his mother, no woman, least of all a white woman, has ever held his hands.

"Trust me," the woman assures. "You will find the words when you give her this gift."

Jake smiles and nods. He does trust and believe this white woman. Kindness is always worthy of trust.

Trying not to be detected by me Jake attempts to whisper, "I must get something for my grandfather, the man who was talking with the bald man with the spectacles."

I duck around a corner so that Jake does not catch me watching him.

The saleslady muffles her resulting laughter by putting both hands over her mouth. "That bald man with the spectacles, the proprietor, is my husband." Composing herself, she then adds, "Look around, and if you need help, fetch me."

Jake is obviously embarrassed that he had referred to this kind lady's husband in this way, but her chuckle at his description is a good sign that Jake has made a friend. He now strolls around, looking at all the gadgets, many of which he has no idea how to use. Sensing that I am close to completing my business with the storekeeper, Jake comes upon a table where piles of books—some old and dusty, some new and clean—are stacked. Jake picks up book after book, blowing off any dust and reading the titles. He seems neither to readily recognize the titles nor even the subject matter.

Likely sensing Jake's confusion, the friendly salesclerk quickly dispatches another customer and comes to his aid.

"Do you read?" the salesclerk asks politely.

"Yes, ma'am."

"What do you like to read?" she asks.

"Oh, I'm not looking for a book for myself but for my grandfather." Jake points to me as I pretend to review the list one more time with the storekeeper.

The salesclerk bends sideways to look around Jake and at me.

"He reads?" she asks with astonishment.

"Yes, ma'am. He loves reading almost as much as he loves our Game."

"'Our game'?" she repeats.

Sensing the urgency of time, and wanting to preserve his surprise for me, Jake responds, "Lacrosse, our Game. It is a French name for the Game that the Creator gave to the people to help us grow the crops, cure the sick, honor him who gave it to us, and sometimes train for war."

"Really?" she exclaims with raised eyebrows. "Train for war?" she adds placing one hand on her chest and one hand on her forehead as if she were about to faint.

Jake quickly assures her, "Training for war was in olden days."

The salesclerk is relieved to hear that the Indians are not going on the warpath. She chooses a book, inquiring, "What about this one, *The Story of Robin Hood*?"

"Who is he, ma'am?"

"Oh, he was an outlaw who stole from the rich and gave what he stole to the poor."

How noble to give to the poor! Jake probably thinks, even though the part about stealing and being an outlaw is likely somewhat discomforting to him. Jake shakes his head negatively.

"What about this one?" Jake asks, picking up a worn, dusty book.

The salesclerk takes the book and dusts it with her handkerchief. "Oh, this is the story of Christopher Columbus. He discovered America, you know," she says proudly.

I wonder how it is that the white man can lay claim to discovering the land where the Indian people have lived for thousands of years.

"No, I think he read that one already," Jake politely replies.

"Oh, yes. Well then, here is a perfect book," she says assuredly, handing him a beautifully leather-bound volume, "unless, of course, he has read this one too," she adds, looking at Jake suspiciously.

Glancing over my shoulder, I notice on the cover are white men in what appears to be a long canoe with many paddles. An Indian stands in the front of the canoe, about to hurl a long spear at a large white fish that is even bigger than our lake's sturgeon. Jake moves his fingers over the title and reads, *Moby Dick.*

"Yes, this is the one. Grandfather loves to fish," Jake explains.

The saleslady laughs. "I am not sure your grandfather has ever caught a whale, but he can imagine so in a book, can't he?"

"Yes, ma'am," Jake eagerly agrees. "I would like one last thing, please. Leather gloves. With fur inside, please."

The salesclerk smiles and fetches the gloves.

"How much for everything, ma'am?" Jake asks apprehensively, hoping he possesses sufficient funds.

Taking out a pencil and writing figures on the bundle of ribbons, she announces, "Three dollars for the ribbon. Two dollars and fifty cents for the book—after all, it is leather-bound. Five dollars and fifty cents for the earrings. They're sterling, you know. And four dollars for the gloves. Total, fifteen dollars."

Jake reaches into his right pocket and pulls out what he knows he has: thirteen dollars and fifty cents. He desperately rifles through the other pockets in his pants and in his jacket hoping to find loose coins, but to no avail.

Jake looks at the salesclerk's outstretched hand. She takes each coin and totals them up. "Thirteen dollars and fifty cents. Is that all you have?"

Dejected, Jake bows his head and whispers, "Yes, ma'am."

Just as I was about to approach my worried grandson, I notice the saleslady looking around for her husband. Not seeing him, she leans over and assures Jake, "Thirteen dollars and fifty cents is good enough. That will be our little secret." She winks at Jake as she quickly wraps the gifts.

I am sure that other than Miss Doolittle, Jake has never met such a kind white woman.

After negotiating a fair price for the ammunition, spices, buttons, boots, two shirts, four jugs of kerosene, and assorted farm implements purchased for some of our people—too many items for us to carry—I ask Jake to fetch Ulysses to drive the wagon and old Thunder here while the storekeeper bundles up my goods. Jake heads toward the door, proudly holding his wrapped gifts, when the salesclerk calls to him.

Jake freezes. I freeze. The storekeeper bristles, perhaps wondering whether the Indian boy has stolen something.

The saleslady hands Jake a red-striped candy cane.

"I believe you forgot this, young man," she says.

"Well, n—" Jake begins, but she quickly interrupts him.

"Yes, you left it on the counter as we were discussing your purchases," she explains firmly, winking at him.

Understanding her intentions, Jake removes his hat, bows slightly, and thanks her sincerely for her kindness.

"And what is your name?" she inquires.

Jake looks at me for permission to answer her. I nod.

"Jake, ma'am. My name is Jake."

She smiles and replies, "Good luck, Jake. And remember to tuck your hair up under your hat or into your collar."

Embarrassed, Jake immediately tucks his errant braid up into his hat.

Although I am jaded from these many years of dealing with white people, I believe this woman's interaction with Jake has been sincere, and for that I am appreciative. We all laugh as we observe the broad smile on Jake's face at his first taste of the red-striped candy cane.

—

His mission accomplished, I sense that Jake cannot wait to return home to see the looks on the faces of his sisters, Miss Doolittle, and I when we open his gifts to us, but mostly, I believe he cannot wait to see the look in Sarah's eyes. He is so excited that he hardly pays attention to where he is going.

I step outside the store as the proprietor is ringing up my purchase to assure that Jake does not dally on the way back to the livery. Jake is running by that loud, foul-smelling place where the scruffy man had been thrown to the ground. Suddenly, I am shocked to see him fall headlong onto the sidewalk, tripped by one of the good-for-nothings sitting on a chair outside the swinging wooden doors. Jake's candy cane breaks into many pieces and scatters on the sidewalk like broken glass.

Amid the raucous laughter from the men standing nearby, Jake quickly rights himself and begins to dust off his new jacket with his new hat, forgetting what he had hidden within: his braid is now fully exposed. The men are struck silent as they realize what stands before them.

"An Injun!" one of the drunkards exclaims.

Now all the men slowly and menacingly draw near.

"Ya better watch where yer goin', Injun boy," another slovenly drunkard growls as he drops his half-full whiskey bottle on the wooden sidewalk to free his hands for trouble.

"Yeah, what's an Injun doin' walkin' on our sidewalk?" another slurs, spreading his arms to indicate apparent possession of the area where Jake now stands.

Spitting a wad of chewing tobacco at Jake's feet and wiping his mouth with the back of his hand, a fat, sweaty, stubble-faced man, just aching for a fight, hikes up his filthy trousers and walks ominously toward Jake, who is now trembling.

Raising his fist toward Jake, the drunkard yells, "Ya better skedaddle before someone scalps ya." He demonstrates by pulling his own greasy hair up with one hand and running the forefinger of his other hand across the front of his hairline, grunting a guttural ripping sound.

Just as I begin to run to Jake's rescue, he has already gathered his packages. He looks off into the distance and shouts, "Grandfather!" The men stop and look into the distance. Seeing his opening, Jake dashes off the raised wooden sidewalk, knocking one of the men backward onto the dusty street.

The hilarity of the drunkard lying like a turtle on his back draws laughter from the crowd and saves Jake as he flies down the street toward the livery. Jake runs recklessly, carelessly bumping into people before again falling headlong into the street.

"Hey, watch where yer goin'!" shouts a white man driving a black horseless carriage as its wheels come perilously close to crushing Jake's ankles.

Jake lunges out of the way and falls to the ground a third time. Rolling up from the street, he looks back at the crowd of drunkards, who have picked up their comrade and have returned to their bottles. Jake stops running but hurriedly stumbles along.

Jake must realize that every white eye in the vicinity is focused upon him now. With his braid bouncing free from his hat and his jacket, Jake sticks out like a sore thumb. Apparently thinking that an Indian carrying packages and running with great haste will gather further unwanted attention, he slows to a quick walk. He stows his packages within his jacket so as not to be accused of thievery. I bet Jake almost wishes he were white, at least until he arrives at the livery, for then he would be invisible among these men. Jake hustles down the street, trying not to look suspicious and not daring to walk upon the raised wooden sidewalks. I pray for our ancestors to carry him above the fray to the safety of the livery.

Straining my neck to catch a glimpse of Jake's escape, I hear the well-dressed man in front of the moving picture lodge shout out in a typical hawker's loud enticing way to him, "Hey, chief, only cost ya a Liberty Head nickel or five new Lincoln Head pennies."

Catching Jake's attention just for a moment, the man grabs Jake's arm, hooks Jake's other shoulder with his cane, and forcefully draws him toward the doorway. "Ever see a Hawaiian girl dance? Feast your eyes," the man blares, pointing to the white wall.

Having seen this demon device that captures a person's spirit and casts his flat image upon a wall in Albany once, I remember up on the wall is a moving picture of what appears to be an Indian woman with flowers in her hair, wearing nothing but a skirt of sweet grass and a flowered necklace that moves as she sways her hips.

"There's plenty more where that came from, kid," the hawker intones, grabbing Jake by the elbow to escort him inside.

Hearing the men inside whistle and howl at the flowered Indian woman on the wall, I am thankful that Jake spins out of the hawker's grasp, and runs down Salina Street toward the livery, where I hope all will be calm and safe.

14

JAKE TO THE RESCUE

What happens next is recounted to me by a panicked-looking Ulysses, the livery hand. Out of breath, more from nervousness than physical strain, Jake finally arrives at the livery stable and braces himself upon our buckboard. Jake struggles to catch his breath and regain his composure. Although he is still alone, somehow he probably feels a bit safer touching our wagon. Jake examines his new jacket, new hat, and his bundles to assure that they have not been damaged. Satisfied, he strains his neck and calls out for Ulysses.

Suddenly, his attention is drawn to a girl's muffled scream in the alleyway between the livery and a warehouse. Jake tosses his bundles into the back of the buckboard and quickly turns the corner to investigate. Three scruffy white boys are dragging a struggling young woman down the alleyway. She fights them mightily, flailing her arms, kicking her legs, biting, and scratching.

"Help me!" she screams in desperation. A dirty-blond boy with an extraordinarily pimpled face tries to muffle her screams with his grubby hand. He yelps as she bites him, immediately letting go of her and nursing his wound. Just as he is about to slap her with his bloody hand, the crying young woman ducks and back-kicks a freckled-face redhead, the tallest of the three attackers, hitting him squarely on his right shin with her high-heeled boot. Squealing in pain, he bends over and vigorously rubs his wounded leg. The remaining ruffian, a dark-haired boy with two broken front teeth, laughs at his two companions, giving the young woman an opportunity to escape his grasp.

"Leave me alone!" she cries, momentarily free. Broken Tooth immediately grabs her around the waist from behind. With extraordinary quickness, she again frees herself, wheels around, and punches her attacker squarely in the nose with her right hand while scratching his face with the left.

Feeling the rasp of her nails across his face, Broken Tooth slaps her with the back of his hand, saliva and blood flying from the corner of her mouth as she falls to the ground. "No-good squaw!" he shouts as he menacingly stands over her.

Jake looks on with shock. She *is* an Indian girl, but somehow she does not look Indian to him. She wears a beautiful white-and-blue cotton dress, heeled boots, and had a laced bonnet that now lies crumpled in the dirt. Her skin is light, even lighter than Sarah's, but not quite as light as Miss Doolittle's. However, her long braids reveal her true identity. Having greatly under-estimated the resolve of the Indian girl's resistance, the three wolves set upon her again to regain control of their prey with greater force if needed but not so much as to viciously maul her.

"Stinkin' half-breed. I'll fix ya," Pimple Face sputters angrily as he violently grabs the girl by her throat with one hand.

"Shush! Quiet," warns Broken Tooth. "Stop yer yellin' before the police come a-runnin'. I don' t'ink dey'll take too kindly to funnin' a woman in de streets like dis."

Freckle Face, blood rapidly staining the bottom half of his trousers, screams back, "She ain't no woman. She's a breed, and dat don't count."

The girl spits blood and curses her attackers.

Angered by her continued resistance, Pimple Face punches her on the side of her face with his closed fist and knocks her to the ground.

His full weight preventing her from moving, Pimple Face sits upon his fallen victim and begins tearing her blouse. "Yeah," he hisses, "I ain't molestin' da white side, only da Injun side."

Try as he may, he cannot pry the girl's legs apart with his knees. Thinking quickly before she succumbs, the girl raises both of her knees and strikes Pimple Face directly between his legs. Moaning in agony, he rolls off her, giving way to the other two. As they are about to pounce on their hapless victim, Jake's stern voice commands them from up the alley: "Stop! Leave her alone!" The ruffians and the girl freeze, she with a look of shock mixed with relief, and the boys with stares of pure malice.

Leaving their victim on her back, the three attackers rise to their feet and stand shoulder to shoulder, facing the boy who dares challenge them.

"Oh, lookee here. Another damn Injun," sneers Pimple Face.

"We're overrun by dese filt'y savages," Broken Tooth adds.

"Hurry up, finish what yer doin' and leave some for me while I take care of Sittin' Bull over here," Freckle Face directs.

Pimple Face and Broken Tooth pounce upon the helpless girl again, tearing at her like wolves ripping apart a deer. Yet the girl will not submit and fights them with all of her waning strength.

Freckle Face, still in pain from the girl's second kick, charges Jake, cocking his right arm back as he runs, hoping to hit Jake with a flying haymaker. But as the ruffian begins to swing forward, Jake ducks and rolls his body on the ground, cutting the tall boy's knees from under him like a scythe cutting a swathe of field hay.

Jake rolls and immediately springs to his feet in one fluid motion. He then wheels about and quickly hurls himself at the other two boys, who are sitting atop the still-struggling girl, mowing them over like a storm wind toppling an old tree.

With all three attackers now on the ground, the girl is momentarily free.

"Run!" Jake shouts to her. "Run for help!" he pleads, knowing that this fight is not over and preparing to face the attackers again.

Rising painfully and slowly but realizing the urgency of the moment, the girl finds energy to jump over the stunned tall boy. She momentarily stops, turns back, and—risking further assault—for good measure kicks him squarely on the other shin. Holding his newly injured leg with both hands, he writhes on the ground in pain like a bear caught in a trap.

Scrambling to his feet, Jake attempts to dash toward the livery, but Freckle Face, struggling to his feet, blocks the way and draws a knife from his coat pocket. The long, shiny blade opens with a menacing click at a flick of his wrist. Jake freezes as he hears two more clicks from the other attackers.

"Whatcha' gonna do now, Injun?" Pimple Face asks with a bloody smile.

"Now ya know what Custer must a' felt like before he got it," taunts Broken Tooth. "Hey," Freckle Face casually suggests, "I never scalped an Injun before."

"My granddaddy was wit' da cavalry out west durin' the Injun Wars. He said he scalped plenty a' dem. Women and children too. Looks like I'll be keepin' up da family tradition," Broken Tooth adds proudly.

Just then a voice calls out, "Jake! Take dis!" All four boys hear the voice of Ulysses, who hears and watches the scuffle but is too scared to intervene himself. From the corner of his eye, Jake sees an object sailing through the air, which he instinctively reaches up and catches—his lacrosse stick. Jake had taken my advice and left his lacrosse stick, which he never went anywhere without, behind in the wagon so as not to unnerve the white citizens of Syracuse should they see an Indian walking through town with an object that resembled a war club.

Truly, nothing is more dangerous than an Indian and his lacrosse stick. About four feet in length, half of which is the foot-wide webbing, it is a formidable instrument of war if its holder intends such purpose. Jake likely feels the spirit of his ancestors in his wooden friend, strength and confidence pulsate through his veins. Twirling his stick quickly from hand to hand mesmerizes his attackers. Finally, snapping out of his momentary trance, Pimple Face shouts, "Let's get 'im!"

At once, all three charge Jake, who makes no attempt to retreat or escape. He stands his ground, both hands on his stick, his legs as taut as a deer alert to the twang of a bowstring just before leaping. When his attackers are about a stick length away, Jake torques his hips and spins his body like a top. Holding his stick straight out from his chest, the spinning Jake strikes each of the three in succession, mowing them all down like Samson dispatching the Philistines with the jaw of an ass.

Jake hovers over the three now lying in the dirt, rubbing their heads and wondering what hit them.

"Dirty Injun," Pimple Face shouts as he scrambles to his feet and charges Jake again. This time Jake crouches low and lunges with both arms straight out from his body, jabbing his stick so fiercely into Pimple Face's ribs that his attacker is suspended in the air as if impaled. With a mighty heave, Jake tosses Pimple Face up and over his head onto the ground behind him.

Curled up in a ball on the ground and holding his ribs, Pimple Face cries, "My ribs! My ribs is broke!"

Incensed and embarrassed for his friend, Freckle Face struggles to his feet and charges Jake, limping discernibly. "Dat's it. Dat's it fa' you, Pocahontas!"

Again, Jake momentarily hesitates, undoubtedly wondering why this attacker would call him by a girl's name. Just as Freckle Face is about to stab Jake with a thrust of his knife, Jake quickly steps to the side, spins, and whips his stick around to impact his attacker on the back of the shoulders, knocking him face-first into the dirt.

Seeing his two friends in pain in the dirt, Broken Tooth employs a different strategy. "OK, Geronimo," Broken Tooth begins, "jus' you an' me."

Jake once again stands his ground with his lacrosse stick at the ready and shouts in exasperation, "Stupid white boy! Geronimo was a war chief of the Apache. I am grandson of a Sachem of the Onondaga tribe, once the keepers of the council fire of the Haudenosaunee people. My ancestors hunted and fished this land when your ancestors were picking fleas off each other in some cave in Europe."

Broken Tooth just shakes his head and laughs. "Ya stinkin' savage. Ya think yer smarter dan me?"

"Let our wisdom be judged by our actions, white boy," Jake vows as he prepares for one last assault.

Charging a few steps, Broken Tooth stops and hurls his knife at Jake.

Jake ducks and deflects the knife from his face with his lacrosse stick. Jake then reaches out with his stick, cups it over Broken Tooth's head, and entraps him like a bird in a leather-laced cage. Jake swings Broken Tooth around; when he lets go of the stick, the motion propels Broken Tooth down the alley, depositing him at the feet of newcomers to the fray. Two burly, mustachioed policemen, each wearing a blue tunic with gold buttons and a silver star, stand with their arms crossed over their chests, each lightly tapping a small club against his shoulder.

"Hey! What in flamin' hell is goin' on here?" snaps one of the officers.

"What mischief have ya fallen into there, Cochise?" inquires the other policeman as he pulls Broken Tooth up by the collar.

The boy immediately accuses Jake. "Dis Injun attacked us fa no good reason, officer," the boy states with as good manners as his ill breeding can muster.

"Yeah," chimes in Freckle Face, taking a cue from Broken Tooth, hoping that courtesy might give them a pass. As he dusts off his bloodstained pants, Freckle Face continues, "For no good reason dis Injun jumped us. Prob'ly wanted ta rob us."

Seeing his opening, Pimple Face adds, "He beat us wit dat Injun war club."

"Grandfather!" Jake cries as I arrive in the alleyway.

I pick up Jake's lacrosse stick, for it is sacrilege to let it lie in the dirt.

"Dis kid belong to ya, chief?" one of the policemen asks.

"He is my grandson," I calmly reply.

"Yeah, well, he's goin' to jail. Ya can come along if ya want," the policeman says as he sternly grabs Jake by the arm.

"Stop right there!" a woman's voice rings out from up the alley. "Let that boy go, if you please," she commands with authority.

"But, Mrs. Graham," the first policeman explains, "look at what dis little savage did to dese here t'ree boys. Dey're a bloody mess but dere's nary a scratch on da Injun. He obviously attacked dem." All three young hoodlums nod in agreement.

I speak the obvious in defense of Jake. "Why would a single Indian boy attack three white boys in a blind alley?" Then, pointing to the blades lying in the dust I add, "Especially three boys with knives?"

Now smiling at my presentation of the evidence, the woman chastises the policemen. "You idiots! Can't you see what happened here?" The two policemen shake their heads, looking very confused. Exasperated, the woman continues, "This boy intervened to save a young woman whom these hooligans were assaulting."

"Young woman?" Broken Tooth mutters with scorn.

"Young woman?" Pimple Face laughs with sarcasm.

"Don't see no young woman aroun' here," remarks Freckle Face.

The well-groomed woman steps to the side, revealing the mixed-breed girl, dirty and bruised. "She is my house girl. She ran to me for help and would not have escaped except for the heroics of this young Indian boy."

The woman looks upon Jake with kind eyes and snaps at the policemen, "Now unhand this boy and arrest these three low-life scoundrels!"

The three boys protest, crying loudly as they are dragged down the alley by the burly policemen, who whack each of them a few times with their clubs out of anger for appearing so stupid as to have fallen for their false story.

"Come, Madeline," Mrs. Graham waves to the half-Indian girl, "come meet your savior, your hero."

Madeline approaches with quick steps, looking down at her feet in embarrassment. She holds her torn blouse together. Although her face is dirty, cut, and bruised, Madeline has an aura of purity about her.

Mrs. Graham gently lifts the girl's head by reaching under her chin with a hand gloved in black lace and gently reminds her, "Always stand erectly. Comport yourself with dignity. And never look down at your feet like a Chinawoman."

Although her bottom lip is swollen, her braids are a tangled mess, and her cheeks are sullied with dirt and blood, the girl dutifully obeys her mistress. With a forced air of dignity, she curtsies before Jake, murmuring, "Thank you, young sir."

Dumbfounded, Jake quickly looks at me, unsure whether a response is required. Then, in his own sincere way, he simply says, "You are welcome, Miss."

"That's better," says Mrs. Graham. Then, as an aside, she continues, "I spend so much time and money trying to educate these children, but in times of trouble, they revert to their old ways like children of the devil."

She looks at me for overt, if not tacit, approval. I smile and nod as neutrally as possible, for I am insulted by her arrogant view of our people. *But what is it about this woman?* I wonder. Then I recognize her as the impatient woman at the General Merchandise store. *But what else? Where else have I seen her?* She is a comely woman, with hardly a wrinkle on her alabaster face. Her gray hair is tucked up under a large brimmed hat with a thin black veil covering her face. She has a tiny waist and ample bosom. *Wait! Could it be?* Now it is my turn to be dumbfounded.

"Well, Madeline, have you something more to say?" Mrs. Graham prompts her charge.

"Thank you again, kind sir," the girl repeats as she curtsies, holding the sides of her torn dress out with both hands.

Jake is about to speak when the woman steps between them, looks admiringly at Jake, and purrs, "Such a handsome boy. Does he read?" she politely asks me.

"Yes, ma'am," I reply.

"If he learned to read on the reservation, he probably hasn't learned all that well," she insists. "Well, never mind. Will you join us for tea?"

Jake looks at me eagerly, but the day is late and I politely decline.

Taking a piece of paper and pencil from her purse, she scribbles something and hands the paper to me.

"Take this," she says. "This is my name and address." She then lifts her veil over the brim of her hat, revealing the ruby lips I had never forgotten, and extends her gloved hand to thank Jake and me.

I am shocked. I am speechless. I am breathless. It is…it is she: the mistress who read to me when I was a boy, the woman who held me close to her soft bosom. But I do not understand. How can it be? She is older than I, yet she has many fewer signs of age than I. And her name was not Graham—the name on the piece of paper she's handed me—back then.

She continues, "My name is Charlotte Graham. If you bring the boy to me, I will take extraordinarily good care of him." As she further eyes Jake with a smile, she explains, "I will teach him to read properly. If you become lost, most people know where I live." She points to a mansion on the hill in the distance.

I do not remember that house, I think.

"I used to be a minister's wife but, alas, the poor man died of consumption, and so circumstances dictated that I remarry," Mrs. Graham explains. "Fortunately, I married one of the owners of this town. Poor man. He too died suddenly. It seems my men cannot keep up with me," she chuckles slyly.

How beautiful she is after all these years! Time has indeed been kind to her. She is still sassy and is still enamored of Indian boys.

Madeline cannot take her eyes from Jake, her hero. She is dazzled by her knight in shining armor.

Madeline's gazing is interrupted by Mrs. Graham, who begins to leave. Before returning her veil under her chin, she hesitates, looks back over her shoulder, and demurely inquires, "Do I know you? Have we met before?"

She scrutinizes me as she had Jake. Obviously less pleased, she murmurs, "No, impossible." And with a twinkle in her eye, she slowly turns away again.

I watch her walk ever so elegantly down the alleyway. Spinning her small umbrella, she occasionally glances over her shoulder flirtatiously. She beckons Madeline, who dutifully scurries after her. The girl too admiringly looks back occasionally at Jake. Catching up, the Indian girl and Mrs. Graham walk arm in arm until they reach the street and turn the corner from our view—but not from our memories.

I pick up Jake's hat and begin to dust off the back of his trousers with it.

"Seems like I am always dusting you off, my son," I comment as Jake retucks his shirt and brushes his jacket. "You know, the Great Spirit did not give you the gift of the stick to use as a war club."

"But I did not use it as a weapon, Grandfather," Jake protests.

"The trickles of blood running from the three white boys' heads and faces seem to indicate otherwise," I patiently reply.

"Grandfather, have you not taught me to use my head in the Game? Have you not taught me that there are times when we must attack our opponents' goal and other times when we must defend our own goal?" the boy asks.

"Yes, but what are you getting at?" I respond.

"Today, did I not use my lacrosse stick in defense of a girl in distress? Is it not the same as defending our goal?" Jake asks with a sheepish grin, knowing that he is right.

I smile. Patting Jake on the back, I note, "You are becoming wiser each day. Are you in training for the Game or to replace me as Sachem?"

"I could never be you, Grandfather. I only want to make you proud of me."

I suddenly stop as if struck by an invisible object. I cannot let this moment pass. Placing both my hands on Jake's shoulders, I say with all sincerity, "Every man walks his own path, my son. Some trail off. But others, like you, walk the path of a human being. A man can be no prouder of his grandson than I am of you."

"Horse an' wagon ready, sa," Ulysses announces with a big smile. "Ya sho' showed dose boys a t'ing or two, young massa. Damn, I likes it when de white man gits a taste a' his own medicine fo' a change. Y'all welcome here anytime," Ulysses adds sincerely.

We shake Ulysses's hand. In return, he tips his tattered straw hat, backs away with a big smile, and scurries out of sight.

We stow our bundles inside the wagon. As we ready to climb on, Jake embraces me. I draw him close to my heart. No words need be spoken. Our embrace reflects our eternal bond. On this day, Jake has grown, not so much in body but in maturity, wisdom, and experiences that will serve him well into the future. I cluck old Thunder on, eager to return to the safety of our country. We tarry no longer in Syracuse, for if evil lurks there by day; I shudder to think what we may encounter there at night. I urge Thunder to a pace quicker than normal, for I have had enough excitement for one day, as has Jake, his head already bobbing as calm washes over him.

"Cluck, cluck, giddyap, Thunder. Take us home, old friend."

15

HEADING HOME

I hope that our journey home will be peaceful. The excitement of visiting the big city and rescuing a young woman has been extremely fatiguing for Jake. Compared to the hustle and noise of the city, I am relieved that our journey home through farmland and hills is pleasantly quiet. The cacophony of the creaking wagon, the jingle of the tack, and the clippity-clop of Thunder's hooves are a lullaby for Jake, whose head begins to bob as he sits back with his arms comfortably folded across his chest. Soon he is leaning further back, with his dusty hat over his eyes and his dusty jacket folded as a pillow to protect his neck from splinters in the wooden backboard. As we travel south, the sun warms our right cheeks.

Seeing Jake perilously list to the side as he dozes off, I decide to stop and arrange a nest in the back of the buckboard for my young sleeping prince. I whoa Thunder and gently call, "Jake… Jake."

Jake awakes with a start and grabs his hat as it begins to fall to the ground.

"Yes, Grandfather," he replies sleepily, "are we home?"

"No, no, my son, but it is dangerous to sleep high up on the buckboard. What if a bee stings Thunder on the backside or the wheel hits a rock and we jerk forward? You will tumble to the ground, possibly breaking an arm, and then where would you be with the Game just two days away? Crawl into the back. Make a nest among the blankets and goods. Sleep. Dream of the Game, my son."

"Yes, Grandfather," Jake uncharacteristically but most willingly replies.

The boy must have been truly exhausted; if not, he would have argued that he could sit erectly and alertly for the remainder of the time like any man, and probably would have insisted on driving as well.

"Pass up some water before you lie down," I request.

"Yes, Grandfather," Jake sleepily obeys, somewhat annoyed as his nest beckons. I drink mightily from our jug. Before I can hand it back, Jake is loudly snoring from under the buckboard seat shading his face from the setting sun. I smile to myself, content that we have survived the city fairly unscathed and have accomplished our missions. Most importantly, I have seen Jake grow taller as a man today.

"Giddyap, Thunder," I command with a gentle snap of the reigns and a cluck.

My mind wanders back to Mrs. Graham. I am truly amazed at how beautifully she has aged. Her warmth, her smell, and her touch come back to me from my memory. I smile quietly, silently thanking her again for teaching me the love of reading and the love of a woman's body. I begin to hum, then sing a song of thanks to the Creator, for I have had much to be thankful for on this day.

As we return to our country, all apprehension and anxiety associated with traveling to the city disappears. The look and smell of pine, hemlock, and sweet grass fill my senses. We pass occasional farmhouses, some leased by white families and others inhabited by our people. The road twists and turns as it mirrors the Onondaga Creek, which we follow deeply into the heart of our nation. The hills at distant right glow in the sunset. The wind blows its music through the trees, beckoning us home.

After a while, just before we cross an old wooden bridge, weather-beaten and worn like the many wagons that have traveled upon it, a strange thing happens: my eyelids become heavy, subject to the same rhythmic cadence of our movement plus the warm setting sun on my back. But I feel no fear in my heart, confident that if anything happens to me, Thunder will find his way home.

As I cross between the world of the living and of dreams, I sense a large shadow pass over me. To my right I see in the sky a rapidly approaching object that blocks out the sun. I whoa Thunder, drop the reigns, pull back on the brake lever, and stand.

Covering my brow with both hands to better observe the object, I finally realize that I am looking at a bird—not just any bird, but our brother the majestic eagle, the symbol of our people. But the wings and body of this extraordinary bird block out the whole sky as it swoops down upon me. In its talons this eagle carries what I believe to be a snake, oddly still and not wriggling in its death throes. As the great bird nears, our eyes meet. The wind generated from its mighty-but-graceful wings knocks me over the back rail of the wagon's raised seat. I fall right atop Jake.

Startled, Jake jumps, violently striking his head on the underside of the buckboard's seat.

Rubbing his head, Jake whines, "Grandfather! What are you doing? Why have you jumped on me?"

Embarrassed, I apologize. "I'm sorry, my son. I must have dozed off and fallen backward," I say, anxiously looking up and all around.

Still rubbing his head, Jake too looks up and around, wondering what I am looking at or for. Seeing nothing, Jake states with concern, "You have never done that before. Are you feeling all right? Are you seeing things that are not there? Have you seen a spirit? Do you want me to drive?"

Still searching the sky for the mighty eagle and wondering whether I was, indeed, dreaming, I assure Jake I am fine. "You may as well sit up with me. We are almost home," I comment as I look again over both shoulders for what may have been a feathered specter.

Jake grabs his hat and climbs up and over the buckboard seat. I wonder whether I have just witnessed Jake's dream eagle. Is it a messenger from the Creator, or is it a great eagle that simply flew too closely? Not seeing or hearing the great bird, I shrug my shoulders and whisper under my breath, "Must be getting old."

Climbing back up onto my seat, I notice three spots on my jacket sleeve: blood. I immediately swipe Jake's hat from his head and run my fingers through his hair, desperately looking for a cut or abrasion but find none.

Fussing and squirming, Jake jams his hat back on with both hands. Most annoyed now, Jake shouts, "Grandfather, are you going crazy?"

Shocked by his voice and by my own behavior, I slowly sit down and try to gather myself. I stare straight ahead wordlessly. Then, thinking that the great bird still may be in the sky, I again look over my shoulders several times for some confirmation of my experience. Seeing nothing but billowing clouds to the east and fiery, low-lying clouds to the west, I shrug again and chuckle at Thunder's raised tail as he passes gas. With a gentle snap of the reigns, we continue on the final leg of our journey home.

Jake looks to the sky, then at me, then to the sky again. He shakes his head, tips his hat forward, folds his arms, and closes his eyes.

I cannot help but stare again at my jacket sleeve. The three droplets of blood stare back at me but offer no explanation. *Were these drops from the bloodied faces of the three white ruffians in Syracuse?*

I gently touch the spots. They smudge. They are fresh. *Or has the great eagle carrying the stick from Jake's dream bled upon me? Am I now a part of Jake's dream? Will our paths intertwine in a remarkable way, more than the customary relationship of grandfather and grandson?*

Saying nary a word to each other after this episode, we finally turn the last bend before home. Thunder seems to perk up as the familiar smells of his barn waft to him. Like Thunder, my heart skips a beat or two as I see our house in the distance and we hasten up the dusty hill.

In spite of needing paint, a few roof patches, replacement of some rotten porch boards, and grease on that squeaky screen door, no more beautiful a home can I imagine. Its porch and barn lights are beacons, beckoning tired travelers. I hope that my three cherished granddaughters are long asleep.

But how could a creaky wagon and a large-hoofed horse approach unannounced? Our old, semi-blind, battle-worn, mixed-breed dog Bear announces our approach with a strained, raspy bark. He is not much of a hunter anymore but can still scare off varmints and warn of intruders.

Passing the house and heading for the barn, I see three ghosts, their white nightgowns flowing behind them. But their angelic voices belie their ephemeral appearance.

"Grandfather! Jake!" they shout in unison.

Although annoyed that they are not sleeping, I return a broad smile and a tired wave at my beautiful granddaughters.

"Well? Well? Well? Did you accomplish everything?" they shout as they jump up and down with anticipation.

"Shush," I whisper, hoping that they will recognize and adopt the low tone of my voice. "You will awaken Sarah and her father over yonder."

The girls immediately fall silent.

"Now move away from the wagon lest you lose a few toes under the wheels," I add.

They hop back in unison, like three little rabbits.

"Wait for us on the porch, and I shall tell you all about our trip," I calmly say.

Clapping their hands and squealing in delight, they race back to the porch, chirping all the while about gifts.

Although happy to see his sisters and undoubtedly eager to tell them of his adventures in Syracuse, Jake is too tired to talk tonight.

Driving into the barn, we are greeted by our chickens and the rooster. Jake and I crawl off the wagon and begin to unhitch Thunder. Silenced by fatigue, we mechanically go about our duties. Jake's final chores are to draw water for Thunder, throw some hay into the stall, and place a bucket of oats on the hook just inside the stall door. Unhitched and without coaxing, Thunder plods headlong into his stall, quickly turns himself around, and whinnies contently as he buries his nose in his bucket.

With the lamplight guiding our way, Jake and I trudge up the path to our house. As we approach the porch, I don't believe we can take many more steps.

I wonder where my three little specters have gone. Raising my lamp, we can see three sleeping figures cuddled together under a blanket on my rocking chair. So peaceful are they—little Mary's face snuggled onto her oldest sister's chest, both older girls with their arms firmly encircling her—that I am reluctant to move them. But the night air is chilly, and there is much to do in the morning that requires fully rested children with strong backs. Jake and I carefully untangle the girls from each other's grasp and gently carry them off to bed one by one.

Now, finally heading toward our respective bedrooms, Jake wearily asks, "Grandfather?"

Too tired to answer any more questions, I stop, smile, and lovingly reply, "Goodnight, my son. Let us sleep now." I turn my bedroom doorknob and enter. The night is not for talking, only dreaming. I wonder if Jake and I will dream as one tonight.

16

GIMME SOME A' THAT OL' TIME RELIGION

As I begin to stir, leaving the world of dreams for the world of the living, I feel a weight on my chest. *Has the great eagle returned to me in my sleep and perched upon my chest?* I wonder. Breathing rapidly, and with some trepidation, I hesitantly open one eye and then the other. Although fearful of what I may see, to my relief and delight, I am feeling not the weight of the great bird of the sky but the combined weight of my three granddaughters.

Clutching and jabbing me, they tease, "Come on, Grandfather! Wake up! Are you going to sleep all day?"

"Rah!" I bellow as I sit up with my arms raised, fingers swiping the air like the claws of a mighty bear.

"You have awakened your brother the bear," I joke. "Now I will eat you little bunnies for my breakfast."

Half-wondering whether I have shape-shifted into a bear, the girls scream but then burst into laughter as I lovingly clutch them to my chest. Only momentarily enjoying the warmth of my embrace, they quickly return to their purpose.

"Stop playing, Grandfather," each one chimes. "Come on. This is a busy day."

And so it is. This is the day before the Green Corn Festival. Each of us in the household attaches a different level of importance to the festival.

The council meeting of chiefs, held four times per year, is a most important time for me as Sachem and Faithkeeper. Our clan mothers, the wisest and most respected of our women, are empowered to nominate and elect only men as council members, from whom our Sachems are chosen. Each of the clans is equally represented. The council, as a body, hears grievances, resolves disputes, discusses civic projects, listens to Firefly's promises, and recounts the many blessings that the Creator has bestowed upon the people. And, most importantly, as the Faithkeeper, I will be called upon to give the thanksgiving prayer this year.

For the girls, Saturday night means singing, dancing, and wearing their finest clothes. During the day, the older girls will giggle and fawn over the handsomest boys, whom they will attempt to distract from viewing the Game.

For Jake, nothing else matters but the Game. Every Haudenosaunee boy dreams of being invited to play in the Game with the men. I am not sure if there is anything equivalent in the white man's culture. I have read of African boys having to slay a lion with little more than a knife as a rite of passage and of boys from India having to kill a tiger with a spear. But for a Haudenosaunee boy, even more than the hunt, his first Game is most momentous. Although not as death-defying as hunting a lion or tiger, the invited boy's reputation and stature as a young man are measured by his first performance in the Game. The invitation to play is special but does not miraculously transform a boy into a man. What that special boy does with that special moment counts most.

Not every boy is offered this opportunity. While most of the older boys and men play among each other recreationally nearly every weekend, the Game is played against other tribes during some of the main yearly festivals. During these special times, the Game takes on greater importance, becoming a matter of tribal pride. Jake, at age seventeen, is the youngest of our people and the only new player to be given the honor of playing in the Game with the men during the Green Corn Festival.

The white spectators often comment that our Game is like the gladiatorial contests of ancient Rome. But such a comparison demonstrates the white man's lack of understanding our Game. The gladiator of ancient Rome fought for his very life; in life or death, his primary motivation was personal glory. Not so with our people. An Indian lacrosse player is taught to think little of personal glory; giving every ounce of strength, speed, and skill glorifies the Creator. Jake understands and respects the spirituality of the Game, but he surely also wants to shine for that special person in his life, Sarah. For this, he prays for the Creator's forgiveness.

—

Because our festival extends through the weekend, including Sunday, we agree with the Christian ministers that our children will attend Sunday school on Friday morning.

"Hurry along, children," I urge, "or you will be late for church."

"Why do we have to go to church today?" Mary whines. "It is only Friday."

Before I can, Molly calmly explains, "You know why we must attend church today. Our festival is celebrated on Saturday and Sunday. The minister has requested to hold services on Friday, knowing that we are unlikely to attend on Sunday."

I smile at Molly's calm demeanor and wisdom. Although not as book-learned as her brother or as experienced as her older sister, Molly is innately intuitive beyond her years and as steady as a rock. Both girls, Molly and Maggie, may one day become clan mothers, but Molly is clearly already in training.

"Besides," Molly continues, her words now bolstered by my approving looks, "Grandfather has made a deal with the minister that all the people have agreed to abide."

"Deal? What is a deal?" little Mary asks of her wise sister.

Maggie now interrupts, "A deal is an agreement between men."

Here I quickly add, "...that is forged by women but for which the men take credit."

Maggie and I smile at each other because only she and I understand the meaning of my words. Even Jake looks somewhat perplexed. Not wanting to appear ignorant after so many moments of shining brilliance lately, he only smiles and nods in agreement.

Mary impatiently blurts, "Deals? Deals? Deals are none of a child's concern. The sooner we finish with church, the sooner we can meet Grandfather under our Sacred Tree. And eat corn cakes with maple syrup!"

The girls race out of the house in their prettiest white woman's clothes, long white dresses with short sleeves tied off with ribbons, and some Indian beads. They wear bonnets but eschew leather shoes in favor of the comfort of their deer hide and rabbit-fur moccasins.

Jake wears the only other shirt and pair of pants he owns. He had dusted off his jacket the night before and hung it outside on a tree limb so that the cooler air and morning dew might freshen it. He wears black-laced boots, the tops barely reaching the bottom of his pants, which always seem too short for him. He races after his sisters, the screen door squeaking and slamming behind him, trumpeting the children's departure.

Ah! Peace at last, I think.

I grab my cup of coffee, appreciating its enticing smell, and locate my spectacles as well as the dime-store novel about Wild

Bill Hickok that I purchased in Syracuse. Settling into my rocking chair, I reach underneath for my corncob pipe and tobacco pouch.

Suddenly, I am startled by a thump on the porch and the squeaking of the screen. Jake bursts in. He thrashes about in his room like a mad bull, finally emerging and panting and hiding something behind his back.

Whispering, "Almost forgot my lacrosse stick, Grandfather," Jake flips it upward into the air, just missing the ceiling beam—and the tip of his nose—as the stick falls. Without breaking gaze from my astonished look, he reaches out with his right hand and snags the spinning stick before it hits the floor. With a wild war whoop, Jake raises the stick above his head and blasts off the porch and onto the ground without touching a stair. As he races down the dirt road, I hear him singing an Indian song of bravery and courage that I taught him. I watch him flipping his stick in the air, spinning and catching it, scooping up stones and throwing them at the crooked, splintered wooden posts that barely hold up old rail fences. Quickly catching up to his sisters, Jake emits horrifying warrior screams, scaring them so terribly that little Mary begins to cry before she realizes that it is only her brother.

Jake is beginning to feel the fever that every warrior, soldier, and player feels before going into battle, whether in war or in the Game. That fever will glow hotter as Jake undergoes our pregame rituals.

—

Although the church is the only building on the reservation always freshly painted and sparkling white, its interior is always dark, gloomy, and filled with stale air.

A dozen rows of hard wooden benches are exceptionally uncomfortable for an Indian unaccustomed to sitting straight-backed with both feet on the floor. The windows are small and few; some are made of a colored glass and never opened. Not a breath of fresh air is to be found after the doors are closed for the service, which is particularly stifling during the hot days of summer, often producing ill effects on the people.

I have seen ministers from all Protestant denominations come and go during my many years on the reservation. After a year or two, they request to be transferred, most out of frustration because few of the people ever truly embrace Christianity.

After the war between the Americans and the English, the Haudenosaunee were guaranteed possession of their land in return for peace with the white man and the acceptance of Christian ministers onto the reservation. The Americans thought that Christianity would help subdue the people's warrior spirit. But our warrior spirit had less to do with religion and more with preservation of our culture and identity.

We, the Haudenosaunee, have practiced our own religion for many years. The white man and his preachers, who mistakenly believe that non-Christian Indian people worship multiple gods or animals, call us pagans. The Haudenosaunee and most of the Indian peoples from the Atlantic to the Pacific universally believe in one god, whom we call *Ha Wen Neyu.* We are no less monotheistic than the children of Abraham.

One of our older and most venerated clan mothers, laughing, tells me about what transpires in church before I meet the children under our sacred tree. About half an hour into the service, little Mary's head begins to nod until she finally dozes off. She surely does not understand a word the young minister shouts at her. Maggie places Mary's head on her lap, and Molly places Mary's feet on her lap. Apparently seeing little Mary sleeping from his pulpit perch, the minister begins shouting even more loudly. Veins line his forehead like tributaries of a river and pop out on his neck from under his stiff white collar.

"Leave the body of the child!" he shouts, his hands stretched, fingers spread open, as he glares at the sleeping cherub. "Leave the body, evil one. Take not her soul to perdition. Be gone, Satan! Be gone!" he commands.

The entire congregation now stares at the three girls but soon realizes that little Mary is merely sleeping, no less possessed by the devil than the minister himself. In his mind, however, the preacher must reason that the child has swooned from a malevolent spirit. Otherwise, she would surely be awake and alert, absorbing his every word as part of her salvation.

After a few minutes of ear-numbing shouting, an elder clan mother stands and calmly speaks: "With all respect, pastor, sleep is usually brought on not by evil spirits but by boredom. Please return to your sermon and try to be quieter about it. You are hurting my ears."

At first, the people are stunned into silence, but as the truth and humor of the old woman's words sink in, they begin to laugh. The young minister, angry and embarrassed, turns red, slams his book shut, tucks it under his arm, stomps down the pulpit stairs, and hurriedly exits the church through the back door. The people are surprised at the young minister's unexpected departure, but no one calls him back. Even the true Christians remain silent.

The old clan mother rises again, saying, "Very rarely do young men understand humility, whether in white or in Indian culture. Our young minister, with his stiff white collar that chokes him as he speaks, does not yet realize that the word of the Creator cannot be shouted at and forced upon people. The Creator's words are gentle. They come to us in the rain that cleanses Mother Earth. They come to us in the hunt. They come to us in our songs and dances. They come to us in our dreams. They come to us in our Game."

The people nod in agreement at her wisdom.

"Some of the people attend church because they have accepted Christianity. But most of us attend church to keep peace with the white man, his government in Albany, and the BIA. But I say to you who will hear me that the Christian god is really not much different than our Creator. Did not one god create the heavens and earth? Did not one god create man, animal, and the fruits of the land? Are we not all equal in God's eyes? It is the white man's delivery of God's word that troubles me," the old woman concludes.

At that, little Mary stirs with a loud grunt and snore. The people burst into laughter. Her timing could not have been more perfect.

The clan mother raises her hands to quiet them. Smiling at Mary, she notes, "So much truth is spoken from the mouths of babes."

The people clap with approval. The loud clapping, unusual in this church, finally awakens Mary. Slowly rising and rubbing her eyes with both hands, she sleepily asks, "Is it over?"

"Yes, my little sleepyhead," Maggie whispers.

"Is it time to see Grandfather?" she asks.

The girls and the other children look for approval from the old clan mother, who replies, "Yes, you may all go. Grandfather awaits you under our Sacred Tree."

With respect, each child lovingly runs to the old clan mother, hugs her, and scampers out of the church.

Laughing and squealing with delight, the children eagerly but gently tug on the clan mother's dress to urge her to hasten her step to me, as I am awaiting under our sacred tree. They run by a visiting white family dressed in black. The man comments to his wife, "Must have been a particularly inspiring sermon. Let us pay our compliments to our brother pastor."

Walking toward the church, the white family and the clan mother hear a sharp snapping sound coming from the woodshed behind the building. Urging the children to proceed along without her, the clan mother observes the white man cautiously approach and slowly open the woodshed door. Sneaking a peek herself, both she and the man watch in horror the young pastor, ministerial tunic removed and body stripped of all clothes but his white collar, steadily beating himself over his back with a leather strap. With every lash, the strap draws blood from the young pastor's skin as he cries and begs forgiveness. Witnessing such a pitiful, frightening sight, the clan mother and the visitor shudder and slowly back away.

As his wife approaches out of curiosity, the man, obviously disturbed, silently looks at our clan mother, slams the shed door behind him, and braces it with his back as if he has captured Satan himself within. He then abruptly steers his wife away from this place and incoherently mutters something to the effect that they visit the pastor another time.

17

THE SACRED TREE

"Grandfather! Grandfather!" the children cry out. Like wild turkeys, they flock to me, settling quietly under a great white pine, our sacred tree. Out of respect, Haudenosaunee children refer to all of their elders as "Grandfather" or "Grandmother." Likewise, we of advanced age look after all the children and refer to them as if they were our own sons and daughters.

The great white pine tree reaches skyward with the majesty of any man-made European cathedral. The symbol of the Haudenosaunee from the earliest days of the Iroquois Confederacy, its branches signify shelter as well as the protection and security that the people find in their union with each other. The roots, which stretch to the four corners of the earth, signify the extension of peace to embrace all mankind.

"Come and sit, my children," I beckon them. "Gather closely, my little ones, and quiet yourselves if you wish to hear my stories."

One little boy, of perhaps seven years, impatient with the others and apparently hungry, stands up and commands, "Yes, be quiet to hear Grandfather, or you will not get corncakes." He points to the women cooking at the outdoor ovens up the hill near our ceremonial longhouse.

Another little girl, about the same age, also adds confidently and hopefully, "With maple syrup on them too."

All the children rub their stomachs and smack their lips, imagining the tasty delight.

"Is that the only reason you come to the Great Tree after church?" I ask.

"No! No!" they protest. "We love you, Grandfather."

All the children cheer. How proud my three girls are that these many children love and respect their grandfather as much as them!

Sitting quietly upon Mother Earth is part of Onondaga training for our little ones. We believe that a child who cannot sit still is a half-developed child. We strive to teach our children to look where there is apparently nothing to see and to listen intently when all is seemingly quiet.

Although I enjoy my rocking chair, sitting upon the ground brings me closer to our Mother's power, enabling me to think more deeply and feel more keenly.

For the first time, Jake does not sit with the children. He stands some distance away, leaning against a fence rail along the side of the road between our Great Tree and the longhouse complex. Down the hill lies the field upon which the Game will be played. I realize that Jake can no longer sit among the children for he is no longer one of them. Not yet a man, he stands halfway between each world, remembering the one and eagerly anticipating the other.

And I suspect Jake has another reason for selecting this location. By the cooking ovens, I see a young, lithe figure moving among the older clan mothers. It is Sarah. She pretends to busy herself but intermittently looks at Jake, who returns each glance with a smile. The connection between the two of them is obvious and warms my heart.

"Children," I begin, "what did you learn in church today?"

One girl giggles, "Mary snores."

All the children laugh.

"Other than my little butterfly's sleeping habits, what did the new young minister teach you?" I ask with sincerity.

Trying to return these gigglers to some semblance of seriousness, Maggie stands. "The minister explained that we cannot be Christians if we do not believe in the Father, the Son, and the Holy Ghost," she reports.

Another girl, a bit younger than Maggie, arises. "Grandfather, why does the minister want us to believe in three gods? Isn't one god enough?" I marvel at the wisdom of these children. At this young age, they are aware of concepts that have troubled me for years.

I think a moment about how to answer this question. I am cognizant of BIA ears lurking about. I do not want to say anything that will undo our unspoken rule that neither the people nor the Christian preachers will disparage each other's religion.

Our people have had our own religion for over one hundred years. Around 1800, Handsome Lake, half-brother to the renowned Seneca war chief Corn Planter, had a vision as an old man. In this vision, the Creator revealed certain lessons of life called *Giahwihoh*, or the good word, which formed the basis of the longhouse religion. Its fundamental precept is to live in peace with the white man without forfeiting our spiritual and cultural identity. Handsome Lake stressed peace among families and among all people—no violence and no war. He preached respect for all people, Indian and white, no thievery, no murder, and no alcoholism. He taught the people that they are obliged to share with others less fortunate, thus no poverty and no need for orphanages.

"There are many more whites than Indian people," I explain. "Although I am not certain, I think that because they are so many, white men believe that they need more than one god."

Another more precocious girl asks sheepishly, "How could Jesus be born of a mother who had not been with a man?"

The older children duck their heads a bit and snicker. Little Mary looks at the older children who giggle and, somewhat annoyed, asks, "Grandfather, why are they laughing?" That question, of course, brings louder laughter.

"This story is not unique to the white man. The story of creation that has been passed down to me by the many grandfathers before me is similar. Do you want to hear it?"

"Yes! Yes!" they all clamor.

"Grandfather, excuse me. Before you begin your story, may I pass out these delicious corncakes?" asks Sarah, her face partially hidden by the fragrant steam rising from the large wooden plate.

"With maple syrup," a little boy reminds her.

"Yes, with maple syrup," Sarah assures him with a sweet smile.

Maggie stands to help distribute the corncakes, but before she can reach out, Jake darts to Sarah's side.

"Thank you, my sister," Jake begins somewhat arrogantly, "but you have much to learn from Grandfather's teachings, and I do not want you to miss anything while passing out corncakes."

"Thank you, my brother," Maggie answers with a sly smile. Turning to Sarah, Maggie continues, "You are indeed blessed with special powers, my sister, to encourage my brother to help serve food. We have never seen such assistance at home."

Maggie willingly returns to her place on the grass, accepting Jake's unintended teasing in order to facilitate his real design: to be near Sarah.

"Thank you, Jake, for your assistance," Sarah says politely. "Be careful not to burn your hands before the Game. The cakes are hot."

I observe this exchange between my grandchildren and Sarah with gladness in my heart. I notice Jake cannot take his eyes off Sarah. Apparently so enamored is he of Sarah's presence, Jake does not hear her warnings and carelessly grabs a stack of corncakes. At once, he tosses them into the air with a loud cry.

"Aiee! Aiee!" Jake shakes and blows on his hands. He runs to a nearby horse trough and immerses his hands repeatedly. The corncakes lie scattered all over the grass. Nevertheless, the children gladly pick up the now-cooled corncakes, carefully brush off the few particles of dirt, grass, clover, ants, or ladybugs, and return to their places. Sarah makes her rounds, pouring maple syrup on each cake.

Embarrassed and worried about his reddened hands, Jake heads to the outdoor kitchen, where one of the clan mothers generously applies butter and honey to his wounds. Blessing both of his hands, she assures him that these sweet ingredients will draw away the pain of the burn.

I glance at Sarah, who after distributing the tasty treats to these happy little ones, returns the wooden tray to a table near the outdoor kitchen. The clan mothers nod their approval.

What I next see and hear convince me that there is something more than a spark between Jake and Sarah and that perhaps I should discuss a courtship between them with the clan mothers who typically arrange such matters.

Now turning toward Jake, Sarah reaches out and gently takes hold of his hands.

"Do not worry," Jake assures her. "Grandmother has blessed my hands."

Almost crying for Jake's pain, Sarah empathetically raises both of Jake's hands to her lips, gently kissing both and whispers, "A kiss is sweeter than honey."

Hearing a clan mother call to her, Sarah runs off with a smile.

Jake stands frozen. His mouth agape, he stares at his hands in awe. I do not believe Jake has ever been kissed by a girl and so had no idea that a girl's lips could be so soft. With all respect to the clan mother, I think Sarah's kisses surely are the best remedy for his hands.

Closing his eyes, Jake raises his hands to his lips and softly kisses them, pretending they are Sarah's lips. His brief interlude with his own hands is interrupted by a clan mother nearby, who clears her throat as a signal that she disapproves of Jake's public display. Jake walks down the hill toward me with a silly smile.

"All right, my little ones," I begin, "here is the story told to me by my grandfather, who was told the story by his grandfather, and so on.

"Long ago, instead of land, there was the Sky World, where the Tree of Life grew laden with many kinds of fruit. Below the Sky World was a dark, watery world with flying birds and swimming animals.

"Sky Woman, wife of the Chief of Sky World, was expecting a baby. One night she dreamed that the Tree of Life was uprooted. The Chief interpreted her dream to mean that the people of Sky World should make this happen.

"Do Sky People still live in Sky World, Grandfather?" a little boy asks.

"Listen and you will learn," Molly intones, having heard this story before.

I continue, "The Chief urged the young men in the Sky World to uproot the tree, but they failed. Finally, the Chief of the Sky World summoned all of his strength and uprooted the tree himself. A huge hole formed, and the curious Sky Woman accidentally fell through it. As she fell through the hole, Sky Woman pulled seeds from the Tree of Life and held onto them tightly."

"Oh," all the children moan, thinking that Sky Woman had surely fallen to her death.

"As Sky Woman was falling, a flock of geese saw her, caught her on their backs, and lowered her toward the water. Thanking them, Sky Woman noted that she needed dirt to live on. Many water animals dove under the nearly bottomless waters to find some dirt, but each failed. Finally, one small creature, a muskrat, was able to bring a tiny bit of dirt up to Sky Woman. Sky Woman placed that dirt on the back of the Great Turtle, who had offered his shell as a resting place. As Sky Woman sang and danced on the turtle's back, the dirt and the shell grew larger and larger until it became the whole world."

"Yay!" all the children cheer.

"Sky Woman then spread the seeds she had pulled from the branches of the Tree of Life into the soil. When she finished, plant life on Earth began."

"Do we live on the back of the Great Turtle today, Grandfather?" a little girl asks.

"Yes, my little one. All that you see today is from that spot of dirt our brother the muskrat brought up from the sea and placed onto the Great Turtle's back."

The children eagerly dig into their corncakes as I take a moment to stand and stretch my legs. Seeing my difficulty in rising, the little girl who has been sitting directly in front of me offers her corncake, hoping that it will make me spryer.

When I return to my grassy seat, a young boy eagerly waves his hand. "Grandfather, tell us about good and evil."

All the children murmur. Most have never heard that part of the story.

I clear my throat, determined to tell the story in a way that will not scare the little ones. When I was young I heard the story from my grandfather, who left out no detail. The conflict of good and evil is frightening to a child. But it is part of the circle of life that I have a responsibility to teach.

"Soon Sky Woman gave birth to a daughter, Tekawerahkwa. Eventually the daughter became pregnant with twin sons by the Spirit of the West Wind. The twins were very different. The right-handed one, called Good Mind—or "Sapling" in some story versions—was soft-skinned and patient. The left-handed one, called "Bad Mind"—or "Flint"—had hard, tough skin and was very argumentative.

So intent are they to hear my words, the children stop eating.

"Good Mind was birthed the normal way, but Bad Mind forced his way through his mother's armpit, killing her. Sky Woman became terribly sad and angry. When she asked her grandsons who had done this terrible deed, Bad Mind lied, accusing Good Mind. Unfortunately, Sky Woman believed this lie and ordered Good Mind away from her sight."

"What happened to Sky Woman's daughter?" a little girl wonders aloud.

"Shush," Molly again whispers. "Be quiet and you will see," she says with a smile.

"Sky Woman put her dead daughter's head in the sky to become Grandmother Moon and buried the body, from which grew the three foods important to our people: corn, beans, and squash—the Three Sisters."

I pause, momentarily losing track of the story.

"And is not the beauty of our nation the result of Good Mind's work?" Maggie prompts me.

"Yes, after he was banished, Good Mind was not angry or bitter at his grandmother and resolved to spend his days making the earth beautiful. He created the rivers, the mountains, and the trees. He planted many vegetables, fruits, and healing herbs. He taught the birds to sing. He made rainbows and helpful rains. He became in charge of the day."

A little boy who had heard the story before immediately jumps to his feet, "And there was a fight between Good Mind and Bad Mind, was there not, Grandfather?"

"Yes, little one. There was a fight, a fight between Good and Evil that goes on even today. But let us clean up and get comfortable before I go on."

Maggie and Sarah help wipe the children's sticky hands with warm, wet towels. Now that they have finished their corncakes, many of them lie down on their bellies, propping up their heads with both hands under their chins.

"Watching his brother creating beauty, Bad Mind became envious. He set out to create the opposite of all the good his brother had made. Bad Mind made all that is bad, such as destructive storms, dangerous rivers, bony fish, thorns on berry bushes, and monsters. He planted poisonous roots. He became in charge of the night."

That same little boy impatiently shoots upright. "And…and?"

At that, little Mary also stands. "Why do you not sit down and be patient so that Grandfather can finish his story?"

All the children clap. Somewhat embarrassed, the little boy immediately falls to the ground and buries his face in the grass.

Seeing his embarrassment, I quickly add, "There is nothing wrong with being excited, especially over one of our great stories." I nod kindly at the little boy, who returns a sheepish smile.

"Let me continue. One day, Bad Mind took all the helpful animals and hid them in an underground cave. When Good Mind realized that all of these creatures were gone, he was very sad. A mouse told him what his brother had done. Good Mind went to the cave and caused the mountain to shake until it split and the animals were free. Good Mind was very angry with his brother, and they fought for many days. For weapons, Bad Mind used an arrow and Good Mind used a deer antler. Finally, Good Mind won."

With that the children spontaneously jump and cheer in celebration.

"Although Good Mind banished Bad Mind to live in caves beneath the Earth, the evil brother awaits to return to the surface where he will look for good little boys and girls to snatch," I conclude, quickly reaching out for the two nearest children. They instantly scream in terror but are reassured as I gently wrestle with them on the grass, laughing mightily. With that, all the children jump upon me joyfully.

"My children, my children, you are smothering your grandfather," I playfully cry.

Thinking that I am in real trouble, my own three girls attempt to pull the children from me as I lie on my back, gasping for air. They help me sit up and brush me off as I regain my composure.

"Thank you, my daughters. Sit down, everyone, and I will finish up for today," I say, brushing grass off my sleeves.

"I have one more question for you," a young girl with two long braids, her shoes off and her toes caressing the grass, quietly interrupts. "Grandfather, why do you not go to church?"

The children are aghast at her irreverence, although that is likely not what she intends. Perhaps sensing she has asked an impudent question, she quickly apologizes. "I am sorry, Grandfather. That is not my business."

I assure her that no insult is taken and try to end our session with some humor.

"Do you want to know why I don't go to church?"

"Yes," they all reply. My three girls, Mary, Molly, and Maggie, look at each other with trepidation, hoping that I will not be too insulting to the white man's religion.

"Long ago, when I was a young man, before any of you were born, an old, balding, bespectacled minister from Boston had preached fire and brimstone to us for weeks on end."

A young boy in long pants with one suspender attached and the other flopping off, inquires, "Grandfather, what is fire and brimstone?"

"Oh, you do not know what fire and brimstone is?" All the little heads shake negatively. "Fire and brimstone is shouting fear at the people. Every week, this minister promised we would burn in the flames of hell if we did not accept Jesus as our savior."

"Hell?" a quiet girl scared almost to tears asks. "Where is hell? Is it over the mountains?"

The rest of the small children, trembling at the thought of burning anywhere, draw closer together.

"Children, children," I say soothingly, "there is no such place. The white man tries to scare his people with death. If you do not believe in his god the way he wants you to, the white man says you will be punished by burning in hell. But be assured, we, the Indian people, do not fear death, which is part of the circle of life. If you walk the straight path of a human being, then you have nothing to fear. Upon your death, you will join your ancestors around the great council fires in the Sky World, which the white man and some of the people call heaven. There you will know joy, peace, and kinship. The great council fire is not there to burn you, but to draw you near to our people from past generations."

"What if someone does not walk the path of a human being?" a boy close to Molly's age inquires.

"Then that person's spirit is destined to walk the earth aimlessly, lost in the wilderness, without his people, without his ancestors, searching for the council fire that he will never find," I explain.

"And why don't you go to church, Grandfather?" Maggie reminds me.

"Oh yes, one Sunday after a particularly loud and fiery sermon, I approached the minister and asked, 'When you die, where are you going?' The minister confidently replied that he was going to heaven. He then asked where I wanted to go when I died. I hesitated, looked the old minister straight in the eye, and replied, 'I want to go to hell.'"

The children gasp in horror.

"Shocked, the minister asked me why. Do you know what I said to him?"

The children eagerly lean in to hear my answer.

"I said to the minister, 'Because if you are not there, then at least I can get a little peace and quiet.'"

Taking a moment to understand my meaning, the children begin to laugh a little, then uproariously as my message sinks in.

"Go off, get along, all of you," I laugh, as my three girls pull me up to my feet, my knees creaking the whole way. The children scamper in all directions to return home, to be with their mothers at the outdoor kitchen, or to collect nuts and berries for the next day's festivities.

18

A SACHEM'S DILEMMA

A boy nine or ten years of age, who lives across the valley and whose father had taken to the bottle after recently losing his job at the lumber mill, lingers behind. His hands fidget by his sides. His head bowed, his eyes staring at his shoes, he asks me, "Grandfather, will you please answer a question that has greatly troubled me?"

Gently attempting to pick up his chin, I glimpse the swollen bottom lip and the black-and-blue eyelid of a boy who has been beaten. Rarely are children spanked in our culture. Sometimes an unruly child may have water splashed onto his face but never beaten.

Holding my anger for the moment, I ask, "What bothers you, my son?"

"Grandfather, what so angered the white man's god that he allowed the soldiers to nail his son's hands and feet to a tree until he died?"

"Why do you ask such a question, my son?" I ask gently.

Hesitantly, he explains with obvious anguish, "I am worried that my father will get angry again and do that to me. The white man's laws will do nothing to punish him because their god allows such things."

I caringly place both of my hands on the tortured boy's shoulders with sincerity and sympathy, for I feel the pain in his heart.

A single tear rolls from each of his eyes.

So as not to patronize or embarrass him, I speak somewhat formally about the matter as if I were a philosopher. "I have often thought of your question. And after many years, I still do not understand why the white god allowed his son to be taken and killed in a most ghastly manner by enemy soldiers. Was he without power? Did he not care? Was he angry with his son? I do not know the answer. I will probably never know. The white ministers often explain that their god wanted his son to die for all men's sins. That is not in our nature. Placing such a great burden on one man is contrary to our beliefs and customs. We share all burdens together."

The boy looks disappointed. He believes that I, as Sachem, am wise and all-knowing. Surely I should have a better answer. But I am a man—no more, no less—with strengths and weaknesses such as all men possess. I am not the oracle he has hoped I would be.

Obviously disappointed that I have answered his question with more questions, the boy turns and slowly walks away. Unlike the other children, he is not eager to run home, where he will most likely be met with violence and abuse.

"My son," I call to him, "the Creator will watch over you and guide you. Listen to his direction. I can tell you now that he will never allow your father to nail you to a tree, nor will the people permit your father to abuse you anymore. Where is your mother?"

He points to the kitchen and begins to run away.

"Where is your father?" I shout before he disappears into the woods.

He points to the back of the kitchen where I spot three men who appear to be chopping wood. As I strain my eyes to recognize them, I notice the glint of the sun reflecting off a glass bottle. I suspect that the men are drinking more whiskey than they are chopping wood.

The boy runs back to me. With a frightened face, he hugs me around my knees. As he looks up at me, tears streaming down his face, I see that both eyes are misaligned in their sockets and their gaze peering somewhat toward his nose. I wonder if his father's beatings have caused the boy's eyes to move into this odd position. The thought enrages me even further.

So outraged am I by this boy's pain that I stomp over to where the men are supposed to be chopping wood for the many fires that will light up the sky tomorrow night. I see a nearly empty amber bottle by the chopping block. The three men sit on tree stumps, laughing as I approach. They become more serious as I stop in front of them.

One man slowly stands. "Great Sachem, are you here to chop wood? Surely that is a task beneath your greatness," he snickers as he teasingly holds out the wooden-handled log splitter. The other two begin to laugh, a reaction they will soon regret. More quickly than a flash of lightning, I grab the chopping maul from the unsuspecting man's hands and split a log with one chop, my follow-through intentionally shattering the bottle that lies near the chopping block and splattering its contents all over the ground.

Dropping the ax, I feign an apology. "Sorry, my brothers, for I did not notice your bottle. I guess I did not realize my own strength."

I intend to depart peacefully lest I use that ax to split their stupid heads, but the man who I suspect is the cross-eyed boy's father quickly pursues me.

"Hey, old man!" he shouts, roughly grabbing me by the shoulder and whirling me around. "That bottle cost me four bits."

Looking at his hand on my shoulder and then straight into his eyes, I speak softly but angrily, "Remove your hand from my shoulder, or I will break it."

This drunken wretch, now having drawn the unwanted attention of some of the people milling about the outdoor kitchen, fiercely exclaims, "You cannot tell me what I may do. You do not own me. I will teach you to mind your own business."

He draws his right arm back and attempts to throw a punch at me. But I quickly duck, simultaneously catching his hand in my own. I quickly step to the side and twist his arm behind his back. In one fluid motion, I spin him around, away from my face, and, with my boot firmly on his backside, shove him headlong into a tree. He bounces off the tree with a thud and collapses backward in a heap.

Before he can regain himself, I pounce on him with the speed and ferocity of a mountain lion, hold him to the ground by his throat, and angrily whisper in his ear, "Do not ever raise your hand in anger again, either to me or any of the people, especially your wife and son. If you do, I shall ask the council to banish you from this longhouse and our country. And do not think for a moment that the council and the clan mothers will not support me on this."

Finished with my warning and revolted by the stench of whiskey on his panting breath, I release him. Then an old woman quickly approaches us, wielding a cast-iron frying pan, not aimed at me, thankfully, but at this hapless shell of a man, whom she drives out of sight.

Still seething, I grumble something inaudible as I pass by the other two who make way for me with apologetically bowed heads. Wondering whether I have overstepped my bounds, I glance over at the clan mothers who say nothing and nod approvingly. I pass the boy's mother, who uncomfortably but I believe gratefully smiles. However, I am surprised at the expression I see on the young cross-eyed boy as I draw near him. He stares stone-faced at me, neither approvingly nor disapprovingly, for I have simultaneously embarrassed his father yet have saved him and his mother from further torment.

My adrenalin still surging, I stomp down the hill toward the road, my stride somewhat elongated by the slope of the hill. There I meet an awestricken Jake, standing in silence. He has never seen me raise a hand in anger in his life. I have always taught that physical punishment is unnecessary among a thinking, loving people. As I approach Jake, though he seems still apprehensive about my next intentions, as my hands are still trembling, I abruptly stop. To every observer including Jake's relief, I bend over, put my hands on my knees, and laugh uproariously.

Shocked at first by this sudden change in demeanor, Jake uncomfortably laughs with me, although I can tell from his expression he does not understand what is so funny. Regaining my composure, I stand erect and reach out one finger to scoop butter and honey off the tip of Jake's nose, probably unknowingly deposited there during his earlier romantic interlude with his own hands.

Putting my finger into my mouth, I exclaim with delight, "Umm! I guess I can use some sweetening up."

We both laugh again and embrace. As we walk arm in arm, I am comforted by Jake's strength, which steadies me after this emotional event. I abhor violence. It is contrary to our people's teachings. I pray to the Creator to forgive me and to grant me wisdom to abstain from future violence.

As I think about the cross-eyed boy, his mother, and the three drunken men, my heart grows heavy. Recognizing my melancholy, Jake smiles as if to say, *It's OK grandfather. You are only human.* But soon a pall falls over me again as I think, *By this time tomorrow, rather than honey and butter on his nose, Jake's body will be covered in dirt, sweat, and blood. He will transform from a lovesick boy to a warrior in one sun's passing.* I silently pray to the Creator to look favorably upon my grandson, to make him strong, and to protect him in the battle to come.

I squeeze Jake hard until he shouts in protest. I am not ready to let go of my grandson, physically or emotionally, but I know that I must, sooner or later. I just wish it were later.

19

GIFTS AND GRATITUDE

After helping the clan mothers clean up and after meeting with me under our sacred tree, Mary, Molly, and Maggie come running and tumbling down the grassy slope from the outdoor kitchen toward Jake and me. Giggling with her sisters the whole way, Mary playfully asks, "You two were not going to leave us here all alone, were you?"

Perhaps anticipating that Jake will present them with their gifts from Syracuse upon their arrival home, the girls seem eager to depart.

"Come on, Maggie! Last one home does not get a gift," Molly teases.

Maggie and Molly instantly fly down the road. Mary takes three steps and soon realizes that her little legs cannot keep pace with her older sisters. Disheartened, she falls to the road and begins to sob.

Seeing her distress, Jake quickly reaches for his lacrosse stick, slung over his shoulder with a deerskin thong. With one swift motion he draws his stick under Mary's bottom and scoops her up off the road. With supreme confidence and no hesitation, Jake flips Mary up and over his head, her bottom remaining firmly in the leather webbing of his stick as he carefully deposits her upon his shoulders.

Mary is stunned by the swiftness of her brother's actions. Momentarily dazed and now realizing that Jake has placed her on his broad shoulders, she squeals with delight. "Come on, horsey. Giddyap! After those two foxes ahead," Mary commands.

Pawing the ground, pretending to be old Thunder, Jake heads off. Mary holds Jake's braids as her reigns and urges him on with a few gentle kicks against his ribs and a tap on his shoulders.

"Faster, faster, they are getting away!" she shouts. Jake runs even faster until he catches up to and passes his other two sisters just before I lose sight of them over the hill.

I thank the Creator for this day and for the blessings of my grandchildren. I only wish that my daughter and her husband were alive to share in this happiness and to marvel at how well all four are walking our people's path of life.

As I approach our house, I see its many imperfections and shake my head, wondering whether Jake and I will be able to make all the repairs before the winter snows fall. Such a task as winterizing the house would be overwhelming were it not for the contentment I feel in the four beautiful children who dwell within.

I slowly walk up the weathered porch steps, wondering whether the creaking sounds come from the boards or my knees. I cautiously look down at the steps, which bend under the weight of my body. I am startled to see Jake waiting for me on the top step, wondering how he has appeared without the accompanying squeak of the screen door. Am I going deaf, or has he now developed the stealth of a warrior?

"Jake, are you so swift now that you appear without your grandfather hearing or seeing you?"

"Do not worry, Grandfather. You still have the senses of a hawk," Jake reassuringly replies, motioning toward the railing.

We both laugh as I see a grease can by the railing, still slightly dripping on the porch floor.

"I know how that squeaky screen door annoys you, Grandfather, especially when you are reading," Jake notes. "I do not want you to be disturbed when you read this."

From behind his back, Jake produces the most beautiful book I have ever seen, leather-bound and beautifully embossed in gold letters. I retrieve my reading glasses from my shirt pocket, gently placing them on my nose and around my ears. I read aloud, "*Moby Dick* by Herman Melville" and move one hand over the cover, feeling the depressed lines that outline the picture of a great white whale emerging from the depths below and crashing onto a large canoe filled with terrified men. I have heard of this book but have never read it. Observing that the terrified men carry what appear to be long spears, I quickly deduce that this is a book about hunting on the sea. I clutch the book to my chest and smile.

"I bought this book for you in Syracuse," Jake says proudly. "I hope it brings you much knowledge and pleasure."

I hug my grandson, proud of his thoughtfulness even though I already knew he had purchased the book in Syracuse. He has grown in so many ways this summer. But his first true test of manhood will come tomorrow in the Game.

Suddenly the girls pop out of the screen door like bunnies out of a hedge.

"Jake!" they all clamor. "Have you forgotten anything?"

"Ah, why, no, I do not think so," Jake pretends.

Crestfallen, the girls sadly turn away.

Never wanting his sisters to feel sadness for too long, even if part of a joke, Jake ends his charade with a feigned voice of surprise: "Oh, do you mean gifts from our trip to Syracuse?"

The three girls immediately whirl around, fondly grabbing and hugging Jake. Little Mary wraps herself around his legs like a vine.

"Wait! Stop!" Jake pleads, as he gently shakes them off. "Calm yourselves, my sisters. Now close your eyes."

As all three comply, Jake produces a pretty box from under his shirt. The girls stand breathlessly, hands to their mouths, not quite covering their smiles. Jake slowly opens the box.

Thrilled by the treasure within the box, the girls uncontrollably screech, "Which is mine?" not daring to touch the beautiful ribbons before Jake gives permission.

Sensing Jake's quandary as to which ribbon should be given to whom, I remind them, "The gift is given by the giver. It is not for you to take."

Understanding my meaning, Jake determines to distribute the ribbons one by one to each girl rather than risk their fighting over a particular one. He has obviously thought long and hard on the way back from Syracuse about which ribbon would best suit which sister. "First, to you, Mary, for you are the youngest, I give the white ribbon, which matches your bright smile and the purity of your heart." In her exuberance, Mary quickly snatches the white ribbon from Jake's hands, forgetting to thank him for the moment, and rubs her fingers up and down the long strand, cooing over its smoothness.

"And to you, Molly, my middle sister, destined to be a clan mother, I give the purple ribbon, for that is the color of the rulers of Europe about whom we read in Miss Doolittle's class." Molly delicately plucks the ribbon with just two fingers so as not to soil the exquisite fabric. She too has not yet thanked her brother.

"And finally, Maggie, my eldest sister and the best seamstress in our country, I give you the gold ribbon, for it denotes the wealth you have in your abundant talent." Maggie's eyes light up as the gold ribbon shines in the sunlight. The brightly colored ribbon seems to cast its own light. Maggie too is speechless.

"Two ribbons remain in the box, a blue one and a red one," I observe.

Mary always speaks what others are only thinking, for that is the privilege of youth. Folding her hands and gazing at the setting sun, she croons in a dreamy voice, "And blue is the color of my beloved's eyes, like a beautiful pool of water."

All three sisters begin to giggle as Mary playfully reaches into the box, pretending to snatch the blue ribbon, until her annoyed brother slaps away her hand.

"Hey, do not touch that ribbon, you little devil," Jake demands embarrassingly. I can see that Jake is angry at being mocked, especially after he has been so generous toward his sisters. He likely thinks they are ungrateful; however, I know they are only teasing him.

But Mary's song is the truth. Jake stares at the blue ribbon, and I can see he might be imagining Sarah's beautiful blue eyes, that are, indeed, like perfect pools of water. But he certainly needs not be reminded of his beloved by his sisters.

"And the red ribbon?" I inquire, rousing Jake from his dreamy stare.

"That is for Miss Doolittle, Grandfather. It will compliment her red hair," Jake explains.

I marvel at Jake's eloquence in his presentation of gifts. He is becoming a gifted speaker. A great speaker is motivated by his heart first, but his words must always be tempered with wisdom. I wonder whether Jake will be a Sachem one day or if he will leave the reservation and never return. I sigh at the thought of losing him to the outside world, but this is no time to become sentimental; we have things to do.

"Girls!" I call.

"Yes, Grandfather?" each responds as they return to the porch, busily tying their ribbons around their braided hair.

"Have you something to say to your brother?" I ask.

Embarrassed by their lack of manners and truly grateful for his generosity, all three simultaneously fling themselves upon their brother. Jake bends over so each can kiss him on his cheeks. Picking up Mary, Jake confirms, "You know, my sister, you are right about Sarah's eyes. They are as blue as this ribbon and a pool of water."

With hugs and kisses, little Mary whispers in her brother's ear, "I love you, my brother. I will always love you. I want to marry you someday."

But before Jake can explain to Mary that brother and sister do not marry each other, the other two girls echo in unison, "We love you, Jake," before vanishing inside.

"They know you love them, Jake," I say. "They are eager and proud to see you play in the Game tomorrow."

Jake sits down on the porch against the railing post, caressing the blue ribbon and looking off into space, undoubtedly dreaming about Sarah. I let him dream on for the moment, but soon he will need to direct his focus toward preparation for the Game.

I sit back in my rocking chair, reach for my corncob pipe, put the bowl in my tobacco pouch, and lightly pack it with my finger. I clean my spectacles on the sleeve of my shirt. I scrape a match along the arm of my rocking chair. The smell of sulfur fills the air as the match lights. I hold the match over rather than on the tobacco and slowly draw the smoke from the tobacco through the pipe stem into my mouth. Immediately calmed, I look at the beautiful, leather-bound book in my lap and wonder what happens to the fishermen who hunt the big white whale.

As I open the cover to begin reading, Jake, who has been sitting with back against the railing post and his eyes closed as the warm sun shines upon his face, hesitantly speaks. "Grandfather?"

I patiently set the book down and take off my glasses and sigh, for I suspect this conversation may be longer than answering one simple question.

"Yes, my son?" I patiently reply.

"That man today. Why...?"

I quickly interrupt, for I do not want to be reminded of my violent behavior, which was most unbecoming of a Sachem.

"My son, the white man is a trickster. He has cheated the red man from his ancestral lands since he came upon our shores. He has tried to force Christianity upon us, reviled our women, killed our fathers, and gouged Mother Earth for gold and minerals. At first we were strong in number and cared little about this puny, insignificant creature. As their numbers grew, we were forced to resist. For a while we were strong enough to stem the tide. But as more white men descended upon us like a plague of locusts devouring everything in their path, the Indian spirit began to break. Now there are just too many of them."

Jake looks at me, wondering what this has to do with a drunken Indian.

"The Indians' resistance has been further broken by the white man's diseases, against which we have few defenses. But his one poison, which some of the people have taken by choice and has been our greatest misery, is alcohol, usually found in a rum or whiskey bottle. The Indian warrior can tolerate the fear of battle, the pain of his wounds, hunger and thirst on the trail, and the exhaustion of the Game. But the Indian has no tolerance for whiskey. Many Indian chiefs have been deceived by the white man while under the influence of whiskey."

"But why do Indian men drink whiskey when it obviously makes them weak-minded and weak-spirited?" Jake asks.

I continue, "The greatest sadness is the effect of whiskey on the people's community and culture. I have witnessed the indignity of idleness and the lack of motivation in some Indian men who have become accustomed to the government dole on the reservation. Those men tend to numb their sorrows in a bottle. I have heard that the sickness of whiskey has plagued our brothers in the West who, less than twenty years ago, were the last of the truly 'wild' Indians before being herded onto the reservations. These brave warriors of the horse culture of the Plains, who lived freely and hunted buffalo, have been pacified on the reservation, in large measure by whiskey."

"Do you mean that government agents actually give the Indians whiskey, knowing its harmful effects?" Jake asks incredulously.

"Yes, my son, sadly, tis true. Some men on our reservation are not happy with farming, working in the mill or quarries, or even playing our Game. They long for something more, like fancy clothes, gold watches, beautiful buggies, and money, all the things the white man will lie, cheat, and steal for. But Indian men can never possess these trinkets that the white man holds more sacred than his own honor, his children, or his respect for the land and the Great Spirit's creations on earth."

"Why do Indian men drink if everyone knows it may mean their ruin?" Jake persists.

"It is this longing to be something else, to be somewhere else, that drives some of the people to whiskey, for in the bottle are dreams of things they can never have, places they will never go to, and people they can never be," I answer.

With great sadness, Jake rests his forehead on his hands splayed across the tops of his knees. I am heartened by his sense of empathy for our people's suffering.

"It is the sharing of our goods, the satisfaction of raising our children together, respecting Mother Earth, and having pride in ourselves as a people that is important. That, my son, cannot be found in a whiskey bottle," I say with assurance.

Jake nods to the truth of my words. No further discussion will be had on the subject. I am confident that Jake will never take to whiskey.

"Umm!" I remark hungrily, flaring my nostrils to draw in supper's familiar smells. "My nose tells me that your sisters are cooking up quite a meal. Eat heartily, my son, for this shall be your last food before the Game. Fasting is the first part of the pregame ritual."

"Eat? But I have my other gifts to deliver," Jake screams in a panic. Here, Grandfather, warm gloves. Hope you like them." Jake hurriedly throws them into my lap. Before I can thank him, Jake is running down the road and over the hill.

Miss Doolittle and Sarah are the last two recipients of Jake's gifts. At the Green Corn Festival, they both make it a point to share with me how impressed they are with Jake's generosity and kindness. Miss Doolittle has previously made it clear that she is impressed with Jake's scholarship and hopes that he may attend a university someday. In her manner of speech, Sarah hints that I approach the clan mothers with the idea of a betrothal.

Jake arrives at the schoolhouse just as Miss Doolittle is closing the front door broom in hand apparently after a day of cleaning in preparation of the students' return on Monday.

"Miss Doolittle! Miss Doolittle! Wait!"

Miss Doolittle is delighted to see Jake waving at her.

"Well, Jake, are you getting in a last run before the Game tomorrow?" she asks.

"No, ma'am, although running is always good for me. I have much to prepare for before tomorrow, but I want to give this to you now." Jake holds up the red ribbon from Syracuse.

"Oh my," Miss Doolittle coos. "How shiny and smooth!" Holding it up to her hair, she asks, "How do I look?"

Miss Doolittle confesses to me that she probably made Jake feel a bit uncomfortable asking him to comment on her looks. After all, she is his teacher, not…not…a woman…with…looks. Perhaps sensing Jake's discomfort, Miss Doolittle inquires about his trip to Syracuse and other gifts he may have purchased.

"Gifts? Oh, I almost forgot. Well, I hope you wear your ribbon well…er…often…er…in your hair. Bye, Miss Doolittle," Jake shouts, heading again down the road.

Jake sprints to Sarah's cabin, reaching into his pockets for her gifts from Syracuse.

Looking pleasantly surprised, Sarah eagerly waves. "Jake, why do you run so? Are the spirits of the woods chasing you?" she inquires, looking around him to ascertain if her playful musings may be true.

"No. No, I am not chased. I am hurried by my many preparations for tomorrow's Game."

"Well, why do you hurry so to me?" she continues, perhaps hoping that Jake will finally muster the courage to say those words she longs to hear.

"Here, I hope you like them." Jake extends his hand, which holds a small box. Inside are the silver North Star earrings, around which he has wrapped the dark-blue ribbon in a bow.

No sooner does Sarah grasp the box, and Jake is again quickly on his way.

"What? Jake? Wait!" she shouts as he speeds up the trail toward his house. "Thank you," she shouts in the direction of the disappearing boy. Opening the box, Sarah cries out at the sight of the beautiful North Star earrings. She clutches the box to her chest and turns toward her father, who sits very still, barely rocking in his chair.

"Do you see, father?" she says tenderly, showing her gifts to his blank eyes. "Jake loves me, and I love him," she proclaims as she runs into the house. I wonder if the old man understands her words.

20

A WARRIOR REVEALED

Jake bounds up the porch stairs, sweating and breathless. "Have I missed it? Supper?"

"No," I reassure him. "It is ready now. Come, let us go inside!"

I sense the beginning of Jake's nervousness about the next day's Game. He uncomfortably smiles, opens the screen door, and gestures that I enter first.

The girls pounce upon a surprised Jake, shouting, "Now it is your turn to close your eyes."

With my arm around his shoulders, I guide Jake into the kitchen. The three girls proudly stand in front of the kitchen table. Depositing Jake before them, I step back and let them proceed.

As they step aside, they proudly beg in unison, "Open your eyes!"

There before him, Jake beholds the most sumptuous, mouth-watering repast of his life: cut yellow squash fried in bacon fat with wild onions; medallions of our brother the deer that we had arrowed a few days earlier, now stewed with carrots and beans; hot corn bread and honey; and pitchers of sparkling water and steaming sassafras tea.

"This is one way to thank you, my brother, for your gifts to us," Maggie says with collective pride.

"A warrior must have strength for the Game, my brother," Molly explains. "We pray that you will play with the speed and cunning of our brother the deer, of whom we partake."

Little Mary adds proudly, "I gathered the sassafras for the tea."

We all sit down to the table, not one child reaching for a single morsel before I give thanks to the Creator.

"Oh, Great Spirit, we thank you for your many blessings. Look favorably upon this family. But most of all, please guide and protect Jake, who plays in the Game tomorrow. Give him strength and courage. Let his ancestors, who sit at the council fires in the Sky World, be proud of their son, who tomorrow will be recognized as a man."

Jake takes a deep, anxious breath and wipes his sweaty palms on his trousers. I smile at him, indicating that I understand his emotions.

As the meal progresses I watch the girls, who hardly eat and mostly giggle, configuring their ribbons into different bow styles around their long black braids.

Jake sits silently, chewing his food more slowly than usual. I know he is deep in thought. I decide to ease his tension with a story.

"I remember my first Game with the men of my tribe over fifty summers ago. It was during the time when the Americans were fighting each other, one war that our people smartly stayed out of."

The girls, now finished eating, could care less about another one of my many "war" stories about ancient times; they excuse themselves and quickly begin to remove their plates to the wash-tub. Jake, continuing to eat slowly and patiently, respectfully listens to my story.

"I remember the night before my first Game. It was during the time of the Green Corn Festival, like now. Our Grandmother the Moon was full but not white; she was a bluish color. I wondered if this was a good omen or bad omen, but nobody could say for sure. I felt as if bees were in my belly. I felt the blood racing through the veins in my hands, neck, and head, which made me hot. I was forced to consciously regulate my unnaturally rapid breathing lest I pass out."

"Excuse me, Grandfather," Jake interrupts. "I have a tightness in my belly right now. Is that what you are describing?"

"Yes, my son. I remember my mother's meal, much like this one but without salt, pepper, or beef on our plates, for the white man's Civil War had redirected provisions normally earmarked for the reservation to the front lines for the soldiers. The white man would not starve his war. It was much easier to starve the Indian."

"But, Grandfather, we have always had our brother the deer, the rabbit, even the elk, as well as the fish in our streams," Jake comments.

"Yes, we, more than many of our Indian brothers to the east and the west, have been self-sufficient on our own lands. We have never been as dependent upon the white man's 'generosity' as others. We have hunted deer, which remain plentiful. We were not wholly dependent upon one resource like the buffalo, which the white man decimated, causing the decline of our brothers in the West. We grew our own crops in fertile ground and were blessed with fish-filled ponds. I have read that our Indian brothers in the Southwest were forced to live on rattlesnakes and rodents when the buffalo were killed or driven off. Their land was unfit to grow anything, even if they had a mind to. Thankfully, our lands have always produced bountiful harvests."

The girls continue to scurry around, cleaning their plates, the pots, and the pans so that they can return to preparing their clothes for the next evening. Jake sits quietly, his stomach so tight that he cannot eat another morsel.

"Grandfather, I am sad when I think about our brothers in the West who have been stripped of their warrior spirit."

"The warriors of the horse culture of the West, who were finally rounded up onto reservations, fell into despair, poverty, and depression. Many of them took to whiskey. On the reservation, these once-proud warriors were reduced to beggars. Their horses, bows, guns, and scalping knives were taken from them. They became walking ghosts without identity. Every day they sang their death songs."

"But it has not been so for us, has it, Grandfather?" Jake reassuringly asks.

"We, the Haudenosaunee, have maintained at least some semblance of our father's warrior spirit through the Game. The Game gives our young men a sense of pride, purpose, and worth. The Game allows a young man to unleash his warrior spirit, his trophy being victory instead of a scalp."

"Has not the Game changed since your day, Grandfather?" Jake inquires. Hearing my voice probably has a calming effect on Jake's nervousness. "Oh, yes," I reply with a laugh. "In my time we played almost an entire day. Tomorrow we will play for about two hours. Our ball was made of deerskin woven very tightly around the knot of a tree or smooth stone. Tomorrow we shall use a ball that is made of rubber hardened from the sap of a tree that grows in the Amazon forests of South America."

"The field was bigger, was it not, Grandfather?" Jake prompts me along.

"Yes, I imagine so. I remember some of the men affixing bear claws to their sticks for strength, or birds' feathers for speed, even an owl's beak for clearer eyesight. We once played a team from the Great Lakes region. The players wore belts of woven horsehair upon which they hung horsetails that fell down their backsides. In my first Game, there were no side boundaries to our field. Our vertical boundary was the goal, which was a single stick that we struck with the ball. Tomorrow we will string nets, like fishing nets, hung upon six-foot-by-six-foot wooden goals. Our field is about one hundred fifty paces from goal to goal and about seventy-five paces wide. While many played in my day, tomorrow we will field ten braves from each team, including the goal protector."

"Some of the old men scoff at the new game that we play, Grandfather. They say we are soft and have submitted to the white man's rules. Is that true?" Jake worriedly asks.

With a laugh, I answer, "Every generation thinks they are stronger and tougher and have lived more harshly than the succeeding generation, whom they think they have spoiled. But the world, like our Game, changes. Nothing stays the same. The modern rules are the rules that the six tribes of the Haudenosaunee have adopted. These rules were developed by white Canadians, who formed club teams many seasons ago. Our Indian brothers to the north, who desired to compete against the white man's teams, slowly began to adopt their rules. Now not only have the white men of Canada adopted our Game, but the white men of England and the Americans have as well."

"But this will always be our Game, will it not, Grandfather?" Jake asks, now intently enjoying my history and anticipating my answers.

"This is our Game, given to us by the Creator. Although our Game has many names, white and Indian people alike now universally know it as lacrosse. The Onondaga name for lacrosse is *Dehuntshigwa'es,* but each of the six tribes of our nation has a different name for the Game. The people of the Great Lakes call the Game *Bagadowe,* which they say means 'bumping of hips.' The people of the Eastern Woodlands and the Southeast have called our Game *Teiontsesiksaheks.* The Eastern Cherokee, who use two sticks, call the Game *Da-na-wah'uwsdi.* Our Game seems to be the only aspect of Indian culture that the white man covets but cannot own. This shows the truth of the Game. The Game not only provides relatively peaceful competition between the whites and Indians but also creates a bond between the players of different cultures like no other activity. Jake, are you listening?"

Jake jumps from a trancelike stare. Has he drifted back in time on the words of my stories?

"Finish your tea, my son, for soon you must offer your sweat to the Creator. Girls, clear the table and sweep the floor, making clean that which is about to receive your brother's hair. Bring a pot of warm water to me as well," I direct.

Jake has both dreaded and looked forward to this moment.

The girls immediately respond to my requests, for they know and appreciate the solemnity of this time-honored ritual.

"Jake, are you ready?" I ask.

"Yes, Grandfather," Jake replies with trepidation.

"Remove your shirt," I tell him. "Molly, turn up the lamp. Maggie, get my leather strap."

"And me, Grandfather?" Mary asks. "What may I do for my brother?"

"Look upon your brother with your sweet eyes, for before you there is a boy. When you awake tomorrow, you will see a young man."

Little Mary reaches out, takes her brother's warm hands from his trembling knees, and places them on either side of her face. She looks at her brother with sorrow because she knows that Jake will no longer be just her brother anymore. Soon he will assume the mantle of a young brave with greater responsibilities to his people. She fears he will no longer spend frivolous time with her.

"I will show you girls how this is done. One day you will be required to do the same for your husbands in preparation for the Game," I explain.

Mary joins her sisters around the kitchen table.

"Are you afraid, my brother?" Mary asks.

Both girls playfully snap at her, "Our brother is afraid of nothing."

"Well," Mary insists, "will you be sad?"

"Sad over what, little sister?" Jake asks.

"Your hair," she whispers.

Jake is silent.

I sharpen the pearl-handled straight razor against my cowhide leather strap.

"Are you ready, my son?" I question.

"Yes, Grandfather," Jake says shakily, closing his eyes.

Just as I am about to put the newly sharpened blade to his temple, a knock sounds on the screen door. Everyone jumps. Breathing a sigh of relief – Sarah enters.

"No! I do not want Sarah to see this, Grandfather," Jake begs.

"Jake, calm yourself, my son. She is part of this ritual tonight. I have invited her here to share in your preparation. She, like the other girls, must learn how to do this for her husband someday."

Jake looks at Sarah, who lovingly smiles back at him. For a moment, Jake drifts off, likely imagining Sarah as his wife—shaving his temples and arranging his tuft of hair before the Game.

"Jake, if my presence here upsets you, I will leave," Sarah says, likely hoping she will not be dismissed.

"No, Sarah, forgive me. I do not wish to be rude. Please sit down with my sisters." The girls eagerly make room for Sarah, whom they love as a sister.

Jake's legs begin to shake, his pants fluttering. "It must be getting cooler outside. I am shaking," Jake vainly explains.

"Calm yourself, Jake. We understand the difficulty in parting with something you have had your whole life."

Mary covers her eyes with her hands and squeals, "I cannot bear to watch."

"When my hair was cut, I remember losing my sense of identity but instantly adopting a new one. I remember my hair falling to the floor as my mother cut and shaved. I remember my sisters crying, for they had lost a childhood friend in their brother, who now sat before them a young man."

I take my first swipe with my razor. As the first locks of Jake's hair, which hangs down below his shoulders, falls to the floor, the girls close their eyes, as does Jake. Only Sarah keeps her eyes open, eagerly watching a warrior—her warrior—emerge.

"There, done," I proclaim proudly, stepping back to admire my work. After wiping the last remnants of his hair from the razor, I hand Jake a small mirror. The girls and Jake now open their eyes. Their faces, wide-eyed with mouths agape, startle Jake. Who is this stranger they are looking at?

Only Sarah steadily gazes upon Jake, looking lost in her dreams of Jake becoming a man, the man she hopes she will marry someday. She is clearly so grateful to be part of this family ritual.

"Girls, stop staring. Retrieve those towels from the kettle, and gently place them around your brother's head," I instruct.

Molly and Maggie swathe Jake's head and face in hot, wet towels. A few nicks of blood around Jake's temples soon close after Sarah gently massages a generous lump of butter onto his scalp.

Mary pushes the mirror toward Jake's face. At first shocked to see space where beautiful, long black hair had just been, Jake moves his head slightly side to side and nods approvingly. A three-inch-wide tuft of hair runs down the middle of his head, trailing down upon his shoulders.

Jake looks to Sarah, whose reaction matters the most. She beams the widest smile of pride, nodding her head approvingly. No words need be spoken.

"How do I look, Grandfather?" Jake asks, as he slowly rises to his feet, caressing the smooth skin on both sides of his head with both hands.

I close the razor, put it in my coat pocket, take Jake by the shoulders, and simply confirm, "Like a warrior, my son, like a warrior.

"I recall my first shave when I first played in the big Game," I continue. "I heard stories from the old men who wore their hair differently during the time when the white man first arrived in our country. They shaved their heads but for a single tuft of hair on the top near the back of their heads, where most white men start to bald. They called this tuft of hair a 'scalp lock.' The men explained that this hairstyle of old was to facilitate scalping by our enemies should we fall honorably in battle. Our enemy, the Huron, and some of our brothers in the Eastern Woodlands of the Algonquin tribes similarly cut their hair in those days."

"Grandfather, I am ready to go now," Jake says proudly.

"Patience, my son. We will go soon. The fire is heating at our ceremonial sweat lodge. But I invited Sarah here for a reason."

All eyes look upon Sarah. She reaches into her deerskin pouch and produces an animal fur.

Sarah begins, "Although my father has a sickness that has rendered his hair white and robbed him of his capacity to speak, he somehow knows that Jake is about to play in his first Game with the men. He has trapped our brother the porcupine and skinned it in Jake's honor."

She spreads the porcupine pelt on the table, the quills black with white tips stiffly stick up from the tanned hide. It is cut narrowly to follow the path of Jake's remaining tuft of hair.

"May I place it upon you, Jake?" Sarah asks reverently.

Jake nods and returns to the kitchen chair. Maggie holds up the mirror as Sarah places the porcupine headpiece squarely down the middle of Jake's head. Four leather thongs affix the skin to Jake's scalp, the front ones tying under his chin and the back ones around his hair to hold the headpiece firmly during the rigors of play the next day.

Looking into the mirror, Jake beams with pride.

Their eyes meeting, Jake and Sarah silently communicate their love.

"Thank you, Sarah. I already feel the strength of my prickly brother the porcupine. Through this 'roach,' his spirit will help me fend off my opponents tomorrow as I slash my way through their numbers."

"Jake, we have something more for you," I announce with pride.

"Grandfather, what more can one person receive in one day?" Jake asks incredulously.

"Just a bauble I picked up in Syracuse," I reply.

From my coat pocket I produce a silver earring. It may have been fashioned for a woman in the white man's world, but in our world a man traditionally adorns his face with necklaces, bead-and-bone chokers, nose rings, and earrings.

"I will place it through your ear," I say calmly as I sense Jake's nervousness once again. "Maggie, one of your sewing needles, please," I request.

With tongs, Maggie holds one of her sewing needles in the fire until it is red-hot.

"Molly, please bring me a small piece of birch bark from the tree outside yonder," I direct, pointing with my chin toward the front yard.

"Sit one more time, my son. The pain lasts for a few seconds only. Do not cry out or whimper. A warrior never shows his pain to another."

Holding the red-hot needle with a leather patch, I place a small piece of birch bark behind Jake's left earlobe and pierce the fleshy part of his lobe with the searing pin. I push the needle in and out several times to assure that the hole will remain open. Unlatching the silver earring, I place the post through the hole. A dab of butter and honey stops the trickle of blood and seals the hole. Closing his eyes tightly and breathing deeply, Jake neither whimpers nor moves.

Once again Jake examines his face in the mirror that Mary proudly holds for him. Jake is now visually transformed. Minutes ago, his boyish looks had been accented by the long black hair of his youth. Now, with his shaved temples, porcupine roach, and silver earring, he resembles Hiawatha, our ancient chief. His jaw seems more squared, his neck thicker, and his shoulders wider.

But the visual change to Jake's face and head are only the beginning of his transformation on this night.

"Well now that you are finished admiring yourself in the mirror, shall we go?" I playfully ask.

Embarrassed at his vanity, Jake confidently announces, in a somewhat unnatural deep voice, "Yes, I am ready, Grandfather."

"We will be home before midnight," I say to the girls. "This young warrior needs his sleep before the big Game tomorrow."

I kneel on the floor with creaking knees, awaiting my usual departure hug from Mary. It will not be long before, like her older sisters, she will not run and jump into my arms but merely meander toward me and peck me on the cheek as part of her filial duty. I love the two older girls and am comforted by their courtesies, but nothing compares to the joyful dashes into my arms by my squirming chipmunk Mary.

"We are going to finish our dresses for the Green Corn Festival," Maggie informs me.

"May Sarah stay with us, Grandfather, to finish her work here?" Molly asks.

"Yes," I quickly agree, "as long as her father is taken care of for the evening."

"Yes, Grandfather. I have set out soup and cornbread for him. The firewood is chopped and gathered. A bucket of cool water with a ladle remains by his rocker. He had been singing in a low tone when I left for here," Sarah explains.

"If he sings, he is happy, my child," I confirm. "You are a good daughter and a fine young woman."

The girls quickly return to their bedroom as I prepare to exit through the screen door. Only Sarah remains behind. Feet together, hands clasped in front of her, her head slightly bowed, I see her eyes meet Jake's eyes as he quickly returns the magnificent roach to the table lest it wilt in the heat of the sweat lodge. He then follows me out. Straining his neck for one last glimpse of her, Jake leaves with the confidence and demeanor of a warrior.

21

THE SWEAT LODGE

Outside and in private, Jake strips away his clothes and with my help puts on one of my old loincloths.

As we walk together, on the meandering white road, I inhale the night's cool air through my nose, preparing to speak, but Jake preempts me.

"Her eyes," he says dreamily.

"Excuse me?" I ask, clearing my throat.

"Her eyes, Grandfather. Have you ever noticed Sarah's eyes?"

"I have not taken particular notice of Sarah's eyes. They are blue, are they not?" I ask with feigned ignorance. "Why do her eyes captivate you so?"

"Grandfather, her eyes are blue, not like the sky but like our sacred pond on a rainy day—almost purple, like the water," Jake describes.

"I see more than that, my son," I reply.

"You see a different color too, Grandfather?" Jake asks.

"Yes, her eyes are a deep blue—almost purple like our sacred pond on a rainy day. But more than that, I see the eyes of a selfless maiden who tends her fields, sews, cooks, attends school, and cares for her ill father, all accomplished without complaint and no less for the wear. She carries herself gracefully. Her words are thoughtful and kind. I see her heart through her eyes. Every time she looks at you, I see her heart."

Jake's attention immediately perks up.

"Really, Grandfather? Do you believe her heart is for me?" Jake begs.

"Enough of this talk now. There is a time for love and a time for war. We must prepare you for the coming battle. You must make certain that nothing from this moment forward will interfere with your thoughts and dreams of the Game."

We continue silently down the dirt road that slithers through the forest like a great white snake.

"The fullness of our Grandmother the Moon is revealed behind those scattered clouds and lights our path well tonight," I note.

Jake does not reply, which a good sign. Jake is beginning to transcend the mundane routine of daily living and enter the spiritual world of the warrior.

I begin to sing a song about long-ago battles. Jake hums along, singing some of the words that he remembers. Our walk slowly transforms into the dance steps of Haudenosaunee men. We tap our hands on our thighs in unison to replicate a drumbeat. Our voices ring out in the stillness of the night. I nod approvingly as Jake sings and dances with me.

Before long, we arrive at the longhouse and outdoor kitchen, where we spent much of our morning and afternoon. Behind the longhouse stands the sweat lodge built many seasons ago by our fathers.

The creatures of the forest are still now. Only the sound of the wind blowing through the trees punctuates the quiet of the night. We hear the low drone of a singer from within the sweat lodge. Jake stops, breathing more heavily and swallowing with difficulty, clearly nervous about entering the mythical sweat lodge. Never had he, or any other boy, dare enter the sweat lodge until invited lest he suffer severe punishment by the men.

"Grandfather, what do I do when I enter? What am I to say?"

"Be yourself, my son. Be true to your heart. When within, thank the braves for inviting you but only after the elders have spoken. Then sweat, think, and clear your mind of all things but the Game. Visualize how you will play tomorrow and it will be so. Sing if you wish. Dream if you will. Take strength in the men who will be around you, for they are now your brothers-in-arms. You will now sit as a young man among men."

I put my arm around Jake's shoulder and urge him toward the sweat lodge entrance. We see smoke billowing from the hole in the roof and smell the aroma of burning apple wood and herbs.

"Wait here."

I enter the sweat lodge. All eyes from within turn toward me. All but Jake and one other have arrived. Bare-breasted, the men sit with their legs folded under their loincloths. Their bodies drip with sweat.

The men greet me in one loud, "Haiah." I greet each man with my left hand raised, as is our custom. No one rises, the respect typically accorded a Sachem. Here there are no Sachems, just brave players of the Creator's Game, all equal in his eyes.

"Brothers, I proudly stand before you as Grandfather and advisor of a young man whom you have invited to take his place with you as a man here in the sweat lodge and on the field tomorrow. I thank you for this honor."

An elder arises and asks whether anyone among them objects to Jake's presence. Seeing none, the elder nods to me.

"Jake! Enter!" I command.

Jake pulls back the deerskin flap, bends forward, and enters. He stands straight, his legs firmly planted and his fists clenched by his sides. The reflection of the fire and burning coals upon his face causes the white, shaven sides of his head to glow. I have never seen such fierceness in his eyes.

"You are the grandson of a Sachem," a white-haired elder of eighty or more winters begins, "but you have no privilege here." Pointing around to each man, he continues, "We, like our warrior ancestors before us, have kept the peace with the white man as had been promised by Chief Corn Planter over 130 winters ago. We have redirected our warriors' natural energy to fight and to kill into the Game given to us by the Creator. In his honor, we play the Game as fiercely as our forefathers fought in battle. We play to help cure the sick and to grow the crops. But mostly, we play because..." He hesitates. "Because we can get out of our houses and away from our wives' sharp tongues for a while."

All laugh readily at such irreverence that only a man of many years can get away with.

Jake does not know whether to laugh or to remain silent. He is probably perplexed as to why a man would want to be away from his beautiful, loving wife.

"Sit here, my son, between me and your grandfather," the old man continues. "We sit in a circle that reflects our unity and equality. The heat of the burning rocks will draw what little evil may dwell within such a young body. The sweat is evidence of your purification. If you are lost to us tomorrow by some tragic accident and are called to our ancestors' council fires in the Sky World, let it not be said that we sent a dirty Indian to the heavens."

The men laugh again at the remarks of this wise but appropriately irreverent old man.

Jake seems to instantly like this old man who tries to lighten the overwhelming seriousness of the occasion with some humor. Jake smiles uncomfortably, sensing that the night's entertainment may be at his expense—sort of an initiation. Players are hazed in such a way. Ultimately, each man in this lodge would die for any brother, including his newest brother, Jake. Each man, that is, but the one who last walks through the sweathouse flap to sit among us.

"Aiee! Youngblood," the men eagerly call out. Jake's chest heaves with apprehension. Everything had seemed perfect until now.

"Youngblood," the elder begins, "this is—"

"I know who he is," Youngblood interrupts. "Welcome, young pup. Do not sit too close to the burning rocks lest you melt like the last pure snow on a spring day," Youngblood disdainfully warns.

The men laugh again, although this time not as heartily as before. The tension between him and Jake is immediately and unexplainably palpable.

Some of the men look to Jake, wondering whether he possesses the temerity to offer a sharp rebuke or rejoinder to Youngblood's disrespectful words. But Jake sits silently. The previous joviality clearly has been dampened by this sudden expression of hostility.

The men return their gaze to the burning rocks in silence, save the occasional song or murmurings of a brave who sits trancelike in the dream world.

As sweat begins to drip from my face, I see that Jake curiously glances around the sweat lodge at each man, undoubtedly wondering what each is thinking. The sweat lodge is where the players last meet before the great Game. Here they bond as one. Here they dream of greatness and bravery.

Here also a brave may bare his heart and express his fears so that his brothers may renew his strength. The group's silence is disturbed by the sobbing of one of the braves, Brown Otter, who laments about an injury to his right hand in the mill. The brother player to his left, Leo Man Killer, takes hold of the hand, spits on it, grabs a handful of burning ash, and rubs it on the hand as he locks eyes with Brown Otter. Neither man cries out in pain. Brushing the burning ash from his right hand, Leo states,

"That is why the Creator possessed the wisdom to give man a left hand."

The men chuckle.

Another brave, John Fast Elk, a generally jovial and ever-smiling brave, sternly expresses his desire to speak. So grave is his expression that a foreboding sweeps over the group. Clearing his voice, he begins, "I am concerned that my manhood is so long I may trip over it tomorrow."

In momentary silence the men do not know whether to laugh or throw dirt upon him for saying something so foolish. Another brave pulls a knife from under his loincloth and holds it up to Fast Elk. "This ought to make you swifter," he says swishing the knife through the air dangerously close to Fast Elk's loincloth.

Sometimes a little playfulness relieves the nervousness some of the men feel. The men chuckle but are quickly interrupted by Youngblood.

"Enough of this banter. If your thoughts are not on the Game alone, then you do not belong here."

The two braves embarrassingly nod and return their gaze to the burning rocks.

Youngblood is correct. It is time to focus all energies on the Game. However, Youngblood's tone of voice is too demanding, too harsh to have been spoken by a brother.

Jake's eyes are now closed. Sweat drips from the tip of his nose and chin. I cannot tell if he is breathing. Although he appears to be sleeping, he may be in a trance.

A dream is the most sacred event in the sweat lodge. Few ever reach the world of dreams, but if and when they do, all who are present recognize that experience as extraordinarily special.

The elder who had previously spoken nods approvingly as my eyes redirect from Jake to him. The other men, who also see Jake in his trance, smile, nudge each other, and grunt their approval.

All but one. Youngblood's foreboding gaze is not focused upon the burning coals, but upon Jake. His dead, grayish eye turns red from the reflection of the burning stones. His glare is so menacing that he resembles a frightening evil spirit.

What enmity lies between Jake and Youngblood? What has caused such hatred? Whatever it is, and before it becomes disruptive to the harmony of the circle, I decide to break Youngblood's stare with a song.

I repeat the verse in a low drone. As hoped, my song diverts Youngblood's hot eye toward me, then toward the burning rocks, and, most importantly, away from Jake.

Strangely, I see only space where I have last seen Jake's sitting body. To my astonishment, he is now lying flat on his back with his legs still crossed under his loincloth. I marvel at such flexibility. Jake appears peaceful.

His peace is soon disturbed as he begins to twitch and to murmur. He is not singing, for there is no melody. No one dares wake Jake because he may be dreaming a portent of events to come in the morning.

Jake begins to mumble more loudly. His face contorts as if in pain, and his head turns quickly from side to side. My friend the elder holds me back, as I am tempted to arise to comfort my grandson. Jake next begins to writhe as if he is being stabbed all over. His crossed legs stiffen out straight in front of him; his clenched fists bang on his sides.

"No!" Jake screams. Frightened, some of the men sitting close to him stand. Suddenly, Jake jerks up to a sitting position. His eyes are wide open, but blank. His mouth is open, his breathing is rapid, but he is not awake. Then, just as suddenly as he sat up, he collapses onto his back again.

All within the sweat lodge stare at Jake in silence. Then Youngblood speaks.

"This boy is not ready to play our Creator's Game among men. He has nightmares like a child."

The elder quickly chastises Youngblood. "That is not for you to say. How do you know what this young warrior dreams? He may have had a vision of tomorrow's events."

"Then why is he frightened?" Youngblood quickly retorts. "There is joy in victory, not fear." He stares at Jake with disdain.

"I have sweated enough, my brothers. Who will bathe with me in our sacred pond?" one of the braves asks, an attempt to break this unhealthy tension.

"Aiee!" they all cheer as they stream from the sweat lodge. Only the elder and I remain. We kneel over each side of Jake's limp body.

The elder begins singing and shaking a turtle-shell rattle filled with corn kernels. I wipe the sweat from Jake's face with a wet cloth. Soon Jake's eyes flutter open.

"The Creator has returned him to us!" the elder exclaims with joy.

"Jake," I whisper, sliding my arm under his head, "Jake, can you hear me?"

"Grandfather?" he replies, his eyes focusing.

"Yes, I am here, my son."

"What has happened? Where have my brothers gone?" he asks, seeing no other braves.

"They have gone to wash away their sweat in our sacred pond. Are you strong enough to join them?" I inquire.

"Yes, I think so," Jake says hesitantly.

The elder and I take both of Jake's arms and help him to his feet. He shakes the sweat from his face and body like a wet dog.

"Let us walk softly into the cool air, my son," I suggest.

As we help Jake through the lodge flap into the night's air, I see the life instantaneously surge back into him. Standing erect with nostrils flared, he deeply inhales the night's cool air through his nose and exhales through his mouth. He repeats this several times, returning the color to his face. He seems renewed.

"Are you strong enough to walk unassisted?" I ask quietly.

"Yes, Grandfather. Where is my lacrosse stick?"

"I have it here. Take it to the sacred pond where we shall bless you and your stick," I direct Jake.

As his eyes become acclimated to the darkness, Jake's slow walk changes to a run and then to a dangerously quick dash through the dark woods on a path with many holes. Jake miraculously dodges or jumps over each one without a stumble, as if he has developed a wolf's night vision or is guided from above.

Reaching the pond, Jake dives in headlong, startling the other braves. They hoot and shout with joy as Jake emerges from under the deep-purple water. Except for Youngblood, the braves seem to be concerned about Jake's health after his extraordinary experience in the sweat lodge.

"Did you have a vision?" one brave asks.

"I…I…I…don't know—" Jake begins but is then interrupted.

"What did you see?" another inquires.

Before Jake can respond, a third brave demands, "Did you see victory?"

Now everyone stops splashing and talking, anxiously awaiting Jake's response.

The silence is broken by the elder's quavering voice. "No man can ask another about his dream or vision. That is private to the individual. If and when a warrior wishes to reveal his vision, he will do so when the Creator wills it so. Now all of you bring your lacrosse sticks to this rock upon which I stand. Here I shall bless you and your sticks."

Sprinkling some burning herbs, sage, and a little tobacco upon the men and the sticks they now hold in their hands, the old man sings, "Oh, Great Spirit. Look favorably upon our warriors. Make them strong. Give them speed. Bring our people victory."

"Aiee!" all the braves cheer, careful that the leather webbings of their sticks do not get wet, which would tighten their laces and reduce their perfectly formed pockets. Even a slightly misshapen pocket may cause a bad pass or a missed goal.

"My sons," the elder calls out, "leave this place for now. I will look for you here after the Game tomorrow so that your wounds may be healed and that you may take a victory swim."

"Aiee!" the men shout back in unison.

I hold Jake's lacrosse stick as he wipes the water from his body with his hands.

"Thank you, Grandfather," Jake says gratefully as I hand his most prized possession back to him.

"How do you feel?" I inquire as we slowly follow the trail through the woods back onto the brightly moonlit dirt road.

Jake pounds the leather laces of his stick with a clenched fist to reshape the pocket and then tightens the outside knots. Holding the stick in front of himself, he is satisfied that it is perfect.

Jake thinks a few moments before he answers. "I feel clean, inside and outside of my body. I feel stronger, taller, and lighter. I feel every muscle in my body. I cannot even distinguish the wooden stick in my hand because it *is* my hand, my flesh, my blood, and my bones. My senses are heightened. I see well, even in the dark. Look! Do you see that firefly in the distance?"

I look but see nothing. Jake stares into the darkness with a wondrous expression.

"Do you see it flicker, Grandfather?" I look again but see only darkness where Jake sees light.

"I feel at peace with myself, yet I am ready for war," he adds.

I simply nod. It is good to hear him speak about his emotions rather than keep them bottled up.

We turn the bend and walk over the last hill I have walked a thousand times before arriving home. I sense I am walking with a stranger yet a friend. This person is not Jake, the boy full of questions whom I sometimes scolded. This person is a young man to whom I will no longer lecture but with whom I will converse.

Neither demanding nor expecting an answer, I finally ask, "Jake, did you see it again tonight?" Jake looks at me solemnly. He understands my words.

"Yes, Grandfather. I saw the great eagle that grew larger and larger until he blotted out the sky. In his talons he carried a stick or branch that dripped blood over the land like rain droplets. But I fear the great eagle no more. It is a sign, the meaning of which I am now determined to know."

After a moment of silence I place my hand upon Jake's shoulder, remarking, "I believe you grew another two fingers taller tonight."

We arrive home, and I am relieved to be walking up the creaky stairs with my creaking knees. Satisfied that today has been a good day, I am eager to plop into my rocking chair, light my pipe, and read about Moby Dick until sleep comes over me.

"Good night, Grandfather," Jake whispers, laboring quietly, and successfully, to open the screen door without disturbing the girls.

Just before he disappears through the door, Jake simply adds, "Thank you."

"For what?" I inquire.

"For being here for me," Jake replies without hesitation, "and for my sisters."

"Sleep well, my son. I shall pray for you."

I sit in my rocker enjoying *Moby Dick* under the lamplight. I light my pipe, inhale, and exhale slowly, pleased with the smoothness of the tobacco. I see similarity between Jake and Ishmael, the protagonist in this book: a young, eager, innocent sailor gone to sea for the first time and tested many times. I do not yet know what happens to Ishmael and the crew of the *Pequod*, but I hope that, like Jake, he fares well in his adventures.

Watching the moths flicker in life and death around the porch lamp, I reflect on Jake's experience tonight. He has grown in many ways. Yesterday Jake was a boy, frightened of his dream. Today I see a young man determined to learn its meaning. I hope I will share in that journey and that the journey will be a good one.

22

TIME TO BE READY

As is typical for Saturday mornings, I am awakened by the usual sounds and smells of bacon sizzling in the frying pan and cornbread baking in the open hearth. My girls scurry in the kitchen like the squirrels in the maple tree outside my bedroom window. My first thoughts this Saturday morning are not about satisfying my hunger but about Jake. I arise slowly from my bed as the passage of time and the debilitating effects of past injuries earned in the Game have taken their toll. I pull on my britches, a pair of clean white socks, and my boots. Instead of lumbering to the outhouse and then to the well to wash, I hasten as quickly as my old body will take me to Jake's room. I hope he has not endured a restless or sleepless night due to either nervousness before his first Game or a recurrence of his dream of the eagle.

I slowly open Jake's bedroom door. A stream of the morning's sunlight beams across the floor where his clothes usually lie. A squirrel calls to his mate from the windowsill. I immediately sense something is wrong. No matter how quietly I have opened Jake's bedroom door on so many mornings before, Jake has always heard and greeted me with, "Good morning, Grandfather." Instead, on this morning silence greets me.

I frantically charge into Jake's room and quickly scan all four corners. Not seeing him, I rush into the kitchen to three sets of startled eyes.

"Have you seen Jake?" I demand with unusual urgency.

"Is he not in his bedroom, Grandfather?" Maggie asks with some concern.

Without a reply, I bolt through the screen door, which squeaks slightly. Just as I am about to bark out "Jake," I am instantly relieved to see our boy resting comfortably under an old poplar tree, as calm and as quiet as a turtle sunning itself on a rock. Breathing a deep sigh of relief, I plop into my rocker, my loud heartbeat nearly audible to anyone within a few feet. I dab my sweaty brow with a kerchief, fumble for my tobacco pouch and pipe under my rocker, and scour my pockets for a matchstick.

I hear the familiar scraping of a match head against the sandpaper side of its box and smell a whiff of sulfur. Molly, my most intuitive granddaughter, stands, cupping her hand around the match flame and urging me with her eyes to draw the flame to the tobacco. As I puff several times, satisfied that my corncob pipe has lit, I smile, thank Molly with a nod, and sit back, exhausted without having lifted a hand in labor this morning.

With an uncharacteristically barely audible voice, I urge the girls to return to their cooking. I sit in my rocker for a few moments, questioning my own concern about Jake's absence from his bedroom. Perhaps I am influenced by the memory of the feelings I had the night before my first Game. I recall that long-ago night, walking through the woods alone and looking for a guiding sign from the Creator. I recall a story of one brave, so overwhelmed by the intensity of the moment that he asked the Creator to take him to the council fires of our fathers to watch the Game from the Sky World. He truly wanted to die to escape the pressure of playing in his first Game with the men of our tribe.

I do not know how long Jake has been lying under the poplar, but I deduce it cannot have been very long, for I do not notice the glistening of the morning's dew upon him as compared to the grass and ferns where he lies. Since he looks at ease, I decide not to awaken him just yet. Instead, after exhausting a bowl of tobacco, I follow my nose and belly to the kitchen to join the girls for breakfast.

As we sit at the kitchen table, crunching our bacon and mopping gravy with our cornbread, Mary breaks the silence of our peaceful meal.

"Grandfather, why is Jake sleeping outside?"

The other girls giggle. Before I reply, I marvel at how the question on everyone's mind is often asked only by the youngest. The innocence of her query makes me smile.

"Many thoughts arise in a young warrior's mind, and many new feelings invade his heart and stomach before he plays in his first big Game. I experienced many queer ideas and feelings in my mind and my body before my first Game, as I suppose your father and my father also did before their first Games."

"What feelings in your stomach, Grandfather?" Mary persists. "Is it like when you have eaten too many green apples?"

Her sisters giggle again. This time Mary giggles with them.

"No," I explain, "it is not like a bellyache. It is more like moths fluttering in your stomach."

"Moths?" Mary asks alarmingly. "How can moths get into your stomach?"

Even I laugh heartily along with Mary's sisters.

"My sweet little one," I say soothingly, rising from my chair. "Even a young woman can feel moths fluttering in her stomach at times. A young woman may have the same feelings as Jake does right now when that special boy she has had her eyes on finally smiles at her or talks to her or asks her to dance at the Green Corn Festival."

"Do you mean Jake is thinking about a girl, Grandfather?" Molly asks, her interest now piqued at the mention of affairs of the heart.

"No, no, darling. He is experiencing the natural nervousness before the Game. He is thinking about how he will perform, what the other braves will think of him, and whether he will make his family proud or fail," I explain.

"Our brother is strong, Grandfather," Maggie states confidently. "He will make us all proud."

"Yes," Molly agrees. "You have trained him well. He is the best player of all the young men."

"Besides," Mary adds, "Sarah will be there. I think Jake likes her."

"Hush up and finish up," Maggie snaps. "How do you know of such things? You are only a little girl."

"I see how they look at each other in Miss Doolittle's class and how they sneak peeks at each other in church and afterward when Grandfather speaks to us from under the Great Pine Tree. I am not blind, you know," little Mary snaps back.

Tis true, I have not noticed as much between Jake and Sarah as the girls have, although I have begun to feel a bond beginning to grow between them. After all, we have considered Sarah another sister for all these many years. Is it possible that deeper feelings have now begun to blossom between Jake and her as they come of age?

Returning to my rocker, I again smoke my pipe and stare at Jake in the morning sun. I think that Jake and Sarah may be a good match. I resolve to speak to the clan mothers about this at the Green Corn Festival. For now, more important matters are at hand: finishing touches for the Game.

As I walk toward the top porch stair and firmly strike my pipe against the railing to dislodge the remaining blackened tobacco, Jake yawns, stretches his arms above him, props himself up, looks around, and wonders how he came to be lying under the poplar tree.

Jake and I make eye contact. He looks rested and has a smile on his face, both good signs.

"Good morning, Grandfather. Why are you awake so early?" Jake sleepily asks.

"Why are you sleeping under a poplar tree, my son?" I reply.

Somewhat perplexed, Jake laughs. "I do not remember coming outside. Did you put me here?"

"No, I did not. Maybe it was your friend the eagle," I state, wondering if Jake has dreamt of the eagle again.

"I do not remember any eagles, Grandfather," Jake muses.

I wonder if that is a good thing. Perhaps if that dream had come to him again in the night, it might have disrupted his sleep and sapped his strength. On the other hand, perhaps that dream might have shown him the path to victory.

With a sudden burst of energy that reminds me of my own youth, Jake rocks back and kicks himself up to his feet.

"Aiee!" Jake shouts, stretching his arms to the sky. "I feel great, Grandfather. But I am hungry. What is for breakfast?"

"Have you forgotten?" I respond. "You must not break your fast until after the Game. But you may drink. Splash some water onto your face. Drink heartily and then walk with me. I know where we might find a sassafras tree. You may bite and suck upon its tender limbs to relieve any hunger pangs."

I watch as Jake first splashes water onto his face and then pours the bucket over his head. By habit, he reaches up to pull back his hair but finds only his bare scalp save for the thin ribbon down the center of his skull. Last night, a boy slept here; this morning arises before me a man, a lacrosse player, and a warrior.

"What time is it, Grandfather?" Jake asks.

Looking at the sun, I answer, "About eight thirty."

I then take out my pocket watch, a keepsake from my father, which he claimed he won from a French fur trapper in a hatchet-throwing contest. The device confirms the time is 8:35.

Jake and I walk down a path behind the barn toward Sarah's house.

"Good morning, Thunder," Jake calls cheerily as he tosses some hay into Thunder's stall. Thunder whinnies back in thanks.

We walk silently. Barefoot, Jake is dressed only in his wet long johns. We both see smoke rising from Sarah's chimney, indicating she is cooking breakfast for her poor, haunted father. I notice Jake stares at the smoke a little bit longer than I.

"Here it is," I say as I locate the sassafras tree. I break off a small branch for Jake and me. With my jackknife, I skin the bark from the stem to reveal the soft, white pulp within. Smiling, we gnaw on our wooden treat. The unique taste numbs our tongues and dulls Jake's hunger.

From the shade of the woods comes a voice.

"Good morning, Grandfather. Hello, Jake."

"Oh my gosh," Jake murmurs, embarrassed and thick-tongued from the sassafras as he tries to hide behind me, far more modest than I ever was.

"Sarah! What are you doing here?" Jake asks in exasperation.

Sarah strains her neck to peek around me at Jake, who bobs back and forth to hide himself from her view. The straining and bobbing reminds me of the mating dance of two wood storks.

"I am walking to your house to help your sisters prepare for tonight and to ready ourselves for the Game," Sarah politely responds. She waits for a reply, continuing her efforts to catch a glimpse of Jake.

I quickly decide to relieve Jake of his embarrassment, which I can now see Sarah is thoroughly enjoying.

"Excuse us, Sarah. Please turn around and avert your eyes from this young man who, after all, must remain modest until his wedding night," I say lightly.

"Wedding night!" Both scream in feigned shock, secretly wishing that it were so.

"Who said anything about a wedding?" Jake asks defensively.

"Yes, who would even think that I…you…and I…that I…that you…that you and I will ever be married," Sarah responds with feigned incredulity, quickly turning her back and folding her arms across her chest.

"Wait, my children," I quickly interrupt. "I do not mean… that is…I am not suggesting…I am not saying that you two will be married," although it is now becoming more clear to me that perhaps this is indeed their destiny.

"I should not think so," Sarah replies in a huff as she quickly walks up the path. I catch a glimpse of a big smile on her face. I believe Sarah hopes that this little charade of anger will make Jake's heart grow fonder.

Jake and I stand silently as Sarah climbs the path toward the house, her body straining against her buckskin dress. The contours of her shape reveal that Sarah is developing into a beautiful young woman from the girl, skinny as a beanpole, who has flitted about with my granddaughters. After ensuring Sarah is out of sight, Jake steps from behind me and asks impatiently, "Can we go, Grandfather? I think it is time for me to get ready."

"Yes, come, my son. Let us make final preparations," I agree.

Jake nervously twirls his lacrosse stick from one hand to the other as we trudge back up the path to the house. He occasionally spins the stick high in the air, plucking it effortlessly from midair before it falls to earth. He flips the stick behind him so that it flies up his back and over his shoulder, snatching it again in front of him before the stick begins its descent. I have never seen a player more adept with his stick.

As we arrive at the barn, I motion Jake to sit and relax on an old tin washtub as I retrieve his gear from the house. Upon my return, I see Jake's right leg nervously tapping up and down as sweat begins to form on his brow. These are good signs. Jake is beginning to focus on Game day. Meeting Sarah in his long johns is already erased from his mind.

I hand Jake his deerskin breechcloth, turning my back to speak to Thunder to afford Jake some privacy. Jake shuffles as he removes his long johns. I gently stroke Thunder's neck and say, "Do you see, Thunder? Do you see the warrior who stands before you? He is no longer that little boy who would sneak up behind you, catapult himself onto your back, and ride you without saddle and bridle, holding only onto your mane like our wild brothers in the West."

Jake interrupts my musings. "Grandfather, can you help me?"

I wonder how much longer Jake will ask me to help him. Soon he will need to make his own decisions and seek his own way without my help. Then, not so many years from now, as my body weakens with age, I will need his help. I smile at the certainty of these things in the circle of life.

Jake needs help adjusting his deerskin breechcloth, which we call a *ga-ka.* Maggie has softened the cloth by meticulously scraping the fat, meat, and sinew away from the hide. To make Jake's breechcloth, I chose the skin of the deer I had most recently arrowed and that Jake had touched. I specifically sliced the hide of the deer's hind leg, hoping that my majestic brother's strength and speed would flow into Jake's body.

Getting the flap of the *ga-ka* even in front and in back requires some assistance. A young warrior first fastens a simple leather thong around his waist. He slips the bottom part of the breechcloth under the thong in front, then under his body, up his backside, and over the thong in the back. The top part flaps over the thong in front. I adjust the breechcloth, which is shorter in the back, by simply tugging the back as Jake simultaneously loosens it in the front until both ends are evenly positioned. I then tighten the leather thong, being careful not to impede Jake's breathing.

Jake slips into his moccasins and laces them as tightly as he can without cutting off blood circulation. He stands up, wiggles his toes, jumps in place and quickly runs front, back, and side-to-side. When he darts too closely, Thunder whinnies and shakes his head as if to say, "Go away, crazy boy."

"I am sorry, Thunder. Did I scare you?" Jake asks as he gently strokes Thunder's neck.

"How do the moccasins feel?" I ask.

Looking down in confirmation, Jake simply replies, "Good. I shall caress Mother Earth with my toes. The extra padding of deer hide you sewed inside by the heel will protect the bottom of my feet from their pounding on the ground, which I suspect will be harder than usual since we have had no rain in the past few weeks."

I am proud to hear that Jake is noticing the small things that can mean the difference between victory and defeat. Whether the ground is wet or dry, soft or hard, is important for a lacrosse player. The wetness determines how swiftly he can cut while running without slipping. The softer the ground, the less bounce the ball will take on a shot. Therefore, the player can shoot the ball farther out from the goal protector on soft ground. If he attempts the same maneuver on hard ground, the ball will bounce over the goal.

"Sit, my son. Let me fasten your porcupine roach."

As I affix the roach of porcupine quills that Sarah's father had trapped and skinned and that Sarah had cured to this perfect shape, Jake confesses nervously, "Grandfather, as I lay under the tree this morning, I looked up at the rolling clouds and saw shapes."

I gently turn his head forward to finish my task. "What did you see, my son?" I curiously ask.

"It is hard to explain. But I saw myself and the other braves on the field. I saw our opponents and even people up on the hill watching us play."

"Go on," I urge, hoping that this will lead to some inspiring revelation.

"But it was not merely unknown faces or bodies or situations. I saw individual faces sweating and bleeding. I saw different light on the field from the different positions of the sun. I saw Sarah's face. My sisters' faces. Even yours. But most strangely, I saw myself running, jumping, dodging, passing, shooting, and scoring. As I looked at the clouds, I saw myself and my teammates mounting an offense. I was breathing hard as the clouds changed forms. My pulse was racing as I saw myself in the clouds, running toward the goal. I could hear very clearly the cheers of the people. I could even see the smile on my face as I scored or helped a teammate to score. Was I having another vision?"

"Yes and no, my son. You were envisioning your play in the Game. This type of vision is common among warriors. You see, before battle, many warriors, like players before the Game, sometimes see themselves as it will be."

"But," Jake quickly interrupts, "are you saying that some men can see into the future?"

"I do not know if a man can as much see the future as he sees his destiny," I try to explain.

"Did this happen to you, Grandfather? Did you have these visions before a Game?" Jake asks, perhaps hoping that my answer will confirm his experience.

"Yes, many times, my son. At first, like you, I was troubled and could not explain these visions. I simply thought they were meaningless, fleeting dreams. But then I found myself, usually at an important moment in the Game, making a play so incredible that my opponents looked as though they were standing still, like I had an advantage over all of them."

"Advantage?" Jake echoes.

"Yes, I had the advantage of having seen that play in my dreams or in the clouds before it happened. I already knew what was going to happen before anyone else. I had seen and felt that moment before."

"Do you think this will happen to me?" Jake asks anxiously.

"I cannot say what may happen to another man. Not every dream I have had has come to pass. But if your vision was so strong and so detailed, I would not be surprised if you are on the field and suddenly you sense that you have been there before."

I finish fastening Jake's porcupine roach. I see his smile of wonderment and anticipation. He is feeling more confident now that he is armed with visions.

"There, done," I say, pleased with my handiwork. "But wait, my son. One last fix. Be still."

I walk around to his front. "Close your eyes," I instruct.

I remove a clay dish containing colored mash from atop a workbench in the barn. I dab one finger into the dish and run my finger down Jake's nose, leaving a black stripe from his forehead to his upper lip.

Jake's eyes pop open.

"What is that, Grandfather?" Jake inquires.

"Every warrior must go into battle with his war paint. It makes him look handsome to his people and fearsome to his enemies. Hold still."

I dab my right forefinger in the bowl of crushed blackberries and draw a straight line horizontally across Jake's face, under his eyes and over the bridge of his nose to prevent the glare of the sun from blinding him.

The vertical stripe down his nose intersects with the horizontal stripe under his eyes, resembling the cross of Jesus. That, I determine, will be my explanation to the church fathers and Quakers in attendance, who often complain that our ancient savage ways, like face painting, are the work of the devil. Sometimes I amaze myself at my cleverness.

"There, finished. Let me look at you," I say as I bend over to inspect Jake more closely.

As Jake stands up, I place each of my hands on the sides of his shoulders and state proudly, "When you look like a warrior, you play like a warrior. Now you are ready."

We both walk back to the house, arm in arm.

I shout, "Girls! We are going."

All four, including Sarah, crowd through the squeaky screen door, coming to a sudden halt as they gaze upon this fearsome but handsome warrior. My three girls then rush to Jake, lavishing him with kisses and wishes of good luck.

"Hey!" Jake complains half-heartedly. "You will mess up my war paint."

The girls giggle at his vanity but accede to his wishes.

Silenced by Jake's handsome visage, Sarah gently waves and smiles as she gracefully descends from the top stair of the porch. Her smile is the extra motivation Jake needs to play the Game well today.

Jake smiles, tosses his stick in the air, and splits the air with his war whoop. My grandson, our warrior, bounds down the dirt road like an elk.

"Wait! Let me walk with you!" I cry. But it is too late. Jake is over the hill before I can finish my request.

"Girls! Do not be late," I chide. "The Game starts at about noon. You have about an hour to finish your preparations for tonight and get to the playing field."

"Yes, Grandfather," the three shout in unison as they hurry back into the house.

At the half-open screen door, Sarah looks back at me and smiles as if to say, *Do you not see how I look at your grandson? Do you not see how he looks at me? I have no mother. My father is plagued by devils. Who will speak to the clan mothers for me that I may be betrothed to your grandson?*

I smile back and wave. I am more convinced than ever of her feelings for Jake. I am now resolved to speak to the clan mothers about supporting a courtship between Sarah and Jake. But that will happen later. Now the Game.

23

TO THE PLAYING FIELD

As I walk toward the playing field located behind the longhouse, I see the women preparing for tonight's festivities. The outdoor kitchen buzzes with activity. From the top of the ridge, the women look like ants swarming about their mound. The clan mothers shout "ahay" to acknowledge my passing presence and the fact that this is Jake's first big Game. Just before I turn toward the field, a woman holding a basket runs down the grassy slope from the outdoor kitchen toward me. I do not recognize her at first; when she is nearly upon me I see that she is the mother of the little cross-eyed boy.

"Grandfather!" she calls out breathlessly. "Please wait a moment."

"Good morning," I say uneasily, for she does not wear a smile.

"Grandfather, I never had a chance to speak to you after... well, earlier."

"The incident with your husband," I interject, helping her to find the words.

"Yes, yes," she affirms gratefully.

"I hope there is peace in your home," I say sincerely.

"Yes, well...yes...now there is," she states hesitantly.

"Good. I am happy for you and the boy," I reply as I turn back toward the field.

"Grandfather," she begs more forcefully, indicating she has more to say.

I stop but do not turn around. I sense sadness in her plea.

After some hesitation, she simply states, "He is dead."

My heart sinks. He was such a pleasant yet troubled boy, small for his age, but polite and brave.

"I am sorry," I say as my eyes begin to fill with tears.

"It is better for us," she continues.

What does she mean? How can the loss of a child be better? I think. I am confused.

"My son and I. It is better for both of us," she explains.

I whirl around. There, holding onto her dress, is the boy. I am instantly relieved to see my young friend.

"Ah, my little warrior, how are you this fine day?"

He ducks behind his mother's skirt.

"Do you wish to tell me what happened?" I ask hesitantly, as it is generally considered impolite to speak of the recently departed except with reverence.

She quickly answers, "Drinking. So embarrassed was he by your words and your physically chastising him that he ran to our house and found another bottle he had hidden in the shed. He lay passed out by the shed by the time we arrived home. I cooked dinner and laid it out by him, hoping that after his sleep and something to eat he would be in a good mood. But when I went back out to check on him, he was gone. He did not come home last night. I was awakened this morning by policemen from Syracuse, who informed me that that my husband's body was found in the ravine by some white men who were hunting around the perimeter of our land. Judging by the broken sapling branches, they determined that he must have run recklessly through the forest and headlong into the ravine. His mind and eyesight were blinded by the whiskey and darkness."

I hesitate before speaking, wondering whether she is somehow blaming me for her husband's death, but I decide to speak nonetheless. "I am sorry for your loss," I say sincerely. "It is a shame the boy will be without a father."

"No, I am at peace. The people on the other side of the valley have been very kind and generous to us."

Relieved that she does not blame me for her loss, I encourage her. "You are still a young woman. Perhaps you will find love again," I affirm as I touch her shoulder. She is a comely woman of perhaps thirty winters or so, shy, and slender. Her son is beautiful, almost like a girl, his face so perfect but for his eyes, which seem to follow his nose. Nowhere on the boy's face do I see his father's craggy features. "Perhaps you will marry again and give this good boy a sister," I volunteer, trying to uplift her spirits.

"Yes, perhaps. It is possible," she replies with a smile.

Knowing the clan mothers, I am certain they are already looking for a match for her, a widower perhaps.

"Well, good day. I am heading toward the playing field. The Game starts in…" I look up for the sun. "…about forty-five minutes."

Sneaking a peek at my watch, I am delighted to note that I am dead-on: eleven-fifteen.

"Yes, I know. We are all so excited. I heard the clan mothers say that it is your grandson Jake's first Game with the men."

"Yes, my family is excited too," I reply.

"My son adores your grandson. He tells me every day after school how wonderful Jake is with the boys in the schoolyard, how great a lacrosse player he is, and how many tricks he can do with his stick. He brings your family great honor."

Taking her kind words as a cue, I boldly ask, "Well, if the boy is not doing anything for you right now, perhaps he can tend to some pregame matters and watch the team warm up with me. I shall watch over him while you finish your duties at the kitchen."

The youngster can hardly contain his eagerness. His mother graciously thanks me for the offer. Kneeling and placing her hands around her son's shoulders, she asks, "Would you like to go with Grandfather to watch Jake and the other men warm up before the Game?"

The boy madly shakes his head up and down with a smile so big that I now notice he is missing an upper front tooth. She extends his small hand to mine, reminding me of the many times that I held Jake's small hand as we walked through the forest or attended the ceremonies of his mother's and father's passing.

"Wait!" she shouts as we depart. "Johnny, your stick." She holds up his lacrosse stick, cut down to a size for a boy his age.

The boy looks at me for permission, concerned that he will cause an unreasonable delay.

I clap my hands. "Go," I urge. "Every boy should have his lacrosse stick in his hands today."

Johnny dashes down the dirt path and snatches the stick from his mother's outstretched hand without stopping to catch his breath.

I urge him on. "Come! Run fast! It is almost the end of the Game. We are losing by one goal. You have the ball." He scoops a rock with ease. "Time is running out. You must find the strength. Fly and shoot at that tree," I point, "if you want to save the day for your team."

Quickly responding to my imaginary Game, the boy dashes by me and throws the rock on the run. *Bonk!* He hits the tree with ease and emits a boy's high-pitched war whoop of "Aiee! Aiee!" while waving his stick in the air, mimicking the older boys and men. Surprisingly, he then runs and jumps into my arms, so proud and so happy.

He reminds me of Jake at that moment. I sigh as I realize that those days are gone. I think of how perhaps one day this happy little boy, who generously kisses me on my cheek with his stick wrapped around the back of my neck, may someday feel as he approaches his first Game like my Jake. I put Johnny down, and we continue toward the field. I occasionally look down at this little boy, who is so unbelievably happy in spite of losing his father. No mortal can explain the Creator's plan for us.

Taking my hand, Johnny hastens my steps toward the field. "There he is, Grandfather!" the boy shouts excitedly as he tugs on me with one hand and points with his lacrosse stick in the other. I see Jake sitting on the hill, overlooking the field.

Why is he sitting and not warming up with his fellow braves? I wonder.

"Jake!" I call out.

The boy reaches him before my words. Jake is shocked as this little boy, so thrilled to be near Jake, trips and falls headlong into Jake's arms. They both giggle as they roll together down the grassy hill. Jake stands slowly as the boy holds onto his leg.

"Grandfather, who is this snail that sticks to me as if I were a rock on the riverbed?" he teases.

"He is my newest little friend. It is a long story. He says he knows you from school."

"I am not sure," Jake begins.

"Jake," I remind him sternly, "He says he knows and loves you for the kindness you have shown him and the other little boys at school."

Sensing my meaning, Jake bends on one knee, feigns recognition, and exclaims, "My little brother from school!"

The boy vigorously shakes his head affirmatively, flashing his big, toothless grin. "You are…"

Jake hesitates and looks to me for help as I mouth "J-O-H-N-N-Y," in an exaggerated manner.

"…Johnny!" Jake concludes.

Thrilled that Jake remembers him, Johnny wraps his arms around Jake and wrestles him to the ground. I truly doubt that this happy little boy had ever enjoyed as many moments of male bonding with his father as he now is experiencing with Jake. They laugh and roll. Perhaps this is just the kind of tension killer that Jake needs to dispel his nervousness.

"OK, you two. Do you want to roll down to the creek? Come, 'tis time."

Jake and little Johnny get up together. Little Johnny brushes off Jake's backside with his hat, and Jake, in turn, dusts off the boy's breeches. The boy, serious now, reaches up and lightly touches Jake's war paint, his earring, and his porcupine roach.

Likely sensing the boy's admiration of his trappings, Jake kneels before the boy and holds his shoulders. "Someday you will wear these things when you play in the big Game. But first you must practice daily, be good to your mother, and listen to Miss Doolittle in school. Then all things grand will come to you."

I marvel that Jake has remembered the words I have spoken to him so often. The universal truth of those words comes so naturally from Jake's lips to this young boy's ears that I am certain Jake will be a good father someday.

Johnny throws his arms around Jake and whispers, "I love you, Jake. Good luck. I shall cheer for you."

"Thank you, my little brother," Jake replies.

"Run down to the field, my little grandson, and fetch the balls that our braves have carelessly let fly far by their goal as they practice their shots," I urge. "We shall be along directly."

The boy gleefully scurries down the hillside, jumping, scooping up rocks, and throwing them as he runs.

"My son, why are you not on the field with your teammates?" I ask.

Jake looks down forlornly.

"Jake, what is wrong?" I press.

"Grandfather, I am…I am scared," Jake whispers nervously.

"Oh! Is that all?" I say reassuringly.

"Is that all?" Jake's voice rises. "Do you not hear me? I am scared," Jake quiets himself lest his teammates hear him.

"Jake, my son," I begin, "what you are feeling is not fear. It is anticipation. It is the same feeling I get when I wait in my tree stand for the first morning's light and the first breaking of a twig by a deer peeking from behind a bush. This feeling comes to all warriors before battle, hunters before the hunt, and players before the Game. It is the last emotion you will feel before the Game starts. But once you take or deliver your first body hit, any feelings of self-doubt and fear instantly disappear, and you enter the world of the warrior."

Jake is not yet convinced.

"Close your eyes, my son," I gently command. "Now draw a deep breath through your nose and exhale from your mouth." I embrace him closely and begin to breathe with him until we achieve a rhythm. "Feel your strength with every breath. Instantly recall the deer you ran down and your thousands of hours of practice in the Game. You are ready, my son."

Jake opens his eyes. They are startlingly aglow, as if on fire.

"Now you have the look of a wolf whose eyes shine in the darkness. Take your stick and run proudly onto the field. Your ancestors run with you today."

We hug and pat each other on the back. And so the two of us, bonded in blood and also in the spirit of the Game, lightly run down the hill to the log bench upon which players rest when not on the field. I hope Jake keeps the fire aglow.

24

MEETING THE MOHAWKS

I greet the braves who have gathered around the bench. Looking up into the summer sky with its few billowing clouds, I matter-of-factly exclaim, "Beautiful day to play lacrosse." They all nod in agreement. "And a beautiful day to defeat our enemy!" I shout.

"Aiee! Aiee!" the men, including Jake, shout back.

"A few of you have not met our newest member, Jake, my grandson," nodding toward Jake. "Give him the benefit of your experience and wisdom."

Those who were not in the sweat lodge welcome Jake by touching him with their lacrosse sticks. Those who had been in the sweat lodge warmly greet Jake again. All but one.

Walking slowly and deliberately, Youngblood, who is shorter than Jake, reaches up and scrapes some black paint from Jake's nose with his forefinger. Turning to the other braves with his finger in the air for all to see, Youngblood proclaims, "Only a warrior who has proven himself in battle may wear a warrior's paint."

None of the braves respond as they finish preparing for the Game.

But Youngblood would not relent until he has had everyone's attention.

"You dishonor us by wearing a man's war paint before being proven," Youngblood shouts scornfully.

As Youngblood raises his hand once more to rub the paint from under Jake's eyes, Jake, with the quickness of a snail darter, firmly grabs Youngblood's hand. Both men's arms begin to shake. Youngblood strains to touch Jake's face. Jake calmly but forcefully keeps Youngblood's hand away. Youngblood's eyes begin to bulge. His face reddens and a vein streaking down his temple begins to pulsate like a lightning bolt in the summer's night sky.

Attempting to break the stalemate, Youngblood throws his left fist at Jake's face. Jake reacts quickly and ducks the punch. In the blink of an eye, Jake spins to his left and twists Youngblood's right hand behind his back. "Argh!" Youngblood cries out as Jake pushes him away. The other braves and I stand silently, stunned at this spectacle. None of the men blame Jake for Youngblood's pain. It was clear that Youngblood was sporting for a fight with Jake and was the aggressor.

Embarrassmed by being bested by the newest and youngest player on the team, Youngblood poises again to lunge at Jake. But before he can spring, the elder from the sweat lodge appears between them. Running Bear is our team's spiritual leader.

"Save your energy and your fight for your opponents, since you will need much today," Running Bear exclaims as he directs every players attention across the field where the opponents have just arrived. There stand the vaunted Canadian Mohawks. The Canadian Mohawks are the fiercest and most skilled lacrosse players of all the Haudenosaunee people. They have traveled south from their lands near Montreal, given to them long ago by the British for having fought with them against the Americans during the Revolutionary War. The Mohawks have crushed every team they have faced this year. In fact, they have not lost a Game to any of the tribes or to the white Canadian clubs in the last two years. They are fearsome, fast, and experienced.

They now spot us as we stare at them from across the field. Running Bear, standing with arms stretched between Youngblood and Jake, greets the Mohawks with a few war yelps, which are returned. The Mohawks unfurl their war pouches, which contain their sticks, lacrosse balls, and odd-looking moccasins.

"Ayah!" I gasp, looking at my watch. "It will be noon soon," I announce to our braves. "Lightly run and throw until you have generated a sweat. Then we will come together one more time before the Game prayers."

Running Bear and I walk across the field toward the Mohawks, looking for our counterparts, who accompany them at every Game. As I approach the Mohawks, whose bodies are painted yellow to distinguish them from us, a gray-haired man of my size, my age, and, judging by his demeanor, my stature with the tribe, greets me.

"Greetings, my brothers," he offers as he approaches with left hand raised.

"Greetings!" We then shake hands the Indian way, using our right hand to grasp the other's forearm.

"I am Gray Wolf, Sachem of the Mohawk of Canada," the old man begins, as is the custom of a visitor to introduce himself first.

"I am Benjamin Fallen Tree Harwood, and this is Running Bear," I reply. "May the Great Spirit look favorably upon both teams today," I say earnestly.

He nods and suggests that we sing to the Creator. We three sing a song of thanks, slowly dancing in a small circle until our song is finished.

Looking over my shoulder toward our braves, Gray Wolf slyly comments, "Looks like a formidable team, my brother. Have you done well this year?"

Feigning mediocrity in the hopes that he and his band will look upon us lightly, I reply, "We have performed with honor."

"We have always known the Onondaga to be worthy opponents," Gray Wolf states.

"And you, my brother, how does your team fare this year?" I ask, expecting to hear stories of glory.

He too answers with feigned modesty, "Like you, we have performed with honor."

Although he sounds sincere, I sense some deception. I break an uncomfortable silence. "We understand that you have played the white man's teams in Canada."

"Yes," he smiles. "We have been fortunate to beat the white teams in Montreal."

Even though Gray Wolf and the Mohawk are our enemies today, the Mohawk are a proud tribe of the Haudenosaunee people and will forever be our brothers. I am, at once, proud to hear that they have beaten the white man's teams and nervous that their skill is probably vastly superior to ours.

Respecting Gray Wolf, and now feeling more comfortable with him, I muse, "Can you imagine? The white man has stolen almost everything from us, and now he tries to steal our Game."

We both laugh.

Gray Wolf replies, still chuckling, "It is the one thing he may try to take from us, but unlike the land, which he has stolen and abused, he can never take the spirit of the Game from the people."

Shaking hands one more time, each of us appreciating the other's wisdom and humor, we return to our respective teams to finish warming up and to prepare for the pregame ceremonies.

As I walk away from my Mohawk counterpart, I am proud to have met a man of such uncommon wit and wisdom. I am also proud that he, like I, represents our people well at the council fires.

Reaching my sideline, I begin to hear some banter between the Onondaga and Mohawk players.

"I'm glad you wore yellow today, my brother, for it will be easier to see your blood upon it," one of our players shouts.

The Mohawk quickly rejoins, "The only blood you will see today, my brothers, will be your own as it drips down your faces from your cracked skulls." He shakes his stick madly at our player.

Our men stare with great fascination at the Mohawks' footwear. They are not wearing traditional moccasins or even playing with bare feet, as some of the older players on our team prefer. They wear black leather boots with what appear to be nails on the bottoms. When the Mohawks run, they leave holes in the ground.

After kneeling and touching this track of holes, one of our older players, who is a trapper and an observer of sign, is disturbed. He shouts at a nearby Mohawk with disdain, "Why do you mark up our field with your pointed hooves? Do you not see that you are stabbing Mother Earth with your white man's boots?"

"How do you know they are white man's boots?" the Mohawk responds.

Our barefoot player retorts, "Because no Indian would scourge our Mother and cause her pain."

Enraged by this insult, the Mohawk hurls back, "The only pain today will be yours as I run over you, leaving holes of blood to trail down your backside."

"Ayah!" Gray Wolf and I call to our teams. "Go to your sidelines," we both shout in unison, shaking our heads, remembering how impetuous we were as young warriors. "Remember when we were young?" Gray Wolf shouts across the field as we watch our teams gather at their respective sidelines.

"Yes, my brother, I remember." "You and I will speak more about our past Games and glory. I invite you to our Green Corn Festival tonight."

"Thank you, my brother," Gray Wolf replies appreciatively. "I was beginning to dread the prospect of a long wagon drive north to our country this afternoon after the Game."

"You and your braves will sleep in our longhouse tonight. Our women will give you food, clothes, and blankets. We invite you to bathe in our sacred pond after the Game," I add graciously.

"You are most generous and hospitable, my brother," Gray Wolf responds with sincerity. "May the Creator look favorably upon us."

"Good fortune," I return.

I strain to find Jake among our warriors, who are milling about adjusting their stick strings, touching up their paint, untying and retying their moccasins, and performing curious pregame rituals. I wonder whether Jake is ready. Sudden and graceful movements catch my eye. It is Jake. He is not difficult to notice being the tallest player on the field. I proudly watch him artfully dodging apparitions, darting back and forth, ducking, spinning, and switching his stick from hand to hand so quickly that he seems practically invisible. Jake resembles one of our best tribal dancers more than a lacrosse player. I see the shine of sweat forming on his body.

Then Running Bear calls the team together. "My braves," he begins in his quavering voice, "like your fathers, grandfathers, and great-grandfathers before you, you are privileged to honor the Creator today in the Game. Look around you," he commands, pointing to the hill that gently slopes to the field, a perfect place from which to view the contest. "See the people as they stream onto the hill to watch you play. We thank them for supporting our efforts. They honor you, for through you the people continue to have hope and pride in our future. Now play together as brothers. Look for the open man. Find open space and move the ball quickly. The ball advances more quickly by passing than with a man running. Look upfield and attack at a fast pace at all times. On defense, we will all swarm to the ball like bees to the hive, for that is how the Onondaga have always played."

"Aiee!" the braves shout together.

That cheer will be the last thing the Onondaga lacrosse team does well together for some while.

25

THE GAME: A GIFT FROM THE CREATOR

The warriors from both teams line up on opposite sides of the field. We take our position along the sideline at the foot of the hill upon which our people have come to watch us. Warriors on both sides anxiously await the spiritual ceremony, which, as Sachem of the home team, I am honored to conduct.

The people gather on the hillside, looking for the best and most comfortable spots to view the Game. The hillside is as much a place to socialize as it is to watch the Game. Typically, little boys, who quickly grow tired of the Game, fall into their own games, mimicking the warriors they watch, even taking on their names. The young girls gossip about what they are going to wear tonight during the Green Corn Festival, laughing and shyly ogling handsome young braves on the sideline or on the hillside. The women discuss the food, the ceremonies, and any betrothals. The men watch the Game, shouting out cheers, jeers, and instructions. Occasionally, I am called upon to escort an unruly and typically drunk man from the hill. The older men reminisce about when they played the Game and how this younger generation plays an embarrassingly tame contest compared to their own.

The people are in a festive mood. This is the most exciting day of the year. Today is the Game; tonight brings the ceremonies, the food, the bonfires, and the dance.

As the people settle in, I look along the sideline for Jake. He is not hard to spot. At over six feet, Jake's height also belies his age. He still has the slender physique of a boy becoming a man. His shoulders are broad and his waist narrow. The muscles of his calves and thighs are prominent yet long and slender. His skin is smooth and unblemished. He stands in stark contrast to some of the shorter, stockier, older players, their thighs, arms, and calves as thick as hardwood and their skin scarred from many a savage stick attack.

Physically, Youngblood is as opposite to Jake as day is to night. Riddled with scars from the Game and the sawmill, Youngblood's skin is as rough as granite. The scars on his shoulders, arms, and ribs are as many as the rings around a tree trunk. Although not the most skillful player, he is surely the most ferocious. Many an opponent has returned home with visible reminders of the weakness of flesh when met with the wood of Youngblood's mighty stick. When necessary, Youngblood does not hesitate to take out, in any way he can, the best opponent. Had he been a warrior of old, he undoubtedly would have been a war chief. Youngblood is Bad Mind to Jake's Good Mind—grandsons of the Sky Woman who created the Earth.

Jake's body glistens with sweat. This is a good sign as a brave should never enter the Game cold. He nervously shifts his weight from leg to leg, spinning his stick alternately in each hand. Every brave exhibits his own physical idiosyncrasies just before the Game. But the mental preparation now gives way to the body as an instrument of the Creator.

Jake occasionally looks over one shoulder and then the other at the crowd as if seeking someone special. Had I not seen the look between Sarah and him on the back trail this morning, I would have guessed he was looking for his sisters, whom he adores. I suppose he can look for both.

A warrior often finds that extra spark to excel to another level of skill and endurance in response to the support of family, friends, and loved ones. Long ago, I remember feeling almost invincible the moment I spotted Weeping Willow, who would one day become my wife, in the crowd.

Then, from among the tumult, I hear familiar high-pitched voices, shouting in unison. "Jake! We are here! Do you see that we see you? Do you see that we love you?"

The crowd turns and laughs as these squeaky voices fill the air. All eyes fall upon a little figure elevated above the crowd as she stands upon three sets of clasped hands. It is little Mary, hoisted up by her sisters and Sarah.

Although all warriors know to keep their faces forward to the field, Jake cannot help but turn around and raise his stick to acknowledge his little sister.

Jake does not take his eyes from Sarah as she and his other two sisters gently return Mary to the ground. With one hand over her brow to block the noon sun from her eyes, and with a smile as wide as the Erie Canal, Sarah slowly and elegantly raises her arm to acknowledge her love. She does not shake her hand furiously because that would be undignified. She gently waves her hand back and forth in a dance-like motion.

Sarah's wave does not go unnoticed by another, whose eyes are not trained on little Mary and her entourage. Watching Youngblood, it is obvious that at first he thinks that Sarah's wave is meant for him. But it quickly becomes apparent that her affections are directed toward Jake, who raises his stick to her.

Taking a swig of water from the team jug, Youngblood shouts down the line, "Boy, no one on the hill can help you now! The battle is in front of you, not behind."

Jake instantly snaps forward. I wonder against whom Jake will be competing today. Battling an opponent and your own inner demons is difficult enough, but to have to battle a teammate is pressure a young brave in his first big Game should not have to endure. I silently pray for Jake.

It is time. I walk toward the center of the field, as does my Mohawk counterpart. We each carry a pouch of offerings—sage, juniper, sweet grass, white birch bark, and tobacco—that represent the common flora of our country. We sprinkle these materials, previously mortared into powder, into the air while facing each of the four directions of the earth in succession.

People now stand and are silent. Looking up to the Sky World and with arms outstretched I speak: "Oh, Great Spirit, your children gather here to honor you and the gift that you have bestowed upon them: the Game. We pray that the warriors of the Onondaga and the Mohawk, two of the six tribes of the Haudenosaunee brought to peace by your first son, Hiawatha, will play with all of their hearts and might. Let your pleasure at this magnificent sight rain down upon the people of both tribes so that their crops may be bountiful, their hearts blessed with goodness, and their health made strong. Bless these warriors that they may weather the battle well. We ask these things in your name. Let my words be heard!"

The people cheer. I must admit that my speeches are getting better every year. Then my Mohawk counterpart and I call the players to center field.

I begin, "You are the best of two great tribes. You are skilled and experienced players. Remember this is still our Game, given to our ancestors by the Creator, even though we play by the rules we have agreed to adopt from the Canadians." Looking at the Mohawks, I continue, "Your Sachem and I will walk among you in the field. You see these reed whistles we wear around our necks? We will blow these whistles when the ball goes off the field, when play needs to be stopped for injury, at the midpoint of the Game, and if you behave badly."

Then Gray Wolf speaks. "We will not tolerate any player intentionally striking an opponent with the stick on any part of an opponent's body other than the arm and hand that holds the stick. You will not throw your stick at an opponent as if it were a tomahawk of your grandfather's day."

The players on both teams chuckle.

Gray Wolf continues. "You may use your body against another who possesses the ball or who is within range to possess a loose ball. If you shoot the ball and it passes the goal and goes out of bounds, whoever of you is closest to the ball when it goes off the field will be awarded possession. No one is permitted in the circle we have drawn around the goal except the goal protector." He hesitates for a moment and looks at the players. All the warriors seem to be nodding in agreement. "Are there any questions?"

Youngblood raises his hand to be heard. "I will abide by these new white man's rules as will my brothers but, I long for the Game played by our forefathers—a warrior's Game where blood is spilled in honor of the Creator." Many of the players on both teams nod in agreement.

Clearly, a change has come over our Game. Some of the older players, who were raised in a Game with few, if any, rules, bristle at the adoption of the Canadian rules. Some of the younger players, Jake among them, readily accept the Canadian rules, for they promote a faster and more skillful Game than that which their fathers played.

An extraordinarily thickly muscled Mohawk—Youngblood's counterpart, no doubt—steps forward and explains, "I am William Brave Bull of the Bear Clan of the Mohawk from the North. I, like my Onondaga brother," pointing to Youngblood, "prefer the Game of our ancestors. I will play within these rules but only to the edge of the rules, for if there is a man among you who finds himself between me and the ball, that man had better love Mother Earth, for I will knock him upon her, and he will be kissing her with a bloody mouth."

"Aiee!" the Mohawks shout as each scowling Onondaga takes a menacing step toward the boastful Mohawk. Gray Wolf and I both push our respective players apart as each side hurls profane epitaphs at the other. Frustrated, Gray Wolf and I blow our whistles, each of which make a different, high-pitched tone that seems silly for the moment. Both teams stop, look at each other, look at us, and chuckle at the pathetic tweets from our whistles. Judging from the intensity of the emotions on both teams, I expect that Gray Wolf and I will be blowing our whistles often today.

"Circle up, my young sons, and make the Creator proud," I command. The goal protectors run to their respective nets. Nine players from each team form a circle around me as I prepare to toss the ball into the air to start the Game. The braves jostle for position. Some break from their positions and run to another side but never within the circle. The pushing and shoving reflect more nervousness than animosity. Gray Wolf keeps his players still until I launch the ball skyward.

Just before I toss the ball, the season's first northern wind blows over our field, a welcome coolness not previously felt during the long, hot days of summer.

Looking upward with nostrils flaring, the Mohawks welcome their familiar Canadian breeze. One Mohawk, clearly invigorated by the cool Canadian wind, shouts, "We are blessed, my brothers, as the Creator has caused our cool Canadian air to follow us."

Soon that sweet, cool breeze will be replaced with the acrid smells of sweat, bear grease, soaked deerskin breechcloths, blood, and fear.

Before the Game commences, all braves surely taste fear, causing difficulty in swallowing. In most instances, that fear is replaced with vigor and courage after the first contact between players.

I call for the ball. My young cross-eyed friend Johnny jubilantly runs onto the field to the cheers of the people, his friends, and his mother, who looks on with pride. Out of breath, panting, and bent over with both hands on his knees, the little boy is quickly restored by the cheers of the crowd. He proudly straightens himself and holds the ball out to me. "Here it is, Grandfather," he offers.

"Thank you, my son. Remember, you are in charge of all the boys who will retrieve the balls that fly off the field, to the side, or past the goal."

Understanding his great responsibility, the little boy eagerly shakes his head up and down. "Yes, Grandfather," he says obediently. "I will do my best. I will not lose one. I promise this to you."

"Do not promise more than you can produce, my little friend," I advise. "Some of the balls may be lost in the tall grass or in the woods up yonder," I say, pointing with my chin beyond the farthest goal.

Embarrassed that he may have boasted too much, little Johnny reaffirms his understanding of his duties and scampers away, to the delight of the people and especially to his mother. He runs to the sideline and falls into the arms of his admiring friends, for his stature, at least on this day, is grander than at any time in the schoolyard. I can hear him bark out commands with the authority of a war chief. I smile and marvel at how even a small bit of encouragement can go such a long way in a boy who has been beaten down for so long.

Some of the players on the field are breathing so hard that they sound like hibernating bears snoring in their winter caves. Others pace or jump up and down.

Jake waits on our sideline with three other substitute players. He, being the youngest, will not start in the Game and will be substituted in only if an injury occurs. I remind him to stay loose on the sideline and to be ready for that call. I explain that the plank that is nailed to two tree stumps is seating for injured or fatigued players, not players who ought to be ready to enter the Game at a moment's notice.

I then look skyward and, with a mighty heave, let fly the ball. I quickly exit from the circle lest I be crushed by the ensuing onslaught. As I clear the circle, even the women at the outdoor kitchen are momentarily drawn away from their duties as they hear the deafening sound of sticks and bodies colliding at once, signaling commencement of the Game.

Although our field's grass is about ankle high, a cloud of dust arises from around the ball owing to a slightly dry August. Nearly thirty seconds passes before the ball, kicked and batted, is finally scooped up by one of our braves, who jubilantly jumps into the air.

The people emit a mighty cheer. But that cheer quickly becomes a collective moan as the brave who earns first possession of the ball, an honor indeed, and who is deep in our own territory, does not notice a stealthy Mohawk player slip in behind him. With the quickness of a mountain lion's paw grabbing its prey, the Mohawk reaches out with his stick and whacks the stick from our brave's hands, causing the ball to fall free to the ground. Exploiting this opportunity, the Mohawk brave quickly pounces upon the ball with the swiftness of a hawk upon a snake. With one great swing of his stick, which he brings with arms fully outstretched behind his back, and with a loud war yelp, he propels his arms and the ball forward with such power that the ball tears through the upper right corner of the net.

Given the tremendous velocity of the shot, our goal protector is frozen in place as if he has not seen the ball fly from the Mohawk's stick. The shot is heard only as it makes a popping sound under the cross bar of the goal. No one blames our goal protector, for not one of us saw the ball enter the goal either.

The Mohawks on the field and on the sideline yell, jump, and cheer at drawing first blood. Dejected, our players walk slowly back toward the center of the field. Their lethargic trek is sharply interrupted by the piercing cries of an irate teammate.

"What are you doing?" Youngblood shouts as he stares at each Onondaga player on the field. He berates his teammate, who gained and lost first possession of the ball. "Why do you raise your stick and stand still like you are a pine ready to be felled?" Youngblood scolds.

"I am sorry, my brother," the embarrassed warrior mumbles.

"Sorry? Here's what's sorry: these pretenders from the North have drawn first blood on our land. They have embarrassed us in front of our people. Now gather around and listen to my plan."

After repairing the net, I call the braves from both teams to encircle me. A sly smile comes upon Youngblood who, only a few moments ago, had been so angry that his dark, calloused skin became noticeably redder. As I hurl the ball skyward, all eyes follow its flight except for Youngblood and some of his fellow Onondaga braves, who exploit the Mohawks' attentiveness to the ball by hacking their opponents' legs with their sticks so mightily that each Mohawk so struck falls to the ground in agony.

I wonder why we recover the ball fairly easily. Neither Gray Wolf nor I have witnessed this blatant infraction because, like the Mohawk team, our eyes, as Youngblood had predicted, had been skyward, looking for the ball among the clouds and not paying attention to the action on the field. I heard the mashing of stick against flesh, and seeing the Mohawks writhing in pain on the ground, I quickly deduce chicanery.

Our players are now on the attack. They easily march down the field, passing the ball deftly to one another with only two or three Mohawks limping after them. The rest of the Mohawks are slow to regain their footing after experiencing this dirty trick. The ball is finally passed to Youngblood, who easily scores our team's first goal, albeit in a dishonorable way.

Youngblood moves his stick, faking high, then low, then high so many times that the goal protector looks like he is dancing in the goal circle. Youngblood then turns to the crowd and smiles. But before the Mohawks are about to jump him, with his back facing the goal, he fires the ball between his legs, which passes through the unsuspecting Mohawk's own legs and into the goal.

A cheer rings out from the hillside. Our players yelp around Youngblood, who, sporting a crooked smile on his jagged face, majestically strides toward our sideline.

I am not as jubilant over our first goal, shaking my head in disgust at Youngblood's intentional humiliation of the Mohawk goal protector. Jake apparently agrees with my sentiment, as he, unimpressed, stands alone, silent, with arms folded across his chest and an obvious look of disgust on his face.

As Youngblood begins to trot along our sideline, holding his stick out to be tapped by our players in recognition of his scoring a goal, he freezes as he passes Jake, whose arms remain folded across his chest.

Youngblood backtracks a few steps and angrily whispers through clenched teeth, "Are your arms tired, boy? I do not recall you raising your stick to honor me as I walked past you just now."

Looking straight ahead, and not at Youngblood's face, which is now only inches away, Jake nervously replies, "No, my arms are not tired; and yes, I did not tap your stick."

Youngblood's face is turning redder by the second. I think that if a hole had been on the top of his head, surely steam would be escaping from it.

"You dare disrespect me, boy?" Youngblood snaps.

Jake remains stoically silent. Looking down into Youngblood's eyes, Jake nervously replies, "You disrespect yourself."

Now Jake's knees begin to visibly tremble, for he has committed the unthinkable. He has stood up to the fiercest and perhaps the most emotionally unstable warrior on the team. Jake probably expects to be bashed at any moment, but the shrill sound of my whistle reclaims everyone's attention to return to the middle of the field.

Observing one Mohawk player being carried off the field grasping his left shin, and many more limping. I call both teams to the center of the field. With Gray Wolf's approval, I command that they pair off, each man facing an opponent, with instructions to remain facing each other until they hear the whistle.

When the whistle blows, a young Mohawk, the first to spot the ball, dashes for it with his Onondaga counterpart fast on his heels. As the Mohawk scoops the ball, instead of drawing the head of the stick that contains the ball toward his body to protect and control it, he turns his back toward our goal and, in one swift motion, hurls the ball backward toward an awaiting teammate, who, by design, breaks toward our goal rather than merging into the center. The streaking Mohawk snatches out of the air what looks like an errant pass, leaving him and the goal protector one-on-one. Instead of toying with our goal protector, as Youngblood had done with theirs, the Mohawk simply shoots where the goal protector is not and scores.

It is an exquisite and honorable goal. The score is two to one in favor of the visiting Mohawks. The remainder of the first half, about forty minutes, is an ebb-and-flow game punctuated with some stellar ball movement by the Mohawks, who seem faster and more coordinated in their offense. They are more spread out and better passers. They slip on loose ground fewer times because of their spiked shoes and so recover more ground balls than we. They possess the ball longer and are seldom careless in their passes. In contrast, we are quick to shoot—often poorly at that—and throw the ball away too often.

I subsequently learn that this style of play is no accident. The Mohawks are influenced by the Canadians, whose play Indian traditionalists disparage. I further learn from my Mohawk counterpart that some of the Mohawks have toured across the great pond to England, where a fledgling league of sorts has started. The Mohawks are a vastly more experienced team.

Our opponents have learned well and are much more experienced at the white Canadian's game than my Mohawk friend lets on. Deception is always a part of warfare.

As the keeper of time, after about an hour and a half of play, I announce that five minutes remain before the teams take a break. Indians are not particularly precise about time. Our days consist of early morning, late morning, midday, early afternoon, late afternoon, suppertime, and evening. Unlike the white man's world, where the day is so precisely divided into the precious minutes that rule his existence, in the Indian world, nothing occurs precisely at any exact time. For example, we gather under our sacred tree after church, not at 9:00 a.m., and the Green Corn Festival will start when the sun sets, not 6:30 p.m.

With the Onondagas losing six to three, the people on the hill are becoming restive. We possess the ball at midfield with only a few minutes left. A Mohawk across the field and away from the ball intentionally uses his stick to strike the ankle of one of our players who is attempting to streak toward the Mohawk goal, looking for a quick pass and shot. The Onondaga tumbles, rolling onto the ground, grimacing in pain, and clutching the back of his foot.

So incensed is Gray Wolf at this blatant intent to injure another player that he banishes the violator from the field for the remainder of the Game. The Mohawk protests little, for he knows that what he has done is a violation of the new rules and, most importantly, is dishonorable.

As we carry our wounded player off the field to be tended by several of the clan mothers and the medicine men who chant and shake gourd rattles on the sideline, Running Bear looks down the line and notices Jake's eager eyes. With his heart likely racing and his muscles contracting, Jake appears to nervously await Running Bear's nod. But disappointingly, he is passed over for one of his more senior albeit less skillful teammates.

We expect to play the remainder of the half a man up owing to the banishment of the offending Mohawk. We hope to score at least one more goal before the half to bring the score to six to four. But the Mohawks play with a determined resolve. They finish the half by intercepting the ball from our goal protector, who, after admirably blocking a blistering shot, mistakenly attempts to clear the ball by throwing it to a teammate in front of our own goal.

Leaping into the air in an attempt to stave off the potential disaster of such a poorly thrown ball, one of our braves lands on the outside of his right foot and tumbles to the ground in pain. I suspect that he has either sprained or broken his ankle. Again, Running Bear looks over his eager charges on the sideline for a replacement. The next player with seniority is given the nod. Jake understands this pecking order, even though he and the player chosen before him know that Jake is swifter and more skillful. Jake patiently awaits his turn.

Looking up at the sun, I estimate it to be about one thirty, which I confirm with my gold watch. I blow the whistle and announce to the crowd that we will resume play after they have refreshed themselves at the outdoor kitchen and used the outhouses.

I hope something refreshing happens to our team.

26

RENEWAL

Our players, sore, bloody, and tired, slowly shuffle to a shady glen behind our goal, as do the Mohawks at the opposite end of the field. We hear jeers and angry calls from some of the men on the hill.

Undoubtedly plied with whiskey, one shouts, "You look like tired old women."

"How can you let those yellow-bellied hens stomp all over you?" another adds.

"Hey, Youngblood!" another calls. "You look better with a saw in your hand than a lacrosse stick."

"No, with a broom, like the kid there," their companion shouts, pointing to Jake.

Youngblood is furious at the first insult, but being spoken about in the same sentence as Jake brings his blood to a boil. Youngblood angrily throws down his stick and runs headlong up the hill toward the drunken sops. Seeing the seething object of their derision tear up the hill like an angry bull, the drunken critics prudently and hastily throw down their bottles and scatter like june bugs in the breeze.

I call for Youngblood to return to his team. After growling and pounding his chest like the mysterious great apes in darkest Africa that I have read about, Youngblood pivots and, with long strides, bounds down the hill. His anger not yet abated, Youngblood intentionally brushes by Jake, knocking him off-balance. Jake and his teammates stare at Youngblood disdainfully. Attempting to attack a spectator, let alone a fellow teammate, during the Creator's Game is unthinkable. But Youngblood is not often chastised for his obvious sacrileges because of his volatile temper. Nobody wishes to suffer his wrath, and so they let his indiscretions pass so long as they are not prolonged or overtly outrageous.

"What are you looking at?" Youngblood roars at Jake, spit flying from his quivering lips as he speaks. "You got something to say to me, boy?" His nose almost in Jake's chest, Youngblood hopes to goad Jake into an ill-advised response. Some of the braves rise and are about to interfere but wait upon Jake's reaction.

Shaking in his moccasins, Jake forces himself to stand straight and remain silent. He closes his eyes, half expecting to be smashed by the stick now returned to Youngblood's trembling hands by an equally trembling teammate.

I can tell from the highly red tone of his skin that Jake is seething inside. Any other brave would instinctively lash out in self-defense or launch a preemptive strike. But not Jake. He stands stoically. Admirably restraining any primitive impulses, Jake does nothing that Youngblood can construe as a response, let alone one with hostile intent. There are times when a man must check his temper and hold his tongue. Jake's silence should not be confused with cowardice, for it is the coward who feigns ferocity. Instead, Jake's self-control demonstrates leadership qualities that will be silently admired by his teammates. A future Sachem must learn to use his anger only in aid of his people.

This is the way of a Sachem but not the way of a logger. Loggers are natural shouters. If they are not, they will be unheard over the din of the mill and the gnashing of saw teeth into a two hundred-year-old tree. The sound of a huge tree crashing to the forest floor, snapping dozens of inferior trees on its journey to the earth, is a sound over which a logger must be heard lest he and others die.

I have always believed loggers to be the angriest of our people. I have a theory that deep inside, loggers loathe their profession and themselves, for are they not scalping their Mother when they cut majestic trees for money? This is contrary to the traditional ways of the people. We are taught from birth to take from Mother Earth only that required to survive and never for profit. I may be wrong in my theory, but how else can a man like Youngblood, a logger, be explained?

Seeing that Jake will not respond, and realizing that his outbursts are not helping what appears to be a beaten team, Youngblood thankfully storms off the field to relieve himself in the woods.

Relieved that Youngblood did not hit Jake, our braves sit up against several trees and return to wrapping cloth bandages around their cut arms, hands, and legs. Looking at them, I see defeat. Defeat is as infectious as any of the white man's diseases, and I see it begin to spread throughout the team. One brave has a gash over his right eye that is so deep I can see his brow bone. The clan mothers and medicine men tend to the wounded as best they can. The brave with the gashed eyebrow cannot be repaired with a bandage. He will need sewing up and probably is finished for the day. Here in the glen sits a most somber group. Other than a few moans and groans as wounds are tended to, not a word is spoken.

Looking like our Apache brothers from out west—shirtless and with painted faces, wearing bandanas around their heads to keep the sweat from their eyes—young Johnny and his diminutive compatriots eagerly return a load of balls in their removed shirts, which they have folded up to use as sacks.

Johnny, smiling in satisfaction at having located all the balls in the brush, looks up to me for approval. But I am too preoccupied by the negative tide that this Game has generated. I am too concerned about our braves' injuries and Youngblood's behavior to readily acknowledge little Johnny's achievement.

Dejected, Johnny and his band of Comancheros shuffle into the high grass, hands on their hips and shaking their heads in disbelief at the lack of gratitude shown to them. They surely feel that they are as much a part of this team as any player. Johnny looks sadly upon his dejected big brother, who stands like an outcast. Jake simply smiles and winks. This acknowledgement, albeit small and unenthusiastic, is all Johnny and his band of ball retrievers need. With a whoop and a yelp, he and his band run and jump away, mimicking the moves of the Game's players. They happily play around our goal, passing and shooting the retrieved lacrosse balls and shouting with glee. Jake smiles. Their boyish enthusiasm reminds him of the natural spirit and beauty of the Game, ideals that presently seem lost to the Onondagas.

Little Johnny's mother is one of two women who brings a water bucket and a wooden tray of cut apples to renew our players' strength. She passes the water bucket to each player, who, using a gourd ladle, dunks and slurps. Just as she reaches Jake, a scornful voice from the edge of the group freezes Johnny's mother in her steps.

"Bring that water to me. He does not need refreshment. He has not played. He has not sweated. He has not bled. He has not earned the gift of water," Youngblood calls out for all to hear.

All eyes pass from Youngblood to Jake, who is about to put the gourd of cool water to his lips. Furious at this last breach of etiquette, I am about to intervene when I see Jake return the gourd to the bucket and raise his hand, signaling that he will speak.

"It is all right, Mother," Jake whispers to Johnny's mother. Now speaking not directly to anyone but loudly enough so that all may hear, Jake boldly states, "My brother is correct. I have not played. I have not sweated. I have not bled. I have not earned water. The water belongs to my bleeding and battered brothers lying here, and I shall humbly deliver it."

Johnny's mother hesitates but obeys as Jake deftly diffuses yet another potential confrontation with Youngblood. Jake stands, gently removes the bucket from her hands, and moves from brave to brave, passing the ladle to his brothers to drink.

"Do not, any of you, my brothers lying here wounded from battle, think for a moment that I would not bleed with you. Do not think that I have not felt your every pain as I have proudly watched you give all of your heart on the field. Do not think that I would not strive to crush our enemy as much as you. I promise you, my brothers, if given the chance, I will be with you as one." Jake speaks loudly enough for all to hear but not as if he were giving a speech requiring their undivided attention.

One of the wounded braves painfully lifts his head and says, "You speak of playing as one. What do you mean?" he asks, spilling half the water from the gourd, which he attempts to hold with broken fingers.

After assisting the brave, Jake now knows it is his time to speak. Repeatedly striking the bucket with the gourd for all to hear, Jake stands up. Waiting for all eyes to meet his, he then speaks, "My brothers, we must play like the wolf pack, which together brings down the mighty moose where a single wolf would be powerless. By coordinating our movements together rather than playing alone, we can beat the Mohawks. When we have the ball, let us spread out in a big circle around our opponents' goal and pass the ball so swiftly around and around that the defenders will become so dizzy with the speed of our passing that they will fall to the ground confused and disoriented. Just as the wolf pack constantly encircles its prey, we will encircle the goal rather than what we have been doing, which is crowding in front of the goal."

I can see some of the braves, who only moments ago had looked downtrodden and beaten, begin to smile and nod with approval as Jake continues.

"We have also done poorly in defending our goal protector. While it is true that the Onondaga way has always been to swarm around the ball like bees which swarm around their hive, by so doing we have abandoned the defense in front of our goal. We must keep three of our biggest and strongest players in front of our goal at all times, just as the biggest worker bees protect their queen."

Our goal protector, seizing the moment to add some levity to Jake's earnest entreaties, playfully interjects, "All of you bow and hail your new queen." The braves chuckle—a good sign.

"You, my brother," Jake continues, pointing to our brave with the thickest legs. "You have the legs of a tree and not of a deer. Plant yourself in front of our goal and stop the Mohawk as if he were a dull saw trying to cut petrified wood, for you will have greater effect there than by attempting to outrun a defender on offense." Jake extends his hand down to this brave and helps him to his feet. Jake points to the brave's legs, and then to his own. The difference in girth is so obvious to all that everyone laughs at Jake's truth.

"You," Jake exclaims, pointing to a teammate with shoulders so broad that his arms hang a foot from his body, "my brother, you do not possess the deftness of intricate stick movement with those huge arms and shoulders." Jake twirls his stick around each of his arms and behind his neck, finally flipping the stick into the air and catching it one inch before it can strike his teammate's head. His teammate looks first at the stick and then at Jake. Both men laugh. "You will be the bulwark of our defense, as impenetrable as a wall of stone. Who among you can run through stone?" Jake asks rhetorically. "Who?" Jake asks again, expecting an answer.

"No one!" the team shouts in unison.

Sensing rising enthusiasm, Jake urges them on. "Who among the Mohawk?"

"None of them!" his team rhythmically shouts back.

"And you, my brother," Jake notes, pointing to a short, stout teammate, "have no curves or shape." His words meet with a cross look from the stout brave. But Jake quickly explains, "You have no neck, no waist. But that is good. You are as stout as a bear. You are thick, fierce, and menacing. I will bet you can even growl."

The stout brave looks surprised. Does Jake really want him to growl?

"Well?" Jake asks. "Can you growl?"

Jake's teammates, now thoroughly enjoying Jake's spirit-lifting performance, begin to chant, "Growl, growl, growl, growl..."

The bearlike brave emits a growl that is barely audible over his teammates' chant.

"You call that a growl, my bear brother?" Jake asks teasingly. "Come on, growl like the fiercest bear in the woods! Come on!"

"Grr!" the brave bellows. Banging his chest with both hands, he growls again.

"Yes, my brother," Jake says, grabbing his shoulders, "now *that* is the growl of a mighty bear."

The bearlike brave, feeling the newly found strength of his spirit brother, hugs Jake with both arms and lifts him off the ground, seemingly squeezing the breath out of Jake. His alarmed teammates jump to Jake's aid, pulling the bear's arms apart as Jake gasps for air.

"Whew!" Jake whistles with hands on knees, attempting to catch his breath. Chuckling as he slowly straightens up, Jake looks at his teammates and earnestly asks, "Do you get my point, brothers?"

"Aiee! Aiee!" All of Jake's teammates jump to their feet, wave their sticks in the air, and pat each other and Jake on the back.

What a few moments ago was a morose, glum, defeated team has now become a greatly reenergized and supremely motivated team. Inspired by Jake's speech and strategy, our braves, even those hurt badly, seem to forget their pain and run toward our sideline with renewed enthusiasm and hope that we can possibly get back into this Game.

That is, all but one.

Using his lacrosse stick as a crutch, Youngblood slowly and unenthusiastically rises from the ground. The heart and soul of this team will be won over either by Youngblood or Jake; at this point, Jake clearly has the advantage with his inspiring oratory. Will Youngblood accept the inevitable, or will he make yet another, perhaps deadly challenge? We have the second half of the Game to find out.

Running Bear approaches Jake as we walk toward our sidelines. "Jake, my son. Are you ready to take your place among the men of our tribe?"

Stunned, Jake looks at me, looks back at Running Bear, and replies simply and confidently, "Yes, I am prepared."

"You are our youngest and our swiftest. Four braves have wounds that will not permit them to play in the second part of the Game."

Jake looks over at his wounded brothers lying on the ground. Understanding his responsibility, Jake states emphatically to Running Bear, "I am ready! I am ready!"

In Jake, Running Bear sees the future, a new generation of player, with Jake as that generation's leader. Putting his arm around Jake's waist and walking him out of earshot of the team, Running Bear confides in him, "Jake, I have heard your words, and they are strong. How will you alert your teammates to your battle strategy?"

"I shall make calls that shall be signals to my brothers," Jake says with untested assurance, having never directed an offense or defense in any Game, let alone the big Game.

"Come together, my braves," Running Bear calls. "Listen to Jake's words."

"My brothers," Jake begins, "when you hear me call out the word 'oak,' form a large circle around the Mohawks' goal, for it is the oak that spreads its branches wider than all the trees."

All of the braves look eagerly upon Jake for continued instructions.

"At the command 'wind,' throw the ball to your adjacent teammate, who will throw to his adjacent teammate and so on as quickly as the wind blows, which will spin our opponents into the ground with confusion."

The braves nod.

"The word 'lightning' is the cue to the player who possesses the ball at the moment of the call to strike at our opponents' goal with the suddenness of a bolt of lightning."

Clearly, Jake is now adorned with the cloak of leadership. He no longer requests or suggests a course of action; he commands it.

"When I shout 'lightning and thunder,' the brave with the ball passes to an adjacent teammate and immediately follows the ball."

"But won't you draw your defender, who might attack our brother to whom you have thrown the ball?" a teammate intuitively inquires.

"Yes, a good question, my brother. But that's the point. If I pass to you and follow the ball to you, I will plant my feet and square my body like a wall toward your defender. You must feign going to the goal with one step and then sweep across the mouth of the goal, running your defender into me, the wall. By so doing, you will thus free yourself of your defender. And my defender, not realizing what has happened, will not be able to jump swiftly upon you, leaving you open for a clear shot. Do you see what I mean? 'Lightning and thunder!'"

"Aiee! Aiee!" the braves shout together, thoroughly accepting Jake's strategy.

Jake confidently continues. "And on defense." All eyes, even Youngblood's, look to Jake. "On defense, I will call 'bees.'"

"Bees?" another brave asks. "Is that not a silly name?"

All the braves chuckle.

"Bees," Jake asks, "do what?"

The braves look at each other with puzzled faces. Jake continues, "They swarm when they attack. Do they not? When I shout 'bees,' only our players within ten paces of the ball, not all will swarm like bees to the ball, stinging our opponent who carries the ball with their bodies and sticks." The rest of our defenders shall match up man for man with the Mohawks nearest the ball.

All the braves begin to jump, shout, and hiss a buzzing sound as they pretend to be swarming bees.

Running Bear interjects, "Calm yourselves, my young sons. Jake is not yet finished."

Jake addresses the braves after recognizing Running Bear's acknowledgement of his leadership. "When I yell 'tree,' 'wall,' or 'bear,' or a combination of all three, you, my brothers to whom I have given these names, must peel off and plant yourselves ten paces in front of our goal as the last defense to a Mohawk charge."

"And you, Jake. What about you? What will you do?" a teammate, now fully believing in Jake, inquires.

"I will use the talents that the Creator has blessed me with. I am not as broad as you, my brothers," Jake says, pointing to the three stout defenders. "I am not as strong as most of you. But what has the Creator endowed me with? I have speed, for was it not I who touched the deer's tail? The Creator has given me height to look over all of your heads. And my hands, well... well...they are magic."

All look intensely at Jake, wondering whether he, indeed, has magical hands. Jake bursts out laughing, followed by his teammates. All save but one.

Jake concludes, "My brothers, use each of your talents to the best of your ability, but let us play together as one. Close your eyes and imagine our plan. Let us put our minds together as one."

"Gather around closer now, my sons," Running Bear directs the team. "Let us close together as one, as our young brother Jake has urged."

"My brothers," Jake requests as he stretches his hand in front of himself. "Put your hands upon mine and upon each other's and repeat after me." All the braves close in, and each of them places a single hand on top of Jake's hand and the other on top of the other teammates' hands. "Many as one."

All the braves begin to chant in unison, "Many as one! Many as one! Many as one!"

I have never seen so many hands upon one another. What splendid symbolism! Maybe I will use that model at my next tribal council meeting. I proudly look upon Jake, who has a unique glow emanating from a true leader's heart.

The braves of the Onondaga team, forlorn at halftime, are now truly inspired. When they break the grip of each other's hands and raise their sticks with a shout, the people on the hillside, who have now returned from refreshing themselves but appear to remain unenthusiastic because of the first half's drubbing, are startled at the team's shout and seem to sense a renewed vigor noticeably absent in the first half.

My girls return early from the outdoor kitchen and from using the outhouse so that they can secure the most strategic location for little Mary's viewing. They naturally come scurrying up to me to announce their presence. I direct them to an outcropping of moss-covered granite, upon which they may sit to view the Game.

Wondering where their brother is, Maggie is the first to point out that Jake appears to be speaking to the team.

"Is that our brother talking to the braves, Grandfather?"

"He sounds like a preacher," Molly observes.

And Mary, ever curious, asks, "Why is our brother speaking to the older men as if he is their father and they are his children?"

The girls giggle. Probably wondering what the girls find so amusing, Sarah stands up on the sideline bench to get a better view. Sure enough, she sees Jake, apparently exhorting his teammates. How proud she must be of him!

Jake is speaking to his fellow braves as a man among men. Sarah must be wondering whether the porcupine quill roach has some magical powers. Just two days earlier, Jake, with long black hair simply parted down the middle, wearing baggy hand-me-down shirts and jackets delivered by the Quakers plus pants that were always too short given his prodigious growth spurts, was not what one might refer to as charismatic. Sarah must be thinking about how Jake hardly speaks although, when he does, it is usually about something plain and simple. She probably cannot recall Jake ever having said anything entirely inspiring. But he has never been called upon to do so—until now.

But that was Jake the boy; now Jake speaks and behaves as a man. I am convinced that events shape a person. Some boys reach the age of manhood but are slow to become men. Other boys become men sooner than most because manhood is thrust upon them, such as when a father prematurely dies. That circumstance is an infinitely more difficult journey for a boy. Boys like Jake are given increasing responsibilities around the house and travel to such places as Syracuse, becoming more mature in the process, but their final step across the threshold from boyhood to manhood is defined by a single event or series of related events. I sense that today's Game will be that defining moment for Jake.

I pray that the Creator helps transform Jake's words into successful action. I pray that the Creator gives him the foresight and courage to make the correct calls at the right times, for if Jake's strategy fails, so shall his passage into manhood be diminished.

27

A FIGHT TO THE FINISH

I walk to the center of the field to meet Gray Wolf and speak first. "Congratulations to you, my brother. Your team is strong. You have learned the Canadians' game well," I say with all respect and sincerity.

"Thank you, my brother," Gray Wolf responds. "Your braves are swift and play with courage, but they do not yet play with a single purpose. Perhaps they are confused by the Canadian rules," he says somewhat bluntly although without arrogance.

But I anticipate something very different in the second half.

I blow the whistle and shout, "Come, warriors of the Onondaga and the Mohawk, to the circle of life, death, victory, and defeat."

The people on the hillside cheer as the second half is about to begin.

The jostling for position begins again among the warriors of both teams, facing each other in pairs. I see that the Mohawks have paired their tallest brave next to Jake, but the Mohawk is still at least two fingers shorter in height. I notice Jake glance at his opponent's face and eyes. Jake can see and hear his opponent breathing rapidly, his hands and feet trembling. Jake is looking at fear. The Mohawk's hands fidget nervously up and down his stick, a signal to Jake that he is unsure of his stick skills.

Lastly, Jake notices his opponent stands flat-footed, not on his toes, meaning he will be less quick to the ball than Jake.

By contrast, Jake is coiled like a snake ready to strike. His hands are steady. His breathing is deep but controlled, and his toes caress our Mother's skin.

I heave the ball into the air. Upon its descent and the blowing of my whistle, Jake dashes in and gets to the ball first. But suddenly a vicious Mohawk's stick check upon Jake's arm dislodges the ball from his stick. In an instant, a multitude of shouting men begin wildly hacking each other within a cloud of dust, attempting to gain possession of the ball. With a crushing body blow, a Mohawk knocks Jake on his backside. Looking up at the chaos around him, Jake probably concludes that being at the center of the face-off is for the stouter, stronger, more powerful braves. On the next face-off, Jake must find a way to position himself outside the fray.

Jake crawls out of the circle of gnashing bodies and sticks. Finally, a loud shout indicates that one of his teammates has regained possession of the ball.

"Here, my brother!" Jake shouts, after straightening his roach, which had moved to the side of his head upon receiving his first body check.

Although hacked viciously, Jake's teammate manages to free up his arms to throw the ball outside of the circle toward Jake. Jake plucks the ball from the air as if snapping a ripe apple from a tree and rapidly advances toward the Mohawk goal.

"Quickly, my brothers!" Jake shouts. "Oak!"

His teammates quickly disperse as Jake fends off several attackers. He whirls, ducks, dodges, and jumps like one of our premier dancers, protecting his stick and the ball from vicious slashes until his teammates are in place. "Wind!" he shouts. Looking right, he passes the ball straight and true as an arrow to his teammate, who, in turn, quickly passes the ball to the player to his right until the ball whips around the Mohawks' goal so quickly that two of the Mohawk defenders run into and knock each other to the ground.

As the ball is thrown quickly around the Mohawk goal, Jake calls out, "Lightning!" The lightning brave slices through the disoriented Mohawks like a hot knife through butter. He vigorously cradles the ball, causing it to rise up in the webbing to the sweet spot from where he propels the ball with the greatest velocity. Like a lightning bolt, the ball screams into the back of the Mohawk net. Goal!

The hill seems to come alive as the crowd jumps to its feet in jubilation. The Onondaga braves swarm their scoring brother, each tapping him on his body with their stick as a sign of respect. They also raise their sticks to Jake in recognition of his successful plan.

I beam with pride.

"Looks like a different team, my brother," Gray Wolf states simply, walking with me to the center of the field. "Did you give them a magic beverage at halftime?" he asks jokingly.

"The magic is here, my brother," I reply, pounding my chest, indicating the heart within. Gray Wolf smiles, for he understands my meaning. Playing with heart is a universal truth that all athletes acknowledge. Now Gray Wolf is surely worried.

For this next face-off, Jake and three of his teammates, who are not thick in stature, surreptitiously back away out of the circle, each facing a direction of the four winds.

After the ball reaches the ground and after a few moments of chaotic mayhem, the ball miraculously pops out of the circle, right into the stick of the smaller brave who has positioned himself to the east. With his southern- and western-facing teammates, he quickly attacks the Mohawk goal. Undaunted, the Mohawk braves scramble to defend their goal.

"Thunder and lightning!" Jake shouts from downfield.

Dumbfounded, the Mohawk defenders stand and watch the ball-carrying Onondaga brave pass the ball to his left and then run after it, as if wanting it back. The passing brave suddenly stops about ten paces in front of and slightly left of the Mohawk goal. The receiving Onondaga brave quickly steps forward and then pivots right, driving his defender, who is desperately trying to keep pace, into the body of the Onondaga brave who has just passed ball. The resulting collision is monumental. Both the Mohawk defender and Onondaga blocker crash to the ground in a heap. The ball carrier is freed from assault with an open shot in front of the Mohawk goal. Leaping off his left foot into the air, the Onondaga rapidly snaps his body like the end of a whip, shooting the ball high to low, finding its way into the net just past the Mohawk goal protector's right foot.

The people go wild. Two goals in as many minutes, an auspicious beginning to the second half! But do not count the Mohawks out yet.

The next face-off is a different story. The Mohawks mirror Jake's strategy of positioning four small and quick players outside the circle. Winning the face-off, the Mohawks are determined to repay the Onondaga in kind.

The Mohawk ball carrier begins to run down the sideline closest to the hill. Jake sees an opportunity to trap the Mohawk and cause a turnover by using the sideline to his advantage. In the old days, the sideline was, really nonexistent. But under the modern rules, once a player goes out of bounds with the ball, he loses possession. Understanding the new rule, Jake views the sideline as a teammate.

"Bees, my brothers. Bees!" Jake shouts.

Five Onondaga players within ten paces of the Mohawk abandon the players they are covering and swarm upon the brave with the ball, so tormenting him with a flurry of stick checks that he becomes disoriented and mistakenly runs out of bounds. Some of the Mohawks berate their teammate for allowing himself to become so entrapped. But just as the hapless Mohawk brave gives up and loses the ball to Jake, a particularly fearsome Mohawk of considerable size charges Jake from behind like a rampaging bull obviously intending to do him great harm.

"Watch out, my brother!" Jake's closest teammate screams. At the last moment before Jake is about to be trampled, Jake falls to his knees, causing the raging Mohawk who has launched himself through the air to miss Jake completely. To make matters worse, the previously fearsome but now ridiculous-looking Mohawk plows into a group of somewhat inebriated mill workers sitting at the bottom of the hill. That Mohawk, embarrassed and bruised, will not return to the field without a few more knocks from the intoxicated men.

Jake takes possession of the ball and anxiously awaits my whistle. On my whistle the Mohawks ferociously attack him. Jake must avoid being pinned against the sidelines like the Mohawk before him. Waiting until the last possible moment, Jake ducks under the three Mohawks who, like their raging bull teammate, stupidly lunge at Jake but topple head over heels off the field and into the midst of the crowd. Now every Mohawk on the field must realize that Jake is the playmaker and probably resolves to eliminate him from the Game—permanently.

Try as they might, all Mohawks who attack Jake are fended off with a duck and dodge, spinning right then left as Mohawks from either side try in vain to pin him between them. One Mohawk player, built so much like Youngblood that he could have passed as his brother, apparently enraged at Jake's superb elusiveness, charges Jake, swinging his stick with certain resolve to do Jake great bodily harm. If contact were made, such an outrageous assault would have meant banishment from the Game for this player, but seemingly he does not care. He looks like his intent is to eliminate this tall, pretty boy and obvious leader from the field of play once and for all. However, as if Jake had eyes behind his head, Jake ducks just as his opponent's stick mows over his porcupine roach. No sooner does Jake duck than another Mohawk dives at Jake's feet, attempting to take his legs out from under him. But Jake unbelievably thwarts that maneuver by jumping up and executing a front flip over the diving Mohawk, amazingly maintaining control of the ball in his stick. The crowd *oohs* and *ahhs* as Jake demonstrates wizardry endowed only by the Creator. Even some of the Mohawks stop to admire the young Onondaga's graceful athleticism. I wonder whether Jake's incredible anticipation of danger is the result of his visions in the clouds.

But the *coup de grace*—a French phrase I learned as a young logger in Canada meaning the decisive act—is Jake's shot. Exhausted from dodging and ducking his many pursuers, Jake comes face-to-face with the monstrous Mohawk who first tried to drive him into the hill. Failing at that, the Mohawk has hurried back to his goal to seize another opportunity to terminate this young upstart's inaugural run. As Jake approaches the goal, he can probably smell the whiskey doused upon this big Mohawk by the mill workers into whose laps he had fallen minutes earlier for I surely can. The Mohawk lowers his shoulders, this time under control, and charges at an exhausted Jake, hitting him on his left side just as Jake attempts to dodge past him. As if being hit by a roaring bull, Jake is violently spun around, momentarily losing his balance and bearings. But regaining his senses and using the force of the spin to his advantage, Jake extends his arms, his spinning body, thus causing the ball to catapult out of his stick, which ricochets off the goal protector's right shoulder into the net. No one has ever seen a shot like this, a shot that would be truly spectacular even if the shooter had been set and standing. But Jake had been spinning. Words cannot adequately describe the majesty of what I call this side arm shot.

The people cannot believe their eyes. The Onondagas' teamwork is truly inspiring in the second half. Even the naysayers seem suddenly elated by the Onondaga team's apparent turnaround.

My little darling girls dance in a circle with their arms around each other's shoulders and laugh with joy. Next to them, by contrast, Sarah stands solemnly with clasped hands near her breast, wearing a smile for one young man's eyes only. Clearly she wants to enjoy these moments of Jake's achievement all by herself. But the Game is not yet won. Although the Mohawks have given up three unanswered goals, which has revitalized the Onondagas, the braves from the north are not easily discouraged. With the score now tied seven to seven, the Mohawks must score to swing the momentum back to their side. On each of the next two face-offs, the Mohawks quickly gain possession of the ball and score two fast-break goals. Down two goals, the Onondagas must deploy plan B.

"My brothers," Jake breathlessly points out in a huddle before the next face-off, "we are leaving our goal protector exposed."

"But when we swarm like bees, we leave some of our enemy open," an equally breathless brave notes.

Jake sees his teammates' dejected faces. It is time to call upon his brothers to whom he has given nicknames.

"Yes, that is true, brother. We shall still swarm, but now my brother with the legs like a tree, my brother with the shoulders of a wall, and my brother with the body of a bear will position themselves before our goal no matter where the ball is on our defensive side. In that way, no Mohawk will penetrate our last line of defense: the tree, the wall, and the bear. Remember, my brothers," Jake raises his voice in excitement, "many as one!"

"Many as one!" his reinvigorated teammates shout, each clasping his hand one on top of the other with stick held high in the other hand.

The score is nine to seven in favor of the Mohawks. The Onondaga braves must play nearly perfectly to get back into this Game. But then we lose another player, this time to a broken right elbow. Since we do not have any remaining substitutes, we are forced to play a man short. To make matters worse, the Mohawks substitute in three fresh players with about five minutes left to play.

With a collective groan from the spectators, the Mohawks win the face-off and immediately press the attack. But as their top ball handler breaks away from the pack, he meets a most formidable sight: the tree, the wall, and the bear. Attempting to elude the bear, the Mohawk ball handler runs headlong into the wall; trying to jump over the wall, he is felled by the tree, losing the ball.

Seeing his opportunity, Jake plucks the dislodged ball from the ground as quickly as a hot potato from the fire. He commences yet another magnificent run down the field, intermittently passing the ball but asking for it back as he dodges his defenders in a classic give-and-go pattern. With time running out, there is no time for wind, only lightning.

Running along the sideline, Jake notes a teammate swiftly cut from right to left in front of him. Seeing this opening, Jake jogs right, temporarily losing his defender. But his streaking teammate's defender stops following him and takes off after Jake, who now suffers two defenders hacking away at his body, each formidable whack flaying open the skin on Jake's back.

Just before unbearable pain brings him to the ground, Jake glimpses his streaking teammate, who has broken toward the goal. As Jake falls, he swings his stick around his right shoulder and behind his neck. This maneuver makes the ball appear to shoot out of Jake's left ear. The ball finds its way into the stick of his teammate who fires the ball over two remaining defenders' heads and into the goal. By the force of the Onondaga's follow-through, the stick strikes a Mohawk defender's head, which gushes a torrent of blood. That Mohawk is finished for the day. A brawl breaks out as the Mohawks accuse the goal-scoring Onondaga of intentionally clubbing the fallen Mohawk. Gray Wolf and I separate the players and agree that no intent to cause injury is apparent. Seething with anger, enduring exquisite pain, and nearing collapse, the players from both teams then settle in for what is perhaps the final face-off. The Mohawks are up by one goal.

Believing that victory is at hand, the crowd chants, "Two more goals! Two more goals!"

The Onondagas win the face-off, to a rousing cheer, but time is not their friend. Jake first shouts, "Wind," but realizing the urgency of the moment, he immediately calls, "Lightning!" The Onondaga brave with the ball is so startled to hear the "lightning" call so soon that he almost drops his stick. But Jake's timing is perfect. Thinking that they can rest a bit as the ball begins to fly around their goal in a circle, the Mohawks momentarily let down their guard. The lightning player dashes madly toward the goal, breezing by the unwary Mohawk defenders and flicks the ball over an equally unsuspecting Mohawk goal protector to score just before he is crushed by two desperate Mohawk defenders. The Onondaga player is carried off the field, holding his stick up toward Jake to signal his gratitude. But the Onondaga team is now short two men.

The people on the hill erupt. Even the drunken sawmill workers are roused to their unsteady feet. Holding my gold pocket watch, I inform Gray Wolf that less than two minutes remain to play. I ask Gray Wolf if I should count down the seconds until the Game ends.

Gray Wolf shakes his head in amusement. "Be careful, my brother, lest the white man's timepiece control your life," he says with a smile.

I am momentarily insulted—although that is not Gray Wolf's intent—and become instantly alarmed that our Game's outcome may be controlled by the white man's clock. I shake my head in agreement. "You are right, my brother," I reply with a confirming smile. I snap my watch shut and return it to my vest pocket, where it remains for the rest of the Game. I address the crowd: "The score is tied. We have agreed that we shall play until one of these great teams scores and is declared the winner."

The players and people are relieved that the white man's watch will not determine when the Creator is satisfied. It is his will that will determine victory and defeat, not the ticking of the white man's watch. "Aiee!" shout the people and all of the players—but one.

Youngblood has been surprisingly quiet since halftime. He has played solidly, mostly as a defender, but not memorably. On the other hand, Jake has been the offensive standout this half, a fact that must gnaw at Youngblood's heart.

The teams circle up for the last face-off. We gain possession of the ball and set up the "oak tree." In his old, frail voice, Running Bear shouts, "Thunder and lightning!" And who are the two actors in this play? Jake and Youngblood.

Jake cannot believe his ears as he hears Running Bear's instructions or his eyes as Youngblood possesses the ball to Jake's right. With a determined look, Youngblood dodges by a slashing Mohawk, who accidentally strikes a glancing blow across Youngblood's right eyebrow, which splits open and squirts a stream of blood. Undaunted by this gaping wound, Youngblood bowls by another would-be attacker only to be challenged by yet another Mohawk defender now struggling alongside him as if they were joined at the hip. Youngblood carries out Running Bear's instruction and passes left to Jake, who has pushed off his defender to create space to catch the ball.

Jake catches the ball and waits for Youngblood to set up. Youngblood streaks toward Jake so swiftly that I fear Youngblood may run him over in some last-minute fit of rage. But Youngblood comes to a sliding stop like a horse from a gallop, kicking up dirt until he stands strong and motionless, ready for Jake to make the next move. Jake jabs left, momentarily freezing his defender, then pushes off his left foot and dashes right toward Youngblood.

Enlisting his last ounce of energy, Jake surges toward the motionless yet strangely smiling Youngblood. Jake's Mohawk defender, hot on his heels, ferociously slashes Jake's back and left arm. Jake is in agony but forges ahead. The spirits of his ancestors protect and carry him. In a moment he will be free of his tormentor, who will unsuspectingly collide into Youngblood's solid body. But as Jake runs past Youngblood, leaving his defender trailing in his dust, Jake's feet unbelievably become entangled.

Suddenly, the whirlwind of action from moments ago slows down. Falling forward, seemingly suspended in midair, Jake looks toward Youngblood, who, incredibly, is laughing. Like a feather in the wind, Jake has no control over his body.

With no time to extend his hands to break his fall, Jake tumbles face-first onto the ground, kissing our Mother the Earth. He tumbles and attempts to roll to his feet while cradling his stick so he can retain possession of the ball. But the ball comes loose. Eagerly exploiting the moment, Youngblood quickly snatches the loose ball from the ground. Forfeiting no time to the impending Mohawk onslaught, upon picking up the ball and without taking a step, Youngblood immediately turns toward the Mohawk goal and unleashes a powerful shot. Like a bullet from a gun, it travels between the bodies of two approaching defenders, who block the goal protector's vision. The Mohawk goal protector dives toward the ball, hoping to block it with his body. But he is a second too late. The ball snaps into the net for the winning goal.

The crowd erupts with joy. Even the mill workers, who are barely conscious, enthusiastically rise to their feet. The Onondagas win a come-from-behind victory. They accomplish what many had thought would be impossible: beating the vaunted Mohawks. The Onondaga braves rush Youngblood and jubilantly heave him upon their shoulders. The throng of cheering people pours onto the field, racing by Jake, who kneels dejectedly in the dirt, to touch Youngblood, the hero of the day.

Nobody but I had been in a position to see what really happened. I do not know whom I feel more sorry for: the Mohawks, who played their hearts out, or Jake, the catalyst of a new and exciting game plan, now kneeling broken, bleeding, and alone in the dirt.

His teammates and the crowd carry an exultant Youngblood off the field like a hero.

"Good game, my brother," Gray Wolf dejectedly but sincerely states from across the field amid the din.

Elated that we won, but sad at Jake's apparent betrayal, and, of course, wanting to remain humble, I reply, "Yes, your braves played well and with honor. Today is a great day for the people of the longhouse."

I graciously invite my brother and his brave band of Mohawks to join us at our sacred pond to bathe. Covered in dirt, blood, and sweat, the Mohawks most eagerly accept my invitation.

"Thank you, my brother," Gray Wolf replies. "I will sing of your hospitality around our campfire when we return north to our country."

"And after you bathe, we wish for you to join us in song and dance at our Green Corn Festival tonight," I invite.

Extending his hand in gratitude, Gray Wolf states, "I doubt my braves will dance much, nor do some even possess mouths that are in any condition to sing, but they will drink your sweet tea, smoke the pipe of friendship, and feast their eyes upon your comely young maidens."

I laugh, for all men, all warriors from all tribes, are ultimately the same. We enjoy the battle, the camaraderie of the bath, good food, good drink, a smooth smoke, and a pretty girl.

Jake slowly stands, brushing himself off and picking clover from his teeth. He reverently removes the porcupine roach he received from Sarah and snaps it against his thigh to remove the dust of battle. A slit over his right eye leaves a trail of blood through the dirt on his cheek.

Placing my hand upon Jake's shoulder causes him to wince in pain. Seeing sadness in his eyes where there should have been jubilation in victory, I ask, "What troubles you, my son?" as I begin to brush off his back, where he cannot reach.

Likely still wondering whether his own teammate tripped him or if the final play had been a dream, Jake asks, "Did you not see what happened? Have I been dreaming, or was I betrayed by one of my own teammates? Did I clumsily trip over my own feet or did Youngblood trip me deliberately? What about 'many as one'?" Jake shouts in frustration and anger.

Jake's anguish is palpable. His sense of betrayal is profound. He knows the truth but either does not want to admit or cannot believe that one teammate could betray another. I cannot find the words to console him. Betrayal is a concept so foreign to a naïve boy that he cannot possibly understand it. I resolve that a lesson shall be learned from this, but I am not sure to what end my words will take us.

I ask, "Are you more angry that Youngblood tripped you or that he scored the winning goal? Are you angry that it is he who is carried off the field by his teammates and not you?"

Jake looks at me incredulously. *Why are you not supporting me? Why can you not feel my pain?* he begs with his eyes. Now beginning to realize and yet not quite sure that he did not trip over his own feet, Jake shouts, "I am angry that my own teammate, my supposed brother, has betrayed me. Youngblood purposely tripped me, did he not, Grandfather?"

I stand silently, for it is difficult for me to concede that one of our own could be so selfish.

Jake does not wait for my answer. "I am angry that my supposed team brother has stolen the glory of the winning goal for himself at my expense."

I can hear the anguish in his voice. Although betrayal is not a foreign word to Indian men, to a boy of any race or of any people, betrayal is the worst of all emotional pain. Betrayal runs contrary to everything Jake has been taught from birth: the unity of the family, the unity of the people, the unity of the team, and the unity of the circle of life.

"Jake, calm yourself. It is I, your grandfather, who sees you and feels your pain."

Jake bows his head in shame and stomps the ground with one foot in frustration.

"I am sorry, Grandfather," Jake responds in barely a whisper. "I do not mean to raise my voice to you. I am yelling at…" he says while looking around desperately for something to yell at, "… this dirt!" he shouts. Jake picks up a handful and throws it down in anger. Realizing that he now is being disrespectful not only to me but also to Mother Earth, he falls to his knees and cries.

Placing my hand on his head in a vain attempt to console him, I calmly say, "Pick up your stick and yourself, my son, and let us go to our sacred pond. The others will be waiting for us there. We can walk together, or you can walk alone. A man sometimes walks alone. I am here for you if you wish."

After congratulating Youngblood and the rest of the Onondaga team, the people scatter. Most hurry home to prepare themselves for the festivities tonight—all but my three girls and Sarah. Before reaching the girls, I stop Jake.

"Jake, is it so important that you score the winning goal? Is it not more important that you inspired your team at halftime when they were forlorn and dejected? Is it not more important that you devised a unique offensive and defensive strategy? Is it not more important that your exquisite stick work caused the crowd into believing in the team again? Is it not more important that your team won the Game? Is it not more important that you carried yourself with honor and, by so doing, you honored the Creator? Is it not more important that, save for a few cuts and bruises," I touch his cheek and an open wound, "you are alive?"

Jake stops to think. Facing one another, I put both hands upon Jake's shoulders, hoping that my words will uplift his spirit. "All in all, my son, you have had a day that most young men can only dream of. Do not spoil it with vanity and anger. Be grateful, proud, and happy."

Acknowledging my wisdom, Jake wraps his arms around my neck. As I embrace him around his ribs, he winces and pulls away in pain.

Shocked at Jake's rejection of my arms, I wonder if my little boy, now a young man and warrior, will ever seek the comfort of my embrace again. Perhaps it is time for the boy to leave me. I cry inside at the thought.

"Sorry, Grandfather," Jake murmurs as he steps away. "My ribs are just a little sore."

Relieved that it is pain and not my son's passing into manhood that takes him from my arms, I calmly reply, "Nothing the cool waters of our sacred pond cannot help. Now go to your sisters and your Sarah, and remember to be humble and gracious."

Respectfully, the girls hold back as I finish my conversation with Jake. Upon realizing that we have finished speaking to each other, as if freed from chains, my three little wildcats run to and jump all over their brother. I can see from the grimace on his face that he is in pain as they grope and hug him, but, in spite of extreme fatigue and pain, he musters the strength to scoop up his little sister from behind with his stick and plop her upon his bruised, cut shoulders. Molly and Maggie pull him along, tugging on hands and fingers that have been smashed countless times today. They hurry him to the path of the sacred pond, not so much that he be cured of his pain and wounds, but under the assumption that the sooner he bathes the sooner they can dress and travel to the Green Corn Festival in the wagon together as a family.

Sarah walks behind Jake, who struggles to keep pace with his tugging sisters. She does not join in the fun of tugging and hugging Jake like his sisters do, for her relationship with him is not as theirs. Her closeness to him must be in private. Jake's pain probably seems bearable under her loving gaze. Her mere presence is like medicine to him. Jake strains his neck back to see her, but his determined sisters see to it that he will not speak to Sarah until later.

28

THE SACRED POND

Jake is the last member of our team to arrive at the sacred pond. Braves from both sides, the Mohawks and the Onondagas, are already immersed in the cool, healing waters. It is widely believed among the people that the waters of our sacred pond cure all manner of ills. Countless stories, some that can be considered no less than miraculous, are well known about the water's restorative powers for diseases of the skin, fevers, gout, stomach cramps, headaches, diarrhea, warts, pimples, and more egregious afflictions such as losing the power to walk, speak, or think well. The sacred waters are much preferred over the white man's medicine, which is usually nothing more than alcohol disguised by a flavor and the shape of a bottle.

I carefully walk down a slippery slope of pine needles and mashed oak leaves just behind Jake. Assured that my little girls have run themselves directly home, I can now focus my attention on the postgame rituals that are as important as those of the pregame.

At first, the braves from both teams keep to their own, with the Mohawks on one side of the pond and the Onondagas on the other. Their separation is not the result of enmity between them, for indeed there is none. Neither team bears the other any malice for even grave infractions committed during the Game.

Keeping to one's own people is simply a reflection of the natural order of things in the world. All creatures, even human beings, feel safe and are more comfortable among their own group.

But we are Indians. Much more, we are Haudenosaunee. We are the same, and we are equal whether in victory or defeat.

Most of the braves on both sides stand in the water, grimacing and gently wiping the dirt and blood from their arms, faces, and legs. Others enjoy the feeling of weightlessness as they float on their bellies, their arms and legs limp, their faces in the water, occasionally raising their heads to breathe, like the otter that slips in and out of the reeds. Others lie on flat granite outcroppings. Some are naked; some still wear their Game breechcloths. Whatever the warriors' state of attire, the sunbaked rocks emit heat that soothes their aching muscles. Some congenial bantering among a few braves from each side in the middle of the pond is accompanied by some playful splashing, but sheer exhaustion dampens what may have otherwise been energetic play in the revitalizing waters.

Jake wearily limps into the pond, his body reminded of every cut and bruise as the level of the water rises up his frame. When waist-deep, he realizes that he is still carrying his beloved lacrosse stick and still carries his prized porcupine roach.

Seemingly without the strength to wade back toward the shore, and perhaps sensing my presence behind him, Jake slowly turns to me. Before he can utter a word, I say, "Toss them to me, my son. I will set them by the rock under this white birch tree."

Too tired even to offer a polite "thank you," Jake smiles, tosses the items, and falls back into the water as if he were dead. He quickly pops up as the water stings his many wounds. He looks over his body and touches the many places where he is cut and bruised. Only now does a warrior realize his pain, for in the heat of battle, the fight and the fierce competition control the brain and make the body impervious to pain.

Seeing my counterpart playfully chatting and laughing with some of his braves, I traverse a rock path and make my way toward the Mohawk side of the pond. As I approach, I marvel over how handsome, strong, clean, competitive, and respectful the braves of both teams are, shining examples of what a Haudenosaunee man should aspire to be.

They become quiet and alert as I approach. I bid warriors of the Onondaga to swim over to hear my words. Like salamanders, they crawl off their rocks and slither through the water and intermingle with the Mohawks. Each man, without exception, greets his counterpart with a respectful nod of his head and an arm clasp, which brings joy to my heart.

"My sons," I begin, "watching you play today in one of the most fiercely fought games I have witnessed in a very long time has made me proud to be Haudenosaunee."

"Aiee! Aiee!" all the players cheer.

"You have brought honor not only to your families and to your people, but also to he who gave us our Game. Remember, my sons, this is one thing the white man cannot take from us. It had been our Game when he first arrived on our shores, and it will be our Game to the end of time."

"Aiee! Aiee!" the warriors cheer again.

"Be proud and grateful, my sons, that you represent your people in the Game. Your playing today as competitors and your meeting here as brothers give our people a sense of pride, unity, and hope for the future. It restores our identity, which the white man wishes to strip from us. By your participation in the Game, the Creator gives you the opportunity to become better men. The lessons you learn in playing our Game, which will guide you on your path as a human being, are the lessons you will apply as the head of your family and in your nation: how to play as one, work together to achieve a goal, and overcome personal pain and fatigue to continue to strive for excellence. Remember the Creator's gift that has been bestowed upon you and never dishonor it."

"Aiee!" both sides cheer.

Gray Wolf, so as not to take anything away from the moment of my words, simply responds, "Thank you, my brother, for your wise words and your hospitality. Will you do us the honor of coming north to our country in the spring during our Maple Festival and play our Game in honor of the people and the Creator?"

I look to our players, who eagerly nod.

As I extend my hand to accept, one of the Mohawks jokingly shouts, "You may need to practice wearing snowshoes, for spring in our country comes later than here."

Everyone laughs.

"Yes, you will need to practice in leggings, long jackets, and fur hats if you come to our country in the spring," another Mohawk shouts.

"Yes, my brother," one of our braves rejoins. "We have heard of your cold north winds. And so I will bring to you as a gift a hat made of the fur of a skunk, which may improve the smell of your sweaty, beaten body."

Every man in the pond freezes while deciding if the skunk remark is meant as an insult or a joke. Thankfully, Gray Wolf breaks the tension with a hearty, infectious laugh, causing all of us to laugh as well. The warriors from both sides splash each other as they shout promises of victory in the spring.

"Now, my Mohawk brothers," I interrupt, "go to your wagons, make a campfire, drink some coffee, smoke your pipes, and let sleep come to you, for when the sun sets, our Green Corn Festival begins. You are welcome. It is not every day that our young maidens, who, I remind you, are girls of virtue, may see such handsome men of the Mohawk nation."

In truth, as a result of these meetings between our young men and women, courtships and marriages between members of different tribes occur. The clan mothers both support and encourage these unions to diversify and strengthen the bloodlines of the people.

The players from both teams emerge from the water together with arms around each other's shoulders. The camaraderie among the players is genuine. Only an hour earlier, they were young men on the field of battle, smashing each other with their bodies and sticks with the intention of doing serious bodily harm; now they walk as brothers. Such is the effect of the Game.

I smile and shake my head as I realize that if the leaders of the foreign nations of the world could agree to resolve their disputes by playing our Game rather than sending thousands of their young men to slaughter, the world could be an infinitely better and more peaceful place.

Joining the walking braves, I do not see Jake among them. For a brief moment, I quickly scan the pond, panicked that he has passed out from fatigue and drowned. To my relief, I spot Jake, naked as when he was born, lying contently on a flat rock in the sun.

"Jake!" I shout. "Are you coming?"

Without even turning his head, so comfortable a position has he found for himself, Jake shouts back with much effort, "Go ahead, Grandfather. I will see you at home shortly. Please let me rest for a while."

Looking up at the sun, I guess the time is about four o'clock. A peek at my watch shows three forty-five. Snapping the watch shut, satisfied that I am within fifteen minutes, I shout back, "It is about four o'clock, my son. The sun fades now. We will probably leave the house when the sun sinks behind our hills in the west. Rest, my son, for there will be much dancing tonight."

Jake wearily lifts his heavy left arm to acknowledge my words. His fatigue is great. I lean up the path, its steepness sometimes causing me to touch the ground. I remember how I felt after my first Game: exhausted and in pain. But there is no better feeling of exhaustion and pain than that earned in battle—in the Game.

As I reach the top of the path, I struggle to straighten my back by placing my hands behind my hips and pushing forward. Satisfied that I am standing as erect as a man of my many years can, I begin to amble along the road home. Just then I see Sarah hurriedly walking toward me, clutching a package as if it contained precious goods.

"Grandfather," she asks, almost out of breath and looking around me as if I were hiding something, "isn't Jake with you?" Panicked, she asks, "Where is Jake?"

"Hold on, my child. Calm yourself. Why do you talk and move with such haste?" I answer.

"Forgive me, Grandfather," Sarah apologizes. "I do not mean to show disrespect with a hurried voice. I just want to offer this gift to Jake before he prepares for the festival tonight. I must hasten to cook my father's dinner and to make him comfortable before I prepare for tonight's festivities."

The more I learn about this girl, the more impressive she becomes to me. Here she is thinking about presenting a gift to Jake when she has so many more things to attend at home and in so few hours.

"Let me give it to him for you," I offer. "You have many things to do before the festival begins."

"Oh, no, no, Grandfather," Sarah replies. "I thank you for the offer, but a gift has little meaning unless given from the heart of the giver."

I smile and think, *I did not know that. I will remember it.*

"You are as wise as you are beautiful, Sarah," I reply sincerely.

Turning and pointing, I direct her. "Follow the path to the pond. You will find him there."

Before I can finish, Sarah is off, thanking me as she runs down the slippery path to the pond. Then I remember that Jake is lying on a rock as naked as a baby.

"Sarah! Announce yourself before you get to the pond," I shout.

But she is already down the hill, and I am not sure that she hears me. I follow her in the hopes of saving Jake the embarrassment of lying naked on a rock.

As I carefully negotiate the slippery slope, Sarah reaches the pond's edge, out of breath, frantically trying to locate Jake. She suddenly stops, most probably shocked at the sight of Jake basking in the sun on a rock. Sarah stands in silence. Modestly averting her girlish eyes at first, she cannot help but to slowly raise her head and absorb the beauty of the naked young man who lies before her.

About fifty paces from her, Jake lies on his back, his left arm under his head and his right arm covering his eyes. His ribs protrude somewhat from his chest as his slender but muscular lower back arches up from the rock. His long left leg, bent at the knee with his left foot flat on the rock, hides his private area. His right leg, slightly twitching as he gently sleeps, lies flat. Jake's skin shines red as the sun bronzes his body. Were he not an Indian, Jake could easily have been mistaken as a statute of a Greek god.

I slow my pace so as not to startle Sarah. As I quietly draw closer, I am touched by what I hear and see next. Sarah begins to weep probably at the sight of her beloved's many welts, scratches, cuts, and bruises on his thighs, under his ribs, and on his left hip. His arms and hands are exceptionally beaten. His beautifully muscled arms are spotted with black and blue bruises and cuts, particularly around his shoulders. Although difficult to see, his fingers are swollen, some grotesquely misshapen. Hearing her sobbing, Jake stirs, raises his head, covers his eyebrows with his right hand, and spies Sarah standing by the water's edge.

She tries to hide her face in her package to silence her weeping. Now shocked at the sight of a girl at the sacred pond, Jake shouts, "Sarah! What are you doing here? Do you not see that I am naked?"

Shocked that Jake has heard her crying, I see Sarah try to compose herself. "Yes, I can see that you are naked," She says playfully.

Jake modestly crosses his legs and hunches over so as not to reveal any more of himself.

"Well?" he asks.

"Well, what?" she retorts, now enjoying Jake's embarrassment.

"Well, are you not going to turn around while I put on my breechcloth?" Jake inquires, nervously looking around for his garment.

"Oh!" Sarah feigns modesty with a laugh as she slowly turns around, giggling to herself and wiping her teary eyes on her buckskin sleeve.

Jake grabs his breechcloth and quickly affixes it, albeit unevenly, around his waist. In one quick motion, he rises, dives off the rock, swims underwater to the pond's edge, and emerges from the water. Like Poseidon, the Greek God of the oceans that I have read about, Jake stands, the drops of pond water sparkling like little stars from the sun's reflection. Jake gently pokes Sarah on the back of her shoulder. With the deepest passion, Sarah turns, throws her arms around her dripping, bronzed warrior, and hugs him with all of her strength. Jake could have lost himself completely in her warm embrace but for her pressing his many bruises earned in the day's Game.

Jake gently pulls Sarah's face back from his chest with both hands and looks longingly into her eyes, which, indeed, are the color of the sacred pond. Sarah clasps her hands around Jake's sore neck. Jake wraps his arms around Sarah's tiny waist, gently lifting and pulling her to him until every part of the fronts of their bodies touch.

Their eyes speaking volumes, their hearts beating as one, their lips gently touch. I am certain that neither has ever kissed another. It is destiny that their first kiss is meant for each other. They kiss tenderly, breathlessly, as if in another world. Although trembling with fear and desire, Jake musters the courage to lift Sarah by her waist and spins her around without breaking the contact of their kiss until her moccasins fly off toward the water's edge.

Gently returning Sarah to the earth she playfully pushes Jake aside, runs to the water, kneels by the pond's edge, and splashes some water upon her flushed face. She slips back into her moccasins and quickly retrieves the package she put down before her impassioned embrace. "I have brought this for you," she says breathlessly, handing the package to a surprised, similarly flushed Jake.

"A gift? For me?" Jake asks, although I am sure that whatever is in this package could not be as beautiful as the gift of Sarah's kiss.

Her composure regained, Sarah replies, "Yes, it is something for you to wear tonight. But do not open it until you are completely dressed, for it is the last thing that I want you to adorn yourself with. Now I must go." Sarah runs up the slippery path to the dusty road. Consumed by her impending duties and her haste, she does not notice me hiding behind a clump of bushes. Nor does she notice the shadowy figure I moments earlier spot lurking in the tree line.

Sonny Two Weasels, Youngblood's henchman, had returned to the pond to what end I was not sure. I saw him retrieve Youngblood's moccasins, which he must have left behind. Momentarily stepping from the shadows, Sonny Two Weasels quickly steps back as he sees Jake, holding a package and bounding up the path, shouting for Sarah.

How, I wonder, will Sonny Two Weasels interpret what he has observed and will he report this encounter between Jake and Sarah to Youngblood? I can only imagine Youngblood's reaction, which may not bode well for Jake tonight.

29

FESTIVAL FINERY

With every muscle aching, Jake slowly pulls himself up the porch stairs by grasping the railing, one hand after another, like a seaman weighing anchor.

"Jake!" the girls shriek as they bolt through the screen door, all three passing before the squeaky spring can snap the door back on them.

"Where have you been?" Molly uncharacteristically scolds. Molly usually tempers her emotions like the clan mother she is destined to be, but she is quite beside herself at this moment.

"What have you been doing?" Maggie, the quiet seamstress exasperatingly demands.

"Do you not know what tonight is?" little Mary begs, looking up almost in tears.

As if he has just climbed the tallest mountain, Jake falls exhausted to one knee on the top step. Alarmed by this unexpected, unfamiliar display of weakness, the girls fall to their knees and begin to cry, trembling at his feet.

"Calm yourselves, my sisters," Jake whispers with effort. "I am all right," he reassures them, although he is not too sure himself. It would be easier to describe the places on his body without pain than with it, so injured does he feel from top to bottom. "Now then, what is this big event you are talking about?"

Their sobbing immediately ceases. The girls incredulously look up, all three mouths agape with astonishment. Forgetting their brother's pain, they wonder whether he has lost his mind as to not remember that tonight is the Green Corn Festival. Their previous expressions of sympathy now give way to a flurry of playful slaps to Jake's face and body as if to beat some sense into him.

"What big event?" all three shout in unison as Jake laughs and shields himself from their loving assault.

But before they can answer for him, Jake taps his head with his fist and says, "Oh, now I remember, the Green Corn Festival."

There is silence, then laughter as Jake's sisters fall into his arms. With an amazing and unexpected burst of strength, Jake reaches down and picks up all three in a bear hug as he arises from one knee, their legs and feet dangling like vines from a tree.

"You had better save some strength for tonight, my son," I jokingly advise as I sit comfortably in my rocking chair, enjoying both my corncob pipe and my children's laughter.

Their dainty feet now returned to the splintered porch, the three tug and pull Jake into the kitchen. Never once does he complain or resist, for he has always succumbed to their girlish attentions.

I silently lament the day when he, then they, will be too grown to carry on this way.

"Sit here," Molly sternly commands, as she slides one of the kitchen chairs back from the table.

"Now close your eyes," Maggie orders.

"Do not peek, Jake," Mary warns.

My curiosity getting the better of me, I arise from the comfort of my rocking chair and creep into the kitchen. Opening one eye, Jake looks to me to betray his sisters' secret, but I too have no idea what they are up to. In response, I simply shrug my shoulders. The three are genuinely excited, for they have something of value to give to their adored big brother.

"Open!" Mary shouts, hardly containing her excitement.

Jake is astonished. Each girl holds out what he can only assume is part of his wardrobe for the night, about which, until this moment, he must realize he has given little thought.

Against her chest, Maggie holds up a most beautiful sky blue shirt made of calico, a fabric that the United States government has promised to the people in perpetuity as part of the treaty made at Canandaigua 150 years earlier. The shirt is loose-fitting, with long, puffy sleeves and tight cuffs around the wrists, unlike most of Jake's shirts, which have cuffs ending at his forearms. Onto the collar, Maggie has sewn an array of colored beads so small that they look like embroidery. Just above the elbow, Maggie has sewn onto the sleeves navy blue armbands that are decorated with white beads in the shape of the symbol of our people: a triangular pine tree bordered on each side by two interlocking squares. The pine tree represents the Onondaga, keepers of the council fire, and is the center and heart of the five original nations of the Iroquois Confederacy. To the left side of the tree, the first square represents the Cayuga, and next to it the Seneca, who are the keepers of the western door. The first square on the right side of the tree represents the Oneida, then the Mohawk, who are the keepers of the eastern door.

Over her legs Molly drapes buckskin leggings that she proudly explains she made from the hide of the deer that I arrowed and whose tail Jake touched. Every part of our brother the deer is used. The leggings are trimmed with buck fringe down the sides. On each legging Molly has sewn beads in the shapes of animal figures. The bottoms of the leggings are bordered with sky blue cloth that features a beaded pattern of the pine tree and interlocking squares.

The intricacy of the beadwork must have required many hours of labor. Molly has even woven knee guards from horsehair gratefully borrowed from old Thunder's tail.

"Now look at me, Jake," little Mary begs, as she holds up a pair of moccasins by the side of each ear, as if they are large earrings. The moccasins are just about ankle-high, with a front flap that is decorated with the beaded symbol of the interlocking squares and pine tree.

"Grandfather cut and sewed the moccasins, but I did the bead work with Maggie's help," Mary proudly explains, looking to her sister to give proper credit.

Finally, Maggie lays out on the table the several strands of colored beads to be worn around Jake's scraped and cut neck, plus a red sash to tie around his waist.

Overwhelmed, Jake is speechless.

Mary eagerly inquires, "Well, do you like them?"

"Yes, oh yes!" Jake exclaims, nearly in tears of joy as he rises to hug and kiss each sister.

"Are you girls not missing something?" I remind them.

They stare with puzzled faces.

"Do you not think that Jake's bottom may feel the wind tonight?" I ask.

The girls giggle.

"Oh, your loincloth, which Grandfather cut for us," Maggie explains.

The loincloth is made of buckskin entirely covered by sewn blue cloth and trimmed with white beads, also featuring the interlocking square and pine tree pattern.

After holding up the garments to Jake's body and cooing how handsome he will look, little Mary notices a package on the table.

"What is in the package, Jake?" Mary asks.

"Oh, that is a gift from Sarah, who wished that I not open it until my dress is complete tonight."

"Well, your dress is complete, so open it," Molly logically requests.

All three nod with excitement. Even I draw close with curiosity.

Acceding to our wishes, Jake carefully opens the package. Everyone in the room gasps in amazement.

"Exquisite!" Maggie exclaims.

No other words can describe the ceremonial headdress that Sarah has meticulously constructed. Jake reverently holds it up and gently turns it in his hands.

"Sarah must have spent one hundred hours making this headdress," Molly states with certainty.

Mary jumps up to reach for it. "Let me wear it."

"No, no," the girls chide, holding her back so that her playful leaping will not dislodge this priceless headdress from Jake's hands.

"Look, my children," I explain as I point to the package. "Oh my, eagle feathers—two of them," I whisper breathlessly, picking them up and turning them in my fingers.

Molly quickly volunteers. "One eagle feather, which we insert into this woven tube on top, stands straight up." Molly places the eagle feather thusly. "The second eagle feather is placed in this tube," she notes as she presses it in and ties it off, "which trails behind the brave who wears it."

"How on earth did Sarah find two eagle feathers?" Maggie asks. "They are as rare as good coffee and sugar around here."

Later I learn that besides all that she does to maintain her home and care for her father, Sarah had helped sew a wedding dress for a clan mother's daughter, payment for which Sarah refused coin. Instead, she begged for two eagle feathers, which the clan mother had possessed for generations.

The *gustoweh* is an Onondaga man's headdress. Round in shape, it is constructed of deer hide stretched over a black ash splint framework and held together with deer sinew. A thick woven-cloth headband sits underneath the framework to ease the fit and to absorb the sweat of the dancing brave. A broad band of intricate beadwork depicting scenes of a man's life, such as hunting deer and playing lacrosse, circumscribes the outer headband. The top of the hat is decorated with ermine fur, porcupine quills, and small clusters of split heron, hawk, turkey, and owl feathers. The tubes that hold the feathers are embossed in silver and wampum shells of old. The magnificent eagle feathers are well preserved. Each tribe of the Haudenosaunee places their feathers differently on the *gustoweh* to mark their tribe's identity. The *gustoweh* that my wife made for me before her passing included decorations that denoted my status as Sachem.

"Well, put it on!" Mary begs.

"No, I cannot. Not until I am fully dressed, for it is Sarah's wish that it be the last thing I do before we leave."

"You have about an hour before we load up the wagon," I note, looking outside at the setting sun and then at my watch.

The girls shriek and quickly dash out of sight.

Still admiring Sarah's artwork, Jake unselfishly asks, "Grandfather, may I help you with anything in preparation for this evening?"

"No, no, my son. I will wear the same things I have worn for years, for it is not I who needs to spread my feathers like a strutting turkey tonight," I comment. "Come, give your sisters some privacy. Let us hitch up Thunder to the wagon, and then we will sit awhile."

Jake and I head to the barn and busy ourselves with the horse and wagon.

"Good boy, Thunder," I coo as we fasten the last harness.

We walk slowly up to the porch. Jake sits on the top step, leaning back against the rail post with his eyes closed. I can tell by his constant shifting that he is still uncomfortable from the many wounds and bruises he had earned in the Game today, but such is the life of a warrior.

Creaking my way up the steps and gently lowering myself into my rocker, I muse to myself, *Smoking my pipe in my rocking chair, reading a good book like* Moby Dick, *and watching my grandchildren grow before me are life's pleasures that I would not trade for anything in the white world.*

I look at Jake through the small flame of the stick match I steady on the bowl of my pipe.

"Grandfather? When did you know you wanted to be Sachem and a Faithkeeper?"

I cough, not expecting that question. I hesitate, think, and explain, "I never set out to be those things. They are honors conferred upon me by the Great Council to which the clan mothers appointed me."

"But did you not seek these positions? Did you not know this is what you wanted to do, what you wanted to be?" Jake presses.

"No, no, my son. At your age, I just wanted to be the best lacrosse player in our nation. I thought of nothing else."

"But did you not think about life after lacrosse?" Jake persists.

"Stop, my son. There is no life after lacrosse. It is our Game, our tradition. I will always love and be a part of our Creator's gift. You were given a stick in your cradle, and you will be buried with your stick at death. Perhaps you mean to ask what I thought about doing to support a family."

Taking a deep breath, apparently in relief, Jake replies, "Yes, that is really what I mean to say. After I graduate from Miss Doolittle's school this year, what will I do? Where will I be? What is my future?"

"Slow down, my son. You know you always have a home here," I reassure him.

"Yes, but, Grandfather, someday I will be married. I must be the rock of my home as my father was and as you are. How will I be that rock if I do not earn a living? I…I do not want to work in the mill, but other than that occupation, I will have to leave our country, which I do not want to do."

After taking a long draw from my pipe, I exhale the smoke, using both hands to sweep it over my face, hoping that the smoke will bring wisdom. I answer, "My son, you have two ways to be the rock of your home. Both are interdependent, meaning you cannot have one without the other. First, you must be the moral authority. You must make sure you raise your children as human beings who understand and appreciate our culture but who possess some working knowledge of the white man's world as well. Second, you must earn a living. You can do that by apprenticing in a trade such as a carpenter, leatherworker, or metalworker. Or you can go to a university and learn enough knowledge to become a professional, such as a doctor, lawyer, architect, or engineer."

"Grandfather, I have dreamed about going to a university, but I am scared. Miss Doolittle believes I could be a fine university student. But I would have to leave our nation, my family, you," Jake says with an uneasy look.

"Perhaps for a while. But after taking the white man's knowledge, you can use it to help your people, for we are like an island in a sea of white. We must learn their laws and their ways of doing things if we are to survive. You can be our bridge to the white man's world. A university education is the wood and nail to build that bridge."

"Why did you not do that, Grandfather?" Jake asks.

I laugh and choke on the smoke that I partly inhale before Jake speaks.

"Because I was stupid and stubborn. I hated the white teachers and white ministers. I thought I could hole up here on our land and never be touched by the white man's world. But I was wrong about that." I laugh again. "I have been wrong about many things."

"But, Grandfather," Jake argues. "You are the wisest man I know. You are Sachem—"

I interrupt Jake's stream of compliments by holding up the book Jake bought me in Syracuse. "All the white man's knowledge is here," I say, pointing to the book. "I have read and have learned much from the white man's books. But without the paper that says you have graduated from the white man's university, you cannot walk on his streets, speak in his government assemblies, or build his bridges and dams as an equal. Instead, without the paper, if it is the white man's world you wish to walk in, it will be as his slave—his red slave."

"Grandfather, I will be afraid to leave you, my sisters, my people, and live among the whites."

"That is a natural feeling, my son. Most people are afraid of the unknown. But you must look at it as an adventure. Your teacher, Miss Doolittle, says that you are the smartest pupil she has ever taught, white or red, from Boston to Albany to here. She believes you can succeed in the white man's university. She is willing to help you accomplish that."

"I will thank her for that," Jake says politely.

We sit quietly for a while. I smile at Jake to reassure him that his destiny will eventually reveal itself. I hand Jake my pipe. Jake looks at it for a moment, smells it, and with a wince that indicates his distaste, returns the pipe to me.

"Grandfather, I think I have done enough new things for one week. Perhaps I can wait for another time to smoke."

We both begin to laugh but are interrupted by screeching voices within.

"What are you two doing? We are almost ready. Please ready yourselves or we will be late. Is Thunder even hitched up yet?"

"Calm yourselves, my little butterflies. Thunder is hitched and your royal carriage awaits you. Jake and I will change in less than a minute."

Jake and I walk arm and arm through the squeaky screen door. Jake puts his head on my shoulder as he did when he was a boy and needed comforting. I am momentarily saddened at the thought that this will probably be the last time this boy, grown to be a young man in so many ways in this last week, will rest his head upon my shoulder. Soon enough, others will come to rest their heads upon him.

30

THE GREEN CORN FESTIVAL

Jake and I are a dressed for the evening and waiting in the wagon up on the driver's seat when my little bunnies come hopping through the squeaky screen door and down the porch steps. The two oldest climb up into the back of the wagon first. They then reach over the sides and, each holding an arm, pull Mary up.

"Whee!" Mary sings as she lands on her sisters, who fall back into the buckboard in laughter.

"Giddyap, Thunder," I cluck, and away we go. The girls giggle under their breath the whole way to the longhouse. Jake sits quietly and pensively. Over and over in my mind I practice the prayer I am expected to give. But I feel a slight sense of uneasiness that I cannot fathom. I look up at the sky, which is clouding. I look around me. The crops are growing strongly. Firefly has delivered our rations of beef, sugar, salt, pepper, calico, and other goods to us without too much delay or graft. And Jake… well, Jake seems like he has sprung from an acorn to an oak tree overnight. I chuckle to myself. I must be anxious about my prayer to the people and resolve that there is nothing to worry about. I hope I will not be wrong about that too.

As we crest the last dusty hill, the delicious food smells from the outdoor kitchen float upon the wind, wafting over us. As the smell announces our destination, all three girls stand and steady themselves by holding onto their brother. I smile. Already he is a rock upon which others support themselves.

As I slowly maneuver the wagon toward the hitching post where the other horses and wagons are already lined up, the girls jump from the wagon with little Mary in their arms and race toward the longhouse. Like a white man's general, I shout, "Halt!"

They freeze and turn. "Yes, Grandfather?" they ask innocently, anticipating my speech.

"Remember who you are and how you have been raised. I feel your excitement. But remember to be polite and humble. And remember well, girls, to watch after your little sister."

"Grandfather," the two oldest girls begin to protest, "must we babysit all night? There will be dancing and, well, the young women wish to talk."

"Hey," Mary complains as she alternately scowls at her two older sisters. "You cannot just leave me. I am still a little girl, you know," she says with a coy smile, hoping to elicit some sympathy from me.

"Girls," I reiterate sternly. "You will watch over your little sister. Now go to the clan mothers and other older women at the kitchen to offer your help. Once you are released from whatever chores they choose for you, you may gather with your friends. But you will look after your little sister all the while. Do you understand me?"

The two older girls bow their heads and barely whisper, "Yes, Grandfather."

"Now go. Shoo," I say, brushing them away with both hands.

Obeying me well, they scamper away, the two older girls practically carrying Mary as each holds one of her hands.

Jake and I look at each other and laugh. After watering Thunder and hooking up his feedbag, we begin toward the longhouse, our arms around each other's shoulders. Walking from the dusty road onto the soft green grass of the hill upon which our sacred longhouse stands, I am comforted by the familiar clanging of pots and pans and murmur of people talking and laughing. Suddenly, a high-pitched cry from a young boy pierces the air.

"Jaaake!"

Johnny, our little cross-eyed ball boy, comes running down the hill followed by a pack of wild-eyed boys.

"Jake! Jake! Jake!" they all scream.

In an instant, squealing admirers jump around Jake like water bugs. They all want to touch him. They all want to be him.

The swarm of adoring children stops Jake in his tracks. The look of surprise on his face is genuine. He has never been the object of such adoration. Jake has not yet realized that his playing in the Game as the youngest player ever and with such skill and aplomb has elevated him to hero status. Jake is the true model of a young man on the path of a human being.

I can tell by Jake's expression that he does not know what to say or what to do. I wonder how he will react. I am about to step in and save him from his adoring crowd when Jake speaks.

"Thank you, thank you, my young brothers," Jake begins. "You do me great honor. Thank you for being at the Game and supporting the team. The whole team together, playing as one, brought us victory. Always remember that the team's victory is more important than a single player's glory."

The boys cheer. This is Jake's second speech, the first being to his team at halftime, and again he speaks well.

No sooner has Jake spoken than a cheer rises up from the people on the other side of the hill. Jake, his throng of admirers, and I walk toward the source of the commotion. Approaching the longhouse, we see the object of the people's adulation: Youngblood!

Gathered around Youngblood are his friends and the older members of the team. All are chanting his name and patting him on the back as he strides like a colossus toward the longhouse. Even the young boys abandon Jake and run toward the Game's hero.

Thus, in a flash, Youngblood, the pretender, overshadows Jake's moment in the sun. *Was it not clear to all,* I think, *that had it not been for Jake's strategy and the team's play, Youngblood would never have been in a position to score the winning goal? Did they not see what Jake and I knew to be true, that Youngblood intentionally tripped Jake, causing Jake to lose the ball to him and allowing Youngblood to score?* For some people, only the winning play is remembered. For others, the more experienced, intuitive students of the Game, it is the team's effort that is more important than an individual's success.

Although I am now diverted to where the members of the tribal council are discussing the night's ceremonies, Jake, somewhat crestfallen at his fleeting moment of fame, does not stand alone; another person stands steadfastly by his side.

Sarah gently touches Jake's shoulder. Startled, he quickly turns. I can tell by his expression that his emotions soar again. His brief feelings of melancholy are immediately replaced by elation as his eyes meet the deep purple eyes of his truest supporter, his love.

"Sarah," Jake breathlessly whispers, his words ending in a broad smile.

"Jake," she coos.

Jake closes his eyes as she gently places both hands upon his face. The warmth and softness of her hands surely uplifts Jake's spirit. But his feelings of elation are as surely dashed by jealous words.

"Ah, my young brother," Youngblood crows. The crowd now gathers around both of them. "You played decently well for a young player," he declares, emphasizing the word "young."

Jake begins to return the compliment, but Youngblood quickly preempts Jake's words, for this will be his moment.

Now pontificating, Youngblood continues. "In time, you may play with the strength and skill of the men you see gathered here." He points to their teammates, whose support he hopes to earn with this charade.

"Yes," Jake begins, wanting to acknowledge his teammates, but again Youngblood, seeking to deprive Jake of the opportunity to express good manners, intentionally interrupts him.

"Perhaps next year, with much practice, you may score the winning goal," Youngblood lectures, now gloating and smiling as if he were the oracle of all wisdom.

Sensing that perhaps I shall intervene by offering a compliment to Youngblood and the team to save Jake the embarrassment—which is clearly Youngblood's intention—Jake speaks up and surprises me yet again.

"Thank you for your advice, my brother," Jake states. "Our victory today did not come easily. Thanks to our teammates," he points to the group, who smile, "whose selfless play permitted your greatness. Thanks to the support of the people," he extends his arms to the grateful faces of the people, "and thanks to the Great Spirit," he looks to the sky, "without whom your scoring of the winning goal would not have been possible." Jake concludes with a courteous but disingenuous smile.

The onlookers respond with nods, smiles, and a few whoops. Youngblood's arrogance is arrested by Jake's wisdom. The other council members return my smile and nod approvingly at Jake's words. I wonder if we are watching a future Sachem.

Youngblood scowls, and then feigns a smile as he pushes by Jake with his sycophants still attached to his side. Some from that entourage pat Jake on the back and smile, including his teammates, for they recognize Jake's contribution to their victory this day. The gathering ambles toward the entrance of the longhouse but is rebuffed by the clan mothers, who say it is not time to enter.

The crowd mills about and breaks off into groups. The young girls, whose eagerness to gossip causes them to be more of a hindrance than help around the kitchen, are dismissed from their chores by the clan mothers and older women.

Under the watchful eyes of their fathers, the young boys play their favorite game, throwing a spear through a hoop rolling down a hill.

The grandmothers take the little girls, including Mary, to the wooden tables, where they eagerly sit and taste fried corncakes doused in maple syrup or honey, or both. They all giggle as their faces and hands become sticky messes, which the grandmothers clean with towels soaked in warm water.

Jake and Youngblood are surrounded by their peers. Youngblood's friends are men in their late twenties and early thirties. Teenagers surround Jake. Each group eyes the other suspiciously and draws apart.

Of course, an impromptu lacrosse Game springs up, played in the small field across the road from the longhouse. Young and old boys, and even girls, join in.

Although thoroughly enjoying the company of his friends, Jake longs to escape their attention to be with Sarah. Feigning attentiveness to his friends' stories, Jake constantly stretches his neck above them to catch a glimpse of his love.

Similarly, Sarah raises on her tiptoes in the midst of the young women and strains her neck to steal a look at Jake. Both seem comforted by just a scant glimpse of one another, at least for the time being.

The clanging of a piece of metal hanging from the corner of the longhouse signals the official beginning of the festivities.

Seven o'clock, I think, flicking the cover of my pocket watch open with my thumbnail and sneaking a furtive look. I smile: 7:05.

The people file into the longhouse. I estimate about two hundred are in attendance and about another hundred straggle in during the course of the night. According to the BIA census, about twelve hundred people call themselves Onondaga, but many of them live off the reservation. In my opinion, this number is inflated so that Firefly can requisition more government supplies, the excess of which he and his cronies skim off the top and sell on the open market, lining their own pockets with the profits. Many of our people are too old and too infirm to attend, although one woman, Mary Sweetgrass, who is nearly one hundred years old, is here. Only a few years earlier, Mary, like her aunt Dinah John—who died at 109—used to walk to Syracuse daily to sell sweet grass baskets at the corner of South Salina and Fayette Streets in front of the First Presbyterian Society Church. Amazing endurance! Had they been men, Mary and Dinah John would have been fine lacrosse players.

The tribal council sits on one side of the room opposite the clan mothers who have elected them. The clan mothers are arguably the most powerful members of the tribe, for they alone select the Sachems. The men and boys stand as a group opposite the women and girls.

I know that the people are getting hungry because I can hear stomachs growling. I patiently await the arrival of our brothers the Mohawks before offering the blessings.

Then the door swings open. We are expecting the Mohawks, but the room is hushed as a mysterious figure enters the dusk's darkness. The twilight has deepened, and the signal is given to light the lanterns, casting a warm glow upon the people and revealing this solitary figure's identity.

Meticulously dressed in native buckskin, white blouse, dress, and apron, with a triangular kerchief upon her head and a red ribbon woven into her hair, a shapely young woman enters. Slowly she raises her head and pulls back her kerchief for all to see.

A hush comes upon the crowd, especially the little ones, followed by an explosion of voices.

"Miss Doolittle!" all the school-age children shout as they swarm around her like bees to the hive. The children closest to her hug Miss Doolittle, and those behind them hug those in front so that all the children are interlocked in a communal embrace around their beloved teacher from Boston.

The people are comforted in the love their children feel for this white woman, who is dressed as finely and as elegantly as the prettiest Indian maiden. So this is the surprise Miss Doolittle promised the children when she dismissed them from their last day of school!

Never have the people seen a white woman dressed in customary Haudenosaunee garb. The children take Miss Doolittle's hands, pulling and tugging her to meet the clan mothers, before whom she respectfully curtsies. She greets the tribal council, each of whose member's hands she shakes, and finally the parents and families. So elegantly and graciously does she comport herself that but for her blue eyes, red hair, and freckled nose, she could easily be mistaken for the finest young Onondaga woman.

I stare at our young white teacher and marvel at how beautiful she is, even for a white woman. But I can see from the reaction of the children that her true beauty emanates from her heart. It is obvious how much the children love her and how much she loves them. Having heard my own grandchildren talk about her, I resolve to personally thank Miss Doolittle, not so much for teaching our children but for not talking down to them like they were poor, uneducated savages. She is not like the ministers and their wives, who come onto the reservation supposedly to save our people's souls. However grand their motivation, in the end our children are made to feel embarrassed about themselves and their families, believing that to be an Indian is to be inferior, dirty, and savage. Without accepting their god, our children are taught that, upon death, their immortal souls will burn in the fires of hell. And there was always a condition, a bribe: Accept our god and our teachings, and you will get bigger BIA rations, more hand-me-down clothing, perhaps a feast at Christmas, and perhaps entrance to the Christian heaven.

Yet Miss Doolittle is unique and not one of those people. She understands that there must be a balance between teaching the children the white man's words, numbers, history, and music, and also helping them to remember their ancestors and to know and be proud of the language and traditions of their culture. Miss Doolittle never consciously does or says anything that would cause the children to lose sight of their identity or to be embarrassed about who they are. This is why, with every white man's song she teaches the children, she insists that the children teach her an Indian song. This is why for every tale of Scheherazade's *Arabian Nights* she tells, the children tell her a story passed down to them through our oral traditions. This is why for every Sunday sermon she insists the children attend, she reminds them to meet me under our Sacred Tree thereafter. This is why she learns the customs and art of the people, plainly expressed in her Indian garments, even including her moccasins, which she cut and sewed herself.

Miss Doolittle is our most honored guest.

But where are our other honored guests?

Suddenly someone shouts that a bonfire has just ignited across the road on the small lacrosse field. Everybody runs to the door and pours outside the longhouse.

From behind the bonfire, which lights the sky, come two lines of men. Three drummers, two rattlers, and two flute players sit on two logs away from the fire. The drummers keep the beat and sing. The two lines of men converge and begin to dance around the fire.

It is the Mohawks, who, in their own way, wish to return the hospitality shown to them. They have gathered the wood that they had kept in their wagons, lit the fire, and set the sitting logs, upon which the older people might find some comfort after the formal ceremonies are completed.

To the people's delight, the Mohawks sing of bravery and honor associated with the Game played that day. They sing praises of our players. Although not as well attired as our own people, for they could bring few clothes in their travel, they are magnificent to behold. Their muscular bodies gleam in the firelight. Their war whoops and songs fill the night air. I am impressed how energetically the Mohawks dance in spite of their obvious bruises, cuts, broken bones, and exhaustion. I notice that some of the people are so moved by the drumbeat and the dancing of our brothers that they spontaneously begin to dance in place themselves. I wonder how I will ever get them to return to our ceremonies. Suddenly, the drums stop and the singing ends with a loud shout. The Mohawks line up shoulder to shoulder and bow to the people. Their showmanship is received by thunderous shouts and applause.

Seeing my counterpart, Gray Wolf, who is one of the singers, I step forward to invite the Mohawks inside the longhouse, where we will begin the ceremonial part of the Green Corn Festival.

I sense some disappointment from some of the people who would rather have stayed outside to begin the social festivities of dancing and singing, having had a taste of what was to come from our Mohawk brothers, but they dutifully file back into the longhouse out of respect for me and the moment. After all again take their places, I raise my hands and look up. The room becomes silent.

"Oh, Great Spirit, who presides over the council fires of our ancestors, hear your children, the Haudenosaunee. We give greetings and thanks to the plant life. Within our plants is the source of substance that sustains life for us. Among them are sustenance, medicine, and beauty. From the time of creation, we have seen various forms of plant life. We give greetings and thanks and hope that we will continue to see plant life for generations to come. Let my words be heard."

I lower my arms and head, bow to the clan mothers, the tribal council, and then turn toward the Mohawks.

"You, my brothers from the north, honor us with your presence. You honor us with your fire, dancing, and song. But most of all, you honor us in the Game, for it is not victory or defeat that measures a man, but how well he plays with his brothers in honor of the Creator. We honor you, for you were valiant foes today. We pray that with the Creator's blessings, good crops and good fortune come to you and to all of us, the Haudenosaunee."

Gray Wolf and his fellow Mohawks beam with pride. All of the people look upon them with smiles and affection. Sensing the people's restlessness, especially among the children, we dispense with further speeches. The next day, the council of chiefs and clan mothers will address reservation issues, replace members who are too ill to serve, make plans for the following year, and, most importantly, discuss how we will deal with continued BIA graft and corruption. But for now, it is time to celebrate.

I stand again, to some barely audible but still obvious moans from some of the people who are expecting more speeches. I stand most solemnly to playfully test their patience further. I raise my hands again. I see some of the young people raise their eyebrows as if to say, *What, another prayer, another speech?* When all are silent I speak: "Enough talk. Let us eat!"

Surprised and relieved, the people shout for joy and stream out the door toward the longhouse outdoor kitchen, where benches and tables have been erected upon the grassy hill overlooking the place where the Mohawks have made the bonfire.

The people cue up, each taking a wooden plate or bowl and wooden utensils, which are carved in the animal shapes of the clans. The people file by the kitchen women, who place on their plates many delectable morsels of food: venison stew and small pieces of venison steak; spit-broiled moose obtained by trading hand-carved, deer antler-handled knives with white hunters who had harvested the moose in Canada; and rabbit and chicken medallions panfried with onions and squash.

Vegetables are plentiful. The three sisters, corn, beans, and squash, have been cooked in every imaginable way. In addition to the staples of cornbread and corn cakes, beans are fried, dried, and rolled in salt. Yellow and green squash are panfried with onions. Salads of lettuces, radishes, carrots, and tomatoes abound.

Our Green Corn Festival is much akin to the white man's Thanksgiving. Ironically, if not for the Indians, the white men in Plymouth, Massachusetts, may never have survived that first winter to even celebrate Thanksgiving. The white man has since demonstrated an odd way of showing his gratitude toward the Indians who saved him. But tonight is not a time for politics. Tonight is our time of celebration, for there is much to be thankful for. The crops are coming in strong; hunting and fishing are bountiful; BIA supplies have, for the most part, arrived on time; and we have beaten the mighty Mohawk lacrosse team.

Illuminated by the bonfire that the Mohawks keep burning into the night, the people sit on benches, at wooden tables, or on the grass, which is now moist with the evening dew.

The people eat well. They laugh and tell stories. It has not always been the case that the Green Corn Festival is so jubilant.

Drought or pests have sometimes decimated the crops, causing hardship and even death as people weak with hunger succumbed to the brutal cold of winter. I myself do not remember starvation, but I do remember tightening our belts when the crops were less than bountiful.

The Haudenosaunee learn from birth not to eat more than what is necessary to satisfy one's hunger. If a family suffers a failed or short crop or is without a man to hunt, by the guidance of our clan mothers and elders, the people will share what they have. For example, Sarah, whose father is no longer a hunter except for small varmints, seldom is without meat. Others, including me, offer gifts of meat, neither expecting nor asking for anything in return. To take advantage of one less fortunate is forbidden and usually met with public ridicule and scorn.

But some persons seek to curry favor with their bounty. For example, more than a few know that Youngblood has passed by a family in need just to bring part of his hunt to Sarah. His explanation is that she is most deserving of his generosity owing to her father's disability. But even this guise of generosity gives way to Youngblood's obviously selfish intentions.

31

DANCE OF DECEIT

Finally, Jake and Sarah will steal away alone together. Jake has confided to me that he is determined to profess his love for Sarah this evening. Just as I had practiced my prayer in my head as we rode to the longhouse, I know that Jake too has practiced the right words to say to Sarah. Alas, being famous often deprives one of privacy. Jake's meal and his opportunity to speak are continually interrupted by well-wishers who truly admired his performance in the Game. Although always humble and gracious, Jake is becoming somewhat annoyed and impatient. He finishes his last bit of venison stew, strikes his palms against the tabletop with authority, springs to his feet, and begins to make his way toward Sarah.

But just then, our people's drums sound, signaling that the feasting is over and the dancing and singing will begin. The girls gather, whisking Sarah away with their group. Similarly, the young men pull Jake away to join them. Both Jake and Sarah slightly struggle against their separation but ultimately submit to their peer groups. The young men and young women stand separately on opposite ends of the fire.

The Haudenosaunee drum, which we call "little boy," is carved from a single broad piece of wood in the shape of a stump with animal hide tightly affixed across the open top. The hollow wood drum is filled with water and inverted to keep the hide moist when not played. When turned upright, each drum, depending on the amount of water contained within, offers a different, rich, hollow sound when beaten with a wooden mallet.

Although all are invited to sing, only a few truly gifted singers lead the songs. For background rhythm, singers shake gourd, horn, and turtle shell rattles with dried corn kernels inside.

Certain ceremonial dances are specific to the holiday. Other dances, more social in nature, are enjoyed at every festival. As in the Game, where only the most skillful are called upon to represent the people, some of the dances that have the most intricate and energetic steps, like the "war dance" and "smoke dance," are performed only by the most adept and athletic of our people. Some of the lacrosse players, who are also the best dancers, sit out, giving deference to their brothers who have not played in the Game so that those men may earn honor and perhaps catch the attention of a young maiden.

The young people dance in rings around the fire, mostly girls with girls and boys with boys. The older men, including myself, rarely dance, preferring to sit by the fire, smoke our pipes, and sometimes hum or sing songs. I particularly enjoy the athleticism of our young dancers. We joke with the young men and boast about our past achievements of dancing all night even after playing a four or five hour lacrosse game.

I hear familiar sounds from the outdoor kitchen as the women begin to clean and pack up the kitchenware until the next festival. Any leftover food is offered to families who may be in need. Over the din, I hear the occasional cries of a little one who has fallen and skinned his knee and the cries of a newborn wanting to suckle at its mother's breast. These are all good sounds, the sounds of life.

Of course, a few men, mostly those working among the whites, carry back to the reservation the white man's curse: whiskey. The

Sachems and other elders know who they are. We watch them sneak behind the longhouse, where they undoubtedly pass the bottle, thinking that they have fooled our watchful eyes. After taking two or three swigs, this troupe of clowns traipses out from the shadows. With heads lowered and struggling to hold back a snicker, they try sliding by us stealthily without detection. But the smell of whiskey following their trail betrays them. We older men look to each other without saying a word for consensus on whether an intervention is necessary, but their actions, thus far harmless, do not warrant any action on our part yet. Tonight is not the time to chastise fools for drinking, unless, of course, they become particularly loud or violent through their excesses. Fortunately, only happy drunks are here this evening.

Last to arrive are Firefly and some other BIA notables, the minister and his wife, and some of their friends from Syracuse who have come to watch the "wild savages" dance, sing, and debauch their souls. Our dancers mockingly take the opportunity to perform their dances with greater vigor and ferocity upon seeing the white people so as to confirm their worst fears of our people's barbarous nature. After all, we do not want the white people to think they have "tamed" us!

One year, a middle-aged white woman was so overcome by the drumbeat, the heat of the fire, shrill voices, and wild dancing that she fainted straightaway. Typically, after about an hour or so, the visitors have reached their limits of tolerance for our savage ways, excuse themselves, and leave. Upon their exit, our people roar with laughter at having given the white man quite a good show.

I am wary of Firefly flitting among the people more than usual, paying particular—in fact bordering on inappropriate—attention to our young people, looking them up and down as if they were livestock. This behavior, odd even for Firefly, makes me uncomfortably suspicious of his intentions. Three white men dressed in uniforms that do not resemble those of a military officer but that clearly denote them as government officials, accompany him. I watch Firefly carefully. He rarely ventures too far from the vestiges of civilization to mingle among the savages. But tonight is different. Smiling and nodding, Firefly actually attempts to joke with the people, who look at him with respectful curiosity and forced half-smiles.

After dutifully paying his respects to the clan mothers, who pay him little mind, Firefly saunters over to where the tribal elders and I smoke our pipes and stare into the fire.

"Good evening, gentlemen," he begins. Nobody responds or looks up. "Lovely evening," Firefly continues, hoping to stir some conversation. Again, no response. "The harvest looks good this year," he continues with his small talk.

Uncomfortable at the silence and obvious embarrassment in front of his colleagues, Firefly attempts to speak again, but I interrupt, "You got one out of two right."

Now somewhat enlivened that one of us has responded, Firefly inquires, "Excuse me?"

"You got one out of two right," I repeat.

"One out of two? Good god, man, what are you saying?" Firefly asks fitfully.

I am amazed at how often the white man invokes the name of his god when he is perplexed or afraid. "You said 'good harvest' and 'lovely evening.' You are right on the harvest. But you are wrong on the evening. There is nothing lovely about it when you come with three big white men in uniforms. Besides, the clouds are forming. It is going to rain."

The other old men look to the sky and nod in agreement.

Quite annoyed by my irreverent and suspicious tone, Firefly patiently explains, "These men are a special detachment from the United States Bureau of Indian Affairs."

We do not need to look up at them. We have seen soldiers before. They do not look like regular soldiers, and they do not possess the arrogance of officers. *Who are they really?* I wonder.

Although somewhat exasperated, Firefly braves on.

"They are here to tell you about a special school in Pennsylvania established for Indian children to help them to read, speak, and write proper English and to learn a trade."

"Really?" I ask incredulously. "Will you teach them to lie, cheat, and steal like the white man as well? Will you teach our children to be your house servants, mine workers, tall building walkers, loggers, and other jobs too dangerous or too dirty for white men? Will we ever see our children again after you take them?"

Stunned by this outburst of hostility, especially from a Sachem, Firefly is momentarily speechless. Then he goads me to further conversation. "Chief Fallen Tree, I have heard that you are well-read. I have heard that you believe in education although uneducated yourself."

I stare into the fire, smoke my pipe, and wonder what Firefly's true purpose is in attending our festival.

Securing eye contact with the three BIA men to assure that they are paying attention, Firefly continues, "It is well known that your grandson, Jake, is the brightest and most athletic of the teenage boys here. Perhaps you should consider his candidacy for this school."

I leap to my feet. Following my lead, all the elders rise after carefully placing their pipes by their seats. Sensing a possible confrontation, the drummers, singers, and dancers stop at once. All in the vicinity look at us for some hint of the problem or for direction in what to do.

My eyes boring first into Firefly's eyes, and then into those of the three burly government men, I state firmly, "I say this to you, Firefly, and to you, BIA agents or whoever you are: you will never enslave one child from this reservation. If there is a child who wishes to go to the white man's university, it will be by his own choice and when he is ready. Mark me well."

Jake and his friends try to press closer to hear this exchange. The government men, however, now feeling threatened, nervously grip the guns holstered at their sides.

Sensing an escalation in hostilities, Miss Doolittle, who has heard part of the conversation, steps between the angry-looking white men and us and speaks. "Gentlemen," she begins.

One of the government men asks, "Are you a white woman or an Indian?"

She looks at him defiantly and replies, "Does it make a difference to you who speaks, white or red?"

The BIA man is speechless.

"I am a white woman born to parents from Ireland, taught in Catholic and public schools, and educated in one of our country's finest universities. But I did not become a human being until I came to live among the Haudenosaunee," Miss Doolittle says with pride.

The people close enough to hear the strength of her words yelp with approval.

Miss Doolittle continues, "Gentlemen," she looks at the government men, "it is true that Jake is one of my finest pupils and without question our finest young athlete, but he is better suited for a university, not some industrial school to learn a trade."

Everyone close enough to hear looks at Jake. Although he cannot hear the conversation, Jake senses that they are speaking about him.

Miss Doolittle presses on. "Some boys may do well learning a trade, but not Jake. He is destined for a university where he will learn a profession," she confirms with pride and smiles at Jake.

One of the government men quietly snickers, "An Indian in a university? Humph, that's about as useful as teats on a bull." The white men try to muffle their laughter.

"Gentlemen!" Miss Doolittle firmly interrupts. "Perhaps we can all discuss this tomorrow morning at our schoolhouse. Shall we say around nine o'clock?"

Sensing the growing uneasiness, the white men furtively nod to each other and slowly back away from the fire that suddenly has become too warm for them. Firefly and the three burly, uniformed BIA men cautiously wade through the crowd of people, who grumble as they pass. By pure accident, their path leads them to Jake. Stopping in front of him, Firefly looks Jake up and down. A sickly smile creeps across Firefly's mouth. He turns to the three government men, then to Jake, then back to the men, and then to Jake again, until the three acknowledge Jake, nodding with similar smiles. The three government men walk by Jake, occasionally straining their necks back for one more look, I suspect, for no reason other than to remember his face.

Sensing the obvious tension and not wanting to end the night on a bad note, one of the clan mothers shouts in her frail voice, "Ojuntaowanna!"

The people shout, "Ojuntaowanna!" This is the fish dance, usually the last dance of the night, in which the single and available girls choose boys of a similar character as their dance partners.

The announcement of the fish dance so excites the young people, including Jake, that nearly everyone quickly forgets that the BIA men had ever even been there. I notice that Jake quickly runs to the wagon to retrieve the precious headdress that Sarah has made for him. He has not worn the hat all evening, undoubtedly for fear of damaging it. I believe that his hat possesses medicine so powerful that Sarah will be inexorably drawn to him and only him.

Jake races back from the wagon just as the drummers begin. He steps in the line of young men, who immediately acknowledge the majesty of his hat and greet him, some with envious smiles. Not daring to touch this exquisite work of art, each takes turns standing on tiptoes for a closer look. The eagle feather that stands vertically on top of Jake's hat bounces gently in the rhythm of the dance, obvious for all to see.

Still angry and unsettled by Firefly's threats, I deeply inhale the night's cool air through my nose and quickly exhale through my mouth several times to calm myself. Having finished smoking my long ceremonial pipe, I retrieve from my coat pocket my favorite old corncob pipe, firmly strike it against a log to dislodge the remnants of its previously burned tobacco, and carefully repack it for one last smoke that evening. I draw upon my pipe and am further calmed. With pride, I watch our young people, the future of our tribe, dance.

Many a courtship has begun with the fish dance. Among other tribal matters, the clan mothers have discussed suitable boy-and-girl matches throughout the course of the night. It is exciting to see who couples up. As they dance, each young woman begins to reposition herself in line opposite a young man whom she may fancy. Sometimes the clan mothers coax and prod the young women to matches.

I have heard whisperings this evening that Jake and Sarah will dance opposite each other. Unbeknownst to them, I have secured the clan mothers' unanimous approval of their courtship. But sinister forces, which sometimes alter fate, are afoot this evening.

—

I look up to the sky, hoping that we shall beat the rain. The winds stir and the clouds, like warriors on horseback, sweep across the face of our Grandmother the Moon. I can hear the tethered horses nickering, indicating an imminent change in the weather.

Rattlers and flute blowers follow the drumbeat in time. The singers begin as the dancers continue to fall into position. The young women typically range in age from fifteen—like Maggie, who is too young to begin a serious courtship—to seventeen, like Sarah, who is of an age where the idea of marriage can be considered. The girls begin to dance in a circle, around the fire neither looking at the fire nor the inner ring of boys, each taking small steps, stepping heel to toe, twice repeated upon each foot in alternation. Just as the beat of the music speeds up, every other girl turns around so that she is dancing with her back facing the boys' line and the remaining girls face the boys. After a minute or two, the girls reverse course and positions. They repeat this movement several times. The girls also begin to shuffle in and out among one another to line up across from the boy who strikes her fancy.

The young men slowly dance in place to the rhythm of the drumbeat. They do not stand erect but rather are slightly bent forward at the waist. With knees bent, their necks cocked forward, and colorfully attired, they remind me of roosters calling to their hens. All the girls now face the boys and still circling them and the fire, they move closer, then backwards, then even closer again. As the music grows louder and faster, the girls keep to the beat by dancing more swiftly around the boys and the fire. They simultaneously move closer to the young men during this last pass before reaching out to select their partners. I strain my eyes to see whether Sarah is positioned across from the tall eagle feather sitting atop Jake's head. *Yes,* I say to myself. *She is positioning herself perfectly.*

I notice that Jake's eyes are closed as he dances trancelike in place. Perhaps he is dreaming of Sarah to come to him. Perhaps he has fallen under the spell of the eagle again. The music becomes even louder and quicker, and the girls move even more swiftly and closer. The young men quiver with excitement as the girls practically race up to their noses, then quickly withdraw, repeating this sequence until the drumbeat stops.

From the corner of my eye, I notice that Youngblood, oldest of the bachelors, has shifted his position down the line of boys, ominously close to Jake. Also moving with him is his brother in crime, Sonny Two Weasels. *Why*, I wonder, *are they moving in tandem? Does no one else see this? Is there skullduggery afoot?*

The drums beat even more loudly and more rapidly. I suspect one more pass will take the girls in front of their chosen ones. Sarah stares intently at Jake, whose eyes remain closed as he dances in place.

Just before the very last beat of the drum, when each girl begins to reach out and touch her chosen young man upon his shoulders, Sonny Two Weasels, feigning a stumble, falls sideways into the unsuspecting Jake, violently knocking him to the ground. Caught unaware, Jake falls sideways and backward. Unable to break the fall with his hands, Jake hits his head and crushes his hat against a tree stump. Youngblood seizes the opportunity and quickly steps sideways into the space that Jake previously occupied before anyone notices.

His broad body blocking Sarah from Jake, Youngblood standing fast in front of her, quickly grabs her hands, and places them upon his shoulders. So swiftly has Jake been knocked out of the line that hardly anyone other than I notice. So quickly has Youngblood replaced Jake that hardly anyone other than I notice Jake's absence. The drummers stop with one final loud pop upon the drum skins. The singers simultaneously end with a loud yelp. Boys and girls are now partnered, to the applause and delight of the observers. The music begins once again, and the couples, arm-in-arm, then commence to dance in a circle around the fire with each other.

Except for myself and a few people nearby, no one has noticed Jake fall behind the line of boys into the shadows, sprawled out and bleeding from the side of his head. As I move quickly to Jake's aid, I spot Sarah with Youngblood, who has interlocked his left arm with her right. Youngblood dances the struggling Sarah away from the prostrate Jake, not as a willing partner but as a prisoner. Sarah is too polite to scream, struggle overtly, or cause a commotion. Her eyes reflecting deep shock, disbelief, and pain, Sarah begrudgingly dances with Youngblood as tears begin to roll down her cheeks onto her festive garb.

As I approach Jake, he slowly rises to his feet with the help of two onlookers. Shaking the cobwebs from his brain, he struggles to discern what has happened. Jake frantically swivels his head to look for Sarah among the dancing young men and women. His heart is uplifted when he spots her. But then he sees the unthinkable: Sarah is dancing with Youngblood, who places a white ermine fur around her neck, an enviable gift if offered and received kindly. The crowd applauds as Sarah smiles politely, although in truth she smiles uncomfortably since the fur is more a shackle than a gift. Jake is too far away to discern Sarah's tears, to know the pain in her heart, or to see Sarah strain her neck back to locate him.

Overcome with the anguish of witnessing Sarah and Youngblood together, Jake clenches his fists by his sides and screams in terrible emotional and physical pain, a sound few hear over the loud beat of the drum. Looking down, he finds the exquisite headdress that Sarah has made for him. Enraged, Jake scoops up the regalia and smashes it against the same tree stump upon which he has almost crushed his skull. Picking up the shattered bits of the headdress, he cries out piteously, as if they were the pieces of his broken heart. Spotting one of the eagle feathers, he reverently rescues it from the dirt before he heads out into the night.

Jake has already disappeared before I can reach him. I turn back toward the dancers and see Maggie happily dancing with a handsome young brave whose family lives over the ridge. Then I see Sarah, a pitiful ghost swept up by chicanery. Happy for Maggie, saddened for Sarah, and worried about Jake, I look down upon Mother Earth for guidance. Among the broken beads, twigs of ash, and fur lies the other eagle feather, which I quickly rescue from trampling feet. Worried, I quickly scan the forest where Jake has fled, but he has disappeared, enveloped by the night's black shroud.

32

KIDNAPPED

Now standing on the road, straining my eyes and ears to see or hear Jake, a strange feeling sweeps over me. I hear voices all around me, but when I turn to locate them, nobody is there. As the wind whips up, causing me to hold my long gray hair from my face, somehow I am commanded to look up; I become entranced by the dark clouds that transform into familiar shapes, each silhouetted by the light of our Grandmother the Moon. The figures in the shapes of clouds and voices in the wind beckon to me.

In an instant I find myself at our tribe's council fires in the Sky World, and while I'm afraid that I am dead, I am comforted by the presence of my ancestors. But then I remember Jake and think that it cannot be my time to die. I fall to my knees and cry out that I must save my grandson.

Then a most strange and wonderful thing happens. My daughter and son-in-law gently bid me to stand and look to the world below. There I spot Jake, alone and afraid. I want to jump down to him, but I am restrained by my daughter, his mother, who without words invites me to remain and observe Jake's journey. I do not know whether what is happening to me is a dream or real, but it does not matter, for dreams and reality are only as different as shades of darkness from when the sun begins its descent until it fully sets. My daughter blows the clouds apart with her breath for me to see below and to hear Jake's thoughts.

From the camaraderie, warmth, and glow of the celebratory fire, I see Jake running aimlessly and alone into the chill and darkness of the night. He does not run along the ashen gray road, his usual guide home, for he does not want to see or talk to anybody. Just as the horses have predicted, a storm is brewing. Jake runs headlong through the forest, stumbling over fallen logs, splashing into streams, slipping on moss-covered stones, and falling to the leaf-covered forest floor. He tears and tatters the magnificent festival clothes his sisters have made for him. He bumps into trees, instantly reminding himself of wounds earned earlier that day in the Game.

Jake runs blindly in circles for hours. Haunted by the image of Sarah smiling at Youngblood, Jake is too angry to realize that he had been pushed out of the way of Sarah's gentle touch. Beset with self-doubt, Jake wonders how he could have passed out just at the moment when Sarah reached out to touch him. *Was I so entranced by the warmth of the fire, the beat of the drums, exhaustion, and anticipation of Sarah's touch that I just fell?* Jake asks himself repeatedly.

Exhausted, thirsty, his head pounding with every heartbeat, torn and scratched by branches and briars, and near collapse, Jake spots a dot of light in the distance. Limping toward what he now discerns is a cabin lantern, Jake recognizes its familiar light. *Is this a dream? Are evil spirits at work? How is it that after hours of running in the dark, I end up at Sarah's house of all places?*

Too tired to think anymore, Jake barely reaches the porch steps before his legs buckle and he collapses onto the cracked wooden steps of the cabin.

—

After a while, Jake slowly opens his tired eyes, wondering whether the events of the festival were just a dream. Next to him is a bucket of water in which there is a gourd ladle. Painfully raising his head, Jake looks around hoping to see Sarah but sees no one other than Sarah's father sitting peacefully in his rocking chair rhythmically rocking, staring blankly straight ahead.

Dehydrated from the Game and his running, Jake eases to his knees, tosses the gourd aside, clutches the bucket with both hands, raises it to his cracked lips, and drinks voraciously. His thirst quenched, Jake pours the remainder of the water over his head. He looks again for any sign of Sarah, but nothing. Sarah's father continues to sit serenely in his rocking chair, each rock keeping rhythm to a song he begins to hum, and then sing in a barely audible voice. Jake wonders whether this enigmatic old man had placed the bucket of water by his head, for he did not remember it being there when he had collapsed earlier.

With no other explanation readily apparent, Jake sincerely but most probably futilely thanks the old man for the water. Jake is still exhausted from his run and the Game, and now, with the wind blowing in his face and a drizzle commencing, he decides to wait out the upcoming storm on Sarah's covered porch and think for a while. He leans back against the rickety rail, almost falling off the porch as the rotten post lurches under his weight. Seeking a more secure back brace, Jake crawls over the porch floor, sits up against the cabin wall under cover, and falls asleep again after a few minutes.

Jake dreams of the Game and the festival, but his dreams do not yet make sense. Frustrated that his dreams offer him no answers, he suddenly awakens. Where is his Grandfather? Where are his sisters? Where is Sarah? Jake, feeling the desperate need to speak to anyone, begins talking to Sarah's father even though his words may not be understood.

"My father, do you hear me? Do you see me?" Jake waits a moment for an answer that he knows will not come. "Matters not," he says under his breath. "I am Jake Harwood, son of Tall Pine, grandson of Fallen Tree, a Sachem and our Faithkeeper. I am your neighbor to the south. I have brought many baskets of vegetables and venison to your table over the years. I have kept your fire lit with wood that I have gathered and chopped. I am a lacrosse player. I played in my first big Game yesterday. I played well and could have scored the winning goal, but I fell at the last minute. I do not know why or how that could have happened."

Jake suddenly stops. He thinks deeply about what he is saying. *Did I fall or was I tripped?* Jake ponders. Closing his eyes, Jake recalls each step of that last play from his memory. Then he recalls his conversation with me after the Game. Now Jake remembers the painful, horrible truth: *I did not just stumble. I was tripped. I was tripped by my own teammate. I was tripped by my own teammate, Youngblood.*

Jake had forgotten that Youngblood had tripped him; the thought of such an overt act of betrayal banished from his memory. Jake had convinced himself that he had tripped over his own feet, the other alternative too painful to accept as true.

Jake now begins to connect other supposed coincidences: first, the day in the mill when he tripped and spilled an armload of kindling; next, the incident on the logging slope when he was almost crushed by falling logs; third, the trip at the end of the Game; and, finally, the dance. The one constant in all of these events—Youngblood. He has always been there. *But what about the dance? Why did Sarah choose Youngblood? Did she even choose Youngblood? How did I fall? Did I pass out, or was I pushed?*

"Pushed!" Jake suddenly screams.

Jake's head begins to pound. All of these thoughts swirling in his mind do not yet make sense. *Why? What have I ever done to Youngblood to earn such hatred from him?*

Although not expecting an answer, Jake pours out his feelings to Sarah's father. "My father, I saw Sarah, your daughter, my love, forsake me this night and chose another. I do not know why. I thought she loved me. Why would she betray me? Does she not love me? But now I am not sure. I am confused. I am not sure what to do or to say. I fear I may have lost her. Lost her forever. I do not know what to do. I do not know what to do," Jake moans as he cups his face in both hands over his bent knees and begins to cry.

Jake is so tired, so forlorn, and so confused that he wishes I were there to comfort him. Then the idea strikes him: *Grandfather! I must get home and seek his counsel.*

But as Jake musters the strength to leave, he hears a faint voice whisper, "Tell her."

Jake quickly turns around, looking for the origin of the voice. Seeing only the old, mute man, he asks incredulously, "Did you speak, my father?"

In all the years since he has known him, Jake has never heard Sarah's father utter a word.

As Jake begins to turn away, he once again hears in a faint whisper, "Tell her."

This time Jake whirls around and kneels in front of the old man. Grabbing his knees, Jake begs an answer. "Do you speak to me, my father?"

Jake is met with silence. Frustrated, Jake places his face upon the old man's knees. Then he hears the voice a third time.

"Tell her," the old man says, blinking his eyes as the wind blows a light rain onto the two of them.

Looking into the old man's face for more answers, Jake implores, "Tell her what? Tell her what?" he desperately asks as he shakes the old man's knees, urging him to give a clearer answer. Jake anxiously awaits the old man's response.

Unbelievably, Sarah's father leans forward and looks directly into Jake's eyes. Shocked by the old man's sudden, apparent return to life, Jake jumps back.

"Tell her you love her, my son. Tell her you forgive her," the old man states with great effort.

"Has she been here, my father? Did she come looking for me?"

Sarah's father sits back, stares straight ahead, and simply nods.

"Has she gone to my house?"

Again, he simply nods.

Elated that he knows what to do, and that Sarah has been looking for him, Jake springs to his feet, grabs the man's face with both hands, and kisses him on the forehead.

"Thank you, thank you, my father," Jake shouts with all of his heart.

Jake jumps over the porch rail and into the mud that quickly forms from a now-steady rain. As he runs up the wet, slippery trail toward his home, he hears the old man singing more loudly than before. Momentarily stopping, Jake looks back and sees Sarah's father standing by the edge of the porch, holding onto the vertical beam between the porch floor and roof with his left hand and the porch rail with his right. The wind blows back his long white hair. The rain becomes a downpour, blowing onto his face and shirt. Raising his head and both arms to the heavens, Sarah's father seemingly rejoices in the rain and sings even louder, as if beckoning the heavens to unleash its fury upon him. Jake recognizes the melody, a song he remembers his mother singing softly to him when he was a little boy, a song about love. The old man sings more loudly, as if to spur Jake on.

Jake waves to Sarah's father and shouts, "Thank you, thank you, my father. Do you not see that I love you? Do you not see that I love your daughter? Do you not see that I am the man who will marry your daughter and give you many grandchildren?"

—

Suddenly I am carried by a cloud in the shape of a horse back to Mother Earth and our home. I am elated that Jake has discerned the right course of action and that I will be joining him and my family in the world of the living. But as I follow Jake to the top of the trail, I am abruptly deposited on my porch with unwelcomed visitors.

Jake runs up the path as fast as he can, slipping and sliding all the way. He hardly notices that the rain is falling even harder now and that the wind has picked up. But the rain is like a cleansing, like a baptism. Jake dodges fallen tree limbs and branches bending in the wind. He finds renewed energy now that he knows what he must do, what he should have done sooner: he must tell Sarah that he loves her and will never leave her. Jake is so elated in the clarity of his purpose that he laughs aloud.

But his cheerful demeanor quickly diminishes at the top of the trail when Jake senses something wrong. Passing the barn, he notices old Thunder pacing furiously in his stall. *Perhaps the old horse is just disturbed by the weather,* Jake thinks.

By the look on Jake's face, I know that he is stunned at the spectacle that unfolds before him. I am struggling with two of the government men who had been at the Green Corn Festival. Jake's three sisters are punching and scratching the burliest of the three, who is violently dragging them by their hair down the stairs and into the mud. Bear, our blind and crippled family dog, lies strangely still in the mud. A steady stream of red mixes with rain and mud.

Sarah stands before Firefly, her hands folded in the way the Christian ministers have taught the children to do when praying, beseeching the BIA agent for something that none of us can hear.

Seeing his sisters and me so mistreated, Bear dead, and Sarah begging, I see rage in Jake's eyes. Losing all self-control, Jake runs and hurls himself headlong into the man holding his sisters, knocking him backward into the mud with a great splash.

"Run, my sisters, run!" Jake shouts as he struggles to regain himself.

Excited to see their brother but still frightened by the government men, they refuse to run away. "No," they cry. "We will not let them take you."

Getting back to his feet, Jake echoes, "Take me? What are you talking about?"

Then I scream, "Run, my son! Run for your life!"

But Jake stands his ground. "Grandfather! What is wrong? Why do you wish me to run? Why are these men here? Why are you fighting?"

Lightning snaps in the background. The heavens open up, and a furious rain pours onto us.

As one of the government men struggles with me, Jake demands, "Why are you fighting with my grandfather?"

"Is that him?" the man who was pulling my granddaughter's hair asks, jutting his jaw toward Jake.

"That's him," Firefly affirms.

"OK, son," the big government man bellows as he slowly walks toward Jake. "Don't make this any harder on yourself than it has to be," he cautions, spitting out a wad of chewing tobacco in the mud at Jake's feet.

The government man I was tussling with now has pinned both of my arms behind me and handcuffed me so that I can no longer fight. "Run, my son, run for your life!" I again implore, as I fall to my knees, helpless and defeated.

Jake now understands that Firefly and these government men are here to take him. But just as Jake turns to run, the man whom he had knocked into the mud wraps his big arms around him in a bear hug. Although Jake's sisters pounce on the man like harpies, biting and scratching his legs, the huge man shakes them off into the mud like fleas scratched off a dog. Jake struggles mightily, but with his arms pinned to his sides and his legs kicking aimlessly as he is held off the ground, he can neither free nor defend himself. Jake is silenced when the other government man punches him squarely on the side of the face, knocking him unconscious.

Jake collapses into the mud face-first. Crying uncontrollably, his sisters remain at Jake's side on their knees in the mud, held at bay by the threat of a sidearm one of the men points menacingly at them.

Firefly firmly holds Sarah by both arms, her hands still clasped together as if in prayer. "Sarah," Firefly speaks softly and reassuringly, "it's for his own good. He is going to a fine school where he will learn a trade. Then he'll come back here and marry you. Both of you will be happy together and have many papooses."

Sarah continues to struggle, but as her strength begins to wane, in one last gasp, she screams, "If it is such a fine school, why must you take students against their will to attend it?"

Exasperated, fatigued, and growing impatient from the struggle, Firefly looks to me to calm the situation. "Look, Chief, you said yourself that education will save your people. In three to four years, you won't even recognize the boy. He'll be a whole new man."

"You mean a new white man!" I shout.

I struggle, one more time with all of my might to free myself, but one of the men strikes me on the side of my head with a small club. I instantly fall on the porch, as helpless as a turtle on its back. The blood that streams from the side of my head mingles with Bear's. "I have caused both of our deaths, old friend," I tearfully lament.

"OK, enough. Take him," Firefly impatiently commands, pointing to Jake's limp, soaked body.

Supporting Jake under each arm, the two government men drag him through the mud toward an awaiting wagon. Each grabbing a leg and an arm, they throw Jake up and over the wagon's side like a sack of potatoes. Jake is thus stolen from his family and thrown into the white man's world.

"Jake! Jake!" I scream. My eyes are so full of tears that I can hardly see. My shouts do not awaken him. I slip, helplessly down the stairs face-first into the mud, next to Bear, wishing I too were dead. I cannot save my grandson. I am ashamed, realizing that Firefly had duped me into allowing this to happen "Why do you tear out my heart?" I shout at Firefly, spitting blood and mud from my mouth.

Firefly bends over to speak to me. Lifting my head up by my hair, Firefly says very calmly, "Don't worry, Chief. The Carlisle Industrial School for Indians will take good care of your grandson. You should be proud that we have selected your grandson of all the young men on the reservation."

I do not have the strength to respond. Firefly lets go of my hair, and I kiss Mother Earth again. I close my eyes and beg the sky people to take me back but to no avail. Here I lie broken in the mud.

Sarah scrambles to my side, turns my face so that it is not in the mud, and cups my head in her lap. "Why, Grandfather? Why? Why my Jake? Why my love?" she repeatedly asks.

I am too ashamed to tell her why, for I was the one who signed the consent papers, authorizing Jake's attendance at this school. I had been played for a fool. At the festival, I had heard Miss Doolittle's words about Jake. I had always believed that he would make a fine student at a university. Firefly had told me that if I signed the consent form, Jake would go to a university. But the Carlisle Industrial School for Indians is not a university.

It is a trade school, beneficial perhaps for some Indians, but not for my Jake. This is not what Jake wants. This is not what I want. I have doomed my only grandson.

"Ya better cuff that wild Indian to the wagon seat or he'll jump on ya," Firefly yells to the government men, who are becoming more aggravated as they become more drenched.

Dutifully obeying, the driver cuffs one of Jake's limp hands to the wagon seat rail. Only Jake's arm is visible; his unconscious body is hidden from view by the wagon's rear boards.

"OK," Firefly shouts. "Move out!"

With a snap of the reigns and a mighty "Ha!" the driver maneuvers the wagon forward. The sudden jolt awakens Jake, who groggily struggles to his knees. He shakes his head, trying to get his bearings. Now realizing he is on a moving wagon, Jake attempts to jump but is abruptly restrained by the white man's chains.

"Grandfather!" Jake screams. "Grandfather!" he screams again, madly jerking his hand up and down, pulling and even biting the chains.

My spirit again leaves my body. But instead of ascending to the Sky World where I wanted to go I am blown towards the wagon. I see my three granddaughters and Sarah below but they don't see me.

"Jake!" All three of his sisters scream as they run after the wagon. But the wagon gains speed and distance as it splashes along the bumpy, muddy road. As the futility of their efforts becomes apparent, exhausted, all three fall to their knees. Huddled together in the pouring rain, they madly grope in the mud as if they had lost something precious. Each girl locates a sharp stone, which she scrapes repeatedly over the top of her head, producing trickles of blood that runs down their faces. Jakes three sisters cry uncontrollably, as if mourning the dead, as they helplessly watch their beloved brother disappear over the ridge.

Escaping the clutches of Firefly and the two government men who chase after her, Sarah frantically runs after the wagon.

Jake clears his eyes enough to see a figure running through the rain after the wagon. He sees it is Sarah.

"Jake!" she screams, as she passes the pathetic little girls sobbing in the mud. "Jake! Jake! Wait! I love you! Do you not see that I have always loved you?" she shouts with all of her might. But the driver snaps his horses to a gallop, gaining distance from a desperate Sarah. "Jake, it was you I wanted at the Corn Festival dance! It was you! It was always you!" she cries. But Jake does not hear her. Exhausted, Sarah finally falls to the muddy road, forlornly moaning to herself, "It was you. It was always only you."

"Sarah!" Jake screams in vain. He tries one last jerk on his chains, but all that gives way is the flesh from his wrist. "Sarah! I love you. I have always loved you. I forgive you. Sarah! I want to marry you."

Alas, Sarah does not hear him either. *Whack*! Jake is hit on the side of his head by the government man's small club. Bleeding profusely and now unconscious, Jake falls down upon the wagon floor. And then a deep breath draws into my lifeless body and my spirit returns to me—I am alive again.

—

I sing out my death song for all to hear. Although alive, I am dead inside. I want to die. First my daughter, then my son-in-law, and now my grandson have all been taken from me. This is too much for an old man to bear. I beg the Great Spirit to take me, but even he cannot hear my words in this deafening storm.

My grandson lies in chains at the bottom of a white man's wagon that rushes away from us, his family, and his people over every pothole on Firefly's "road to civilization." *Will it be civilization or perdition, or are they one and the same into which my grandson has been taken as an unwilling captive?* I forlornly wonder. I do not know. May the Creator watch over you, my son, I mutter with my last breath before passing out as Jake disappears from our world into the unknown.

To be continued…

Read the story of Jake's life at the Carlisle Industrial School for Indians and the amazing conclusion of the ancient prophecy in ***Prophecy of the Eagle II.***

ACKNOWLEDGMENTS

To the boys I coached at Dwyer High School in Palm Beach Gardens, Florida, to whom I told this story around a campfire six years ago, thank you for urging me to write it.

To my many friends and lacrosse comrades who read my early unedited copy and loved the story, the characters, and the message, thank you for encouraging me to complete what I set out to accomplish.

To my first typist, June Brown, who listened to dictated mini-tapes, suffered through my Boston accent, and gave this story its first life—as well as my subsequent typists, my daughter Briana, my associate's daughter Suzanne Lehman, and Michelle Clark, my paralegal—thank you for your important help.

To my son Domenic, who was home from college and studying to enter law school, thank you for performing all the household and barn chores, including taking care of our three horses, so that I could handwrite my book drafts each weekend at my Goodwill desk and chair set up in the tack room of our barn.

To my editor, Diane Bressner, a retired college educator who fell in love with my story, thank you for your advice and skills that helped enrich and polish this story.

To Bill Belichick, head coach of the New England Patriots, my classmate, fraternity brother, and football and lacrosse teammate, thank you for introducing me to the sport of lacrosse in 1971 at Wesleyan University in Middletown, Connecticut.

To CreateSpace, thank you for your competence and professionalism in making my dream a reality.

And finally, to my wife Jean, who tolerated my many excuses for being unavailable every weekend for six years so that I could research and write this story, thank you. I hope this undertaking has been worthwhile.

BOOK JACKET PREVIEW

Prophecy of the Eagle I and II is a two-book, historically based coming-of-age novel. In *Prophecy of the Eagle I,* an ancient prophecy haunts Jake, an Onondaga boy who loves lacrosse, his family, and his girlfriend Sarah. Jake is confronted with the many challenges of reservation life in early 1900s upper New York State and of crossing the threshold into manhood. He is kidnapped and brought to the Carlisle Industrial School for Indians, partially famous for super-athlete Jim Thorpe and for "Pop" Warner, innovative and successful football coach. *Prophecy of the Eagle II* follows Jake's life at Carlisle, where he introduces the sport of lacrosse and ultimately fulfills the Prophecy of the Eagle.

ABOUT THE AUTHOR

Mike Celeste—a former teacher, football, hockey, and lacrosse coach, and athletic director—is a practicing attorney in Florida and current competitive lacrosse player. After a hiatus from lacrosse for twenty years, Mike took up the stick again, and in 2001 became one of the driving forces in introducing lacrosse to northern Palm Beach County, Florida. "I love this Game given to us by the Creator," Mike avows, "and I am determined to remind the non-Native players of the spirituality of the Game. When I die, I hope that my wife and children will abide by my wishes that I be buried with my lacrosse stick."

Made in the USA
Lexington, KY
21 January 2015